I0580181

His Valet

S.M. LAVIOLETTE

CROOKED SIXPENCE BOOKS are published by

CROOKED SIXPENCE PRESS
2 State Road 230
El Prado, NM 87529

Copyright © 2020 Shantal M. LaViolette

All rights reserved. No part of this publication may be reproduced, distributed, or transmitted in any form or by any means, including photocopying, recording, or other electronic or mechanical methods, without the prior written permission of the publisher, except in the case of brief quotations embodied in critical reviews and certain other noncommercial uses permitted by copyright law. For permission requests, write to the publisher, addressed "Attention: Permissions Coordinator," at the address above.

To the extent that the image or images on the cover of this book depict a person or persons, such person or persons are merely models, and are not intended to portray any character or characters featured in the book.

If you purchased this book without a cover you should be aware that this book is stolen property. It was reported as "unsold and destroyed" to the Publisher and neither the Author nor the Publisher has received any payment for this "stripped book."

First printing May 2020

ISBN: 978-1-951662-18-9

10 9 8 7 6 5 4 3 2 1

Any references to historical events, real people, or real places are used fictitiously. Names, characters, and places are products of the author's imagination.

Photo stock by Period Images

Printed in the United States of America.

Praise for Minerva Spencer's Outcasts series:

"Minerva Spencer's writing is sophisticated and wickedly witty. Dangerous is a delight from start to finish with swashbuckling action, scorching love scenes, and a coolly arrogant hero to die for. Spencer is my new auto-buy!"
-NYT Bestselling Author Elizabeth Hoyt

"[SCANDALOUS *is] A standout...Spencer's brilliant and original tale of the high seas bursts with wonderfully real protagonists, plenty of action, and passionate romance."*
★**Publishers Weekly STARRED REVIEW**

"Fans of Amanda Quick's early historicals will find much to savor."
★**Booklist STARRED REVIEW**

"Sexy, witty, and fiercely entertaining."
★**Kirkus STARRED REVIEW**

"A remarkably resourceful heroine who can more than hold her own against any character invented by best-selling Bertrice Small, a suavely sophisticated hero with sex appeal to spare, and a cascade of lushly detailed love scenes give Spencer's dazzling debut its deliciously fun retro flavor."
★**Booklist STARRED REVIEW**

"Readers will love this lusty and unusual marriage of convenience story."
-NYT Bestselling Author MADELINE HUNTER

"Smart, witty, graceful, sensual, elegant and gritty all at once. It has all of the meticulous attention to detail I love in Georgette Heyer, BUT WITH SEX!"
RITA-Award Winning Author JEFFE KENNEDY

More books by S.M. LaViolette & Minerva Spencer:

THE ACADEMY OF LOVE SERIES

The Music of Love
A Figure of Love
A Portrait of Love*

THE OUTCASTS SERIES

Dangerous
Barbarous
Scandalous
Notorious*

THE MASQUERADERS
The Footman
The Postilion*
The Bastard*

THE SEDUCERS
Melissa and The Vicar
Joss and The Countess*
Hugo and The Maiden*

VICTORIAN DECADENCE
His Harlot
His Valet
His Countess*

ANTHOLOGIES:

BACHELORS OF BOND STREET
THE ARRANGEMENT
*upcoming books

$$Chapter\ One$$

London

Stephen sipped his brandy and leisurely studied the woman kneeling before him: she was exquisite. Her name was Sharon and she'd given her age as eighteen, although he suspected she was closer to twenty-five.

That was fine, he'd not chosen her because of her supposed youth, he'd picked her because she possessed exactly the type of body he adored. Although at perhaps five foot six she was a bit shorter than Stephen generally liked. At a shade over six and half feet he simply found very small women too physically challenging.

Sharon had wavy brown hair which fell to her waist when unbound, which it was now. She had womanly hips that narrowed to an impossibly tiny waist, one which his massive hands could easily span, even without her corset. But it was her breasts that were her true glory: full, rounded, with large nipples that were a dark rose. His mouth watered looking at them and it took all his restraint not to seize her and suck her to hard, pebbled points.

But he could do that later, after he'd had his fill of looking at her delicious body.

His gaze slipped from her lovely nipples over the gentle swell of her belly and stopped on her sex.

As he'd requested, she was completely without body hair. Stephen had decided a few years ago that he preferred the sleek look shaving afforded. He also liked the fact that at least their bodies could keep no secrets from him.

Right now, for instance, Sharon's pudendum was flushed and swollen and her bud peeked from between her lips: she was aroused.

The fact that she couldn't hide such a private fact from his probing eyes only served to make him harder.

Stephen smiled at the twisted thought and took another drink. He knew his deeply suspicious nature coupled with his almost pathological need for control made for a personality that was far from attractive.

He also knew that when it came to sex, his desires were not normal. Luckily, he'd accepted both those facts about himself long, long ago. But just because he knew the truth about himself didn't mean he shared that truth with others. Indeed, he shared nothing of himself if he could help it. Especially not with the whores he paid to satisfy his needs.

People thought his excessive reserve was standoffishness and most disliked him for it. He had few friends, but friends were something he'd never wanted. He'd learned to his detriment, long ago, that it was better to live without *friends* and not have to wonder about the inevitable betrayal or lies or manipulation.

Worrying about his business partners was bad enough, although after years of working with the three men he was less wary of them than anyone else in his life. Even so, he was never foolish enough to trust them. If he'd ever possessed the capacity to trust another human being, he didn't recall it.

"Open yourself for me," he said, his voice gruff from disuse and arousal.

She parted her lips.

Stephen's pulse—already racing—quickened; she was wet. He believed she liked being studied and admired like a beautiful object. He'd discovered many of the women he engaged found such admiration an aphrodisiac. He loved watching but couldn't help wondering why anyone would like *being* watched. Was it just because it was different from a typical client's behavior? Were most men in a hurry to fuck, viewing a woman as nothing more than a vessel waiting to be filled?

Stephen was also planning to fill her at some point this evening—likely soon—but for him, this process—this silent exchange—was an important antecedent to ejaculation: it was a dialogue without words.

Stephen set aside his glass and began to unbutton his trousers, savoring the way her eyes dropped to his lap, where the fine wool could not hide his arousal.

He lifted his hips to slide off his trousers and drawers, pushing them to the floor. When he wrapped his hand around his shaft, he had to grit his teeth against the swell of pleasure, controlling himself against too precipitate a release, subjugating his body the way he controlled every other aspect of his life. He would come when he'd taken sufficient pleasure from her and not before.

Control in all things; that was his way.

His mouth pulled into a wry smile; perhaps he should draw up a family crest like a pretentious cit and have that motto scrolled across it in Latin?

He gave himself a swift, firm pump, not that he needed it. He was primed for her: slick and hot and hard. He wanted to fuck her, but he also loved the way her eyes caressed his cock. So it appeared he *did* enjoy being looked at, after all. At least when it came to his prick.

Even in his hands—hands that suited his oversized frame—Stephen's erection looked large. That's because it *was* large. While he appreciated being proportionate, his size was sometimes a problem for women. The way her pupils flared told him it wouldn't be a problem for Sharon.

Stephen stroked himself from root to crown, his balls tightening as the tip of her pink tongue darted out and moistened her full lower lip. He'd been uncertain as to which of her entrances to fuck first, but that action decided him.

"Come here."

Her lips curved into a wicked smile and she dropped onto her hands, crawling toward him on all fours, and taking her time about it.

He felt his face shift into an expression it rarely wore: a smile. "Very pretty," he praised.

She lifted his feet and freed him from bunched up wool and fine muslin before pushing his knees apart. Her eyes were heavy lidded as she dipped her head, using her hot, wet tongue to caress his sac.

"Yes," he hissed, pushing his hips toward her, while his palm slid over his weeping slit and he slickened his shaft. "Take them in your mouth."

She sucked first one and then his other testicle with her silken mouth, rolling his full ballocks with her tongue.

Stephen dropped his head against the back of the chair and gave himself up to pleasure, his hand absently stroking. She tongued and sucked and kissed, her mouth worshipping him until he was aching for release.

She covered his hand and he let go, eager for her expert handling. A wicked tongue probed his slit and she lapped up the moisture, humming with pleasure.

"Suck," he murmured.

Again, he had to leash his lust as she stimulated the tiny hole and sensitive crown, tormenting him until he groaned and shivered. A slender, wet finger moved from his balls, going back and back and back, until the soft pad probed his pucker in a way that was humorously polite.

Stephen hadn't used Sharon before, but she must have done her preparation to know he enjoyed a finger up his arse while he was being brought off. He pushed his hips forward in invitation, his body tense and expectant.

The wet heat of her mouth disappeared from his cock and he heard the clink of the glass stopper on the big bottle of oil that sat on the table beside him.

When her lips and tongue returned to his swollen head, her hand slathered him with oil from his sac to his hole.

Stephen wanted to dig his fingers into her thick hair and yank her lower, plunging into her hot softness until he bumped against the back of her throat, but he forced his hands to lie flat on the arms of the chair: he'd see what she had to offer before he took from her.

One hand massaged his jewels while she took his shaft deeper with each suck. She'd risen up high on her knees to take him but he knew the angle was a challenging one. She took her time, lightly prodding with her slick finger, deeper each time.

"Yes," he hissed as she stretched the tight band of muscle. "Deeper," he urged, grunting when she complied. "Harder. More."

She didn't stop until her knuckles rested against his sensitive flesh, and then she turned her finger and beckoned.

Stephen gasped and stiffened as she prodded the spot that erased the last of his restraint.

"Oh God, yes," he murmured, lost.

***

Jo knew it was terribly wrong to spy on one's employer while he was engaging in sexual acts with a prostitute.

Actually, wrong wasn't nearly strong enough: it was morally reprehensible. And it was also more than a little dangerous when one's employer was as suspicious, strict, and controlling as Mr. Stephen Chatham.

Even so, none of that was enough to make her stop what she was doing—what she'd *been* doing for months now.

It was inevitable that Mr. Chatham would catch her and when he did, he wouldn't just give her the sack, he'd exact the same thorough revenge he'd taken on the newspaperman who'd tried to bribe one of his servants about him, or the whore who'd thought to blackmail him by claiming she was pregnant with his child.

Mr. Chatham hated liars more than anything else in life and he'd have every right to his vengeance against Jo because she'd been lying to him since the day she met him.

Mr. Chatham had told her, on the day he'd offered her this exceedingly well-paid position, that he did not tolerate lying. Nor did not tolerate servants who were indiscreet when it came to him or his business or personal affairs.

Jo had not been indiscreet—gossiping about one's employer was a betrayal of trust she found reprehensible—but she lied and abused his privacy daily.

And she knew she would keep doing it.

Jo flicked open two trouser buttons, just enough to slide a hand down her tight, quivering belly to her shaved sex. Six months ago Jo had finally used the razor she'd kept in her kit for over fifteen years. She'd not used it on her face, but to shave off all her body hair, including that covering her sex. She'd done it for *him*, although he'd never know.

Jo stroked her smooth lower lips, which were swollen and sensitive after watching him for almost half an hour. He was sprawled in his big leather chair in front of the fire and he'd kept the whore kneeling before him. The woman was bloody gorgeous—just the type Mr. Chatham liked. Just the type Jo liked, too: lush, womanly, and submissive.

Mr. Chatham's long, muscular body was impressive even in repose. He was a titan of a man, a good head taller than most others of the male species. Jo, who was herself tall for a woman—and even for a man—still had to look up from her five foot ten inches. Not that she often looked him in the eye.

After all, it wasn't her place: he was her master and Jo was his servant.

Of course it also wasn't her place to be lurking in his bedchamber, peering through a crack in the door, and frigging herself while her employer got sucked off.

Only an hour ago Jo had promised herself she would restrain her impulses this time and just watch. But when he took out his big, beautiful, slab of a prick she lost all control, just as she always did.

It didn't take much work to bring herself off and she was gasping and shuddering in less than a minute, biting her lip hard enough to draw blood to keep from crying out.

She hunched against the door frame as the waves of pleasure receded, breathing so hard she was stunned neither of the people in the next room heard her.

But when she peered through the crack again she knew she could have howled like a beagle and her employer wouldn't have heard it. The woman must have slipped a finger up his arse because he was dead to anything but his pleasure.

As for the possibility of the whore hearing Jo? That was even more unlikely since throating that huge cock and breathing at the same time were probably occupying all her attention.

His head had dropped back and his thin lips parted as he breathed in rough, labored gasps. His eyelids were covering those too-penetrating eyes of his.

Even somebody who lusted for and perhaps even loved Mr. Chatham could not say he was handsome. Neither was he ugly. Rather his face—unlike his tall, muscular body—was average. If the same face had been on a smaller man, Mr. Chatham would have gone unnoticed most of the time.

Unless a person was to look in his eyes. Oh, how she loved looking *at*, if not into, his huge, hooded gray eyes. It wasn't so much their color—a rather common slate gray ringed with a darker shade of gray—but their weight, if that made any sense.

While his mouth always remained flat and stern, his eyes glinted with interest, annoyance, curiosity, and even dry amusement on occasion. But they could also peel away a person's flesh layer by layer. Luckily Jo had only suffered that particular visual dissection on one occasion.

As cutting as his gaze could be, Mr. Chatham had never raised his voice with her. Indeed, the more displeased he was, the softer and more slowly he spoke.

Mr. Chatham was the most self-contained person, man or woman, that Jo had ever met. Except for times like this, and she loved watching the person who inhabited that huge, glorious body unravel.

Imagining that it was her mouth he was fucking made her greedy for another climax, but Jo wanted to watch and enjoy his orgasm and she couldn't do that when she was caught up in her own.

So she reluctantly slid her finger from her slit, used her snow white handkerchief to wipe off her hand, and buttoned herself up.

The woman—Sharon—was impressively coordinated. She was fingering him in rhythmic thrusts while her mouth accepted every inch of his gorgeous shaft. He was built like a bloody horse and Jo had seen his cock gag more than one woman—but not Sharon. Jo tried to decipher her technique, but it was difficult from this distance. Not that it mattered; she'd never get a chance to employ this technique or any other on Mr. Chatham's body.

He grunted and began to thrust, his powerful hips pumping. Sharon absorbed his brutal thrusts, taking him deeply. When his movements became jerky and uncontrolled, he slid a hand around her skull and pulled her lower.

There was the briefest instant of resistance in the woman's body before her training took over and she submitted, her soft, luscious form becoming pliable as she opened completely to his invasion.

Jo's eyes threatened to cross at the intoxicating sight of the woman's throat distending with each brutal thrust. Mr. Chatham wasn't just thick; he was long and he pummeled her without mercy. Jo imagined her own throat being stretched and savaged and it was the last straw. Somehow her hand had worked its way south without her permission and a second orgasm ripped through her just as Mr. Chatham sheathed himself to the balls, his body jerking violently as he spent.

Jo shuddered silently along with her master, the contractions of pleasure wringing her out like a dish cloth, until she was limp. Until all she wanted to do was crawl to him and fall asleep at his feet.

But of course she did nothing of the sort.

Instead, she took one last look at the slack muscles of his face and shut the door with infinite care, not making even the whisper of a click.

And then she sagged against the wall and closed her eyes. Behind her lids she relived the scene she'd just witnessed, but with another woman kneeling before him.

Why can't it be me?

Jo knew the answer to that pitiful plea even in her sex-dazed state. It could never be her—not only because she wasn't the type of woman he favored, but, more importantly, because Stephen Chatham believed Jo to be Joseph Edward Leather, his valet of almost two years And if he ever found out the deception she'd played on him there would be no crevice deep enough or cave dark enough to hide her from his wrath.

Chapter Two

It was past two in the morning when Stephen returned home from Number 14, the gambling club he owned with the other three men who belonged to the syndicate.

As ever, Leather was awake and waiting for him when he entered his chambers.

"Good evening, Mr. Chatham."

"You should have gone to bed," Stephen said—which is what he always said.

"I was awake, sir." Which is what *Leather* always said.

Stephen had serious doubts the man ever slept—or was even human, for that matter. Except for one day every month, the first Monday, Leather was always waiting for Stephen whenever he returned home. Two o'clock in the afternoon or two o'clock the morning, Leather was there, impeccably groomed and dressed, his face an impassive mask. He was the ultimate servant, a man who seemed to live only for his job. That was fine with Stephen; he was the best damned valet he'd ever had.

Leather was a tall, bone thin man who didn't have to stand on his toes to help Stephen in and out of coats or waistcoats as his last valet had. He moved with quiet efficiency, helping him slip out of his coat, but leaving Stephen to pull off his cravat. Leather had known, without Stephen having to tell him, that Stephen didn't like anyone's hands except his own near his throat.

He was remarkably adept at anticipating Stephen's every need, want, or desire before Stephen did. He certainly knew as much about Stephen's likes and dislikes as Stephen himself.

But, most importantly, Leather was discrete and reserved and demonstrated an unprecedented degree of devotion to his job.

Although Stephen didn't trust him completely, he trusted him a great deal more than anyone other than his three business partners.

"Will you be engaging in your usual routine in the morning, sir?"

Stephen's usual routine was to wake at five and spend an hour and a half in his private gymnasium, which he'd equipped according to the principles of MacLaren, although with more emphasis on solitary exercises.

"I'll have a lie-in tomorrow, Leather. Wake me at half six."

"Very good, sir."

"Also, we'll leave two days hence on the six-fifteen from Paddington Station. You'll need to pack enough for a stay of two weeks, although we may be back sooner."

"Very good, sir." The other man's eyes—so distorted by spectacles it gave Stephen a headache just looking at him—caught his in the mirror as he draped Stephen's coat over the wooden clothes horse.

The brief glance reminded Stephen of something. "We shall be out of town on your first Monday. You may either take tomorrow or have your day while we are away."

"May I enquire where we are going, Mr. Chatham?"

Stephen finished the last button on his waistcoat and Leather helped him out of it. "Glasgow."

"Very good, sir. I shall take tomorrow off if that serves." His face remained as impassive as ever, but Stephen thought he saw something in his eyes.

"Have you been to Scotland before?" Stephen asked.

Leather's full mouth—the only generous feature on a face that was spare and angular—twitched into something that approached a smile but did not quite make it. "I have, sir, but not for many years."

Stephen thought about asking where and when, but then decided he didn't want to breech the wall of reserve between them. Although they often spoke about his business dealings or news items of interest, Stephen had tried to avoid personal questions.

His last valet had chattered so incessantly about his family, his sweetheart, his bloody butterfly collection, and half a hundred other subjects that Stephen had finally needed to discharge him just to get a moment's peace.

Although he doubted Leather would be such a blatherer, it was best not to open that door.

Stephen lowered his long body into the well-padded chair just outside the dressing room and Leather dropped to his knees and unlaced his ankle boots with the same deft, efficient motions he did everything. Stephen idly studied the man's bowed head as he worked. Leather's hair was a mousy brown that he kept cropped so closely Stephen could see the pink of his scalp through the short, spiky hairs. It was a severe style that suited his rather austere person.

Joseph Leather had the sort of average, non-descript build and looks a person always forgot. Even though Stephen saw his face every day, he was always slightly surprised when he'd been away a few hours and saw him again.

Indeed, Leather would make an excellent spy.

Stephen's mouth pulled into a slight smile at the thought of his mild-mannered valet getting up to political hijinks for the government or getting up to hijinks of any kind.

It wasn't just his face that was bland, it was his temperament. He'd never seen the man exhibit anger, happiness, sadness, joy, discomfort, or anything other than a nod of satisfaction when Stephen praised some aspect of his work.

Stephen believed he was an easy master to serve as far as valeting. He was particular about his clothing and how he dressed, but he was not a dandy. And while he had the occasional late night—as he had this evening—he otherwise he kept early hours.

All in all, Leather had plenty of time on his own, not that he ever went anywhere except on his one day off a month. Stephen had wondered more than once what he did on those Mondays.

Did he visit family? A lover? A wife and children? He supposed any of those things was possible, although the idea of Leather with a sweetheart stretched Stephen's imagination to the breaking point.

Although Stephen had been raised in a household with servants until age six—when his parents sent him away—he'd done without live-in servants of any kind for most of his adult life, until he'd suddenly woken up one day and noticed that he was living in cramped lodgings on the east side of London when he was worth hundreds of thousands of pounds.

Since that time, his household increased with every year that passed: valet, butler, housekeeper, footmen, countless maids, grooms, and a host of other strangers. How amazing that he could live cheek by jowl with all these people and know nothing about them, when they knew so much about him.

And nobody knew more about him than Leather. The man knew even the most intimate details of Stephen's life. Somewhere along the line Leather had even taken charge of arranging Stephen's amorous entertainment at times.

His face heated at the thought; he simply could not recall how such a thing had come about. It wasn't that he employed Leather in that capacity all the time, only on those evenings when Stephen needed release and couldn't find the time or energy to go to one of the houses he favored—those places that catered to very wealthy men like him, where any fantasy could be made real.

Stephen certainly hadn't *intended* to make his valet his procurer but the man managed the selecting and fetching and dispatching of whores with the same detached efficiency he employed choosing his clothing. Although he appeared not to mind, or even notice, his ever-increasing list of responsibilities, Stephen couldn't help wondering what the man thought about him. To Leather, Stephen's sexual tastes appeared to be just another preference to be memorized—the same as Stephen's predilection for rare beef.

Leather stood up, stockings in one hand and shoes in the other. "Will you be going straight to bed, sir, or should I run you a bath?

Stephen stretched and groaned as his various joints popped. "A soak is exactly what I need."

"Very good, sir." Leather disappeared and Stephen heard the sound of water splashing in the bathroom adjacent to the dressing room. Leather returned just in time to crouch and retrieve Stephen's drawers and trousers as he stepped out of them.

"Is your shoulder paining you again, sir?"

Stephen realized he was rolling his right shoulder, which had never been the same since it had been pulled out of the socket. "It's stiff. I think it must be the cold weather."

"I'll fetch the warming liniment and apply it while you soak."

Stephen opened his mouth to tell the other man he needn't bother, but then closed it and nodded. Leather, for all his apparent subservience, always seemed to carry through on anything he suggested. No matter how diffident he looked or sounded, he possessed a quiet will of iron on some subjects, especially those concerning Stephen's person.

Stephen padded in bare feet toward the bathroom, which was already deliciously warm and steamy. Leather had filled the tub with almost-too-hot water, which Stephen found perfect.

Stephen had purchased the townhouse from a barrister who'd also been a bachelor. He'd done very little to anything other than his own bed chambers and the study after moving in. But the one change he *had* made was to bring in a custom bathtub to suit his extra tall person, so when he slipped into the hot water he could stretch out to his full six feet six inches.

It was bloody heaven and he laid his head against the sloped tub and considered the meeting earlier tonight.

"It's *your* turn to go up to Glasgow and deal with these bloody shipbuilders," Gideon Banks reminded him—for at least the third time. "Edward and I went last time and Smith before that." He shrugged. "I'd go again but I've got a bit of personal business to take care of."

Stephen knew that Banks wanted one of them to ask him *what* personal business he had to take care of, but the rest of them knew Gideon would tell them without any encouragement.

The others began to gather their possessions while Stephen finished up with the evening's notes. He was the syndicate's unofficial secretary, mainly by virtue of his meticulous—some would say obsessive— organizational skills.

"Is he going to answer me?" Banks asked nobody in particular.

"I think he's ignoring you," Fanshawe said as he straightened the scattered papers in front of him.

Edward Fanshawe had been the one to suggest they needed to increase their shipping fleet. This time, rather than build new ships, Edward proposed they look at older ships in dry dock, most of which needed serious repairs but could be picked up at a substantial discount.

"Are you pouting, Chatham?" Gideon asked.

Stephen cut him a cool, dismissive look. It was almost impossible not to smile at Gideon Banks's petulant tone, but Stephen managed it.

"I told you, Banks, he's ignoring you," Fanshawe said, tucking the fat stack of documents and drawings into a worn leather satchel. "I wish I could ignore you even half as well."

Stephen and Smith—and even Banks himself—laughed at that.

"I'll take my own railcar," Stephen said, more to himself.

"It speaks!" Banks said.

Everyone ignored him.

"Ah," Smith said, "that's right, Chatham. I recall you just had your car redone."

Stephen grunted and Smith pulled out his silver scrolled case and extracted one of his vile cigars—which was usually Stephen's cue to leave the room. He abhorred smoking of all types. It reminded him of that summer.

"I think he's pouting," Banks said again. When nobody responded he added, "Cheer up, Chatham, you'll get to visit one of my favorite places." He turned to Fanshawe with a lascivious smile. "*You* recall Glasgow, don't you Edward?"

"Shut up, Gideon," Edward said, but his words lacked heat. He buckled the last of the straps on his satchel and stood. "Have a good trip, Chatham." He paused, a curious expression on his harsh face. "As much as I hate to agree with anything Gideon says, I do recommend the place in Glasgow—Frau Meisen's in the Possilpark area. It's a very . . . unusual establishment." He gave an abrupt nod. "Good night gentlemen."

Gideon barely waited until the door closed to say, "Edward's no fun now that he's married."

"Edward was rarely any fun *before* he was married," Smith pointed out.

"That's true. But at least he could be counted on to be adventurous on occasion."

Stephen knew where this was going before Gideon spoke.

"I'm going to the Birch Palace," Gideon announced. "Either of you want to join me?"

"I'm for home, my dear Gideon," Smith said, standing with a groan. "These old bones need their beauty sleep."

"What about you, Stephen?" Gideon asked.

Although he tried to sound casual, Stephen had detected a strain of desperation Gideon's voice lately. The younger man was a whoremonger of monumental proportions but he appeared to be getting even worse these past months, as if even the depths of debauchery he wallowed in were no longer enough to satiate his needs.

Stephen had once, years ago and in a moment of weakness and foolishness, accompanied Gideon to a brothel and had almost immediately regretted becoming ensnared in the man's extravagant, out-of-control whoring. He'd never gone with any of his partners after that, although he suspected Fanshawe and Smith behaved with more decorum.

No, he preferred to whore in private.

"He's ignoring you," Smith said, his hand on the door handle. "I shall see you in two days Gideon, and you in two weeks, Chatham."

Stephen grunted.

"Wait," Gideon said, getting to his feet. "Will you drop me at Tosca's?"

"I thought you just said you were going to the Birch Palace?"

"I was, but Tosca's is on your way and I sent my carriage home earlier."

"I will drop you off at Tosca's, you young reprobate." It amused Smith to call Gideon young even though there was barely five years of difference between the men. Of course Gideon behaved like he was twenty. Or twelve, even.

Gideon winked at Stephen and gave him a grin that was supposed to be charming. "You could learn a thing or two from me, Stephen: you see how adaptable I am when it comes to my amores?"

Stephen barked a laugh at that. "Adaptable? You'd fuck a knothole in a fence, Banks."

Gideon was rendered speechless—a rarity—but Smith roared.

"Come on," Smith said, brushing actual tears from the corner of one eye as he grabbed Gideon's arm and dragged him out the door. "You should know better than to prod the lion. The next time you do he might take off your entire bloody arm, not just your hand." He winked at Stephen. "Ta, Chatham, see you in a few."

Stephen snorted as the door closed on Gideon's complaining. The man was a perennial juvenile who carried none of the tools of a successful businessman: no bag or satchel or even a pen. He never took notes or did anything that even remotely resembled work. Yet he possessed a bloody brilliant mind that could recall any detail, no matter how minor or from how long ago. He was a walking, talking compendium of every piece of information he'd ever absorbed. It was one hell of a gift when coupled with Gideon's engineering skills. It was too bad he was so distracted by whoring that he was driving himself—and everyone else around him—mad.

Somebody cleared their throat and Stephen jolted, sending hot bathwater sloshing over the sides of the big tub.

"I'm sorry, sir," Leather said. "I didn't know you were sleeping."

"I wasn't sleeping, just thinking over the day's business."

"I thought you might like some tea while you soaked."

Stephen saw that a tea cart had miraculously appeared on the right side of the tub. On it was a cup and saucer, pot, and a plate of Stephen's favorite butter biscuits. He picked up the cup, took a sip, and then sighed with genuine happiness.

"I don't know what you do, Leather, but you make the best tea I've ever tasted."

"It is my pleasure, sir."

Stephen could hear the truth beneath his words—unusual in the man's generally toneless voice—and he marveled anew that Leather took so much pleasure in his job.

Leather was his fourth—and hopefully final—valet and Stephen did not want another. Especially when Leather seemed to have been put on Earth just to serve Stephen's needs.

He gave a soft snort at the arrogant thought—so arrogant it might well have come out of Gideon's mouth.

The steam shifted and swirled around Stephen, and Leather's voice came from behind him, "May I proceed, sir?"

"Yes." Stephen took a deep drink of almost scalding tea and then set down the cup before stretching his arms on the warmed copper rim of the tub.

Leather's hands, when they touched him, were slick and warm, the smell of something astringent, but not unpleasant filling the air.

"Ahh," Stephen groaned, his body going limp at Leather's strong, massaging fingers. "That is pure magic," he murmured. "What is that plant, again?"

"Eucalyptus, sir."

"Are you coming down with a cold, Leather? Your voice sounds rather hoarse."

The valet's hands paused and he cleared his throat. "Just the wretched fog outside today, sir." His fingers resumed their work.

Stephen grunted. "It *was* bloody nasty. I daresay it will be better in Glasgow," he added on a yawn.

Thinking of Glasgow made him recall both Fanshawe's and Gideon's words earlier in the evening. He'd heard both men speak of the exclusive brothel in Glasgow several times. Apparently the clients often made themselves available to other patrons, sometimes in private, sometimes in very public showings.

Stephen was intrigued by thought of watching something so public. When it came to his sexual encounters he'd always been intensely private, but he wondered if voyeurism might enhance an experience. Would he like being watched by other men while he got his cock sucked? He wasn't so certain. Nor was he certain about fucking a woman in public, although the notion was titillating. He suspected he would only enjoy both activities if his identity were concealed.

His cock had begun to swell at the erotic thoughts and he spread his legs a little, enjoying the sensation of hot water caressing his engorged shaft. Leather's hands were still working his shoulder, the fingers carefully pressing between the joints, prodding just enough to hurt— but it was a pain that was oddly pleasurable.

"Does this still ache?" Leather asked in a low voice, his thumb pressing against the spot that usually pained him the most.

"Not as much as before," Stephen admitted, his voice husky with arousal or exhaustion or a combination of the two.

"I'm going to work on the other side a little."

Stephen gave a sleepy grunt as Leather's hand moved to his other shoulder, his own hand moving to his erection, which had begun to throb.

He gave himself a gentle stroke and yawned, thankful the room was too steamy for Leather to see his swollen prick or he might think Stephen had untoward designs on his virtue.

His lips twitched at the thought and his smile stretched into another yawn. God, he was so very tired. And Leather's hands just felt . . .

***

Jo had to concentrate on her breathing to keep it normal. These nights when he came home exhausted and let her massage his injured shoulder were the best nights of her entire life. And, yes, she was fully aware of just how pathetic that was.

He relaxed in his tub believing his valet was rubbing an ache out of his shoulder and all the while her arousal was sliding down her thighs, dampening her black woolen trousers, and providing masturbatory material for later tonight.

His body beneath her hands was like silk-covered steel. He was such a big man, but not bulky, his muscles long and toned from his rigorous daily exercise regimen.

She knew why he'd stayed still for so long and allowed her to work on his shoulder when she heard his deep, even breathing: he'd fallen asleep.

Jo smiled into the swirling steam and blew air out through pursed lips, the movement stirring the steam and allowing her a ghostly view of his long, hard body. And oh how very hard and long it was tonight.

Her mouth flooded at the sight of his thick rod, which one hand loosely cradled beneath the water.

What had he been thinking that made him hard? She knew it wasn't her hands—he'd never gotten an erection from her shoulder rubs in the past. Jo would have noticed because she made bloody sure to snatch every opportunity to look at him: while handing him a towel, while bustling around the room under the guise of tidying up, or while drying his body or shaving him, but really staring and spying.

She allowed her hands to dip a little lower, to massage the sculpted muscles of his magnificent chest. Jo tilted her head enough that she could see his tiny nipples, which had puckered from either the cold or arousal or both.

Jo would have given all the money she kept hidden in the lining of her mattress to put her mouth on one of those little pink disks and suck

18

until he squirmed with pleasure. She knew for a fact he enjoyed nipple stimulation.

Her hands brazenly slid lower, kneading and prodding, and she dared a feather-light touch on his nipple; his body jolted as though she'd passed a bold of electricity through him.

"Wha—?" he mumbled, slipping slightly in the tub before grasping at the sides and sitting up.

Jo immediately removed her hands from his body. "I'm sorry Mr. Chatham, did I hurt you?"

"Huh? Uh, no," he lifted a dripping hand to shove his thick chestnut hair from his eyes. It had curled in the steam and made him look younger, more vulnerable. "I must've fallen asleep," he said, sounding exhausted. He laid his big hands on the copper rim and pushed himself up.

All the moisture that had just filled her mouth drained away as she looked up at him. He'd turned to the side to step out of the tub and she had a perfect view of his softening, but still jutting shaft, the thick blue vein visible from this angle, his sac heavy and pendulous.

"Fetch me a towel, Leather." Mr. Chatham's tone was impatient and Jo shot to her feet. Shame that she'd been gawking rather than doing her job overpowered arousal and she scurried to grab one of the towels she'd laid over the warming bar in front of the fire.

She knew it was beyond pitiful, but it was a matter of pride to *always* have what her master wanted *before* he wanted it—before even *he* knew that he wanted it. So even this slight slip in her duties was mortifying.

"Here you are, sir."

He took the cloth and she stole a glimpse at him in the steam-shrouded mirror: dark smudges below his heavy-lidded eyes as he wrapped the large towel snugly around his muscular hips.

"I'll dry myself and you can shave me in the morning," he said on a yawn, padding toward his bed chamber. "I'm dead on my feet."

Jo stared down at the trail of large, wet footprints he left in his wake, her own body humming from touching him.

She wouldn't be sleeping any time soon.

Chapter Three

Jo waited until after she'd shaved and dressed Mr. Chatham to remind him that she would be taking her day off today.

"That's fine," he said, looking at something in the paper, his expression distracted.

"I'll be back tomorrow morning rather than afternoon, sir. That will give me an entire day to prepare for the trip north."

"Mmm," he shook his head and she knew it wasn't at her, but at whatever he was reading. "Make sure you pick up my new suit—the gray one you returned to the tailor for adjustment."

"It's already done, sir."

Thinking about that suit reminded her of the excessively enjoyable experience of adjusting Mr. Chatham's inseam.

Yes, she most certainly needed her day off.

"I shall see you tomorrow, then," Mr. Chatham said dismissively, never looking up from the paper.

Jo closed his door soundlessly behind her and paid a visit to the kitchen. She spent very little time socializing with the servants and knew they thought her aloof. She *was* aloof, but not for the reasons they suspected.

Mrs. Dane was giving instructions to one of the maids when Jo entered. She immediately stopped and turned to Jo. "Ah, good morning Mr. Leather. What can I do for you?"

"I'll be taking my day early this month. Please tell Charles he is to valet the master while I am gone tonight, but I'll return tomorrow morning."

"Very good, Mr. Leather. I hope you enjoy your day off."

"Thank you, Mrs. Dane." Jo nodded to the other servants milling around the room and left, aware they'd enjoy talking about her once she'd gone. She knew speculation was rife about where she came from and what she did on her mysterious days off. God willing they would never know more than she'd begun her service in the household of a duke. That piece of information was usually enough to maintain distance and quell any friendly overtures.

Up in her room she took out her small overnight case, which she kept packed and ready and locked. Jo allowed the chambermaids into her room, but only when she was in the house. She kept anything that might incriminate her—there was pitifully little—under lock and key; she didn't take foolish risks. Some people might say keeping hundreds of pounds sewed up in one's mattress was foolish, but after what had happened, she always kept enough money on hand to leave quickly, should she need to.

Jo put on her hat and picked up her case, taking the servant stairs, not because Mr. Chatham made her use them, but because they were faster.

She never took a carriage to Bernina's directly from the house. It was probably an unnecessary precaution, but she didn't want anyone at Mr. Chatham's to ever ask a driver where he dropped Mr. Leather.

Yesterday's nasty brown fog had cleared slightly and she walked longer than she usually would before hailing a handsome. The driver's smile at the address told Jo that he knew her destination was an exclusive brothel.

Jo seated herself and stared out the grimy window. The driver might know it was a brothel, but he likely wouldn't know just how unusual its services were. Few people did, except those who employed said services: people like Jo.

Bernina's had once been called Madam Cecile's but had needed to close its doors in a hurry after word leaked out that Madam Cecile's catered to sodomites. It had taken Cecile two years before she could open again elsewhere. She now made an effort to disguise the true purpose of her business and Bernina's offered services for *regular* patrons.

Jo had discovered the place—inadvertently—from her last master, a retired, highly decorated colonel whose tastes had run along unconventional lines. Colonel Whitby had been Jo's second gentleman after she'd left the Duke of Tarland's employment and she'd stayed with him for almost four years, until his death.

The Colonel had once become ill and had sent Jo to Bernina's to cancel his appointment. The first time Jo walked into the brothel and met Madam Cecile she felt as though she'd come home.

Jo had always wondered if the sharp-eyed old officer knew her secret, but he'd never spoken of it. If he'd known she was a female, he must have received some enjoyment from her impersonation because he'd left her a very handsome bequest in his will: for *excellent services rendered.*

Jo smiled at the euphemistic phrase; yes, she'd given good service to the old gentleman and had been glad to do it. Back then—before she'd discovered Bernina's—she'd thought there was something wrong with her for becoming aroused by serving others.

Not until she'd walked into Bernina's did Jo understood that she wasn't alone—that there were other people like *her.*

Cecile had taken one look at her and smiled, seeing beyond her exterior to the person who inhabited Jo's somber black suit. It had taken Jo a little longer to see past Cecile's lovely exterior, but then she didn't have the other woman's wealth of experience in such matters.

The carriage stopped in front of the nondescript gray building and Jo paid the grinning driver.

"'Ave a nice day, sir."

She ignored him and mounted the stairs. This early in the day she had to knock. A liveried footman answered the door, his stern expression breaking into a smile when he saw her.

"Jo—what a pleasant surprise."

"Hello, Daniel, how are you?" she asked as she stepped into the handsome entry hall and handed him her hat and cane while she stripped off her gloves.

"Ship shape, sir. Would you like to see Madam first?"

"I'd better, since I know you weren't expecting me." Jo smiled and handed him her gloves. It was probably the first genuine smile to grace her face since the *last* time she'd been to Bernina's. Sometimes she wondered how she'd survived before she discovered this special place.

"Don't wake her if she's sleeping," Jo said.

"I don't think she ever sleeps," Daniel said in a stage whisper.

"I heard that, Daniel."

Jo glanced up and saw Cecile at the top of the stairs.

"Did I sleep through the week, Jo? Is it already Monday?" Cecile asked in a teasing voice as Jo mounted the elegant marble steps.

"It's good to see you," Cecile said when Jo reached the top, taking her into a welcoming embrace and squeezing her tight. Until meeting Cecile, the last time Jo had embraced another person was her father, many years ago.

Cecile held her at arms' length and tilted her head. "How about we have something a bit stronger than tea before I send you on your way?"

"Ah, yes—some of that fine brandy?" Jo said, her hopeful tone making the other woman laugh.

The brothel was an old mansion and Cecile used what had probably been the library for her office. It was an elegantly decorated room where the madam often met clients. Cecile called it whore-décor, but Jo thought it was elegant and understated, muted greens and browns with only hints of gold. Lots of leather furniture, just like the guest rooms.

Cecile poured them both drinks in crystal that was every bit as fine as Mr. Chatham's and brought a glass over, lowering her tall, slender body onto the settee beside Jo.

"Confusion to the enemy," Cecile said, the same toast as always.

They clinked glasses and Jo sipped, savoring the expensive liquor. She rarely drank and made it a point to limit her intake when she came to Bernina's: she didn't want to dull her senses while she enjoyed her one luxury.

"Is everything all right, Josie, my dear?"

Jo smiled at the pet name. "We're off to Glasgow for two weeks so I took my day early this month."

"Ahh. *We* meaning you and your delicious employer?"

Jo had been surprised to learn Mr. Chatham had come to Bernina's a time or two, but not since Jo had worked for him.

"Yes, it's a business trip."

"And how do you feel about going back to Scotland?" Cecile asked, ever the perceptive one—sometimes *too* perceptive.

"Where I'll be going is a world away from where I grew up." Cecile was one of only a handful of people who knew about Jo's unusual childhood.

"It never fails to amaze me that you're Scottish: you have absolutely no trace of an accent."

"That was my father's doing. He was a stickler about eradicating all trace of a brogue. He said getting a position anywhere but Scotland would be twice as difficult if I spoke like an Aberdonian farm laddie." Jo pronounced the last few words using said accent and Cecile laughed.

"Before I forget," Cecile said "You did say Glasgow?"

Jo nodded.

Cecile's wicked red lips curved. "Ah, well, you'll regret you took your day off in London." Cecile stood and went to her desk where she leaned over and wrote something before returning. "But if you do find yourself with free time, this place is quiet unusual."

Jo looked at what she'd written and then glanced up. "Frau Meisen's? A house of pleasure, I take it."

"Oh, and a most unusual one at that. The gent who started up the Birch Palace used to be her lover—or business partner, to hear him tell it. What makes the place so unusual is that Frau Meisen often allows *clients* to behave as employees." She gave a throaty laugh. "Quite bloody clever when you think about it. Rich twists come to her with their fantasies and then they pay *her* to sell *them* to either another client—who also pays. Of course she employs plenty of her own people, too."

"How does *that* work? If the clients are rich, aren't they worried they'll be recognized?"

"Masks, my dear. They always wear masks. We have several clients here who've never showed their faces. Wearing masks is not at all unusual. And some of them can look quite charming."

"That's . . . intriguing."

"If you get an opportunity you should go take a look."

Jo didn't see that happening. "Is it difficult to get in?"

"Not if you tell them I sent you—you need a referral. She's dreadfully expensive."

"Oh?"

"As much as £50 for one night."

Jo's jaw dropped and Cecile nodded. "Makes me feel like a right fool for not starting that here, although I suspect the need for discretion is why she has to charge all that money. You know how whores like to talk—she'd need to ensure her employee's silence. Still, it sounds intriguing to visit, if not to run a place like it."

It did sound intriguing. But that was an unheard-of amount of money! What Jo was about to enjoy at Cecile's cost a tiny fraction of that.

She suspected that Cecile gave her some rather special deals as she felt a sense of camaraderie with servants like herself. Jo knew she was extremely fortunate in having found Bernina's. It was the closest thing to a home she'd ever had, which was so sad she didn't even want to think about it.

"I wouldn't be surprised if your employer sought out Frau Meisen's while he was there."

"How do you know that—not that I'm doubting you, since you seem to know everything."

Cecile chuckled. "It's not mysterious. We often see one of his partners, Gideon Banks, here. And he's been there, so I'm sure he told his partners."

Jo squinted at the other woman. "Are you blushing?"

"I probably am," she admitted with a rueful chuckle. "Gideon will do that to people—even old whores like me. The man is—" she shook her head. "Well, I've not seen his equal, that's for sure."

Jo had heard Mr. Chatham mention the man's name, but in tones of annoyance rather than worshipful wonder.

Cecile tossed back the last of her drink, Jo's cue it was time for business. "Gideon's a story for another time, darling." Cecile walked with her to the door and kissed her on the cheek. "I likely won't see you before you go, but I think Daniel may have set up something special for you today."

"How do you manage these things? I never even saw you talk with him—or anyone else."

"That's all part of my charm." Cecile hesitated, and then said. "I'm going to leave a package for you downstairs. Don't forget to check with the footmen before you go."

"What are you leaving me?"

Cecile winked and turned away. "It's a surprise, darling."

"You're a tease," Jo called after her.

Cecile just laughed.

Jo climbed one more flight of stairs and then went to the door all the way at the end of the hall, her pulse beginning to pound as she lifted her hand to knock.

The door opened and a gorgeous blond woman dressed only in a blue silk robe smiled at Jo.

"Hello, darling."

Jo grinned. "Well, this *is* my lucky day. I'd ask how you were doing, Jane, but I can see that for myself."

Jane reached out, took Jo's hand, and pulled her inside. "Come on, there's somebody new here I think you'll like. Her name is Marie."

Chapter Four

Even in his private car with every convenience—well, *almost* every convenience—Stephen was still knackered when he stepped onto the platform in Glasgow at nine-thirty the following morning.

As tired as he was, it was far too early to go to the hotel so he left Leather to deal with the baggage and took a carriage directly to Scott's, the shipyard where he was to look at the first of several prospects.

An unhealthy brown pall hung over the industrializing city but nothing to compare to London. The chill in the air, however, was something else entirely and Stephen was glad Leather had thought to bring along both his heaviest coat and wool muffler because it was bloody freezing for all that it was almost spring.

Stephen had liked his new rail car very well. He was ashamed to admit that he'd sent it out for refurbishment after seeing Edward Fanshawe's car. Edward's proclivities ran parallel to Stephen's when it came to sexual activities and his private car had been equipped as a moving pleasure palace. The bedchamber had subtle additions for restraints, as did the sitting area. There was also a larger than average compartment for bathing and personal needs.

Edward took his wife along on his trips and Nora Fanshawe was a fascinating woman who indulged and encouraged her husband's unusual tastes, so he was getting excellent value from his investment.

Stephen, on the other hand, hadn't wished to take along a companion on a trip that was only business—so it was just he and Leather.

Business had been hectic for him lately and it had been two weeks since he'd last enjoyed a woman. As much as he'd enjoyed his evening with Sharon, it was his practice never to go to the same woman more than once every four or five months. He didn't want to feel any sense of attachment to the women he paid and he didn't want any of them attaching themselves to him.

Besides, as beautiful and skilled as Sharon had been, the small amount of conversation he'd had with her afterward had made him realize the only worthwhile thing she did with her mouth was suck cock.

It wasn't that she'd been stupid; it was that she'd been acquisitive and full of artifice, which had dulled his ardor for a repeat performance.

Stephen reminded himself that Sharon had delivered on what she'd promised—sexual release—and that he was a fool to expect more, especially when he never gave anything of himself. He was sure Sharon hadn't liked him much, either. No doubt she'd found him brooding, domineering, and remote, which was how he always behaved with these women.

Stephen stared at the grim Glasgow streets as he considered how jaded he'd become.

No doubt part of that was the inevitable result of being so wealthy he could buy anything he wanted, including people. It had warped his view of humanity to know that any woman was his if he was willing to pay for her.

Stephen wasn't stupid; he knew using whores was lazy and, quite frankly, a power imbalance that mitigated against developing anything other than a master-servant relationship.

But whenever he started to question the wisdom of paying for physical gratification, he just reminded himself of Louisa.

He grimaced just thinking that name.

Whoring might leave him feeling empty, but feeling empty was far better than feeling gutted and betrayed.

The cab shuddered to a stop and Stephen looked out the hazy window: he'd reached the Clyde River. He picked up his satchel and put sex and women and pleasure from his mind; it was time to get down to business.

***

Jo counted the money yet again: two hundred and ninety-two pounds. Although it wasn't her life's savings—she'd always sent the bulk of her wages to Mr. Withers, the solicitor her and her brother had used to manage their father's small estate—it was still a goodly chunk of money, which she'd been saving for years.

She'd been working since age seven, when she'd started as a page for the Duchess of Tarland. When she turned ten, she'd begun to work under her father's tutelage. Albert Leather had been the head valet for the Duke of Tarland for almost fifteen years by the time Jo started to work for him.

She hadn't actually waited on His Grace until she'd turned fifteen, when she'd become her father's chief assistant.

At eighteen, she'd replaced her elder brother Ben as valet to His Grace's heir, the seventeen-year-old Marquess of Staunton.

Jo had served the marquess for a little more than a year before leaving the duke's employ at nineteen to accept a position—almost unheard of at such a tender age—with a mid-level banker who'd not been able to afford a more seasoned manservant.

Jo had stayed with her first master two years before accepting an offer from the colonel.

She'd saved a good deal of money over the years, rarely needing to spend any on herself. After all, a valet had their meals and housing paid for and Jo's masters had always allowed her access to their books for her entertainment. Her only real expense was clothing. Her father had taught her and Ben to buy only the best, which meant rarely having to replace anything.

It wasn't until Jo discovered Cecile's that she began to spend anything at all on herself.

Jo stared at the money in her hands, as if it would tell her what to do. As if she didn't *already* know what she was going to do, despite how wrong it would be.

Jo couldn't help thinking about the message Mr. Chatham had given her before he'd left this morning: a message addressed to Frau Meisen in Possilpark.

It had to be some sort of sign that Mr. Chatham was contemplating going to the very brothel Cecile had mentioned? Or perhaps it was just because Frau Meisen's was the best and Mr. Chatham never took anything less?

Either way, it was *exactly* what she'd hoped for.

But if she acted on her impulse and got caught then she would likely be a twenty-seven year old valet in need of a new position. Well, if Mr. Chatham left enough of her to find a new job.

"This is a sickness, Jo," her brother Ben accused the last time they'd met for their monthly dinner. "What you *are* has always been dishonest. But to *lust* for a man unbeknownst to him?" Ben's expression had brimmed with disgust after he'd somehow guessed Jo's feelings toward Mr. Chatham. "You must leave him *now* Jo, before you do something unforgiveable."

Jo had busied herself with her roast beef, hoping he'd leave the subject alone if she ignored him long enough. But that had been wishful thinking.

When she'd not answered, Ben had leaned across the table and hissed. "Jo. Are you listening to me?"

She'd put aside her fork and knife, no longer hungry. "I can hardly *not* listen to you, Ben."

"This is a bloody mess." Ben eyed her in a way that was comprehensive—a way that let Jo know that he didn't just mean the fact she was infatuated with her employer, but that *everything* about her was a mess. "I hate to speak ill of the dead, but our father should've been horsewhipped for what he did to you."

"He only did it to save me from mother's fate."

"It didn't bloody work, did it?"

Jo stiffened at his cold, mocking tone. "I don't want to talk about this."

"You *need* to *do* something about this, Jo. It's—it's bloody *unnatural!*"

She'd shoved her chair back so hard it hit the wall. Heads turned in their direction and Jo could see her brother cringe at her behavior. Their father's very first rule: never draw attention to yourself, strive to be invisible.

Jo threw some coins on the table and snatched up her hat and cane and left. She walked a block before she heard the sound of feet pounding behind her. "Jo! Dammit, Jo. Hold up."

Jo chewed the inside of her mouth but stopped and swung around. "What do you want now, Ben? To insult me more?"

"Why is it insulting to tell you the truth?" He grimaced and leaned close enough to hiss in her ear. "You're a woman, Jo. You're not a man and you never will be. It's time you accepted it."

"And do what, Ben?" she didn't bother keeping her voice down and people on the sidewalk glanced at them. Jo knew they'd be having a difficult time matching what they saw with how she was behaving: a gentlemen's gentlemen who was apparently drunk and ready to fight another gentlemen's gentleman. "What would you have me do?" she repeated. "Take a job as a char woman? Wait," she said with exaggerated comprehension, "I won't even be able to get *that* position with the recommendations I have." She got right up in his face. "Just *what* would you have me do?"

A muscle in his jaw twitched as he stared at her. They looked so much alike, Josephine and her elder brother Benjamin. So much alike that their father had never had any difficulty passing Jo off as his younger son—except that one time.

"Good God, Jo didn't you learn anything from what happened with Staunton? What will it take to teach you a lesson?" When her jaw dropped Ben lifted his hands in a placating gesture, as if he were blameless for the words pouring out of him. "Somebody has to say it, Jo—Father certainly never did. What his lordship did was wrong, but do you really believe you don't deserve your share of blame?"

"I cannot believe you're saying this. Is this what you've thought all along? That I caused all that?"

"I don't blame you for what happened—I blame our father for that, after all, he drummed his motto into me, too: The perfect valet exists, first and foremost, to serve all his master's needs. *All* his needs. Do you think I don't know what he meant?" Ben demanded and then shook his head. "But none of that matters—I'm talking about what you're doing *now*. I'm sorry to have to say it, but—"

"Save your apology. And also save your advice. I love my work and if the way I live doesn't bother me, why should it bother you?"

"Because Father is no longer here, Jo. Who will have to clean up after you, this time?"

"Not you, Ben, don't worry. Nobody even knows I *have* a brother. You can just pretend like I don't exist."

"I wish it were that easy. But we *are* related and as much as you don't want to accept it, we're linked in name, if nothing else. God, Jo, you're my *sister.* Are you happy to live your life never having a family? Children?"

Jo probably should have told him the truth at that point, but she'd just been too bloody angry. "I don't have plans for either, not that that's any of your concern."

"But about *me*, Jo? What if *I* marry? Do I tell my wife about my younger sister or my younger brother? Do I tell her I have a sister pretending to be a man lusting for the man she's deceiving daily? Have you ever once considered how your behavior affects *my* life? Have you—"

"I'm leaving, Ben," Jo had said. "Don't contact me again if this is all you have to say." She'd left him standing there, too hurt and furious to speak without saying something she'd regret.

That argument had been six months ago and they'd not spoken since—the longest she'd ever gone without talking to her only remaining relative.

Jo missed Ben so *much*, even though they'd argued more often than not these past years. But once, when they were children, they'd been as close as two peas in a pod. Once Ben had not cared that Jo wore trousers and they competed for the same household positions and their father's praise.

But as much as she missed her brother, she could not give up who she was and what she wanted to please him. Indeed, in the months since she'd last spoken to Ben her feelings for Mr. Chatham had only become stronger. Every day with him was an agony of lusting and wanting and, yes, *loving.* She was tired of subjugating her desires; she was going to do something about it even if it ended in disaster.

So today, when she delivered Mr. Chatham's message to Frau Meisen's, she would deliver a message of her own at the same time. Who knows? It was entirely possible that Mr. Chatham would want something completely different at the unusual brothel. Perhaps Jo would spend all that money and end up with very expensive whores. But she had to try—when would she get a chance like this again? Never.

Jo drew a deep breath and then carefully folded up the banknotes and tucked them into the inner pocket of her black sack coat. The looser style of coat was not as popular among valets, but if she wore it rather than a more fitted coat then she didn't have to bind her breasts at all—not that there was hardly anything to bind.

Jo looked around Mr. Chatham's room one last time to assure herself everything was the way he liked it. When he'd left the Glasgow station he'd told her not to expect him until just before dinner, but she liked to have his room perfect in case he came back on a whim.

Once she was finished in his rooms she went to her own and picked up her gloves, hat, and umbrella.

It was drizzling lightly and Jo opened her umbrella and headed north. She would hire a carriage once she was far enough away from the hotel. The brothel was a few miles away, on the fringes of the industrial area known as Possilpark.

If everything went as she'd planned, she'd be returning to the hotel in a few hours a great deal lighter in the pocket.

Jo smiled to herself and then caught her reflection in the plate window of a watchmaker's shop. She stopped, arrested by her image. A man looked back at her, a gentleman's gentleman—dressed in a sober black suit of excellent tailoring. The man was slim—some might even say too thin. He wore fine black leather gloves—one of Jo's few extravagances— and a black bowler. His overcoat was black wool and the toes of his black boots were buffed to a mirror shine. His face was narrow and pale and overpowered by thick gold-rimmed spectacles that distorted his pale blue eyes.

She rarely ever studied herself in the mirror, only enough to ensure her person was clean and well presented. The image she saw didn't surprise her; this was the way Jo saw herself—as a man—and always had. But if her plans were successful, she would soon have to don her first ever dress and strive to look enough like a woman that Mr. Chatham would actually want her.

What would she do if he saw her and didn't want her? The thought was like a huge brick on her chest—on her heart.

A woman appeared in the window, gesturing to the tray of watches Jo had been unseeingly staring at.

Jo shook her head and then turned on the heel of her sensible ankle boots and resumed her journey.

***

Chatham was beyond knackered when he arrived back at the hotel. He'd taken dinner with one of the higher ups at Scott's—a casual meal at the man's small but elegant gentleman's club—and hadn't returned to the hotel until after dark.

As ever, Leather was waiting for him.

"You must be exhausted, sir," his valet said as he lifted Stephen's damp wool overcoat from his shoulders. "Shall I have dinner sent up or will you be going down to the dining room?"

"Neither," Stephen said on a huge yawn. "I ate already. What I *would* like is a cup of your tea, a shoulder rub, and a soak."

Leather grimaced slightly. "I'm afraid the bathtub would only fit half of you, sir."

"Ah, of course."

"They do have a new shower-bath, sir."

"Well, I suppose it shall have to do," Stephen said, starting on the buttons of his waistcoat. "But I still want the tea and shoulder rub—this damp, freezing weather is playing havoc with the bloody thing."

"Of course, sir. Did your business go well today?" Leather asked as he shook out the waistcoat, examining it. Stephen knew his valet handled a good deal of his laundry himself, not trusting his clothing to hotel laundries, or even the woman Stephen paid in London.

"It did," Stephen said, removing first his collar and then slipping the plain gold cufflinks from his shirt and handing them to Leather. "I looked at two of the ships they have on offer," he admitted, "But that is just the beginning as there are another dozen or so scattered at the various shipyards."

Leather deposited the cufflinks in the small leather box he kept for such items. "The city appears to be bustling, sir. I understand the ship building trade has caused rather a drastic shortage of housing." Leather took his shirt, laid it on the growing pile of discarded clothing and then knelt in front of the bench where Stephen sat.

"Yes, ship building has created both excess *and* shortage, a good and bad problem to have. I think my business won't keep me here the full two weeks—more like ten days," he added as Leather unlaced his shoes.

34

"Very good, sir."

Leather was sensitive enough to Stephen's moods that he always seemed to know when to ask Stephen about his day and when to be quiet, never bothering him with questions or comments if Stephen was tired or distracted. His questions were always intelligent and Stephen often found himself discussing business matters at some length without realizing it. More than once he'd solved some problem or other after verbalizing the issues to his attentive valet.

Now that he thought about it, he conversed more with Leather than he did with his business partners. In general he preferred to conduct his communication with the members of the syndicate in writing. He liked letters and the clarity and control they afforded.

Leather removed his stockings and then stood, the stockings in one hand and Stephen's shoes in the other. It was the same thing he'd done hundreds of other nights but for some reason tonight Stephen was suddenly curious about his reserved servant's activities in this strange city.

"And what did you do today, Leather? Did you see any of the city?"

Leather could not have looked more surprised if Stephen had broken into song and dance. His eyes, already enlarged by the thick lenses, appeared to double in size. And his cheeks—so pale and hairless Stephen doubted he needed to shave more than once a fortnight—striped with dark red slashes. Good God, who knew Leather could be so discommoded by such a simple question?

"I went for a walk to Buchanan Street, sir, which is accounted the finest shopping area in the city."

"Ah." He was going to leave it at that but the imp of the perverse—with whom Stephen was not very well acquainted—decided to pay a visit. "And how was it?"

Leather blinked. "I'm sorry, sir?"

"Buchanan Street? Was it good shopping? Did you drop a packet? Spend more than you should have?"

The valet's lips pulled up ever so slightly on one side, his face once again an unreadable mask. "I was somehow able to restrain my impulsive nature, sir."

Leather had a sense of humor? Who would have guessed?

"*Do* you have an impulsive nature, Leather? Somehow I would not have expected that."

"It springs forth on occasion, sir, er, rather . . . impulsively."

The dry words surprised a chuckle out of Stephen.

"I will start the shower-bath for you." Leather turned away abruptly, almost as if he were concerned the grilling would continue.

A huge yawn seized him and Stephen stretched his aching body, arching his back and moving his head from side to side to work out the knots and kinks. Just what was it about travel that made one so bloody sore and tired? He had to admit that he'd wanted to go to tantalizing-sounding brothel on the edge of Possilpark, but he was simply too exhausted tonight. He'd much rather have a hot shower, some decent tea—the tea at the shipyard had been dreadful—and a shoulder rub.

The door to the bathroom opened and steam billowed out. "The shower bath is ready, sir."

"Thank you, Leather," he said, the last word distorted by a yawn. He slipped out of his robe and handed it to his valet before stepping into the tub and pulling the curtain. Naturally the water was at a level for a man of normal height and Stephen had to bend nearly double to wash his face, neck, and head. As he soaped his chest and stomach he thought about what he might write to the madam. Did he really want to put his desires on paper? Or should he simply show up tomorrow night and do as the whim took him?

He had to crouch low to rinse the soap from his body, and contortions were necessary to clean his genitals and arse properly. The water was still hot when he finished, but the cramped stall left him with no desire to linger. He turned the handle and pushed back the curtain.

Leather handed him a towel and used a second one to dry the back of Stephen's body.

He'd never employed a valet who was quite so sedulous of his care and although he'd been rather leery of such intimate assistance at first, he'd come to not just tolerate the extra attention, but to expect it. Stephen could only suppose that Leather's commitment to his employer's comfort came from once having served a duke.

Stephen wiped his face and front with the warm, slightly rough towel while Leather dried his back, starting at his neck and vigorously rubbing down his shoulders, back, arse, and kneeling to dry his legs, calf, and feet. He had to admit the vigorous toweling made him feel . . . decadent. Was it strange to enjoy the attentions of another man? Even if the man in question was employed to be his body servant?

Stephen glanced down at his cock, which had been shriveled when he stepped from the shower and was now rather heavy, if nowhere near erect. He chewed the inside of his mouth and then, on impulse, slightly spread his feet. Leather's hands hesitated so briefly Stephen wondered if he imagined it. But then the man continued toweling the tops of his feet, his ankles, and then worked back up his leg, drying the inside of his thigh now, not just the back.

Just when Stephen wondered whether he might keep going and dry his cock and balls Leather switched legs, starting perhaps an inch below Stephen's sac. As he worked his way back down to his feet, Stephen was almost fully tumescent and his breathing had quickened.

He swallowed, his hands shaking slightly as he wrapped the towel around his waist. He must be tired; he'd always become easily aroused when he was either excessively tired, or, most strangely, bedbound with some chill or head cold. He supposed that was when his self-control and defenses were at their lowest.

Yes, he thought as he wrapped the towel around his waist, that must be it: he was tired.

***

"Where would you like your tea, sir?" Jo was proud that her voice was as low and bland as ever when her body was so hot and sensitive she felt ready to fly into a thousand pieces.

"Bring it to me in the study, I've just remembered I have a message I need to send. You'll deliver it for me when I'm done." Mr. Chatham slipped into his robe and used the towel he'd had around his waist to ruffle his thick, damp hair; it had a slight curl, which he wore sternly slicked back from his clean-shaven face.

"Very good, sir. Do you wish me to wait and go after you've had your tea and I've worked on your shoulder?"

"No," Mr. Chatham said, the word sharp. "I've decided I'm too tired tonight and I'll retire after I jot down my message. Go fetch an extra warming pan for my bed, I'm feeling chilled." He strode to the other room.

"Yes, Mr. Chatham." Jo stared for longer than was wise, as if his broad back might tell her something. She didn't mention to him that she'd already ordered extra bed warmers and had employed not two, but three to make sure the bed was adequately warmed for his long body. She knew to do that because he liked to keep his rooms in London on the warm side.

Jo chewed the inside of her mouth until it bled: it was the toweling—she'd gone too close to his private parts. She cursed herself for behaving so boldly with him. She should have gone slower, brought him around to such intimacies as slowly as she'd brought him around to everything else. But when he'd spread his feet, she'd lost her head, her body pulsing at what had seemed not like an invitation—but almost an order.

Wild horses couldn't have stopped her from taking a second opportunity to handle his long, muscular legs. He had hair in all the appropriate places, but he was not what Jo considered hirsute, as her last master had been. Mr. Chatham's legs and broad chest were lightly dusted with brown hair—and of course he had a thick nest of brown curls at the base of his cockstand—but his arse was firm and muscular and pale and all but hairless.

His scrotum—and he had an impressively heavy sac compared to the others Jo had seen in her time—had been somewhere between tightly bunched to his body and pendulous, telling her that he was becoming aroused.

She'd been very close, so deliciously intimate, that she'd been able to inhale the masculine smell of his clean body deeply into her lungs.

Good Lord but he smelled and looked divine.

Jo throbbed hard; she was so swollen that the slight brush of her well-worn cotton drawers against her stiff bud would almost be enough to bring her off.

But then came the memory of his dismissive tone—and his rejection of the ritual evening shoulder rub—and it was like a douse of cold water. For months and months she'd incrementally made herself more indispensable to him.

This included taking on increasingly intimate duties. First she'd suggested rubbing his sore shoulder through his robe. Next she'd offered the liniment—an excuse to touch his naked skin. One evening, when his shoulder had been so sore he'd had difficulty drying his back, she'd offered to dry him, conveniently doing the same the next time even when his shoulder was *not* sore.

But tonight she'd moved too fast and now there would be restraint between them. There was nothing she could say or do, only wait and see how he would respond. And pray she'd not ruined everything.

She busied herself with his discarded clothing, the routine work soothing her anxiety. Once she'd finished in his dressing room she picked up the boots he wore today and took them to her bedroom to polish. Her room was part of Mr. Chatham's suite. It was smaller than his dressing room but, fortunately, had its own tiny toilet and sink in one corner and a door that opened onto a service corridor. Having her own facilities meant she wouldn't have to compete with other servants to use the common bathing and toilet areas. That was always a tension-filled activity as she often had to wait long past the point of comfort before a bathroom might be empty and safe to use.

It was lucky for her that Mr. Chatham did not often socialize so she wasn't thrown into servant quarters in other houses. In fact, in the almost two years she'd worked for him he'd never visited either friends or relatives. Really, all the man seemed to do was exercise his body, work, and fuck the occasional whore.

That last fact had not bothered her . . . at first. But by the time she'd worked for him for three months—when it became impossible to deny that she'd become smitten by her employer, if not actually in love with him—it had eaten at her to think of him off with some other woman; somewhere she couldn't watch. Jo had been beyond thrilled—and more than a little surprised—the first time he'd sent her to collect a woman and bring her to his house. Thankfully, at least for Jo's sanity, that was the way he'd conducted his business for the past ten months—once again relying on Jo for intimate services.

The bell that was above her narrow bed jingled and she set down the ankle boot she'd been polishing and stripped off the cheap cotton gloves she employed for that purpose before opening the door to Mr. Chatham's suite.

He was sitting at the secretary desk near the fire, an empty cup of tea beside him.

"Take this to the direction on the envelope," he instructed, his dark eyes seeming to bore right through her. His face, always stern and serious, seemed even harder than usual. "I want you to deliver it personally to the name you see printed—not to a servant or messenger. Understood?"

Jo bowed. "Yes, of course, Mr. Chatham."

He stood. "See that you don't wake me when you return," he tossed the words over his shoulder, disappearing into his bedchamber and shutting the door.

"Very good, sir," she said to the closed door. She knew before she looked down at the envelope what the name and direction would be.

Chapter Five

Stephen realized he'd been staring at the same diagram and ledger page for a good ten minutes. He pulled out his watch; it was only ten after two. That meant he still had to wait another seven and half hours.

He glanced around Albert Swan's office—the manager of yet another shipyard—as if somebody might be spying on him—before taking the folded envelope out of the inside pocket of his coat and staring at it.

The letter had been on the breakfast tray Leather brought him this morning. "When did this come?"

"I was told to wait for a response and brought it back with me last night, sir."

His valet's words had given Stephen a surprising twinge; not only had he kept Leather working late but he'd done so after Stephen had been abrupt with him for no reason. But Stephen had forgotten all about that when he opened the letter.

It was barely past midday and he'd already re-read it five times. He unfolded the paper and read it again:

Mr. Chatham:

I'm sorry you were not able to make it in this evening.

Indeed I do recall Mr. Banks and Mr. Fanshawe. I'm pleased to hear they shared their pleasurable experiences with you. I also recall those particular evenings, when they engaged with a female client—the wife of one of our most valued customers.

It just so happens I have only today been contacted by a woman who has an unusual, and intriguing, request.

The lady in question will marry in eight days. Her betrothed is a very old gentleman who does not care for bed sport. Not only has he given the lady permission to enjoy herself, but he's purchased five nights of unfettered pleasure as a wedding gift to her.

This is her second marriage and she's eager to experience some variety in the bedchamber as her first was rather staid.

She is commencing her visit with us tomorrow and has indicated she is amenable to either my employees or any client whom I think would appeal to her.

Given what you told me in your brief message, there is a slight possibility you might suit. She is tall, which you stated as a preference—five foot ten. However, she is slender rather than voluptuous, as your letter indicated was your taste.

She does have several conditions, and I've listed them below. If you are interested, I will arrange for you to meet tomorrow at ten o'clock. At that time you may both decide how to progress, or whether to part ways.

> *1.   She requires somebody who is both experienced and adventurous.*
>
> *2.   You will know her only as Josephine—no surname*
>
> *3.   Her betrothed requires that she wear a mask to conceal her face and identity, at all times.*
>
> *4.   She is not permitted to reveal any details which might allow you to guess who she is.*
>
> *5.   She must leave no later than three o'clock each morning and cannot arrive any earlier than ten o'clock.*
>
> *6.   She indicated she is open to the following services my establishment offers: birch lectures, chevalets, Berkeley Horse, restraints, public displays, multiple partners of either gender, and erotic aids."*

Stephen had to read number six several times. He'd never even *heard* of some of those items. Perhaps he was not as sexually sophisticated as he'd believed.

Neither of you are obligated to see each other again if, after you meet and converse, you decide you do not suit.

Please reply before five o'clock tomorrow evening if you are interested. If you do not reply, I will present you with different options when you arrive.

> *With the greatest respect and humility,*

Frau Helge Meisen

Stephen was half-hard just from reading it. But part of his brain—the larger part—did not believe in something that sounded too good to be true: a woman who only wanted sex—no marriage? No romantic attachment?

He gave some thought to what she'd enumerated. A mask did not bother him. Neither did the requirement that he know nothing about her. The stricture that they meet only between ten and three o'clock was likewise acceptable.

As to those of Madam's service she might be amenable to?

Well, he'd never heard of a Berkeley Horse but could guess what it was.

He knew birch lectures were whippings. Although he would not agree to being on the receiving end of a whipping, he'd delivered plenty and enjoyed it with the right partner.

As to multiple partners? He assumed she meant another woman, which he'd occasionally employed. If she meant another man? Well, that was another matter, entirely. The woman sounded too intriguing to rule anything out, but there would be firm limitations on several of these activities, should he choose to engage in them.

He adored restraints but, again, would not submit to being bound.

The part about public displays also gave him pause. He knew Gideon had somehow convinced Edward—generally reserved—to participate in a very public erotic display. So, yes, Stephen was more than a little intrigued. But he'd need to have a good deal of specifics before he agreed.

All in all, he found the letter very appealing. He confessed to a great deal of curiosity to meet a woman who was willing to participate in sexual adventures. While he could always get what he wanted by paying, he'd never engaged in such open sexuality with somebody on an equal footing.

He put the letter back in his pocket and tried to concentrate on the information before him. As far as these things went, it was not a particularly riveting subject.

The plans he was examining were for a ship that was half the price of any of the others on his list. Unfortunately, it was also one hundred years old and had a hole in the hull the size of a carriage.

He stretched his neck and winced at the pain in his shoulder. Which reminded him of his valet, which in turn reminded Stephen of why his shoulder was still aching today.

This morning Stephen had looked into Leather's bland, plain face and wondered what the devil had come over him the night before.

It was true he'd been a bit ashamed that he'd become hard because of another man's hands on his body, but he was more embarrassed about his reaction afterward.

This morning he'd accepted the fact that what had concerned him the most is that Leather would believe Stephen's arousal was to Leather's *person* rather than the pleasurable sensation itself.

As it happened, that was true—at least partly.

Yes, he'd enjoyed the sensation itself, but he'd also become aroused—perhaps even more aroused—by Leather's immediate submission when he'd opened his legs. His obedient response led to the obvious question: just how far would Leather go to please his master?

For good or for ill, *that* was a question that made Stephen very hard, indeed.

Stephen's fascination with dominance and submission was an integral part of his sexuality and nothing new. But it *was* new to entertain erotic thoughts about a man—especially an employee. It was not unnatural to believe Leather would think his job was at stake if he didn't respond to Stephen's every demand—spoken or unspoken. Stephen had never been the sort of employer to chase maids around the bed—that was a type of power imbalance he did not care for.

The truth was that he'd snapped poor Leather's head off last night because he'd been shocked by his own behavior, not his valet's.

Not that Leather had looked as if his feelings had been injured— neither last night nor this morning. Perhaps what seemed snappish to Stephen had meant nothing to Leather? Perhaps he'd not even noticed—or, if he had, he'd attributed Stephen's abruptness to being tired.

Yes, that was probably exactly how it was. After all, to Leather's way of thinking Stephen was merely his job—a job he was exceptionally skilled at.

Stephen was behaving like a fool to let such bourgeois morality bother him if it didn't bother his servant. From now on he would enjoy all the services Leather offered. And if Stephen did something that bothered his valet—like sporting an erection—Leather could tell him directly. After all, they'd dealt honestly with one another for over a year and a half, there was no reason they could not continue to do so.

***

Jo's hands wouldn't stop shaking. She'd gone through the regular motions, waking Mr. Chatham at the usual time, shaving him, dressing him, and sending him off into the world.

Her employer had seemed pensive this morning and Jo could only surmise it was the letter he'd found waiting for him on his tray. Not until Mr. Chatham stood coated and hatted and holding his walking stick did he mention the letter.

"I left a reply on my desk, Leather. Please deliver it first thing to the same woman."

This time Jo had taken one of the hotel carriages and headed directly to the quiet gray stone building and handed the missive directly to the Prussian Madam, who'd opened it and then nodded at Jo without speaking.

It had been all Jo could do not to leap and yell *huzzah!*

Frau Meisen had shown no emotion at all. And why should she? No matter what happened tonight—whether Mr. Chatham took one look at her and turned away or decided to stay—the woman was already hundreds of pounds richer.

Jo now had £23 8 s 2 d in her possession.

Well, it was too late to regret her impulsivity. Frau Meisen had given Jo what she asked for—or what Jo had told the woman her mistress wanted—and the Prussian had charged dearly for it.

While much of the letter Mr. Chatham received had been a lie, it was truth that these next five days—or maybe only tonight—really *were* one woman's fantasy: Jo's.

After leaving Frau Meisen's Jo had gone to a small hotel that was midway between the brothel and where they were staying. It was there that she would transform every evening. She'd taken the room under the names Mr. and Mrs. Joseph Leather.

Jo opened the case Cecile had left for her that day in London, marveling at the other woman's insight. She picked up her friend's brief letter and re-read it:

Jo,
You'll never have a better opportunity than this—don't let life pass you by.
I'm giving you a few essentials to help you on your way if you have the courage to seize your dreams.
The gowns are not new, but they are still lovely and I know you're skilled enough with the needle to take them in where needed. Pleased don't think of them as castoffs, they are a few of my favorites—and also great favorites with some of my most enjoyable clients.
The mask is one I wore to a party two years ago. I thought of you immediately because it will take care of hiding your identity and concealing your shorn head while making you look mysterious and, I suspect, adorable.
I hope you use these few gifts to have the night or nights of a lifetime.
Love, Cecile.

Jo wiped a tear from her cheek; how had she gotten so lucky to have such a friend? And Cecile was right, it was now or never.

The first item she took out was the mask, which made her smile each time she saw it. It was indeed perfect—whimsical yet practical. She'd already tried it on and it fit snuggly once it was laced and secured. Even Mr. Chatham with his love for long hair and rough play would not dislodge it.

There were three gowns, each simple but provocatively cut. They were also more relaxed in design, not requiring crinolines or bustles or any infrastructure at all—the type of gowns a whore would wear: designed for pleasure.

Jo discovered the far less fussy and columnar style of gown suited her tall, slender frame, the soft draping somehow making her breasts— which were worryingly smaller than what Mr. Chatham usually liked— appear more generous.

The gowns were a black velvet, a crimson silk that looked like red water poured over her slender body, and a peacock blue that made her eyes a darker blue.

Jo possessed just one corset—the only one she'd ever worn or owned. She'd worn it with lovers at Bernina's, but never for a man. She'd considered buying something to go under each of the three dresses, but her money was already stretched thin. She would wear nothing under the red and blue gowns, and—she thought after trying both dresses on—*nothing* looked quite nice.

She'd purchased black leather opera gloves—which had cost more than all of the other gloves she'd ever purchased put together—in a dress shop off Buchanan Street, where she'd also bought a black wool cloak of good quality and a wide brimmed hat with a veil.

She'd spent a shocking amount of money to bribe one of the doormen to wait for her between three and four o'clock each night at the service entrance to the building, so she could slip back up the room undetected.

Jo looked at her disguise, laid out in all its pieces, and took a deep breath. Tonight she would put hundreds of nights of desire into action.

***

Stephen had been so restless all day that he'd been less than productive, not making his way through even a fraction of the information he needed to examine. For the first time in forever his brain had been willful and disobedient, until all he could think about was tonight.

He'd gone back to the hotel early, ordered his dinner at an unfashionable hour, and was lingering over his toilet, and it was still two hours until his appointment.

"You seem to be carrying a great deal of tension in your back and shoulders, sir," Leather commented as he shaved him.

"I'm bloody stiff from crouching over that desk all day," he admitted, rolling his shoulder and wincing.

Any lingering concerns he'd had about there being any awkwardness between himself and Leather had been dispelled by the man's matter-of-fact greeting at the door when he'd arrived back at the hotel.

He'd ordered Stephen's meal, undressed him, and pushed him into the shower. And then he'd given him a repeat performance of the night before, drying his body thoroughly, clearly not connecting the action with Stephen's irritation the prior evening.

And now he was offering to rub his shoulder. Stephen should be bloody grateful the man was too impervious to his abrupt behavior to notice.

"Have you ever experienced therapeutic massage?" Leather asked as he bathed Stephen's freshly shaved face with a hot towel, an after-shaving luxury that always made Stephen want to purr.

Stephen frowned into Leather's distorted eyes in the mirror; where the hell had that question come from?

"I have not," Stephen finally admitted, feeling a distinct lack of cosmopolitanism.

"My last master was an elderly gentleman who suffered several wounds while in the army and required full-body therapeutic massage for the pain. Prior to engaging me he went to a bathhouse where that service was offered. But after several months in his service he paid the bathhouse owner to give me several months of training." He hesitated, and Stephen realized that was the longest statement he'd ever heard the laconic man speak. Leather removed the towel and stepped back, his eyes on Stephen's in the mirror. "The colonel often said an hour-long session made him feel like a new man. If you would care to try a therapeutic massage, I would be honored to provide that service for you, sir."

Stephen considered that for a moment. A therapeutic massage? Well, why not? "Yes, I believe I would like that."

"Very good, sir. I do not have the special bench the colonel possessed, but if you lay on your bed, face down, head at the foot end, that will allow me to work on you more easily."

Stephen had hesitated for just a fraction of a second and Leather, careful observer he was, noticed.

"I'll stop at any time if you do not care for it, Mr. Chatham," Leather said in his calm, toneless voice. "May I take your robe, sir?"

Stephen pulled on the sash and slipped out of the heavy black and gray silk robe.

"Please make yourself comfortable and I will fetch a towel from the warming rack."

Stephen didn't feel exactly comfortable, but he laid face down on the bed as Leather directed. The valet returned with a hot towel that he draped over Stephen's hips. Stephen had to bite back a groan of pleasure.

"This should keep you warm until your blood gets flowing. I'm going to use a little bit of oil on my hands if that is acceptable."

It sounded bloody delicious, but Stephen just grunted.

Leather took a moment to do something—presumably rub said oil on his hands—and then went to the foot of the bed and began with Stephen's shoulders.

God! The man's remarkably powerful hands felt even better with oil on them. It was also far more comfortable to lie on a soft surface like a bed rather than recline in a tub.

Stephen relaxed and let his mind wander and, predictably, it made a beeline for tonight. What would she look like? Not that he would see all her face if she wore a mask. He'd not asked her age, not that it mattered. While he often engaged young women that was largely because they were the ones working at the brothels he frequented. He supposed the life of a prostitute was a hard one and didn't want to think too closely about what happened to women when they were no longer desirable to their clientele.

Leather's fingers were pure magic as they worked their way down his body.

Why had Stephen never thought to extend such pleasure from his shoulders to his back? It even felt good on his waist, which Leather kneaded and probed hard enough to almost be painful, leaving his muscles invigorated.

When his valet's hands reached the towel, he stopped and then came around to the side of the bed; Stephen heard the clink of glass. Leather had been right about the massage warming his body; he didn't notice at all when Leather removed the warm towel.

Stephen jolted when the other man's hands landed on his naked arse.

"Is aught amiss, sir?"

"Er, no," he muttered. "Go on."

Leather began to massage his taut muscles.

"Good God," the words slipped out of him and again Leather hesitated.

"Did I hurt you, sir?"

Stephen smiled at the anxiety in his voice. "No, Leather, you certainly did not. I'm afraid you will now have even more work on your plate—although I'll try not to give in to selfishness and use you every night."

There was a brief hesitation. "Thank you, sir. I'm glad to make use of my training." And then the magic hands resumed.

Stephen forgot about everything: about the man whose hands were on him, about how little work he'd done today, about what he would be hopefully doing in few scant hours—everything. He just floated, reveling in sensual pleasure.

"Mr. Chatham?"

Stephen blinked, his mind fuzzy as he struggled to recall where he was. Ah yes, his hotel room, therapeutic massage. He must have fallen asleep.

"Are you ready to turn over, sir?"

"Yes, of course," Stephen mumbled his limbs heavy with sleep. "I must have dropped off for a bit," he confessed as he pushed himself up.

"That is quite normal, sir."

Stephen rolled onto his back, which is when he realized he had an enormous erection.

"That is also perfectly normal, sir," Leather said in his level, emotionless voice as he poured oil into the palm of one hand and rubbed them both together. Stephen thought his strange, distorted eyes looked darker and realized it must be the odd angle: when was the last time Stephen had needed to look up at another person?

"Leather?"

The valet looked up from his glistening hands. "Yes, sir."

"You know you don't need to do this if it makes you uncomfortable." Stephen gestured to his cockstand.

"I'm not uncomfortable, sir." He laid both hands on Stephen's right arm. "I'm going to begin with your hand and work my way up, sir."

Stephen nodded, staring up at his expressionless face.

"When I trained at the bathhouse I practiced on various clients. A great many of them became erect at some point during the massage. It appears the stimulation does a great deal to get the blood flowing."

"Hunh. And did this," Stephen gestured with his free hand to his groin, "happen to your colonel?"

"Yes, sometimes." Leather hesitated and then added. "The colonel was a very elderly gentleman and was always thrilled by his body's reaction."

Stephen chuckled, but Leather's expression did not alter. His eyes were focused on Stephen's hands.

"Bloody hell that feels good," Stephen said. "I wouldn't have imagined it would feel so good on hands and arms. You'll have me babbling uncontrollably soon."

Leather gave a slight flex of a smile.

Stephen felt strange lying on his back staring up at the other man—it made him aware of the human being who was giving him such pleasure. Even conversing—surely one of his least favorite activities in life—seemed preferable to lying silent with his cockstand jumping.

"How long have you been a valet, Leather?"

His enlarged eyes flickered slightly. "I worked as an under-valet for my father at first," he cut Stephen a quick look. "You may recall he was head valet for the Duke of Tarland."

"Head valet? You mean the man had more than one?" And Stephen thought *he* was pampered.

Leather gave what might have been the first genuine smile—although miniscule—Stephen had ever seen. "His Grace had two valets in addition to me and one other young gentleman.

"That seems a lot of people to care for just one man."

Leather's fingers moved over the surprisingly tight and sore muscles of his forearms. "His Grace was a very busy man. He had seven estates and frequently kept a full staff in the country as well as one in London."

"Does your father still work for the duke?"

"My father passed on several years ago, sir."

"Ah. My condolences," Stephen said awkwardly. He let the man work in silence after that. The conversation reminded him of why he disliked conversations in general. It was too easy to wander into areas like death and tragedy, and the only way out was often like this had been: awkward and abrupt.

Stephen closed his eyes and forced himself to relax. But the truth was he was highly aware of Leather's hands and the state of his cock, which had only increased its throbbing as Leather's fingers moved up his arms and then onto his chest.

He couldn't help a peek from beneath his eyelashes when Leather approached the tightly woven muscles that stretched over his lower abdomen. But Leather's expression didn't change, his fingers just digging and prodding and smoothing. Didn't the man ever get tired?

Didn't he notice the red, hard organ bobbing and waving shamelessly for attention?

Apparently not. His eyes didn't even flicker as he worked close to, but never touched, Stephen's erection.

Stephen studied his impassive face and he knew, with certainty, that Leather would give him release if Stephen gave him the slightest sign. He throbbed hard at the image that thought created: this selfless man—who appeared to live only to serve him—would take him in his soft, strong hand and bring him off. Or would he take him between those surprisingly full lips—surely the only generous part of his spare body?

"Will you open your thighs a little for me, Mr. Chatham?"

The words startled Stephen out of his pleasant and erotic musing and he spread his legs.

"Thank you, sir."

How the hell could Leather possibly say such a sexually charged sentence with any change in his countenance? Was he giving Stephen some subtle sign?

But the man looked as much like a wooden totem as ever, even while one of his hands delved between Stephen's thighs and his fingers resumed their vigorous massaging.

Honestly? It just felt too damned good for Stephen to care about Leather's thoughts. Instead, he spread a little wider, giving him as much access as he wanted and giving himself up to the hedonistic pleasure of Leather's skilled fingers

***

Jo said goodnight to Mr. Chatham, waited until he'd left the hotel room, and then hastened to her small chamber, where she'd shut the door and slumped against it: never in her life had she experienced such exquisite pleasure and crippling terror at the same time.

Having her master lying naked and hard beneath her hands was, quite honestly, the single most erotic experience of her life. The only way it could have been better is if he'd instructed her to bring him off, or, even better, suck him off.

Naturally, those were improbable fantasies.

Still—and it might have been wishful, lustful thinking on her part, but—for just a second, she'd thought he was considering the possibility of allowing Jo to relieve him. She knew plenty of men did not believe that taking sexual pleasure *from* another man made them a sod.

The way the colonel had viewed it was that it was something one did when the situation required it. She recalled the first time he'd asked Jo to fist him. Although *ask* wasn't quite the right word. After a lifetime of command, the old man had simply told Jo to, "give him a hand" when he became erect.

They'd never spoken of it, but it had become part of his massages— although not every time, or even most, as he'd had difficulty become hard.

Jo hadn't been ashamed of what she did. Indeed, she'd enjoyed giving him so much pleasure so easily. However, she'd known her willingness to do such a thing had meant she was beyond the pale, deviant, cast away, and a dozen other words for the type of woman who'd service a man and actually enjoy it.

Jo now knew that what she'd done for the colonel wasn't particularly unusual. She'd learned, again at Bernina's, that plenty of valets serviced their masters. She'd even heard that that some masters even reciprocated.

Jo had never allowed her imagination to go so far as to imagining Mr. Chatham touching his staid valet. In fact, it would be a disaster.

But she did know that if he let her do *this* to him every week—or even just once a month—she would be satisfied and not try to get more from him. Or so she told herself.

She'd been so very close to offering, but was terrified of pressing the small advantage she'd gained. Jo was fairly sure he'd known what she was thinking. If he had, she'd opened the door tonight. And she would continue to make miniscule advances both in the bathroom and on the massage bed. Provided he became hard, of course. If this erection was merely an aberration she wouldn't persist.

Jo heaved a sigh and pulled out her pocket watch: it was twenty past nine. She'd put Mr. Chatham in his coat and hat ten minutes ago and all but shoved him out the door. If he hadn't returned already for some item he'd forgotten then he was likely gone for the evening and Jo could get ready.

She locked the door to her room just in case—by some freak accident—he came back before her and summoned her for something.

It took her longer than she liked to get to the Royal Scotsman Hotel, but no more than twenty minutes to strip out of her clothing and into her first ever dress. The corset took longer than she expected with no other hands to assist her; she'd have to add an extra five minutes to her plans tomorrow if she decided to wear it again.

Tomorrow. The word gave her pause. Would there be a tomorrow? Would there even be a *tonight*?

Jo couldn't think about that now.

Instead she shook out the mask, brushing the long hair that hung down the back before pulling it over her head, lining up the tilted cat-like eye holes before snugging the lacing that ran down the back, tightening until the soft black leather was smooth over her face. She tied the laces in a double knot and took out the small tin of lip rouge and dabbed some on with her finger. She looked in the mirror once she'd spread it around. Without her distorting glasses—which she needed but would unfortunately have to do without—and with long brown hair hanging to mid back and red lips making her mouth seem larger, she no longer looked like herself. She took out the small kohl pencil she'd purchased on impulse and darkened just the corners of her eyes, as the woman at the costume store had told her. She'd to hold her glasses over her eyes to see her image clearly, but what she saw pleased her.

She put on her hat, careful not to bend her small ears, lowered the veil and then slipped her cloak over her shoulders. She was ready.

Chapter Six

Night One

Stephen studied the odd, dark landscape painting above the crackling fire that filled the big hearth and sipped the excellent scotch the madam supplied.

"I am pleased to have any friends of Mr. Banks and Mr. Fanshawe," the madam had informed Stephen in her heavy Prussian accent, her slick crimson lips bared in a carnivorous smile.

In her way, she was an attractive, if not exactly appealing, woman. Tall, bone-slender but cinched into a corset that gave her a dramatic silhouette, she had exceptionally white skin and huge kohl darkened eyes, which were a sensual counterpoint to that slick red mouth.

But she also possessed an openly predatory nature that made him restless and Stephen was grateful when she left him alone in the room. He sipped the scotch—a taste he was gradually acquiring—and glanced at his watch. It was ten after ten. Well, that was a female prerogative, being late. Not that he usually had to tolerate it from the women he paid. But he wasn't paying this woman. Instead, they were both paying the madam.

Stephen snorted; she was a remarkable businesswoman. Perhaps he should talk to the other syndicate members and see if they should bring her in.

The brothel itself was unlike any he'd seen. No effort had been made to create the sumptuous, decadent feel of most whorehouses. Indeed, the room was so stark it was almost monastic. Stephen found the black leather furniture, white walls, and snowy white bed linen a welcome surprise from the over-upholstered plushness. The only touches of color were the occasional splashes of crimson—the same shade as the madam's lips.

The room held several armoires and he opened one; it held the usual selection of whips, floggers, even sticks, canes and birch cuttings.

The armoire beside it held more erotic, personal toys. Stephen found the notion of using such items, which had likely been used by many, distasteful.

His body felt remarkably relaxed after a day of far too much tension and anticipation. He knew it was the massage Leather had given him that was responsible. Good God but that had been enjoyable. How often could he reasonably expect such a service? He would double the man's wages if he could have something like that a couple nights a week. He could see himself—

"Good evening."

Stephen turned at the sound of the low, sultry voice and his breathing stuttered at the vision in the doorway. As promised, she was tall and slender, garbed only in black. But the thing that robbed him of breath was *that mask*!

She cocked her head. "Mr. Chatham? Or am I in the wrong room."

"No, you are most certainly in the right place—Miss Josephine?" He set down his glass with a clumsy *thunk* and strode toward her.

Her full red lips pulled up into a genuine smile—as if she were truly *happy* to see him. "Josephine will suffice."

"Call me Stephen," he said, taking her outstretched hand. When he lifted it to his mouth her cloak slid back to reveal an arm sheathed in black leather well past the elbow leaving only a few inches of tantalizing white flesh before the black velvet of her sleeveless gown—a gown that reminded him strongly of those Nora Fanshawe wore. He felt his lips curving against the soft leather of her glove and very reluctantly released her and straightened. She was a tall woman—easily five foot ten—but her sparkling blue eyes were still a good six or seven inches below his.

She boldly held his gaze while her hands went to the clasp of her cloak.

"Let me," he said, lifting it from her shoulders and draping it carefully over the back of a nearby chair. When he turned to her she'd removed her hat and Stephen actually chuckled. "Madam Meisen indicated you would have a mask, I did not expect it to be so . . . piquant and charming."

Her eyelids lowered in a gesture of modesty that was at odds with both her adventurous list and presence here tonight. Stephen liked the combination of shy and bold and wondered if it was artifice or real.

She laid her hat on the chair and strolled slowly around the room. "I haven't been in any of the rooms before tonight." She cut him a quick look, her eyes a flash of blue surrounded by black leather. "I just met with Frau Meisen in her study."

"This is my first time here, as well," Stephen admitted. "Would you like something to drink?"

"Yes, whatever you are having," she said without turning, looking at the various wall hangings and furniture, slowing her steps when she reached the bed and dragging her still gloved hand over the luxurious bedding.

"Have you been to other such places?"

Stephen glanced up, surprised by her question. She wasn't looking at him but had opened the door to one of the armoires and was studying its contents.

"I have," he said, watching her out of the corner of his eye as he filled a crystal glass.

"And how does this compare?" She closed the armoire and moved on, swinging her arms in a brash manner that was at odds with her very feminine person.

"If you mean how does it compare in appearance? It's very different—none of the visual and sensual excess that many owners believe men want. But if you mean how does it compare when it comes to service?" He gave her a slight smile. "I couldn't say."

"Many people view brothels as something evil," she said in a musing tone. "But they are just providing a service, like so many other businesses, aren't they? If there was no need for them, they wouldn't exist."

Stephen smiled. "That's a rather radical outlook that would land you in hot water in most places."

She grinned, an open, engaging smile that exposed slightly crooked but white teeth. "I hope I'm safe in this room."

She was, Stephen decided, already proving to be an interesting woman. She wasn't what he'd expected, but then he wasn't sure if he'd actually had any notion of what an adventurous-soon-to-be-remarried woman would be like.

"I won't tell if you don't." He met her halfway across the room and handed her the glass.

"Thank you." She took a sip and stared up at him, her pupils huge.

He had to admit her bold openness was arousing. "What do you think of your first brothel, so far?"

"I'm not sure yet. But I'm hoping you and I discover that together."

Stephen's eyebrows shot up at her forward words and she swallowed, the action drawing his eyes to the smooth column of her throat. Yes, she was most interesting.

Whatever she saw on his face spurred her to begin walking again, her gait a little wobbly. Instead of continuing her inspection of the room, she walked around Stephen, examining his person.

When she stopped in front of him, he asked "Am I satisfactory?"

Her lips pursed thoughtfully. "That remains to be seen."

Stephen chuckled, realizing he'd laughed and smiled more in the past few minutes than in the past month. He was behaving like a giddy boy.

He gestured to the chairs and chaise in front of the fire. "Would you like to sit?"

"I would."

He followed her to the warmer area, amused when she draped her long body on the chaise, almost as if she were presenting herself for his inspection.

Stephen took the chair nearest the chaise, which afforded him an excellent view.

"May I ask you some questions about this?" She waved a hand around to encompass the room.

"You mean Frau Meisen's?"

"Not so much about here, but I'm curious as to how such things generally work." She gave him a slight, almost shy, smile. "You appear to be very comfortable and confident while I—well, I'm a bundle of nerves."

Something about her honesty softened his reserve. "It's understandable to be nervous—we are complete strangers."

"Were you nervous with your first stranger?"

Stephen blinked. "I beg your pardon?"

The part of her face that he *could* see pinkened. "I'm sorry, I shouldn't have asked that. Especially since I cannot answer any of your questions."

"I have no reason to hide who I am, I was just surprised by the question. To be honest, my first time was so long ago it is shrouded in the mists of antiquity."

She laughed, a girlish, open sort of laughter.

Stephen sipped his scotch and looked at her masked face, which couldn't hide her good humor or genuinely curious eyes. What could it hurt to answer her questions? Nothing that happened here could be used to blackmail or shame him. Going to whorehouses was something every man of his station did. If anyone would be hurt, it would be her. For once, he could afford to let his guard down. Just a little.

"I was fourteen my first time."

Her eyes widened. "That seems very *young*."

"For women, perhaps, but I think most boys have the combination of curiosity and opportunity that brings such a situation about much earlier."

"Did it happen in a place like this?"

Stephen smiled wryly. "No, it happened in an alley behind an inn. I was a stable lad and she was a serving wench. She was an *older* woman—eighteen." He met her rapt gaze, amused that she was so interested in a stranger's story of his deflowering. "I don't recall too much about it other than it was, er, brief." For God's sake! His face actually heated at that admission.

"Thank you for telling me."

"It's not much of a story," he pointed out, taking another drink of scotch as he thought about that serving wench for the first time in nearly thirty years.

"You don't seem like the sort of man who once worked in a stable." Her voice had become softer, less certain.

"Don't I? What sort of man do I seem?"

She tilted her head, the action making her look more like a curious kitten than a full grown cat, an observation Stephen enjoyed in private. "You're clearly very successful, so you mustn't have stayed a stable lad for long."

"No, not long," he agreed, having no intention of discussing that part of his life with her, or anyone else.

She nodded, as if he'd spoken out loud, and Stephen could see she was at a bit of a loss. He considered asking her a few questions about what she wanted, but it was her evening and he could be patient.

"As I mentioned in my letter, my b-betrothed," Stephen heard the slight stumble, "is a much older man who doesn't grudge me physical pleasure even though he's no longer able to enjoy it himself."

Stephen wondered how any man—even if he'd lost the ability to summon a cockstand—wouldn't at least want to *watch* this woman do … well, just about anything. And why was he marrying such a young woman if he didn't want to bed her? But those were questions he was not allowed to ask.

He did want to get one thing out in the open. "I hope you'll pardon my bluntness, but you stated you were married before and it was, er, staid?"

Although she blushed, she looked at him directly. "Yes, that is true. I've—" she paused and unconsciously licked her lips, an action that drew his attention to her full mouth. "My last husband died some years ago, so it has been a very long time. Um, a *very* long time." She squirmed a bit. "It was not a love match and we were not married long before he died. The truth is," she swallowed noisily, her neck flushed, her chest rising and falling rapidly. "My husband and I only had relations a few times."

"Oh?" Stephen wasn't sure what else to say.

"I—well, you would be the first man that I've actually chosen to welcome into my body." The odd choice of words made his heart hammer. Her big blue eyes blinked rapidly. "If you want me, that is."

His prick, which had already been half-hard, stiffened fully at the thought of teaching her the joy her body could give and receive. Still, he wasn't sure exactly what was going on here—was the woman the next thing to a virgin?

"I want you—have no doubt about that, Josephine." Stephen couldn't help feeling flattered by her obvious relief. "But it might be a bit uncomfortable after so much time."

Her body shifted in a way that was unspeakably sensual, and she asked, "Will you be gentle the first time you take me?"

Christ! Stephen's curiosity—normally an emotion he easily kept in check—was tugging at him like a fierce, insistent dog on a leash.

"I'll be very gentle," he said, his voice gruff with desire. Was he really so in need of release? Or was it this woman?

Stephen suspected it was the latter. She was attractive enough, but it was something else—something more than just her body. It was the way she was looking at him: as if he were everything she'd dreamed of. Stephen was a wealthy man, so he'd become accustomed to women playing up to him, but this woman had nothing to play up to him *for.* She was getting married in a little more than a week. Could it be she simply was attracted to him? Not the wealthy man, Stephen Chatham, but *him.*

"I know part of my letter was—" her lips again pursed. "Well, it was Frau Meisen who explained what s-services she offered and advised me to list what I might consider. Did you have any opinions on that part, Stephen?"

He liked the sound of his name on her slightly accented tongue—a soft Scottish brogue that was barely audible.

He smiled and wondered if the expression looked as predatory as it felt.

"Yes, your list. Well, I will *play* with anyone you select. However, I don't allow men to fuck any part of my body."

She jolted at his words.

"I hope my plain speaking doesn't shock or disgust you, Josephine." Not that he would change the way he spoke for her, or anyone else.

"No, I l-like hearing you speak like that." She swallowed. "I want you to."

Stephen held her gaze. "As to restraints and whips, I will not be the recipient of either, but I do enjoy restraining and whipping my lovers, if it contributes to both our pleasure."

She nodded jerkily, as if she couldn't speak.

"I would be amenable to public fucking but I would need to know the details before I agreed to participate."

Again, she nodded.

"I'm curious to see what you have in mind," Stephen said, in what had to be the understatement of the century.

She inhaled deeply and held it before saying, "I intend to make the most of it—to explore every possibility. You see, once these five days are over, I will likely not get such an indulgence again." She tilted her head and her eyes swept him from head to foot in a way that stirred him. "But I don't want to limit my experiences to what I can imagine. That's why I asked Frau Meisen for a man who has accumulated some experience in his life."

"Before I received your letter, I thought I was adventurous. But I have to admit there was at least one item I didn't recognize on your list. I might not be as experienced as you think."

"I think you're being modest."

"Modesty is not one of my failings."

She laughed, the sound low and caressing. "Do you mind if I ask your age?"

"I'll be forty-three this June. And you?"

"You should never ask a lady that."

"It's too late—I already did," he pointed out.

"I'll be twenty-eight on April twenty-first." She sipped her whiskey, which Stephen saw she'd barely depleted. So, she didn't want to lose control of herself—good, he wanted her sober and alert when he slid into her body.

A slight shiver shook her slim form.

"Are you cold?" Stephen asked. "Should I—"

"I'm not cold. I was merely shivering at the expression on your face."

Stephen raised his eyebrows. "Such honesty—I like it." And he did, too. Very much. "What expression did I have on my face?"

"Tell me what you were thinking, first," she countered.

All this conversation was outside his usual experience. But he decided he was enjoying it—perhaps because of its very novelty.

"I was thinking about how I am going to take you." His prick throbbed at the slight widening of her eyes.

"Oh, and how is that?" her words were breathy.

His nostrils flared and he let his eyes travel over her stretched out body, perusing her at his leisure before saying, "Deeply and thoroughly."

The hand that held her glass shook and Stephen couldn't help smiling at that tiny display of excitement.

"But I want to know what *you* prefer, Josephine—you are the mistress here."

She lowered her chin in a submissive gesture but her eyes blazed out of the black leather. "I would like to place myself in your hands, Stephen. I would like you to be my . . . guide. I want you—if you do not mind committing to all five nights."

Stephen almost laughed out loud—as if committing to five nights of fucking her was some sort of hardship. Instead of laughing he threw back the remains of his glass and set it down on the nearby table, never taking his eyes from hers.

"Before I accept your offer, I have one condition of my own. I'm sexually stimulated by submissive lovers. Do you know what I mean?"

Her chest was rising and falling faster. "You m-mean you like to give orders?"

"Yes. And when I do, I expect obedience." Her eyelids fluttered, but her eyes remained open. Stephen bloody ached at the silent sign of arousal. "If you give me your obedience and trust me, I will be honored to spend these nights with you."

The cords in her neck tightened as she swallowed and then swallowed again. "I can obey and trust you, Stephen."

Her words made him feel a thousand feet tall. They also made his balls clench painfully. His trousers were damp from his weeping prick but he wanted more than to just shove himself into her and spend. He wanted to make his time with her something neither of them would ever forget.

So, Stephen leashed his rampaging desire. The sheer amount of will it took to deny—or at least postpone—his orgasm was itself arousing.

"I want to taste you. Now." His voice was harsh and ragged.

Her knuckles became so white he was surprised she didn't break the glass. Was this a very good act or was she really this moved? His suspicious nature made him inclined to believe she was a superlative actress. But why would she lie? After all, she was paying for this—she could do whatever she wanted and she'd just said that she wanted him.

Stirred by that thought he stood and went to the end of the chaise, his body on fire for this intoxicating combination of sensuality and innocence.

"Pull up your gown," he ordered.

***

It was happening. It was happening. It was happening.

Jo had to keep that mantra running through her head or she would faint or fall gibbering at his feet.

She'd seen him with dozens of women, dozens of times. But she'd never understood what it felt like to be on the receiving end of his forceful stare. No wonder so many whores had appeared almost entranced when they were with him. Jo had always assumed it was his size—but it wasn't that alone, it was the sheer force of his attention. His heavy eyelids had lifted and he was focused on her with every ounce of his will.

Then there was the fact he was actually *conversing* with her.

Stephen Chatham occasionally spoke with the women he paid, but not like this. Did this mean she was different? Special? Or was it just a unique situation? She was not his whore, she was paying, as was he; they were each other's whores.

He knelt at the end of the chaise and took one of her slippered feet, his big fingers opening the buckles of her plain black satin shoes. The gesture was such a familiar one but reversed. In his hands her long thin feet looked dainty and small. He set down her shoe and then slid his hand up the openwork on the instep of her black stocking.

"Very pretty," he said in a voice that pulsed with desire. For her.

Hysterical laughter bubbled up in Jo's throat, this was her master: the man whose shoes she polished and clothing she mended and whose hair she cut, nails she trimmed—this was her employer, her fantasy.

His hand stopped shy of her knee, his expression questioning. "Is aught amiss, Josephine?"

His hands were so big and warm it was difficult to think. "Your hands feel wonderful," she croaked.

His lips curved into a smile she never thought she'd see directed toward her. "Lift your skirts higher for me."

Her hands responded to his order just as they always did, and his gaze dropped to her thighs. He'd somehow managed to take off her other slipper without her being aware of it.

"I want to leave your stockings on," he told her as she lifted her hem, exposing her shaved sex.

Heat flared in his eyes, dark, smoky and explosive—just like the savage, uncontrollable peat fires Jo had once seen when she'd been a girl. "God, yes. You are exactly the way I like," he murmured. "So smooth, soft, sleek."

Jo opened her mouth to say, "I know," and caught herself just in time.

"Beautiful." His thin, stern lips twisted into a smile she'd only seen him give to other women before. He stood and came up beside her. "Sit forward, I want to remove your gown."

Jo obeyed and he nudged her with his hip before lowering beside her, his hard, warm body pressed against hers.

"I want your obedience, Josephine, but you must stop me if I do something you don't like. I want to give you pleasure, not hurt or disgust you. Do you understand?"

"I'll stop you if you do anything I don't like." Jo hesitated and then bravely added, "It helps me feel less nervous when you talk to me."

His eyes remained on the tiny buttons he was unfastening but his lips flexed slightly. "It's not my usual way to be so talkative, but I think tonight is a first for both of us in several ways." He looked up from his work. "I like your manner of dress—I dislike crinolines and bustles and the like. A friend of mine's wife dresses in such clothing," he said as his fingers worked. "I believe it is called artistic dress?"

"Is it?" she asked in a breathy voice that was not her own.

He reached the end of the fastenings and stood. "Lift your arms and bottom," he ordered and then raised the heavy velvet garment carefully over her shoulders and head. "I should hate to crush your very adorable pussy ears."

Jo couldn't help laughing at his delightful sense of whimsy. Who was this man? A far different version of her stern, serious employer, that much was clear. Even with his other women he'd hardly ever smiled— and he'd never laughed or jested, at least not that she'd seen.

Once the gown was off, he gazed down at her body, which was clad only in gloves, corset, and stockings. A low, animal grunt—not whimsy this time—rumbled in his broad chest. "You're very, very lovely."

Jo shivered and had to bite her tongue to keep from saying something foolish—like *I love you!* Or simply falling into a pile and weeping. He thought *she* was lovely. A woman who'd spent her entire life being a man. Jo knew he was only being kind; she was far too spare when compared to the women he usually favored.

But the emotion in her chest—love? Lust?—swelled at his words; it didn't matter to her if he meant them or not.

"I want you to leave your gloves on." His mouth pulled up into a half smile that was hard yet promised unspeakable pleasure. "I like the look of them on your long, elegant arms." He reached down and slid a big hand around her leather sheathed bicep; his eyebrows rose. "You're actually quite muscular."

She felt her face heat. "Yes, I'm sorry, I know they're rather mannish. I do a good deal of—gardening."

"Don't be sorry," he said sternly, his eyes devouring her in a way she'd never dared to imagine. "You have absolutely nothing to be sorry about. You are perfect the way you are."

She was perfect. For as long as she lived—and no matter what else happened—she would remember this.

"Spread your thighs for me, Josephine."

She trembled slightly at his words, an echo of those she'd taken so much enjoyment in saying to him earlier, and she slowly opened her legs.

He moved to the end of the chaise, his eyes on her sex. "Wider, and then put your feet flat on the floor. Good girl," he praised, when she complied.

He cut her a quick look, as if he couldn't bear to tear himself away from her body. "I'm going to put my mouth on you—do you have any objection?"

"No." The word was breathy and weak.

"What made you shave yourself?" he asked, using one big finger to lightly stroke the seam of her lips. "It's quite unusual."

"I—well, I read a story. A very wicked story," this was partly true—she *had* read more than a few stories at Cecile's. "It talked about—*this*," she made a vague gesture to her sex.

"Ah. And is that how you got all your ideas? You've read . . . other stories?" he asked, a teasing glint in his dark eyes.

He was killing her, just *killing* her.

"A few," she admitted. She'd decided this would be an excellent way to explain her knowledge of certain acts and implements, rather than having to keep pretending at complete ignorance of sexual matters.

"So you know what I'm going to do—and it doesn't repulse you?"

"No, it doesn't repulse me." *At. All. And it is actually something I'm very, very good at, myself.* Jo smiled at the wicked thought.

His eyes dropped and he parted her with gentle fingers. "Shhh," he murmured when she shuddered, rubbing beneath her clitoris with his thumb.

Jo squirmed.

"Yes?" he looked up, a line of concern between his eyes.

"I'm . . . nervous." Jo was such a little rat. "Perhaps you could keep talking—tell me what you are doing?" She hated to be such a liar, but the truth was she wanted more of *him* even more than the wonderful things his body could do to her. When would she ever get the chance to hear him talk this much again? Never.

His eyes glittered with amusement. "Certainly—at least as long as I am able to talk."

She caught her lower lip between her teeth to keep from crying out as he circled her, his touch skilled and confident.

"This is a wonderful jewel," he said, his slickened finger proof of her arousal. "It's the source of so much pleasure—for you, and for me. I don't think I can't wait much longer, Josephine," he murmured as he leaned low, his stroking more insistent. "I'm going to suck and tongue until you shake and cry out. And then I'm going to do it again." And then his hot mouth descended on her aching organ and Jo closed her eyes, but not in time to keep the tears from leaking out.

Chapter Seven

Stephen couldn't get enough of her sweet cunt. He'd already teased her through three climaxes, until her body was limp and her chest and throat were mottled and slick from pleasure. But she was too sensitive right now, so he let her stiff little bud rest, languidly tonguing her opening, his motions suggestive of what he would soon be doing with some other part of his body.

He pushed her thighs wide, stroking the long, firm lines of her legs. It had been a long time since he'd enjoyed touching a lover so much. Although she was far thinner than the women he usually enjoyed, she possessed a spare elegance that was very appealing. Even more appealing was the way she was openly embracing sensual pleasure.

A soft touch in his hair made him look up. She smiled down at him, her lip rouge smeared, her eyes heavy and sleepy.

He knew it was juvenile—something his business partner Gideon would likely think—but Stephen bloody *loved* that cat mask and couldn't wait to fuck her mouth while looking down at her lips wrapped around him, her perky little ears standing up.

"Stephen?"

"Yes, Josephine?" He held her eyes while he caressed her entrance with his tongue, probing her.

She shivered. "I want to s-see you."

Stephen had been exerting iron control over his aching cock the entire time he'd been feasting on her, but the raw want in her voice and darkened eyes were simply too much to resist.

"Please," she whispered.

"I like hearing you beg, Josephine." He unfolded his cramped body from the chaise, biting back a groan; he would be needing Leather's healing hands sooner rather than later.

She swung her long, long legs over the side and rose to her stocking feet, her movements steady and graceful. "I want to valet you."

Stephen first removed his tie and tossed it over the chair. "I'm in your hands."

Her expression was serious as her nimble fingers unbuttoned first his coat and then waistcoat. She helped him out of both and then yanked his shirt tails from his trousers and ran her leather clad fingers over his naked chest and stomach.

Stephen groaned. "If I had you for a valet I doubt I'd ever get dressed."

She shuddered at his words, an odd spasm crossing her face.

Stephen laid a hand under her silken jaw and met her eyes. "Is something wrong?"

"No, I'm just a wanton to be in such a hurry. But I only have these few nights to try . . . everything. I just . . . well, I just *want*."

He bent low to kiss her rouge-reddened lips. "There's nothing wrong with wanting."

She thrust her tongue into his mouth, plunging into him and exploring him without hesitation. Stephen couldn't recall ever being probed so . . . aggressively. Josephine had absolutely nothing to be ashamed of when it came to her kissing skills.

"Up," she said in a breathy voice and he realized she'd stripped him to his shirt, removed his cufflinks and unbuttoned him.

"You *are* an excellent valet," he muttered, amused and aroused.

She tossed aside his shirt and sank to her knees in front of him, her fingers going to his tented, damp trousers.

She paused and then looked up. "Stephen?" she said his name haltingly.

He stared down at her cat face, her long brown hair brushing her pert arse, and he just about doubled over with lust.

"Yes, Josephine?"

She caught her lower lip with her teeth. "I want to—to taste you, as well."

He wouldn't last five minutes at this rate. He cleared his throat. "All right."

"But I've never done this before."

He throbbed at her words. "I'm glad I'm your first." Yet another understatement; what an honor to be the first man to have those lips around his cock. "I'll show you." He thumbed her lower lip and then nudged his thumb into her mouth. "Suck." Her pouty lips wrapped around his thumb as if it were a candy. Yes, her sucking was clumsy, but her obvious eagerness to please him went a long way to making this one hell of an erotic moment.

"Use your tongue to caress while you suck."

She immediately complied and he groaned; who knew getting one's thumb sucked could feel so bloody wonderful?

"Good girl," he murmured. "It feels good when you exert pressure." He gave a sound that was part moan and part laugh at the hard suction. "Yes, I think you'll be very good at this." And Stephen would have to remind himself to be gentle—when was the last time he'd been sucked off without savaging a woman's throat? Not for years—not since before he'd begun paying professionals.

She released his thumb and her fingers unbuttoned him quickly for all that they were shaking. When she pulled down both his trousers and drawers her expression was one that every man should see at least once in his lifetime: worshipful, wanting, aching desire—it was all there in her hungry eyes. For him.

Stephen could only stare down at her in wonder; he'd known her not even an hour and he was already captivated. When had a woman—*anyone*—looked at him with such yearning?

My God, how on earth did I ever get this lucky?

***

Jo was woozy and had to remind herself to breathe. He was so very, very beautiful, and she could do whatever she wanted with him. She frowned, if only she knew *how*. Watching him with women was all very well—*very* well—but it hadn't taught her how things were done. She'd not lied to him when she said he was her first. At least in the only way that mattered.

His hand slipped around his thick shaft and he angled the ruddy, bell-shaped head toward her mouth. There was liquid in the little slit and more smeared across the head. She smiled: this was all for her.

"You're a vixen," he accused softly. "You knew you were teasing me and you were enjoying it."

70

Jo didn't argue, instead she inhaled him deeply, filling her lungs with him, willing the familiar yet exotic scent to sink into her very bones. She wanted to be able to summon his unique aroma at will, the way she could recall the smell of fresh bread or the tang of the moors after a hard rain.

Jo made her tongue into a point and probed the little slit.

He shuddered. "God, yes. Again."

She licked and sucked, rolling the salty taste of him on her tongue. He was like the sea, sharp and salty and a little metallic.

"That's good," he encouraged in a rough voice he'd never used on her before. "Now take the head into your mouth and tongue the part right beneath it, where the flared head meets the shaft. That is where I'm most sensi—ah, yes—" He shuddered.

He was *so* big. Jo had never imagined how much space he would take up in her mouth and she now had even more respect for the women who'd not only taken him into their mouths, but into their throats. She shivered with pleasure at the thought—that's what she wanted tomorrow, to see him with—

"Loosen your jaw and curl your tongue. Mmmm, just like that. Now take my prick in your hand; I need the use of both mine so I can play with your ears."

She choked back a laugh and he chuckled with her—the sound surprised. Never had she expected to hear his laughter; it was almost as delicious as his cock.

Jo slid a hand around his thick shaft, sliding her hand up and down the hot, satiny skin while he made noises of encouragement and his fingers lightly played with her ears, tracing the lacing at the back of the mask, his big hand cradling her skull and making her feel so fragile, so small, so *his*.

His hips began to pulse a little, his small hole producing more liquid. It was difficult to remember to suck, lick, and not graze him with her teeth, but she wanted to please him—more than she'd ever wanted to please anyone in her life.

His hand slid beneath her jaw and slowed her, pulling himself out and leaving her bereft. "Show me your tongue—your kitten tongue," he said hoarsely.

Jo did as he asked and he stroked his length against her extended tongue, their eyes locked while she cradled and tongued his shaft.

He smiled and reached down. "That was excellent for a first time—or even a twenty-first." He lifted her to her feet and captured her mouth with a savage kiss.

Kissing was something she knew and Jo gave as fiercely as she got, their teeth and tongues clashing until they were both breathless.

He pulled away and trailed kisses up the leather mask to her small ear hole—her real ear, not the cat ear.

"You were right when you said you knew how to kiss. I don't recall ever enjoying kissing so much."

Jo had never seen him kiss any of the women he paid. Yet another way she was different—special.

He nuzzled her, his hips pushing against her corseted midriff. "I want to put this inside you, but it may hurt a little as it's been so long. Are you sure you don't want to wait until—"

"No," she said sharply. "I want it tonight—every night. I want you to do it."

"Very well," he said, his words a satisfied purr.

Jo wondered if he was anywhere as excited as she was. But then she remembered this was not a fantasy he'd been craving for over a year and a half. She was just another woman he would fuck, albeit not a whore.

"Remember, if it hurts, you must tell me."

Something in his tone made her realize he was genuinely concerned. Given the size of his organ, she could understand—she was concerned, as well.

"What is it?" he asked, his sensitivity to her expressions surprising—and worrying—her.

She decided to tell him the truth. "I've been, well—."

He stilled. "You've been . . . what?"

She tried to look down but he took her chin and made her look all the way up at him. "Tell me, Josephine."

Jo was suddenly, foolishly, shy—as if she really *were* the near-virgin she was playing at being. She couldn't look at him—she had to close her eyes to say the words. "I've been practicing."

"Practicing?"

She swallowed. "Yes, to make sure it didn't hurt too much the first time."

When he didn't speak, she opened her eyes.

He wore an intense expression she'd never seen before, not even when she'd spied on him with other women. "How have you been practicing?"

"Frau Meiser told me what to get—she told me it would make the first time . . . less traumatic." She chewed her lip as his eyes burnt holes through her. "Frau Meiser said sometimes men liked to, er, well, use it on their women. I brought it—do you want to see—"

"Yes," he answered. "Yes, I certainly do."

Jo was glad to turn away because her face was scalding. It wasn't until she began to walk toward her case that she recalled she was almost naked. By the time she returned to him she was probably blushing all over her body.

He took the box and opened it, his expression unreadable as he extracted it and turned it in his hands. Was he not going to speak? Why didn't he—

When he looked up, he was grinning—not smiling, but grinning. And it made his stern, harsh features look boyish—like a wicked boy. "I'm going to want to use this on you—later." He strode to the nightstand and placed the box on it. When he turned, his face was serious.

"Come here."

She swallowed and felt like the few feet between them were miles, his eyes avidly roaming her body until she came to a halt before him. He slid his hands up and down her arms, from the soft leather to the sensitive skin of her upper arms and shoulders.

"Aren't you worried about a child?"

The thought of his child growing inside her was something she only fantasized about in the most private hours of the night. Unfortunately it really *was* a fantasy.

She dropped her chin, unable to hold his gaze, and pressed her lips to the soft skin and hard muscle of his chest. "I know how to prevent conception."

He hesitated a moment and then slowly turned her around, his fingers going to the laces of corset. "I want your gloves and stockings on." He spoke the words against the top of her mask, his breath hot even through the leather. "I have to admit I loved the feel of soft leather on my cock, Josephine."

She shivered.

He gave a soft snort. "I can't seem to shut up around you—you've bewitched me."

"I like it—I like—"

"Hmm?" he pressed his ridge against her back and paused his unlacing. "What do you like—tell me?"

"I like it when you're . . . vulgar."

"Ah, well you're in luck. I can do vulgar quite well." He chuckled and this time she thought it was happiness she heard. Happiness from this man whom she'd never before seen happy? It was an intoxicating thought.

"When I get this corset off you I'm going to throw you onto the bed, spread your legs wide, and then fuck your cunt until you scream."

A shudder shot through her body, leaving her head so dizzy she worried she'd faint.

"Wanton," he hissed as he pulled down her corset, helping her step out of it before turning her around.

"Mmm," he said as he looked her up and down, his gray eyes pitiless and probing as they took in every inch of her body. His mouth dropped to one of her nipples and he sucked her to hardness. His hand slid between her wet thighs and he caressed her with his long, powerful fingers while alternating breasts, sucking and nipping and teasing.

Jo had been with quite a few female lovers, and all of them had been very skilled. Even so, this was the first man she'd been with—and also the only person she'd ever been with whom she loved and wanted. His touch was somehow . . . different. It wasn't just his skill, it was *him*.

He kissed his way up her chest and then picked her up around the waist and tossed her onto the bed, smiling slightly when she gave a startled yelp.

He crawled up on his hands and knees, his eyes heavy, his jaw hard. "Spread for me, I want another taste," he ordered.

Jo hastened to obey and then let her head fall back onto the bed.

His soft hair tickled her thighs, his breath hot on her exposed sex. "Your pretty lips are so plump, swollen, and pouty. I love them like this—it exposes you." He probed her seam and flicked her stiff, sensitive bud before sucking her between his lips and massaging her with his tongue, working her easily toward yet another climax.

Jo buried her hands in his hair and held him pressed against her greedy sex while her body shook and clenched. He tongued another orgasm out of her before the first had even receded. But when his clever tongue began to drive her toward another, she pushed his head away.

"No, please, Stephen, I—I can't."

He released her clitoris from between his lips and chuckled into her spread sex.

"I'll have mercy on you. Besides," he said, rising up on his hands and knees and moving up her body. "I'm selfish," he spoke those words against her belly, moving inexorably upward. "I want to be inside you now," he said against the think skin of her breast.

When he reached eye-level she felt him position his hot, slick head at her opening.

Jo bit her lip.

"Should I ease in slowly, or do you want me to get it over with?"

"Get it—"

The marble phallus had not prepared her for the sensation of his thick, hot, and remarkably long organ sliding into her body.

"My *God* you're tight," he whispered against her ear when he paused. "Is it terribly painful? Should I give you more? Or wait?"

More?! She'd thought he was already all the way in. He was bloody huge and Jo was afraid she might scream if she opened her mouth so she clenched her jaws tight and whispered, *"More."*

He gave a pleased grunt and then flexed his powerful hips and continued his merciless invasion. Jo spread her legs wider, as if that would somehow make taking him easier, but when his body finally pressed against her widespread sex she felt as if he were poking her backbone.

"Shhhh," he whispered. "I'm going to keep you filled for a moment to stretch you and accustom you to my size." He kissed her throat. "You feel divine Josephine—so hot and tight and wet. It's like your body was made for mine." His voice shook slightly, and she knew he was not as controlled as he seemed. "Listen to me. I sound like some fool poet, and a bad one at that."

Jo wanted to tell him to keep talking, but then he began to move, pulling out slowly, until only the big head stretched her opening.

"Breathe, Josephine."

She did as he bade her and then held her breath as he slid all the way in again.

"Yes," he whispered. "So fucking tight." His body was shaking as he held her full. "I want to pump you full of come so badly, Josephine." Her inner muscles clenched at his filthy words and they both gasped with pleasure. "Do you want me to make it last or be quick this first time?"

"Quick, please." She barely forced the word out she was stuffed so full of him.

"That's just as well because I won't last." A groan ripped out of him and he pulled out and then sank in. Hard.

And then again, and again.

He kept the weight of his massive body on his arms, but he drove into her with hips that pounded as hard and pitiless as a machine. His breathing became more ragged, until it sounded as if he were in pain.

Jo was certainly feeling more discomfort than she'd expected and didn't know how much more she could take when he hilted himself with a savage thrust and stiffened, his taut body spasming and jerking as he filled her. Jo gloried in the feel of each and every contraction of his thick organ, burning the moment into her mind.

She closed her eyes, unsurprised when she yet again felt tears. Not tears of physical pain—but the pain of knowing one night was almost over and she only had him for four more days.

***

Stephen woke with a start and looked around at the dimly lighted room, confused for a moment before he remembered: he was at Frau Meisen's with . . . he sat up and looked around, frowning. Where was she?

When he pushed off the bed, he heard the crinkling of paper and saw a note on the pillow.

76

Stephen,
I hated to leave you without saying goodbye, but you were sleeping so peacefully.
I'll be back again tomorrow at ten o'clock. Josephine

He was smiling when he read her name, but then he frowned—how the hell could he have fallen asleep? He never slept in whorehouses; he never even slept with whores in his own bed.

But she's not a whore.

No, she wasn't.

Stephen squinted at the clock on the bedside table—it was almost three o'clock. Something about falling into such a deep sleep irritated him.

He dressed quickly, too annoyed to care that he jammed his arms into his coat hard enough to rip a seam. He slammed his hat on with more violence than necessary. Only when he looked in the mirror to tie his four-in-hand did he calm down. Why was he behaving this way? He couldn't have fucked her again even if he'd remained awake. The evening had been delightful and there were four more.

He knew that was true, but still felt annoyed to have missed the opportunity to talk more.

He gaped at his startled reflection. *Good God! What's wrong with me? I want to talk?*

Stephen was grateful Frau Meisen wasn't about when he went down to the main entrance. He'd sent the hotel carriage back without telling them to return so the footman hailed a cab for him.

Only when he was ensconced inside the carriage did he allow himself to relive the evening. He would have claimed that he'd behaved so strangely—laughing, talking—because he was drunk, but he'd only had the one drink.

No, the reason for his behavior had been Josephine—this mysterious and strangely wonderful woman.

Stephen shook his head, that same question running around and around in his head: who the devil *was* she?

And why was she throwing herself away on an old man who couldn't even make love to her?

Stephen blinked at the thought and frowned. What bloody business was it of his? He was behaving like a boy with his first grind!

It was a sobering thought. He'd behave more like an adult tomorrow night—there'd be no more mortifying yammering.

Yes, he thought as he stared out the window at the streetlamps that flickered past. *I'll behave more like myself tomorrow.*

Chapter Eight

"I'll be back before six but off again at nine-thirty," Mr. Chatham told Jo for the second time that morning.

Jo bit back a smile at his unaccustomed distraction. "Very good, sir. Dinner in your room, then?"

"Yes, in the room," he muttered, staring at his reflection unseeingly as he tied his tie for the third time. Jo's finger's itched to tie it for him, but she knew he didn't like her near his throat.

She stood off to the side and watched him while supposedly taking lint off the coat she'd soon be putting on his shoulders.

He'd been a revelation last night. Funny, kind—almost loving—and so very, very passionate. It had been gut-wrenching to leave him at twelve-thirty but Jo had desperately needed to get back to the hotel and take a shower-bath. She'd been so very sore—was *still* sore—that she knew she'd likely not be able to take him again tonight.

The realization infuriated her. *Blast and damn!* She should have practiced more with that bloody phallus.

"Leather, can you *hear* me?"

Her head swung up and she blinked into his annoyed face.

"Are you ill?" Mr. Chatham asked.

"No sir, just caught up in my thoughts. I beg your pardon."

"Hmm, seems to be some of that going around this morning," he said almost to himself.

Jo helped him into his coat and then went to fetch his overcoat and muffler. "It's raining out, sir. Do you want your umbrella?"

"No, I'll just go from the hotel to the carriage to the office at— dammit, where am I meant to be going today?" he said this last part under his breath.

"To Baker's yard, I believe," Jo supplied.

"Ah, that's right. Much obliged, Leather," he said absently, picking up his satchel and then having to put it down again to pull on his gloves.

Jo met him at the door, which she held open.

"I'll see you around six," he said for the third time.

"Very good, sir." Jo closed the door and went to the nearest chair and dropped into it. Good God this was hard—far harder than she'd expected—seeing him and not touching him as she wanted. How could only one night threaten to overpower the habits of months and months?

And he'd seemed so distracted and irritable this morning—was he angry that she'd left? Had he woken and wanted more and been disappointed she was gone? He'd not come back until late—had he engaged another woman for more pleasure when he'd found her gone?

Jo shoved the pointless thoughts away.

Only four more days—or nights, rather.

He'd looked stiff this morning and she couldn't help thinking it was due to the delightful activity on the chaise longue. She knew it was bad of her to hope he was sore, but if it meant another full body rub, well, then she'd have him kneeling in a cramped position again tonight, too.

She shifted in the chair and winced; she was so bloody sore. The man was built like an ox. Jo grinned; just what would he want to do to her tonight?

***

To his enduring shame, Stephen left the Baker offices not at five or five-thirty, but at three. His brain was simply useless and all he could think about was tonight. This bloody woman had tied him in knots. Although his wits were scrambled, he'd not felt so alive in years and years—if ever. He was walking on air one minute and cursing his idiocy the next.

He as a fool. But he was a happy fool.

As he rode through the rain and Glasgow's congested streets he could not stop thinking about their evening—about the taste of her and being inside her.

His prick—which had been half-hard all day—ached at the memory of her sweet cunt. God! She was so bloody tight. She'd felt exquisite as he'd buried himself deep inside her body.

Stephen's face flushed at the memory of the far too hasty coupling. Truly, the last time he'd spent inside a woman so quickly was when he'd lost his virginity. Still, it was better that way. He'd suspected she was in some discomfort, although she'd not shown it.

Christ! She was so sensual, why had she not sought physical pleasure all these years?

Stephen couldn't wrap his mind around what she was doing: five days of physical love and then nothing? What kind of man would let his betrothed give herself to a stranger a week before she was to marry?

What kind of man would take her?

Stephen frowned at the thought. She *wanted* this and her husband-to-be was paying for it. That was all he needed to know. The rest was none of his concern. His only concern was to be grateful he'd been the man fortunate enough to be selected to receive such a gift.

Yes, that was exactly what he needed to keep in mind.

And she *was* a gift. Josephine could have had her choice of men, he knew that, but she'd chosen to give herself to him. He wanted to give her . . . *something* to commemorate the importance of last night.

You're behaving like a smitten youth.

"Piss off," Stephen muttered under his breath. Was there something *wrong* in doing something nice for another human being? Is that what he'd become? A man who was afraid to give a gift because it would make him appear *weak*?

That is how you behaved with Louise.

That taunting dig stopped Stephen in his tracks. *Was* that the truth?

Perhaps he'd been less guarded than usual last night but—

You behaved like a smitten youth.

Suddenly the little voice that constantly urged vigilance, suspicion, and control irritated the hell out of him.

It was *not* behaving like a smitten youth to want to show appreciation to a lover. Especially not when you were that woman's *first* lover in years. Men gave their mistresses gifts all the time.

The carriage rolled to a stop in front of the hotel entrance and a hotel employee ran out to shield Stephen with an umbrella during his short walk to the lobby.

Once they were inside the doors Stephen paused for a moment to allow a very grand older lady to pass in front of him. She was wearing an enormous lavender head-dress of feathers with her neck swathed in glittering stones. She sailed by Stephen as majestically as a royal barge.

"Who is that?" he asked the concierge, who seemed to have sprung from the tiled floor beside him.

The short, unctuous man stood on his toes and whispered. "That is the Duchess of Tarland, sir."

Stephen stared after her as she disappeared into the hotel restaurant, a drab little woman—likely some beaten-down relation—scurrying after her like a tugboat to the duchess's barge.

Tarland? The name was familiar, although he couldn't place it. But the duchess *had* helped him decide what to buy. The one thing Josephine had not worn last night was any jewelry—it would be a thoughtful, lasting gift.

"I need the name of the finest jeweler in Glasgow," he told the concierge. "I am going up to my room for a moment but I'll want a carriage waiting for me when I come back down in a quarter of an hour. Give the name of whatever jewelers you come up with to the driver."

"Very good, sir."

Stephen went up to fetch his umbrella—it had begun to rain even harder—and was surprised to find Leather gone. So, the man *did* go out into the world. Well, good for him.

He returned to the lobby but hesitated at the doors; it had become a deluge of Biblical proportions. Perhaps he should wait? He glanced around at the people sitting in small groups or reading newspapers. What the hell would he do at the hotel but pace?

Besides, what was a little wet?

The same liveried man as before walked him out to the waiting carriage.

"The shop isn't far, sir, just down Buchanan Street," the servant told him.

Stephen had only gone a block and was still considering the wisdom of his decision when something out on the sidewalk caught his eye. He squinted. It was Leather, hunched under an umbrella.

The only reason he recognized him through the pissing rain was because of his unusual umbrella—at least unusual for Leather, a man whose clothing was conservative—boring, even: except for his stylish black and white umbrella.

Stephen knocked on the roof of the carriage and when the panel opened he said, "Pull over. I think I know that man with that striped umbrella." The carriage rolled to a stop and Stephen cracked the door. He couldn't help smiling; even with the shelter of an umbrella poor Leather looked like a soaked cat.

"Leather!" he called, waving a hand out the window.

The tall, slender valet straightened and glanced around, rather like a gopher popping out of its hole. When he spotted Stephen, his mouth formed a comical O of surprised and he came toward him.

Stephen flung open the door. "Get in, it's bloody bucketing down."

Leather closed his umbrella and climbed in, removing his hat as he lowered himself onto the opposite bench.

"Thank you, sir," he said with a shiver. "It was not raining quite so heavily when I headed out."

"Hmph. Where the devil are you going on such a day?"

"I was working on your black Trickers and realized I'd not brought a spare lace, sir."

Stephen stared uncomprehendingly.

"A lace for your shoe, sir," Leather explained. "The one in it is near breaking."

Good God! The man *was* devoted. "You'd risk drowning for a shoelace?"

"The rain is not that bad, sir," Leather demurred in his mild, toneless voice.

"Where the devil does a person purchase a shoelace? I know I must have bought one at some point but I appear to have put it out of my mind."

"These are particular, sir. But there is a small cobbler's shop two streets past Buchanan."

"Buchanan is my destination."

"I see, sir." Leather extracted his handkerchief from his pocket and was looking at Stephen with his usual incurious expression on his face.

"I'm going to a jeweler's," Stephen blurted, and then wanted to kick himself.

"Is that so, sir?" Leather removed his spectacles and glanced down to dry the water spots with his handkerchief.

Stephen realized he'd never seen the man without the ridiculously thick glasses. He looked quite different. He looked—

Leather looked up from his task and went still. "Is something wrong, sir?" he asked, hastily slipping his glasses back onto his face, his distorted blue eyes exhibiting their usual polite disinterest.

Stephen shook his head, not sure what had so arrested him. "No, it's nothing." He realized he'd been holding his breath and released it, his mind moving back to the task at hand. "I find myself in need of a bit of glitter. You can come with me to the jewelers and offer your assistance."

Stephen didn't say what he was really feeling—that he was nervous to be buying his first piece of jewelry for a woman at the advanced age of two-and-forty.

***

Jo had never stepped foot inside a jeweler's in her life and had no idea what to expect. She also had no idea why she was standing in front of a glass counter looking at bracelets she was certain cost more than she made in five years.

But, most of all, she couldn't believe how stupid she'd been removing her glasses in front of Mr. Chatham, who'd given her a piercing look that had chilled her worse than the rain.

Luckily, he appeared to be even more distracted by his errand.

"I want to see that one," Mr. Chatham pointed to one of the few bracelets the poor jeweler *hadn't* taken out of the case over the course of the past forty-five minutes.

The man pulled out the black velvet tray that contained only three bracelets.

"Put on that one," Mr. Chatham said to beautiful woman whose job it was, apparently, to model pieces of jewelry. Jo had been amazed to learn such a job existed; how tedious that must be, standing around all day like a human jewelry rack.

The jeweler fastened the bracelet to the woman's delicate wrist and she did her job, turning the piece of jewelry this way and that, the rather large reddish stones somehow secretive and almost sullen as they caught the light.

"Hmmm, I don't know," Mr. Chatham said, looking from the girl's wrist to the tray of possibles he'd pulled out.

Jo found Mr. Chatham far more fascinating than the entire store's contents. Never had she seen him exhibit even a second's hesitation over *anything*. Even last night, when he'd been divesting her of her pseudo-virginity he'd been in control and confident. And yet choosing this bauble—and yes, she knew it was for Josephine, who else?—was scrambling his wits.

He turned to Jo, his brow furrowed. "What do you think?"

Jo knew she shouldn't, but when would she ever get this opportunity again? "Perhaps you might describe the lady. sir?"

His brow became even more wrinkled and Jo thought he would ignore her request.

But then he said, "She is tall, slender—delicate but not fragile. Her hair is an attractive light brown, her lips full and shapely," his stern mouth suddenly flexed into a smile that was like a punch to her stomach, "and her eyes," he blinked rapidly as if realizing what he was saying and where he was saying it, and then added in a rush, "Her eyes are the fresh blue of the sky after the storm clouds have cleared away."

The shop was silent but for the sound of perhaps two dozen clocks ticking.

Never in Jo's life had it been so hard to maintain the bland, impassive façade her father had drummed into her since the moment she could walk.

She pointed to one that had stones that were an unusual shade of blue with striking white crosses that seemed to shift depending on how you looked at them. "These stones are very interesting and the setting is subtle."

"Those are star sapphires interspersed with diamonds and pearls," the jeweler supplied. "They are the first stones of that quality and brilliance I've worked with—*very* unusual star pattern."

Jo winced; that sounded expensive. "Oh. Well, perhaps that one there might—"

"No," Mr. Chatham said picking up the star sapphire bracelet. "This is the one—you are correct, Leather."

Jo stood by in something of a daze as the jeweler prepared the item in an attractive case.

And when he gave Mr. Chatham the total she almost swallowed her tongue: £300.

*£*300 for a *piece of glitter*!

Jo was having difficulty breathing and turned away from the transaction, walking toward the jewelry shop window, staring unseeingly at the rain battering the empty street.

The expense of his purchase was shocking. But the truly shocking thing was that Mr. Chatham had purchased something for her—*just for her*—and Jo would never be able to wear it.

Chapter Nine

Night Two

The weather was far worse when they left the jeweler's shop and even with skipping Leather's errand to the cobbler's it had taken almost an hour to get back to the hotel.

Stephen told the coachman—who'd been utterly drenched—to pull in somewhere and get out of the rain and horrid congestion, but the man claimed there was no place in which to shelter.

By the time they returned to the hotel it was almost six-thirty. Stephen picked at his dinner until seven-thirty and then commenced his toilet.

In the middle of his shower-bath the water had stopped. Luckily Leather had been in the dressing room and heard him call out because the water had stopped just when he needed to rinse the soap from his body.

Cans of water arrived quickly and Stephen knew it was a testament to Leather's relations with the staff that it had appeared *at all* with the entire hotel out of water.

"They are deeply apologetic and are working on the problem," Leather told him as he poured lukewarm water over Stephen's back. "I beg your pardon, sir, but could you lower your head just another inch?"

Stephen complied and Leather dumped an entire can over his head. He straightened and wiped the water from his face and hair and pointed to one of the cans. "I'll take that."

Leather handed it to him and Stephen sluiced the soap from his cock and arse.

"Shall I fetch more cans, sir?"

"No, this is ample. I must say I'm glad you shaved me before my shower," he said, stepping out of the tub and taking the proffered towel.

Leather dried his shoulders and back. "The concierge assures me the water should be back before tomorrow morning."

Stephen grunted, his feet moving apart to accommodate the other man's hands before he was even aware he'd done it. Well, he thought with some amusement as his valet briskly rubbed his feet, calves, and thighs, the towel lightly grazing his sac, it hadn't take him long to accustom himself to such service.

"I stoked the fire in your bedchamber, sir, if you have time for a massage."

He bloody needed a massage. Badly. "Yes, I have time." Stephen strode toward the other room, his body so tense with anticipation for tonight that his shoulder screamed.

He assumed his position on the bed and Leather was close behind him. "I'll put two towels on you, sir, you seem a bit chilled." He covered Stephen's bare arse and legs and Stephen gave a slight shiver of pleasure. It was *cold.* And if it wasn't for the lure of Josephine tonight, he would have taken his massage and then crawled into bed and looked over some of the papers he *should* have looked at today.

But proverbial wild horses couldn't keep him in tonight.

Leather's magical hands began working and Stephen exhaled deeply and forced his body to relax, imagining Josephine's reaction when he gave her the bracelet. Would she like it? Or would she think it presumptuous? They'd only spent a single night together, perhaps she would think him overly sentimental. Or just plain odd. After all, it was likely she could not wear it once she was married.

An unpleasant thought suddenly struck him, would she think Stephen was treating her like a mistress and—

Stephen realized he was behaving like an idiot again.

The little he knew of Josephine made him believe she would accept the gift in the spirit he intended. After all, there had not been even a moment of awkwardness between them last night. That was what had made the evening so singularly enjoyable—or at least part of it.

"Sir, are you ready to turn over?"

Stephen roused himself enough to roll over, not surprised to find he was, once again, hard. Well, that's what came of thinking of Josephine.

Leather worked him with the same efficiency as always, although he did accidentally jostle Stephen's cock when he removed the towel to work on his abdomen.

"I beg your pardon, sir." His politely apologetic tone was the same one he used when he laced Stephen's shoe too tight. Once again, his matter-of-fact behavior made Stephen see just how much the man viewed him as a job that needed doing, and nothing more.

The massage soothed his sore body but did nothing to calm his hard prick. By the time Leather finished with him Stephen was so eager for tonight that he would come if Josephine merely looked at him—a thing he refused to allow after his performance last night.

So, while Leather laid out his clothing Stephen retired to the bathing chamber and shut the door. And then he fisted himself, coming in mere moments just like the fifteen-year-old boy he apparently was.

There was a horrific snarl of carriages about a mile away from the brothel, which made him fifteen minutes late. The footman who met him at the door told him Miss Josephine had not arrived.

"I'd like to speak to Frau Meisen," Stephen said, his mind on what he'd planned for tonight.

"Of course, sir."

His conversation with the madam was quick and Stephen was up in the room—their room—a mere ten minutes later.

He glanced again at his watch: a quarter to eleven. Perhaps she was not coming? He went to the decanters and took the heavy crystal stopper out of the scotch. Perhaps she was—

The door opened and he turned, forcing the fatuous grin from his face and replacing it with a cool smile. "Hello, Josephine."

"Good evening, Stephen." Even though she was wearing her mask he could see she was flushed and flustered.

He lifted his glass. "Would you care for something to warm you?"

"Please. I'm sorry I am so late," she said, tossing her hat onto a table. "It was absolutely wretched and a cab collided with a beer wagon." She removed her cloak before he could assist her.

Stephen had just taken out the stopper to pour another glass and froze.

She tossed her cloak over the chair back and turned, coming toward him. But she stopped when she saw his face. "Is something wrong?"

Stephen swallowed.

"Stephen?"

He cleared his throat—twice. "You look magnificent."

She glanced down, as if only now remembering what she was wearing. Her hands smoothed the sleek gown over her hips. "Oh. I'm pleased you like it." The gown was blood red silk and it flowed over her curves like oil.

Stephen took a rather deep drink. "Like is not the word I had in mind," he said gruffly.

Yes, it had been wise to toss one off before coming here tonight.

She gave a husky laugh and the material shifted enticingly over her flat belly and firm, high breasts; she wore nothing at all beneath the gown. How could a woman be garbed but appear so very exposed?

Her nipples had stiffened to hard peeks under his lascivious staring and it took a herculean effort to raise his eyes. "You look better than magnificent—you look delicious."

So much for no foolish babbling tonight.

Her charmingly shy smile made him want to babble even more. "Thank you." She stretched out her arms, which were sheathed in the same black opera gloves. "I'm afraid I could not find gloves to match."

"That *is* a tragedy," he agreed with a barely-there smile. "But I daresay I shall somehow muddle through. Here," he said, pulling his scattered wits together and striding toward her with the glass of honey-colored liquid.

"Ah, thank you." She reached out and misjudged the distance, jostling the glass and spilling scotch on his hand and cuff. "Oh, I am so sorry, S-Stephen!" Her expression was far more mortified than the occasion demanded.

"It's no bother," he said, pulling his handkerchief out of his pocket and wiping off the liquid.

"Did it get on your clothing?"

"My valet is a wizard and enjoys such challenges," he said, smiling.

She still looked almost . . . agonized. "I'm sorry," she said again. "I'm afraid I don't see distances accurately sometimes."

"Ahh," he tucked his handkerchief back into his pocket. "And you are too vain to wear spectacles?" He used a teasing tone, hoping to put her at ease.

"Yes," she admitted. "I need them quite badly but hate wearing them."

"I imagine you would look charmingly in them—like a stern school mistress."

She chuckled and then sighed heavily. "It's been dreadful all day," she said, allowing him to lead her to the chaise, on which he had a burning desire to see her stretched out with that thin red silk the only thing sheathing her body.

"Is it like this often in Glasgow?" Stephen asked. He was not interested in the weather, nor was he skilled at small talk, but she seemed . . . *anxious.*

"Too often," she said as she draped herself over the black leather.

Stephen took the same chair and forced himself to sit back and relax, rather than covering her like a desperate street cur.

"I missed you when I woke up last night."

Stephen's face flared as hot as the fire raging in the big fireplace; where the bloody hell had *that* come from?

Her eyes darkened and her lips parted, the hungry expression suddenly making Stephen glad he'd spoken so foolishly. "I couldn't bear to wake you—you were sleeping so soundly and you looked contented."

"Next time, wake me," he ordered.

"I will." She lowered her eyes to her glass in one of those submissive gestures that made him remarkably hard. Or course everything about her made him hard.

She glanced up. "May I ask you something?"

"You may ask me anything." Oddly enough, he meant it.

Her smile was arch. "You may regret that."

"Ah, I didn't say I would answer, just that you may ask."

Her rich, low laughter vibrated the air between them. "What kind of business are you pursuing in Glasgow?"

The question surprised him. "I'm here about ships, but we have a multitude of holdings."

"We?"

"I belong to a small syndicate that purchases businesses which are struggling financially and bring them around. One man in our group finds the prospects or conceives of ideas for new endeavors; another is a brilliant engineer; and another is a strategist who is able to see all parts of the whole and how they best fit together."

"And what is your part in the group?"

"I am merely the accountant."

"I find it difficult to believe you are a 'mere' anything?"

It was his turn to look away and the uncharacteristic flash of embarrassment was more unnerving than his non-stop chattering. Stephen Chatham, embarrassed? No, that simply didn't happen.

"Last night you told me you wished for me to plan our evenings." He wanted confirmation that what she'd said had not been spoken lightly. "Are you sure?"

"I'm sure." Her full lips curved into a sudden, wicked smile. "I'm lazy and want only pleasure while you do the work."

Thank God!

"Anything in particular?"

The tip of her pink tongue moistened her lips. "I want it all, everything. I want to be tied, whipped—" her voice broke, but she cleared her throat and continued. "I w-want to be watched." That came out barely a whisper. "I want it all," she repeated. "And I want you to decide what and when."

He'd memorized her arousing list and simply could not believe his good fortune. "Do you have any particular curiosities or desires you'd like to have satisfied this evening?" Stephen asked mildly—certainly more mildly than he felt.

Her lips trembled slightly as they curved into a smile. "I—"

"Yes?"

"You mentioned you'd like to t-take me in every way."

His pulse sped, and he didn't trust himself to do more than nod.

"We tried two things last night. Can we try the other way?"

Stephen had an odd feeling that he was in a dream. A very, very good dream. His cock was as heavy as a brick—there was no way he could become harder or more aroused.

"Are you sore today?" he asked her.

She caught her lip with her teeth—a reaction he found endearing. "Not too much."

Stephen suspected she was lying, but it was a pleasing lie. "You will be considerably sorer after I take you in back." He paused "Unless you've been practicing there, too?"

"No, I haven't. But—" her pupils were huge as she looked up at him. "I want it—with you. I want it quite badly."

Christ! His prick wept as though he'd already ejaculated; he simply had to gain control over his body.

He stared at her for a long moment, his speculative look causing her to blush. His calm increased inversely to her agitation, but he still throbbed dangerously as he considered what he was about to say.

"It pleases me greatly that you want to give yourself to me in all ways, Josephine." He tossed back the remains of his glass and set it down before leaning toward her, his forearms resting on his thighs as his lips curved into a predatory smile. "I fully intend to take every part of you."

***

"I fully intend to take every part of you."

The words were spoken softly but they were saturated with want.

Jo had told him the truth this time: she really hadn't had anything up her arse before. She had no idea why she felt so guilty and deviant asking Mr. Chatham for it, she'd seen him take women anally many times. She'd also seen their rather shocked face when he entered them. Would it hurt? Likely. But she wanted to be hurt by him so badly it was almost driving her mad.

"Go fetch my bag," he ordered, his voice shaking her from her terrified, hopeful, frantic musings.

Jo stood immediately. It was easy to obey him; she obeyed him every day—and loved it. But now when he gave orders, she knew there would be pleasure at the end of them. Painful pleasure, perhaps, but she would treasure these memories for the rest of her life.

She recognized the satchel he'd brought with him and her sex clenched. It was bad of her, but of course she'd looked inside it. She knew what waited in there. For her.

She handed him the case and he set it down beside his chair. "Strip for me—you can take off your gown and gloves and shoes, but leave your stockings."

Jo's hands shook as she opened the few buttons that ran down the side of the gown beneath her arm. Cecile had purchased it and whores knew to buy clothing that could be removed quickly and easily. She cast a quick glance at his crotch and smiled to herself as she lifted the gown over her head: she wasn't the only one who was aroused.

She began to toe off her shoes but he shook his head. "You'll ruin them that way. Come and put your foot here," he spread his thighs and pointed to the bit of chair showing between them.

Jo did as she as he bade and he unbuckled her shoe, caressing her foot, ankle, and calf before setting the shoe down.

"The next."

He made the same, slow love to this foot and leg, his eyelids heavy as he laid her foot on his straining cock and groaned. Good Lord he was big—he even made her foot look small.

He rubbed himself against her arch, his jaw tight, his nostrils flaring as he stared up at her. Jo could only swallow; it was so intoxicating to give him pleasure she felt positively drunk.

He sighed, gave her a hungry look, and then lowered her foot to the floor. "Continue."

Jo stripped off her gloves, employing the same leisured pace as he had.

"Good girl," he murmured, his big hand resting on his tented trousers, stroking lightly. "I like to be teased."

Once she was wearing only her stockings and belt, he gestured her toward him again. When she reached his thighs, he turned her around, shoving her feet wide with his foot until the tendons and muscles in her thighs ached she was spread so wide.

"Rest your hands on your knees and bend low."

Jo hesitated for only a moment and he slapped her cheek—hard. She contracted and shuddered, but she did as she was told.

His hand slid between her spread thighs, his big finger pushing into her wet entrance. "Mmmm, I can see already you like that," he said in a cool, conversational tone, his breath hot on her bottom. "I am eager to see what a crop will do to such beautiful skin." Jo clenched involuntarily and he sucked in a sharp breath. "What a beautiful, tight cunt you have. Is this sore?" His finger slid into her, not hard, but deep.

"Yes, a little."

He kissed her cheek and removed his finger. Jo yearned to change her answer—to say whatever she needed to say to bring back his touch. But before she could say anything his hands spread her cheeks.

"So lovely," he murmured in a wondrous tone, his thumb skimming her from her opening to her back entrance, which he gently stroked. "Such a tiny pink pucker; I can't wait to stretch it and fill you."

Jo's head buzzed and her body tightened.

He chuckled. "I adore your body and the way it communicates. I'm going to plug you," he told her, the clinking of a glass stopper telling her he'd opened the oil. "You will wear it for a while and become accustomed to having something in your passage. It's not enough to get you ready, but it's a start. If I don't prepare you properly, I'll hurt you."

Jo felt something cool press against her hole and shuddered.

"Shhhhh, I shan't put it in yet." The marble disappeared and his warm, slick finger pad pressed against her, circling lightly and pushing but not probing. "You're so beautiful, so tight and pink, Josephine, that you'll give me pleasure no matter what. But I want you to enjoy it as well so this will take time and patience." He kissed first one cheek and then the other, his slick finger stroking in a rhythm that became almost hypnotic.

He took his time—too much time—and she pressed back against his finger.

He chuckled. "So impatient," he chided, his finger stroking her harder.

Jo had to bite her lip hard to keep from making noise when he inserted just the tip of his finger, pulled it out, swirled in oil, and did the same again. He penetrated deeper each time, keeping her generously oiled. What had begun as uncomfortable became oddly pleasurable—unlike anything else she'd ever felt.

"More?"

She grunted and he continue his gentle invasion.

When his finger was seated to the knuckles he pumped in and out, a bit harder each time, until she was pressing against him, her body demanding more.

"Ah, you like it," he whispered, fucking her more vigorously as Jo met him thrust for thrust, until she was whimpering.

And then he slipped out of her.

"Now," he said, warm, hard stone pressing against her entrance, "relax your body."

The hand that had been holding her cheek open slid around her hipbone, his finger finding her clitoris, which was swollen and eager.

He worked her skillfully, his finger lubricated by her body's juices. "So wet," he whispered, nibbling her arse cheek while breaching her with the plug, frigging her with his hand, and generally driving her mad.

Jo was close to climaxing when the plug widened, and just kept widening; she whimpered.

"Bear down, Josephine, it's almost there."

It was difficult to concentrate on his commands with his gently stroking finger bringing her such exquisite pleasure.

"Take a deep breath," he said, pushing the stone past the tight ring of muscle. The painful stretching stopped suddenly and she felt an exquisite sense of heavy fullness.

"Good girl. You look lovely filled and plugged." His words as much as his finger sent her flying over the edge, her contractions around the stone a delicious addition that seemed to make her pleasure last and last.

He pulled her into his lap as she climaxed, her naked back and bottom pressed against his still-clothed front.

The orgasm was lovely, but it was not complete. As she came back to herself, she twisted around until she could see his profile.

"Stephen?"

"Hmm?" he asked, kissing her temple.

"I want you."

His body stiffened. "You're too sore."

"I want you."

He hesitated only briefly before shifting her body. "Stand for a moment," he ordered.

Jo's feet slid to the floor and she steadied herself on the arm of the chair while he pushed down his trousers and drawers, kicking them aside. When he sat, he spread his thighs wide.

"Spread yourself wide like me and squat," he ordered. One hand held her hip while the other positioned himself at her opening. "Good God," he hissed as his fat crown entered her slowly, only the initial breaching causing pain.

He groaned. "I can feel the marble—it's rubbing against my shaft." His hips lifted. "Does it feel good, or is it uncomfortable?"

She grunted as he stuffed her pelvis full; it *was* bloody uncomfortable, but she still didn't want him to stop. "It feels so very good, Stephen." Jo ground against him, taking him deeper.

He reached around and stroked her pearl. "Can you come for me again?"

"Yes, Stephen." Her head fell back against his shoulder as he caressed her stiff, engorged peak. She could feel his shaft pulsing against the stretched, sensitive skin of her passage.

"Tell me how it feels, Josephine—I want to know."

"I'm so full, Stephen. So deliciously full. I'm close now," she added in a breathless whisper. "I love this. I don't want it to stop." But her voice was breaking and the climax was too powerful.

He knew just when to stop touching her and his hands moved to grip her hips, his own lifting in a powerful thrust.

He bit her throat as he pounded into her, his long shaft filling her with each deep thrust.

"You feel so bloody good, Josephine," he rasped, his hips pistoning. "So tight and hot with both your holes stuffed full." He pumped up into her while pulling her hips down hard. "I can't wait until I tandem fuck you with another man."

***

Stephen enjoyed a private smile as his indecent threat sent her hurtling toward another climax. He knew her orgasm was intensified by the marble plug and she convulsed around his aching shaft so tightly it took everything he had not to follow her down into pleasure. But he didn't want to come yet—he wanted to make his arousal last as he wasn't sure he'd be able to become hard a second time before their brief evening was through. Unfortunately, he was forty-two not twenty-four.

So, he imposed control over his body, taking pleasure in the fact that he could assert dominion, even when it was over himself. He would come when he wanted to come, and not before

He fingered the place where their bodies were joined as she shuddered and whimpered, her cunt like a vise around him.

Her contractions came further and further apart. Stephen thought about the words that had come out of his mouth: a tandem fuck? He'd not thought to actually act on that, no matter that she'd mentioned having others join them. But the way it had sent a shock of arousal to her cunt told him he had to follow through on his promise now—not exactly a hardship, even though he did enjoy having her to himself.

"Stephen?" Her hand joined his where they were joined, their fingers twining.

"Hmmm?"

"I—this—well."

He chuckled, pleased by her well-fucked state of confusion. He kissed her throat, gave a brief thrust with his hips, and then slowly began to pull out.

"Oh," she said, squirming and tightening in a way that threatened to bring him off. "I don't want you to go."

Stephen kissed her again but lifted her delicately boned yet muscular frame off his body.

"I'm not nearly finished with you," he said, swatting her behind once she was standing. "How do you feel here?" he asked, pressing against the plug, pleased when she shivered.

"I love the way it feels."

"That's good," he said, spreading her cheeks, his cock jumping at the sight of the black flanged base that held her filled. "You're going to wear one of these for me tomorrow. You will put it in four hours before you come to me. It will be larger than this one—considerably larger."

"Oh?" her voice was breathy, aroused, expectant.

"Yes. I won't fuck your arse tonight. You're simply too tight. Tomorrow."

"Oh." This *oh* sounded profoundly disappointed.

"You greedy little thing—how many times did you reach your pleasure?"

He heard her swallow. "Er, five."

Stephen growled at that; he loved knowing he could bring her off so effortlessly. He swatted her arse, *hard* and she jumped and yelped. He would bet a good deal of money she was clenched tightly inside. He would need to find time to work in a spanking, or—better yet—a proper whipping. Not with a birch, but something less severe.

"Go pull the bell pull and then lay on the chaise."

He stroked himself to the sight of her slender, hand-printed, plugged body making its way across the room.

Once she was reclining on the chaise she sat with her thighs modestly pressed together. Stephen fucking loved that.

"Who are we—"

There was a soft knock on the door.

"Enter," he said, watching Josephine rather than turning to look at the door, which he knew would expose a beautiful blond woman. Josephine's chest began to rise and fall in a quick, uneven rhythm when she saw the woman and her eyes turned to Stephen, wide with anticipation.

"Come in, Gillian," Stephen said, his gaze fastened on Josephine, whose pupils kept growing. Ah, she liked the thought of having a beautiful woman lover. Stephen hadn't been certain, some women became competitive or jealous in such situations, rather than simply enjoying themselves. "Stand so that we both can see you."

Gillian was indeed very lovely and exactly his type: tall, slender, heavy breasted, and naturally submissive.

"Take off your robe and let Josephine look at you."

The woman gave the sash on her black silk robe a tug. Josephine's lips parted, her chest rising faster, her darkening eyes shooting a bolt of lust straight to his balls.

Stephen watched with greedy eyes as Josephine let her gaze roam the other woman's body, her expression priceless when she saw Gillian's sex. She was smooth shaven—again, exactly the way he liked his women—and a silver ring glinted between her lower lips. Stephen had once had a woman who'd been pierced at a place called Bernina's, in London and had enjoyed playing with her jewelry, surprised to learn it didn't hurt, but rather enhanced her pleasure. He suspected Josephine would also enjoy the novelty.

He looked up to find Josephine watching him, her eyes avid, her slick, red lips curved in a smile he'd not seen before, one filled with lust and avidity—as if he'd chosen the perfect fantasy for her pleasure.

"Spread your legs, Josephine."

She slowly and deliberately set her feet down on either side of the chaise, her smile draining away, her nostrils flaring beneath her mask.

"Frau Meisen assures me that there is nobody in this house better at her job than Gillian. She's a gift for you, Josephine. Open wide to welcome her."

Gillian sank to her knees on the end of the chaise and Jo shifted, her body seeming to ripple.

"This night is for you, Josephine—we, Gillian and I—are yours to use however you wish."

Josephine hesitated only a fraction of a second and then tilted her hips while spreading wider, her position both supplicating and commanding as she opened herself to the beautiful woman kneeling before her. She moistened her lower lip with her tongue, the gesture so raw and erotic Stephen's vision blurred.

Gillian lowered her head, her long blond hair sliding to one side and giving him a perfect view of her raised bottom. When her mouth lowered Josephine caught her lower lip in her teeth and arched her back with pleasure, her heavy-lidded eyes never leaving his face.

Stephen suspected this was going to be yet another evening when he would not last long without shaming himself.

***

Jo thought nothing could be more decadent and divine than last night.

She'd been wrong.

Oh, it had been delicious to have him inside her body after all these long, lonely months, but tonight was not only physical, it was mental, and she was enjoying herself far more than a decent, moral woman should. Luckily she'd given up striving for decency a very long time ago. She wanted to do every single thing she'd been forced to watch him enjoy with others. She knew that would be impossible in the few nights they had left, but this was certainly one of the fantasies right at the top of her list.

It was difficult to say what was more arousing: Gillian's soft, hot mouth on her sex or Stephen *watching* while the beautiful woman serviced her. She decided this might well be the culmination of all her fantasies.

Jo shuddered under Gillian's skilled mouth; her talents were superlative and she worked Jo's body the way only another woman could. Jo could already tell it would be an evening of orgasms.

Stephen's normally cool, impassive face was almost crazed as he watched. His eyes flickered and bounced wildly from the beautiful woman between her thighs, to Jo's face, and all points in between.

Jo shifted in a way she knew would display her body in a way that would stoke the flames of his lust even further, spreading her thighs as wide as she could and lazily stroking from her belly to her breasts, pinching and pulling on her aching nipples in a way he'd ordered whores to do for him in the past.

"Bloody hell, Josephine."

She looked up from beneath her lashes, gave him a smile she hoped showed every wicked thought she was feeling, and then slid a hand into Gillian's hair and pulsed her hips the way he had last night.

An agonized moan escaped his tightly clenched jaws and he looked so beautiful in his suffering that her cunt convulsed as Gillian teased out her first orgasm. She was breathing like a lathered horse as she rode out her pleasure, her gaze fastened to his big hand, which circled the base of his cock.

She could see he was squeezing himself, hard enough to hurt and certainly hard enough to control his erection

"Does it hurt?" she asked, her voice a harsh gasp as she arched her back, yet another wave of pleasure rippling through her.

His eyes glinted dangerously and he did not answer her question.

Oh, he was going to make her pay for this—and she could hardly wait.

Jo stared at him and deliberately slid her second hand into Gillian's hair and pushed her head down, grinding into the blond woman's mouth with increasingly savage thrusts.

His expression was one of disbelief and lust. It was beyond delicious to watch him want and suffer . . . but it would be even more delicious to get what she'd been fantasizing about.

"Take her, Stephen," she said. "Take her while I watch."

He blinked hard and she knew his passion-addled brain was struggling to translate.

Without ceasing her expert sucking, Gillian spread her knees to the edge of the chase and canted her bottom in clear invitation.

Stephen muttered something incomprehensible as he surged to his feet, his hands tearing at the buttons of his coat and waistcoat. He fumbled with his cuffs, cursed, and then tore the shirt open, sending buttons flying. His chest was moving like a bellows as he slid a hand between Gillian's thighs.

His eyelashes fluttered and his expression was euphoric. "She's so wet, Josephine—she enjoys her job a great deal." He fixed her with his black gaze. "And who could blame her." His arm began to move and Gillian's reaction was immediate: her breathing quickening, her tongue penetrating Jo's entrance in rhythmic thrusts while her relentless thumb caressed her. Yes, Gillian was very, very good.

Jo's eyes locked with Stephen's as he fingered the woman to pleasure and Gillian brought Jo's body arching and shuddering right along with her.

Stephen stroked himself with hard, slow motions, his prick so slick she wondered if he'd climaxed.

"Almost," he said with a smile, and added when her eyes widened. "No, you didn't say that out loud, but I can read your wicked intentions in those eyes of yours." He grabbed his shaft, stroking all the way down to the base while thrusting, the action making his already big cock look twice as long. He crouched low, fit his cock between Gillian's thighs, and slammed into her in one long thrust. His hands looked huge on the girl's delicate shoulders and Jo knew Gillian would be struggling to accommodate his length.

He stared down at her, his face ruthless as he began to thrust. "Gillian is going to suck you to the brink of climax, Josephine. But you'll not take your pleasure until I tell you to do so. Understood?" he punctuated his question with a brutal thrust, his lips curling at whatever he saw on Jo's face.

"Josephine?" he repeated, his thrusts coming faster, his jaw clenching. "Understood?"

"Yes, Stephen. Yes, I understand."

The sight of him using Gillian's body for his pleasure while his eyes were on Jo was far more arousing than the woman's skillful mouth. The chiseled muscles of his stomach and chest bunched with each thrust; he looked like some barbaric conquering king as he towered over her and the familiar ecstasy began to build.

"Not yet," he hissed between clenched teeth, his hips pounding without mercy. "Not yet, not yet, not—*fuck!*" He threw back his head and roared, driving into Gillian so hard that her head bumped Jo's belly.

"Now," he ordered, hilted in the other woman. "Come *now.*"

Jo's back spasmed and arched, until it felt like it would snap, and she hurtled over the edge into oblivion.

***

Stephen knew he was behaving in a disturbing fashion watching her so closely, but he couldn't resist.

He'd returned from his *little death*—one of the most powerful orgasms of his life—to find her sleeping so deeply that she looked unconscious.

Stephen was stunned to discover he was still kneeling and buried inside Gillian.

He stood with a groan and then helped her to her feet before picking up her robe and holding it out while she slipped into it.

Her lips and jaw were bright red from her labors, making him realize just how hard both he and Josephine had used the poor woman.

While she tied her sash, Stephen found his wallet and removed two very large bills.

When he turned back to her, her eyes—which he only then noticed were blue—widened.

He escorted her to the door. "Stay close by. She might wake and want you again," he ordered in a low voice.

She bobbed a curtsy. "Yes, sir, of course. Thank you so much, sir."

He opened the door and then latched it behind her before returning to where Jo lie spread and wanton. She didn't even stir when he carefully lifted her legs and laid them side-by-side on the chaise. Nor did she move when he took one of the blankets off the unused bed and covered her almost naked body from her chin to her toes. He then stoked the fire to a blaze, poured himself a drink, and resumed his seat.

Only now—alone and with a spent cock—did he consider what had just happened.

Stephen only knew of one other 'respectable' woman who considered such deviant activities enjoyable: Nora Fanshawe. Nora's behavior was more understandable because she'd once been a prostitute.

But Josephine? He studied what little he could of her face, wishing he could take off her damned mask—no matter how adorable she might look—and *see* her. She was unlike any woman he'd ever been with.

He sipped his drink unable to keep the question from his mind: why was she marrying this old man?

That is none of your affair.

He tried to force his mind along other avenues—such as tomorrow and how much he would enjoy thinking of her wearing his plug during the day. And then how much he would enjoy removing the plug and fucking her virgin ass.

But the subject of her marriage was insidious.

Why was she marrying this man? Was it money? Could everything she told him about her experience and past possibly be true? But why would she lie? It wasn't as if she were trying to trap him into marriage. Quite the opposite. She must simply be what she claimed—a sensual woman who'd ignored her body's needs for too long.

He thought about her black shoes and gloves, both of which she'd worn twice. He did not believe she was wealthy. Was that why she was marrying?

Stephen frowned. What did it matter? He had three more days with her and then she would be gone from his life forever.

He sipped his drink and studied the little he could see of face. Stephen suspected he'd not be able to read this mysterious woman any better with or without a mask.

Chapter Ten

Night Three

Jo waited until she'd shaved and dressed Mr. Chatham and sent him off for the day before locking herself in her cupboard of a room and reading the note yet again.

"Dear Josephine,

I couldn't bring myself to wake you, either. You must have had a busy day to sleep so soundly—and then we had such a very busy evening.

I wanted to give you this bracelet while we were both conscious, but we don't have enough time remaining to be overly choosy about such niceties. It's a small token of my admiration for you and I hope you will wear it for me tonight. As I mentioned earlier in the evening, I've also left another item for you to wear for me.

With warm regards, Stephen.

Jo clutched the sheet of paper against her bosom, not caring how stupid it might appear that a dull-looking manservant was behaving so dramatically.

She'd woken at a quarter past three last night, terrified, and had sprinted from the brothel with her veil down, clutching her dress in her arms, her cloak wrapped tightly around her naked body.

The servant she'd bribed to let her in had gone, but he'd left a rolled up newspaper wedged between the door and frame.

Jo reminded herself to seek him out and give him a gratuity to reward such behavior.

There'd been no light beneath the adjoining door when she tip-toed into her room and he'd said nothing this morning about her locked door, so he mustn't have needed her last night.

He'd been strangely quiet, wearing a bemused half-smile on his face while she got him ready for the day.

Jo knew the feeling. But she couldn't spend the day standing around with a stupid look on her face—there were things to be done, not the least of which was returning the women's clothing to The Royal Scotsman.

It had been reckless and foolish to come back here dressed as a woman. If the man she'd paid to keep the door open had seen her dressed this way it would be most difficult to explain.

Her hands once again went to the box with the bracelet and she opened it, unable to get enough of looking at this gift from him. It wasn't the high value of the item that pleased her, but the fact that he'd chosen it for her. She'd never had a gift from a lover. In truth, she'd never had a lover, just the employees she paid at Bernina's. And while she'd become friendly with some of the whores, they were not lovers.

Jo placed the box and note in her case and locked it, pocketing the key before returning the case to the small cupboard. She paused before opening the door to shift her hips. She was wearing the plug he'd left for her. It was only slightly bigger, but it seemed far more noticeable as she went about her daily chores. It was also keeping her in a painful state of arousal and her drawers were soaked and chafing her sensitive clitoris. All in all, it was delicious.

There was a chambermaid stripping Mr. Chatham's bedding and Jo gave her a brisk nod as she thought about what he might have planned for this evening. She ran through the fantasies she'd yet to act out with him; there were far more than the few nights that remained to her.

Jo hoped it would just be the two of them tonight—at least for part of the evening—but she also knew she wanted something more . . . taboo, especially after Stephen's words last night: *just wait until I fuck you in tandem with another man.*

Jo groaned as the words stoked the already roaring fire that seemed to burn in her belly at all times. She knew she loved to watch because she'd been watching *him* for months and found it beyond stimulating. In the past, Jo had enjoyed herself with more than one woman at Cecile's. But she'd never been with two men.

Although Jo had told Stephen plenty of lies, she'd not been lying when it came to her experience with men. She never thought about that part of her past in the general course of her life and she didn't want to think of it now. What had happened to her all those years ago had been bad enough, letting it infect this once-in-a-lifetime experience would only give *him* more power over her.

So, Jo pushed the ugly memory from her mind and tried to put her mind on her work rather than dreaming and wondering about tonight.

***

Stephen forced himself to stay at the shipyard until five-thirty. He refused to let the fact that he would be engaging in satisfying sexual relations turn him into a spoilt child.

But staying at the shipyard hadn't meant he'd actually *worked* the entire time, although he'd plowed through two of the ship prospects and could move to the next yard, McCoy's, where he would spend at least four days.

When he reached his hotel room he strode directly to the table where he kept the brandy, poured himself three fingers and drank it in two gulps.

"Good afternoon, sir."

Stephen turned at the sound of Leather's voice. It wasn't until his valet came toward him that Stephen realized he'd not even taken off his coat and hat he was so distracted.

Bloody hell.

He tossed his hat onto the table, unbuttoned his overcoat, and allowed Leather to remove it.

"I'm hungry," he growled, aware that he sounded like a sulking tosser.

"Shall I order dinner up or would you like to go down, sir?"

Stephen stared down at the empty glass on the table, so bloody restless in his own skin he wanted to tear his head off. How could he allow a woman to turn his brain to mush and plunge his life into chaos? Was he so susceptible to female attention that he became pathetic even after just a few days?

What I _should_ do is not even go to Frau Meisen's tonight.

That's *precisely* what he would do—stay here and go through the notes he'd collected and draft his initial findings in a letter he could send back to his partners. That's something he should have been working on already as they'd need that information from him. He'd been remiss and he should work, which is what he'd come here to do.

"I'll take my dinner up here. Roast beef and a bottle of something red."

"Very good, sir."

Leather disappeared with his coats and hat and Stephen slumped into the chair, pouring another drink—ill-advised if he planned to work, but necessary to clear his thoughts.

And just what are your thoughts? Can two nights of sex with a stranger really unman you so easily?

He *was* behaving as if he'd been unmanned. Puling like a cowardly little boy.

Stephen bristled. He would go tonight and prove to himself that it was just like any other night he'd gone to a brothel, the only difference being that the woman he was paying to be with was not a whore.

Stephen knew this was a mistake—this is what happened when you blended the physical with emotional. He should refrain from going tonight. It was too late to abide by his one-night rule, but he could salvage it.

Yes, he should not go tonight. It was time to put an end to this.

"Dammit," he muttered, ashamed and annoyed at his idiotic dithering. If this is what just thinking about the bloody woman did to him then he definitely should stay.

Some other man will go to her tonight if you do not.

His hand poured himself another glass before Stephen ordered it to do so. He put the drink aside. He would *not* allow this woman to drive him to drink along with everything else.

Remember Louise.

A shiver went through him and it wasn't only because he was always bloody cold in this godforsaken city, either. Thinking of Louise always left him chilled; she was the perfect example of what happened when a man let a woman inside his head and gave her free rein. Louise was the reason he imposed such rigid restrictions on his whoring and *had done* for fifteen years.

Stephen picked up the glass and drank deeply.

Living through those weeks after Louise had been like surviving a violent storm, or a volcanic eruption that smothered entire villages.

Josephine is nothing like Louise, the lustful, wheedling voice in his head pointed out. *You were going to* marry *Louise and give her everything. You're only sharing five nights of sex with Josephine—or just two if you don't go tonight.*

Stephen chewed the inside of his mouth so hard it bled. The little voice was correct—she would take somebody else tonight and tomorrow night.

And then he recalled she would be arriving at Frau Meisen's with his plug in her arse.

Stephen shoved aside the glass and stood. Very well, then, he *would* go tonight.

***

Stephen was as nervous as a cat and he'd arrived at Frau Meisen's ten minutes early tonight.

After he'd made his decision to come the evening had seemed to *drag.*

He'd eaten—although not a lot—bathed, had Leather shave him, and then enjoyed yet another embarrassingly invigorating massage, after which he'd fisted himself.

He'd decided to tell Leather he was increasing his wages. After all, Stephen could only imagine what such a massage would cost at a bathhouse. And he much preferred to enjoy such services in the comfort of his own hotel room or home. And he wanted to enjoy it often, so he would compensate him generously for possessing such a skill.

Because he'd already had three drinks at the hotel—two drinks too many—he didn't pour himself a scotch upon arriving at what he now thought of as *their* room.

Instead, he opened the armoire with all the implements.

He stared at its contents without seeing anything, images of the last few nights flickering through his head. What had started out as a wonderful, mysterious sexual encounter had somehow become deadly serious. If he had even an ounce of sense in his head he would—

"Hello, Stephen."

Stephen slammed the armoire door and strode toward her without speaking, pulled off her hat, tossing it aside, and crushed her mouth with his, as if he'd not seen her in a year, instead of only a night.

She gave as hard as she got and they were both breathless when he finally pulled away.

"Hello, Josephine."

She grinned up at him, what he could see of her cheeks flushed. "Thank you," she said. "And thank you for this." She held up her wrist.

The bracelet looked a hundred times more beautiful on her body. "It's perfect for you."

"I adore it."

"I adore you." The words slipped out before he could stop them. And then he compounded his foolishness by saying, "I wish I could see beneath that mask." He traced the edge of the leather with his finger. Her smile faded and Stephen instantly dropped his hand. "Of course I will abide by your rules."

"Thank you," she said simply, her fingers going to her cloak, which she'd not removed because he'd been too busy savaging her mouth.

He lifted it off her shoulders, gorging himself on tonight's gown—a shade of blue that reminded him of a peacock. While the fabric was not as fine as last night's gown, he could still see she wore nothing under it again.

"Have I told you yet how much I like the way you dress?" he asked.

She gave him an arch smile. "I'm pleased to hear that." She took her cloak from his tight grip and laid it over the chair before tugging off her gloves, unfortunately not the long, black leather ones.

She saw him looking at her hands. "I didn't wear the black ones, but I can see perhaps I should have."

"No, I've decided I like your arms bare."

She squirmed slightly before coming toward him. Stephen smiled; it would be the big plug she was feeling.

She slid her arms around his neck and pulled him down. He thought she was going to kiss him again but instead she whispered in his ear. "I'm so excited to learn what you've planned for me. I loved wearing your plug today. Anytime I walked or moved I felt it inside me—insistent—and it kept me in a state of arousal that made me think of nothing but you."

"Is that so?" Stephen asked innocently.

A smile spread across her face. "You knew *exactly* what it would do to me."

"Perhaps."

"You look smug."

"I *am* smug." He grabbed her and jerked her close, branding her with another kiss before growling in her ear. "Take off your clothing—all of it tonight."

It made him insanely hard to watch her hands shake as she removed her gown. It would be another evening of fighting to control his urges—but he knew it would be worth it.

***

Jo stripped slowly, the way he liked it.

He sat in what she now thought of as Stephen's chair, one elegantly sheathed leg crossed over the other, the casual posture somehow heightening her arousal. She was almost naked and he looked the same way he did when he prepared for a business meeting.

"Can you tell me what your days are like?"

Jo was rolling down her second stocking and hesitated at the question. Her heart leapt that he wanted to know her because she understood how rare his curiosity was. But she also ached that all she could give him were lies.

"You needn't if it is prying," he said.

She stood up and tossed her stocking beside her dress. "Well," she said, meeting his strangely flat stare, trying like mad to recall just what the duchess had done all day when Jo had been her page all those years ago. "I answered correspondence in the morning—that is usually invitations and such." She bent to roll down the second stocking. "Sometimes I pay a few morning calls—today I actually stayed home and received calls."

When she stood, she saw his eyes were glinting with amusement. "Morning calls that actually take place in the afternoon, correct?"

"Yes, that is correct." She smiled.

"And why is that?"

Jo chuckled. "I have no earthly idea and have often wondered that myself. Later in the afternoon I might go out to the shops if I need something, or I visit my circulating library, but usually I come home and rest and then get ready for whatever the evening plans are." She shrugged. "That could be a play, a talk, a dinner."

"No balls, parties, and the like?"

"Rarely," she said, not wanting to wander into a subject she'd never been exposed to. She assumed dancing went on at balls, but that was about all she could say about them. "Not particularly riveting, is it?"

He didn't answer. Instead, his lips, which she'd learned were expressive when he wished, curled into a smile so slight it didn't really qualify. His eyes roamed her naked body and his nostrils flared slightly. "Turn for me, slowly."

Jo swallowed and began to turn in a circle, her legs shaky. He was giving her that same look she'd seen him employ dozens of times: the lustful, covetous, cruel look he gave the women he would soon use. Her pelvis tightened and the sensation that radiated out from the heavy marble inside her almost drove her to her knees. When she turned to face him, he was waiting.

He'd uncrossed his knees, his erection a long ridge down the front of his trousers.

"Are you wet?" he asked with same cruelly amused look on his face.

She nodded.

"Come here."

Jo went to him on wobbly legs.

"Up here," he patted the small bit of chair on either side of his thighs. "Kneel for me."

Jo propped first one knee and then the other, her actions clumsy as she lowered her second knee, her thighs wide. He reached between her legs as if he had every right to touch her body in whatever way he wanted; Jo thrilled at his arrogant possessiveness.

His hand stopped before it touched her. "You're so ready to climax I wonder if I even need to finger you." The angles of his face were hard and his jaw was tight; he was not unmoved, quite the opposite.

"Are you ready to come, Josephine?"

"Yes, Stephen, please." She should have been ashamed at the want in her voice, but all she cared about was the insistent pulsing.

"Your lips are so swollen I can see your clitoris thrusting out for attention." He reached out with both hands and spread her with his thumbs, grunting. "You've got a beautiful cunt, Josephine," he said, his eyes never leaving her sex. "I'm going to make you come with that plug inside you." He slid his huge hands around her waist and lifted her. "Put your knees on the arms of the chair and hold onto the back."

Jo squeaked in surprise, her body pulsing at the show of brute strength. She was slender, but she was not light.

"Ah, yes," he said, smirking up at her as he slid lower in the chair, until his mouth was at the correct level. "Hold on," he ordered, and then lowered his head between her wide-spread thighs and sucked her between his pursed lips, flicking her with his tongue. As before, he worked her with a merciless skill that brought her far too quickly toward her climax.

Jo's fingers dug into the chairback as her body shook, each contraction around the unforgiving marble sending intense waves of pleasure rippling through her body.

"Mmmm."

Jo shivered under the vibration of his mouth and pushed her hips toward him when he pulled away.

"Such a greedy girl." He held her hips away from him, tipping his head back to look up at her. Her breathing stuttered as she saw the slickness on his chin, the ruddy fullness of his lips.

He tapped her hip. "Down you go, and turn," he ordered, chuckling as she clumsily turned on legs like rubber. "The evening is only beginning Josephine—are you tired already?"

She shook her head, too dazed to speak.

He spread her feet apart. "Hands on your knees," he said, giving a low grunt of satisfaction when he spread her cheeks. "I'm going to remove this from you and then you are going to give the bell pull a tug." He hesitated and then said, "I've engaged another man to join us." Jo's entire body clenched and he chuckled at her low moan. "I can tell that pleases you." He kissed one of her cheeks and then the other. And then he tongued the skin between her cunt and the plug. "We are going to take you—both of us at once." Jo trembled, swelling and clenching. Once again he gave that low, dangerous chuckle, released one cheek ,and slid a hand between her thighs, one of his fingers entering her. "You're so bloody tight—are you sure you want this tonight? Or are you too sore? We can find other ways to entertain ourselves."

Jo heard the concern in his voice and the emotion that swelled in her was love mingled with lust and the desire to please. "Yes, Stephen I'm sure."

"I don't have to take you here," he pressed lightly against the plug. "The man I've engaged is well-endowed but not so long or thick and—"

"I want you to be the first, Stephen."

He paused and she knew he heard the fervent truth in her words. "Very well. Relax for me while I remove your toy."

***

Stephen hadn't been sure what he wanted to hear more: that she just wanted him, or that she was ready for whatever erotic play he imagined.

"Steady, now," he murmured as he eased out the big marble plug.

She whimpered and squirmed as he pulled the plug to its widest point and left it embedded inside her. "Stephen, oh, please—I"

"Shhhh, Josephine." He released her hips and sat back to enjoy the view. "Remain still. This is not nearly as thick as I am. I want you to have some idea of what I will feel like—you may remove it if it is too uncomfortable."

Her body jerked and wiggled and her breathing was labored and ragged but she did not step away. His rod ached and he'd long ago soaked the front of his trousers. She wanted to please him so bloody badly—he'd never experienced anything like it. The only person he'd ever known who'd worked so hard to meet his needs was Leather, but that was hardly the same thing.

"You're so beautiful," he said in a low voice, stroking himself through the damp wool. "Are you in pain?"

"N-no," she said, her voice breathy.

Stephen grinned. "Liar." He reached out and gently pulled the plug past the thickest spot.

Her body sagged and she exhaled noisily.

Stephen unbuttoned the fly of his trousers and reached inside to extract his cock. "Turn around."

She did so, quickly but still shaky.

"You see this?" he asked, but her gaze was already riveted to the sight of his prick in one hand and the plug in the other. He could tell by the widening of her eyes he knew why he was showing her this. His rod was far thicker than the plug that had just caused her distress. "I believe I was precipitate in planning this. We can enjoy other—"

"No." Her head whipped up and he saw that her eyes were almost black with desire. "Please, Stephen. I want you—I don't have much time and I need to do this before—"

She didn't finish her sentence but both of them knew what she left unsaid.

Stephen forcefully shoved away the knowledge that there was so little time and gave an abrupt nod. "Go summon our companion."

There was a knock on the door almost before Josephine returned to him.

"Enter," Stephen called out, his eyes on Josephine rather than the man who came into the room. Her lips parted and her hands tightened into fists.

"This is Julian," Stephen said as the younger man came toward them with a swagger that was well-deserved. He was quite the prettiest whore who worked for Frau Meisen. Stephen had chosen Julian when he'd arrived, buying him out of an appointment by offering the greedy madam three times his rate. He'd had Julian fist himself to hardness first, so that he could make sure he was not *too* well-endowed. The man had a cock that fit his person, middling in diameter and not too long. Even so, Stephen worried they would rip Josephine apart between them. He would need to be vigilant for signs of distress.

"Strip for us, Julian."

The pretty blond boy smirked, his fingers quickly working open the buttons of his vest. He wore no tie so his simply pulled off his vest and shirt, exposing a body that was well-muscled, fit, and so hairless Stephen suspected he shaved. He toed off his leather slippers and unbuttoned his closely tailored trousers, which fit snuggly across his hips, leaving no doubt about whether he was aroused or not.

He pushed his trousers to the floor and when he stood up Josephine sucked in a sharp breath at the sight of his narrow hips, powerful thighs, and the beautiful cock jutting out, the crown slick with desire.

Stephen watched the two eye each other like two young, fit animals that scented sex. He knew Josephine's cunt would be pounding with desire. Yes, he would very much enjoy watching these two lithe, elegant creatures fuck.

"Julian."

The younger man's head snapped around.

"Yes, Mr. Chatham?"

"Bind her."

Josephine turned to him with an open mouth, her eyes wide when Julian took her hand and led her away to do Stephen's bidding.

Stephen raised his eyebrows at her look of nervous surprise. "Yes?"

"You're going to use r-restraints?"

He couldn't help smiling at her breathy voice and rapidly moving breasts, their tiny points as hard as diamonds.

"Yes."

She swallowed hard and then turned and followed his order.

***

Jo couldn't separate the anxiety from the anticipation. All she knew is that there was no way on earth she was not going through with this. Although Stephen's behavior with the plug told her there would likely be pain, she didn't care. She'd have the rest of her life to recuperate.

"Raise your hands," Julian said in a tone that told her who he believed was in charge. She looked up into his smug face and could see he was greatly looking forward to fucking her while Stephen watched. She could also see he was hoping to have his chance with Stephen at some point and make *her* watch. Her mouth twitched into a smile; he was in for a surprise.

She raised her arms and he tied a black silk scarf tightly around her wrists, tugging hard to make sure the knot was secure before lifting her hands over her head where a big metal hook was suspended.

"I'm going to suck his cock the first chance I get," Julian whispered in Jo's ear, his tone pulsing with amused superiority and lust as his wet, stiff prick rubbed against her belly. "I'm guessing you'll end up hanging here all by yourself while he decides I'm the more enjoyable fuck. And tomorrow night he'll come back just for me."

He stepped back, his face expressionless, only the glint in his eyes convincing her that he'd said what she'd thought he said.

He took a second scarf, folded it in half, put it around one of her ankles and drew the two ends through the loop, pulling it tight. He flipped up a piece of flooring to expose several black metal rings in a row. He selected the second ring from the end and passed the ends of the silk scarf through it.

"Please move your leg closer, ma'am," he said loudly enough for Stephen to hear, his tone far more respectful than the one he'd used when he whispered in her ear.

Jo complied. As Julian secured the knot she looked up to find Stephen watching her with an amusing half smile. He'd moved to a chair that was at an angle rather than directly behind Julian.

Julian secured her second leg and once again she was asked to stretch.

"A little more, please," he murmured respectfully, his head bowed so that Stephen could not see his lips curved into a mocking smile.

Again Jo complied and Julian kept tightening the silk scarf until she was spread so wide her hips ached. She stared straight ahead, willing her breathing to slow. She didn't want to make Stephen stop, and she knew he would if he believed she was in distress. All the times she'd seen him with a woman he'd never hurt or frightened one.

Once her leg was secure Julian disappeared behind her and Jo realized what he was doing when her arms began to tighten: he was pulling the hook up. The movement stopped.

"A little more."

Jo looked up at the sound of Stephen's voice. His hand was slowly stroking his erection and his chest was rising and falling faster than normal.

Julian kept tightening, until her arms ached and her breasts were thrust high.

"That's good," Stephen said in a voice so raw with lust it had the inevitable effect on her body. She'd just had two orgasms but she needed another before she could think.

She stared at him, so very close to climaxing just from watching his big hand on his prick and his hungry look.

"You may enter her, Julian." He said the words as if he were asking for another drink or summoning a cab. Every muscle in Jo's body tightened and her mouth opened.

"Hold one moment," Stephen said as Julian laid a hand on her hip, his other hand around his shaft, preparing to guide his erection into her body. "Josephine, do you wish to stop?" Again she heard the concern beneath the desire.

She looked at Julian rather than Stephen; she couldn't look at him right now, she was too full of emotions to contain them all. But Julian stirred nothing inside her except lust. Yes, she found him arousing, even though he was a taunting little toad.

"I don't wish to stop," she said, pleased at how strong her voice was.

Julian's lips curved into a snake-like smile and he held her hip while he brought his crown to her spread sex.

"Is she wet?" Stephen asked in a voice that could hardly sound more bored.

"Soaking." Julian grinned, stroking his cock up and down her swollen, exposed flesh

Her jaw tightened to keep from moaning with pleasure.

"She is enjoying that, I think," Stephen said. "Use your prick to stimulate her to orgasm."

Julian might not want *her* but he wanted to perform for Stephen. He stared at her with a smirk of superiority as he skillfully rubbed her to climax.

Jo couldn't bite back her cry of pleasure as her body shook.

"Enter her now," Stephen instructed coolly while Jo gasped and convulsed, her arms and legs so tightly bound she couldn't move.

Julian slid into her in a single thrust.

"Good. Keep her filled and don't move until I tell you."

Jo heard him speak but couldn't open her eyes, her body so bombarded by sensation she could barely contain them all. Having a hard prick inside her while she orgasmed made everything more intense and drew out her pleasure.

She was vaguely aware of movement behind her. And then Stephen's voice said right beside her ear. "Fuck her. Hard."

Julian pulled out and slammed into her so brutally she gave a startled cry.

"Is that good?" Stephen whispered in her ear. His hands on her waist ignited something inside her and her inner muscles clenched, causing Julian to grunt, his brutal thrusts stuttering before he resumed his stride.

"Tight?" Stephen guessed, his voice filled with amusement.

"Uh," was all Julian could manage as Jo squeezed like a vise around him, her body responding to Stephen's caressing hands rather than the cock inside her.

"You're not to come inside her," Stephen ordered, all amusement gone. "You're here for her pleasure, not your own."

"Yes, sir," Julian wheezed, his jaw tight and his blue eyes boring into her as his hips drummed harder.

"Mmmmm, Josephine." Stephen's hands stroked up her sides and cupped her breasts. His hard ridge ground against her back as his thumbs flicked her painfully stiff nipples.

Jo was stunned to feel the friction of his trousers and coat on her back and she tightened again, drawing yet another gasp from Julian. Why did the fact that Stephen had refastened his trousers and was fully dressed—while she was naked and being taken by another man—feel so very, very . . . erotic?

"I could just stand here and rub and touch and," Stephen kissed her shoulder, biting her, causing her to moan, "and suck and nip. Are you sure you want my hard prick inside you?"

"Want," she gasped, breathless from the violence of Julian's pumping.

He kissed her throat gently. "As you command." His hand was oiled as it slid between her spread cheeks and he stroked her, first one finger, then two—gently probing and scissoring inside her, stretching and filling her. He drizzled more oil on her, letting it run down, soaking her while he worked her. Gradually the stretch began to feel pleasurable.

"Can you do three?" he whispered.

She grunted and nodded, unable to speak. When a third finger joined the first two she shuddered and whimpered.

"Josephine?" His hand paused.

"Please."

After a moment, he resumed his probing, the stretch and burn painful, but not unbearable. Soon, he was stroking her to the third finger joint, twisting his fingers on removal, straightening them for the thrust.

"Slowly now, Julian," he said.

Julian's hips gentled and she could see by his slick chest and face that he was working hard in several ways; he needed to come, but she knew he could not bear failing in front of Stephen. Jo mustered a wink for him and his eyes went wide.

Stephen worked her for a moment more, and when he disappeared, she tried to follow his fingers with her hips. But she was bound too tightly to move.

Something unspeakably hot, hard, and *big* pressed against her and all thoughts of Julian dissipated.

"Shhhhh," Stephen soothed as he caressed her, his presence both a threat and a promise. "You need to bear down as you did before. And after I breach you, make sure you remember to breathe and keep your body relaxed."

"Yes, Stephen."

He kissed her again and said, "Stop, Julian."

Julian pulled almost all the way out, keeping only his crown inside her. His expression went from smirking to worshipful in an instant, which told Jo that Stephen was looking at him.

Stephen pressed his slick head against the tight ring of muscle and she experienced considerably more dull pain than the plug or his fingers. But she refused to cry out with Julian's cruelly amused gaze on her.

"Breathe," Stephen said in a tight voice. He poured more oil on her and it ran down her body to his shaft as he eased in. "Do you like it, Josephine?" he asked in a voice that was rough with restraint.

Jo pressed herself against him, the action pushing him deeper, causing a dull pain to radiate from where they were joined. She felt the change in his body, the subtle loosening of control, like a rope that had been cut and was beginning to fray faster and faster.

"Fuck," he said, groaning. His arm slid around her waist and his fingers fanned over her belly, holding her body against his while he invaded her inch by inch by inch. Just the thought of what they were doing—so filthy and primitive and wrong—made every muscle clench.

"Josephine," he whispered, shuddering.

Jo reveled in his controlled penetration; the more of him she took into her body the more she felt like she was *his*.

Julian was staring at her with obvious envy and Jo narrowed her eyes at him and then deliberately thrust her bottom back at Stephen, biting her tongue to keep from crying out.

He hissed in a breath. "God, Josephine."

"Please, I want all of you, Stephen," she begged.

He complied, invading her inch by inch, not stopping until his pelvis rested against her spread cheeks. Her head throbbed and her body was screaming, but he felt so very, very *good.*

"So bloody tight." He held her impaled and she forced her body to relax around him. "Are you sure you want Julian inside you? We can go on without him."

Jo tightened, the action making them both gasp.

"My good girl," he whispered into her ear, and then, "Take her, Julian. Slowly."

Julian's held Jo's gaze as he pushed inside, not stopping until he was hilted. He wasn't nearly as thick as Stephen but he was long.

Jo whimpered and tried to wiggle her hips, but she was utterly penetrated and restrained.

The sensation of fullness was overwhelming. It hurt—a great deal—but she felt so utterly possessed. She was breathing heavily, working on absorbing the exquisite pain when Julian flexed his hips, driving himself in just enough more to make her cry out.

"Josephine?"

Even in her trance-like state she heard the worry beneath Stephen's leashed passion.

Jo glared at Julian, ignoring the pain. "I want what you want, Stephen."

Stephen chuckled softly, keeping her full for one more agonizing, ecstatic moment before sliding out, until only his thick crown breached her. He gently pulsed, stretching the clenching muscle and biting the juncture of neck and shoulder. She turned her head and he saw her cheeks were wet. "Such pretty tears, Josephine," he murmured as he continued to work her. "Are those for me?"

"Fuck me, Stephen."

She felt his body jolt at her raw command and he thrust all the way in just as Julian slid out.

Jo shivered and moaned.

The men developed a rhythm that kept her impaled at all times, but not with both of them at once. It was an intense pleasure that bordered on pain. Jo wished Julian was behind her and that she could see Stephen. Next time she would ask—

There would be no next time.

She clenched her jaws against the thought.

Stephen whispered in her ear, his voice harsh. "I can't restrain myself much longer, Josephine. Do you want it?"

"Yes, Stephen. . . *please.*"

Stephen must have made some sign because Julian left her body and stepped back, his cock jutting heavy and slick in front of him, his expression tense with the effort of holding back his orgasm. It was Jo's turn to smile and then she closed her eyes and opened her body to the man she loved, heart and soul.

Stephen's pounding became savage, his hips pumping mercilessly now. "I'm going to come in you, Josephine. I'm going to—" he gave loud, guttural cry as he thrust deep and froze, holding her in an unbreakable embrace while his cock spasmed and flooded her with his seed.

Chapter Eleven

tephen dismissed Julian—sending him off with his orders for the kitchen—and carried Jo to the bed.

"No . . . I'm fine. I can walk," she protested in the sleepy, satiated voice he loved to hear.

"Hush." He gave her a hard kiss after laying her on the bed. "I've ordered something to eat and drink and we're going to relax." Stephen went to the small water closet and wet a cloth in hot water, squeezing out the excess.

When he returned to her he parted her thighs, which spread eagerly at his touch. "This will feel good." He carefully bathed her sex, smiling at the soft sounds of pleasure she made.

"Listen to you—purring." He went back and forth a few more times, to freshen the cloth. It had been years—many of them—since he'd seen to a lover's care. Somewhere along the line he'd become the kind of man who didn't give a damn about the women who gave him pleasure. Stephen didn't like that picture of himself; even a whore deserved decency. Stephen turned away from those unpleasant thoughts.

"I'm going to check and make sure I didn't hurt you." He rolled her over, smiling at her grumbling, and spread her cheeks, looking for blood. She was would be sore, but he'd not torn her.

He cleaned her gently, but she still winced. "Did I hurt you, Josephine?"

She shook her head and then rolled onto her back, meeting his gaze. Her lips were curved into a gentle smile and her eyes were lazy behind her mask—a mask he used to like but had come to resent.

Stephen turned away from both her and the disturbing thought, returning to the small bathroom and staring at himself in the mirror as he washed his cock. He'd come into this arrangement knowing the rules: he had no right to be angry about any of it. But saying that to himself and abiding by it were two different things. She'd gotten under his skin, and he was more than a little worried at the wisdom of letting her come so close.

When he returned to the bedroom she'd gotten up and taken one of the robes that hung beside the armoire and wrapped it around herself. She looked up at the sound of his feet, a huge yawn distorting her smile.

"Find me that tedious, do you?"

She chuckled. "I don't know why I'm so tired."

Stephen took her hand and led her to the table in front of the fireplace. "Were you busy today?"

"I think it's this weather. It makes it difficult to do the things I have to do."

"What do you have to do that could be so important as to take you out on a day like today?" He cocked his head. "Except coming here, of course."

Before she could answer there was a light knock on the door and two maids entered, both bearing trays groaning with food.

Josephine looked up at him, wide eyed. "What's all this?"

"I didn't know what you wanted, so I ordered a selection."

She gaped.

"Don't worry, if we don't eat it, somebody will." He turned to one of the maids and waited until she'd unloaded her tray before handing her a coin. "Isn't that right?" he asked. "The food won't go to waste."

She dropped a clumsy curtsy, her cheeks like apples. "Aye, sir."

Stephen gave the other young woman a coin and they both giggled, bolting for the doorway.

"That's more than they make in six months as maids," Josephine observed drily, taking a plate and proceeding to fill it.

"Is it?" Stephen took the seat across from her, reveling in this tiny bit of domesticity more than was healthy for a man who wouldn't see this woman ever again after forty-eight hours.

She heaped the plate with a portion from each dish. "I think you already know that. I suspect you know the expenditures of your house down to the shilling." He'd never seen her eat before and was pleased that she had such a hearty appetite, especially for being so slender.

"Do I give the impression I'm clutch-fisted?" he asked.

She laughed. "No, not at all. Here you are." She handed him the plate.

"I thought this was for you?"

"A lady always serves others from the tea tray first."

"Ah, is that so? Well, thank you."

She set about making a second, smaller plate. "Please, you needn't wait for me," she told him.

He did anyhow, preferring to watch her rather than eat. He noticed one of her cat ears was bent and, for some reason, the sight made him inexpressibly sad: only two more nights after this.

She set her plate down and snapped a heavy damask napkin before laying it across her lap.

"I see you like ham," he said mildly, amused to see not three but *four* pieces.

"I do." She admitted sheepishly. "I'm quite greedy about it. My brother used to—" she stopped and darted him an unreadable look.

"Can't you speak of your brother?"

She hesitated and then said, "Yes, of course. My brother used to trade his ham for my eggs, toast, *and* coffee."

"You sound like a terrible negotiator."

"Perhaps," she said, cutting off a chunk of ham and lifting it to her smiling lips. "Or perhaps I just know what I want."

Well.

"What about you, Stephen? Do you have siblings?"

Yes, three.

"None that I know of—I grew up in an orphanage."

Her forehead furrowed and Stephen shook his head.

"I can see you are imagining sad tales of neglect and abuse," he said. "Don't. I was well cared for." Better than at home, that was for sure. "Do you just have the one brother?"

"Yes, my older brother by two years."

"Does he still talk you out of your ham?" he asked, picking up one of those tiny sandwiches which always made him feel like an idiot while eating them.

"He's—" she stopped and stared at her empty fork and Stephen knew she was seeing something else. "He's angry with me." She shrugged. "We've not spoken for some months." When he didn't speak, she glanced up. "He doesn't agree with the decisions I've made for my future. He thinks I should . . . Well, he thinks I've made some bad choices." She busied herself cutting another piece of ham. "He thinks he knows everything about me," she added, almost to herself. "But he doesn't have the first clue."

Stephen put the sandwich in his mouth, before more prying questions came out of it.

***

Jo had to hurry. Stephen—Mr. Chatham, she reminded herself—had insisted on summoning cab's for both of them. She knew he wasn't following her, but The Royal Scotsman Hotel was on the road that led back to the Cameron. She opened the vent. "Turn at the next street," she told the driver.

"Left or right?"

"I don't care—just turn, I don't want the carriage behind us following me."

"Aye, ma'am."

When she got to the Royal Scotsman she told the driver to wait, that her husband would need transportation to the Cameron Hotel and that he'd be down in a few moments.

"I don't get paid fer sittin' and—"

Jo opened her reticule and flipped him a coin—one larger than his fare. "There will be another like that if you wait just five minutes."

"Aye," he grinned, exposing a blackened smile. "I'll wait."

Jo tore her dress in her haste to get out of it, throwing everything into a messy pile, which was enough to do violence to her meticulous, tidy soul.

It was closer to fifteen minutes when she finally came back out.

"I was 'bout to leave," the driver said as she climbed in. "Yer wife said I'd get another of these." He held up the coin.

"You'll get two if you get me to the Cameron in a quarter of an hour."

The carriage lurched forward so abruptly Jo tumbled back into the seat, the door to the carriage flapping open.

After she'd closed it, she sat back against the worn velvet seat and took several deep breaths. It had been an erotic and magical evening.

126

The best part had been just talking with him as if they were two equals. He behaved differently with her—at least differently than he'd been with all the prostitutes she seen him with over the many months. First off, he spoke to her other than to issue commands. Not that Jo minded being commanded by him. She shivered as she recalled his mastery this evening.

The experience of being taken by two men had been . . . well, although she wouldn't care to engage in such activity too frequently, she'd enjoyed it. She would have enjoyed it even more if it had been somebody other than the smug, snide Julian. Jo allowed her mind to wander over the possibilities. She'd seen one of Mr. Chatham's partners more than a few times at Bernina's—a man named Mr. Smith. One of the women Jo had gone to quite often—Emma—had shared more details than she should have.

"Hung quite nicely for his size and likes both meat and fish. *And* he bleeds money."

Jo knew that last bit had been for her. While she always left an ample reward for those who serviced her, she couldn't afford to bring expensive gifts. Knowing Emma was so indiscrete about her other clients had made that the last time Jo had asked for the woman. That was just what she needed—Emma talking to Mr. Smith about Jo! And perhaps word eventually getting back to Mr. Chatham.

After hearing what Emma had to say about Mr. Smith she'd watched the man closely whenever she'd been in his vicinity. She'd had plenty of chances to study him when Mr. Chatham and Mr. Smith took a three-week trip to Brighton earlier in the year.

Smith was dry, witty, and a considerate master to his valet—Nash, a laconic but friendly man perhaps fifteen years older than Jo—and always had something to say to Jo whenever they chanced upon each other. While Smith had not been familiar with her, they'd been thrown into each other's paths quite often over those two weeks as Mr. Chatham and Smith had worked together almost around the clock.

Mr. Smith hadn't just talked *at* her, he'd often asked her questions—consulting her on matters of business and politics the way only Mr. Chatham had ever done before. She'd learned to like him a great deal—too much, in fact. Indeed, he'd been the only other man Jo knew who'd elicited the physical sensations from her that Mr. Chatham had.

Jo had noticed by the way Nash watched Mr. Smith—with a pensive stare—that there was something more than a master-servant relationship between them, and her realization had both intrigued and titillated her.

Mr. Smith exuded a quiet, compelling sensuality that struck her as being as attractive—and dangerous—as a violent but beautiful thunderstorm. He was the sort of man who people—both men and women—were drawn to, perhaps at their peril.

Jo had no foundation for her fanciful perception of him as he'd always been polite and kind to her, and she knew Mr. Chatham—whose judgement in such matters she trusted— respected Smith a great deal.

The men were complete opposites but had worked long, hard hours together and had ultimately bested their competition and come out ahead in a difficult, tense business transaction. There'd seemed to be some invisible connection between them and Jo had often wondered if they ever—

The vent slid open, startling her from her erotic musings. "You getting' out?"

Jo glanced out the window, surprised to see the Cameron Hotel. "Take me around to the back," she instructed.

He grumbled but complied. She checked her watch and saw it had taken the man twenty minutes. Jo decided to give him the extra money. After all, this was a miserable time of the night to have to work.

When the carriage stopped at the back entrance to the hotel she climbed out, wincing at the discomfort in her behind. Well, Stephen had warned her. She flicked the driver his coin and waited until he'd rumbled away before going to the door. It was locked.

"Damn and blast," she muttered, putting her collar up on her coat with one hand while she knocked with the other. She waited, becoming angrier by the second. After knocking twice more and waiting long enough that her wool coat had begun to get heavy, she set off at brisk jog, back to the front entrance.

It was close to four in the morning. *Dammit!* Jo knew her entrance would be noted and likely remarked on. Luckily there was nobody in the reception area other than a sleepy concierge—not the same nosey man who hovered around Jo whenever she left during the day.

Jo gave him a brisk nod and passed through without stopping.

"Damn, damn, damn," she said under her breath as she took the steps two at a time. Her frozen, wet hands fumbled with the key to her door and at first she didn't hear it. She paused, the dread trickling down her spine even icier than the weather outside: it was Mr. Chatham's service bell.

***

Stephen couldn't sleep. He'd come back to the hotel restless and apprehensive: tonight would be their second-to-last night.

After tossing and turning in his bed for close to an hour he'd given up on the notion of sleep. He didn't have the attention for work and he'd brought nothing to read for pleasure—a pastime he rarely indulged in given all the work he always had waiting—so the only thing to do was to get an early start to his day.

Given the uncivilized hour he decided he would see to his own needs rather than disturbing Leather. But when he'd gone to shave he'd not been able to find his razor. What the devil? Stephen had deliberated a long moment before ringing the bell. After all, Leather could catch up on his sleep at any time during the day. Just how did he spend all his time, anyway?

When Leather didn't immediately respond Stephen assumed it was because he was getting dressed. He decided to take a shower bath, he could shave after. Perhaps by the time he got out Leather would have appeared.

He soaped himself and let his mind wander back to the evening. Good God but she'd been magnificent spread and bound and full of cock. Watching his length slide in and out of her tight little arse had been one of the most erotic sights he could remember. He'd also, quite unexpectedly, enjoyed watching Julian's prick thrusting between her slick, shaved lips.

Stephen chuckled to himself as he recalled the younger man's heated, come-hither looks—as if he'd expected Stephen to spend the evening fucking him rather than Josephine.

Ah, Josephine. She hadn't liked the attractive young whore and Stephen had been perfectly aware of the taunting that had passed between the two. It had given him some excellent ideas, ideas he just might have to put into action tonight.

Stephen was full hard when he turned off the water and stepped out; no Leather awaited him. For the first time in as long as he could remember, he had to dry himself—both front *and* back.

"You're spoiled, Chatham," he muttered to himself. Not only was he spoiled, but he didn't do nearly as thorough a job as Leather before giving up and wrapping the towel around his waist. He padded back to the dressing room and knocked on Leather's door again.

"Leather! I need my razor," he said loud enough to wake the dead, not bothering to hide his irritation. There was no answer and he tried the doorknob; it was locked. Stephen frowned. Now why would he lock his door to Stephen's quarters?

He pounded harder. Nothing.

Stephen dropped his hand, surprised by his own anger. After all, this was the first time that Leather hadn't been waiting and ready for him at any time of the day or night. The thought gave him pause. So why *wasn't* he waiting and ready?

Stephen frowned. What if something was wrong with him in there? A twinge of fear pierced his irritation; what could be keeping him from answering?

"Bloody hell," he muttered, shoving a hand through his hair before turning. He would try his own key in the lock and if that didn't work then he would summon—

"I'm sorry, sir. You rang?"

He spun around to find Leather fully dressed. "Where the hell have you been?" he snapped, his relief leaving him weak and annoyed.

Leather's cheeks had two bright spots of color and he was breathing heavily. "I'm sorry sir, I, er, well, I was out."

Stephen blinked. "Out?"

His flush deepened. "Yes, sir."

"Out doing what?"

"I was visiting somebody." He glanced down in a way that Stephen could only call guilty.

Stephen opened his mouth to ask who the bloody hell he was visiting at this time of the morning and then the thought struck him smack in the face. Lord, what a fool he was: Leather had found himself a lady friend. All the anger he felt drained away. Why shouldn't he go out and get his knob polished? Since when did Stephen ever need him at four o'clock in the morning?

The thought of his staid valet paying amorous late night calls on someone made him smile, but he hid it. The intensely private man would not appreciate teasing.

Instead he grunted. "I wanted my razor to shave. I'd planned to get going without waking you."

"Ah, yes. I'm very sorry, sir. I have it in my room—I'd sharpened it and meant to bring it back this morning when I shaved you."

"Come and shave me right now." Stephen flung himself into the chair they used for that purpose, watching Leather as he bustled around, his movements jerky rather than smooth and silent. He was flustered and it was unusual.

He returned with Stephen's robe, once again noticing that Stephen was cold before he did. Stephen stood and pulled off the towel, relieved the erection he'd developed in the shower had fled. He didn't want the poor man to think he got hard whenever he was around him.

Stephen watched Leather in the mirror as he soaped Stephen's face. His mouth was a thin, compressed line and his color still had not receded. "I'm terribly sorry I wasn't here, sir."

"Don't flog yourself," Stephen said, irritable to be still discussing it. "How could you expect I'd be up at this ungodly hour?"

The question was rhetorical, but Leather said, "Are you having difficulty sleeping, sir? Would you like me to mix a draught for you?"

"No." He closed his eyes, hopefully ending the tedious conversation. Instead, he thought about Josephine. The memory his mind retrieved wasn't erotic, but of her laughing—her pale skin flushed with pleasure at something he'd said.

His lips twitched at the memory. She laughed so easily—and she made *him* laugh. She also made him feel more . . . human. Stephen couldn't recall speaking so much with another person in years.

Not since Louise.

He jerked upright at the thought and frowned. Goddammit! Why did he have to keep unearthing the distant past? Why couldn't he bury the memories for good? He knew the answer to that was because he'd always kept them alive to remind and protect himself. Well, it was—

The sound of a throat being cleared made him open his eyes.

Leather was holding the razor a few inches away from his face, his brow furrowed with concern.

Stephen grimaced. "Sorry for jumping about. Thank you for not cutting off my nose."

"Of course, sir." He resumed his work, his hands moving with a steady confidence that was belied by his tense expression. Really, he needed to get over not responding to Stephen's demented four a.m. summons.

Leather finished quickly and wrapped Stephen's face in a steaming hot towel while he cleaned the razor and put away his shaving gear. Stephen's hands felt restless and empty; normally he would read the morning paper rather than watch his valet work. But he'd have to wait at least an hour for that privilege.

"Do you think I shall be able to get coffee this early?" he asked as Leather removed the cooling cloth.

"I will see to it, sir. Shall I dress you first?" Leather knelt before him and slid his warmest slippers onto his frozen feet.

"No, go fetch my coffee. Perhaps some toast if they have it. I'll be in the study looking at my work." *What a bloody lie*, he thought as he lowered himself into the chair in front of his desk, absently watching as Leather stoked the fire and then hastened toward the door.

Stephen groaned and dropped his head against the high back of the chair once his servant was gone. He didn't know why he was bothering to go into the boatyard. He knew he wouldn't work; he'd just stare at his stacks of paper thinking about one thing—or one person, rather— all bloody day long.

***

What an almost disaster!

Jo flopped into one of the big leather armchairs across from the fire in Mr. Chatham's study and closed her eyes. She could be thankful that she'd locked the door and also that all her non-valet paraphernalia was at the Royal Scotsman Hotel. Tonight and tomorrow she absolutely could not leave things so close, although it was difficult if Mr. Chatham left at the same time. She'd have to think of some way to leave a little earlier—but not *too* early because she didn't want to miss any of their precious time together.

She forced her body to relax after the stress of the past few hours, allowing her mind to wander back to last night. She'd been in such a frantic hurry to get back she'd not had time to savor the evening; she'd be reliving it for a long time to come. Even if she decided to purchase a similar service at Cecile's at some point—with two male prostitutes—it would not be the same because it would not be Stephen inside her.

Jo groaned, unbuttoned two buttons on her trousers and slid her hand between her damp thighs. Her clitoris was sore but already pulsing and swollen and it took little time and effort to bring herself to climax, images of last night flickering through her mind's eye.

When she recovered from her pleasure, she thought about the item she wanted to purchase today. She might not be able to wear it tonight—she suspected she would be sore back there for some time to come—but she wanted to have it just in case. Frau Meisner had told her about the place when she'd inquired about buying erotic toys. It was not far from the few shops she'd already visited, just off Buchanan and Argyll.

Jo gave a huge yawn, her eyelids too heavy to open. She didn't have much to do today. She'd done most of Mr. Chatham's laundry yesterday and had only to shine the shoes he would likely want tonight.

She deserved a bit of rest after the last few hours. Just an hour to sit and do nothing, even if she couldn't sleep. An hour to imagine tonight and relive last night.

Another yawn distorted her smiling face. Yes, just a bit of sleep.

Chapter Twelve

Night Four

*S*tephen behaved during most of the morning and afternoon and completed the evaluations for two of the prospects on Edward Fanshawe's list. At this rate—even with distractions—he'd still finish before the two weeks he'd allotted himself.

It had been Mr. Smith's idea to send somebody up to do these inspections—not because any of them knew sweet bloody fuck about ships, but because the word would get out that he was looking to buy ships that were a burden on most yards: too salvageable to scrap yet too expensive to repair and store.

The Glasgow shipbuilding industry was a close community and already he'd received several invitations to meet with the owners of several yards. Thus far he'd only gone out once, but this morning he'd received a letter from Kyle MacDonald, who was one of the most influential men in Glasgow. The man was leaving town in two days and was only available for an early dinner tomorrow night. Stephen hated to schedule anything on his last evening, but he'd done little enough work already.

Even meeting at six-thirty it would be tight to get through dinner, postprandial drinks, and get across town to Frau Meisen's. He might have to arrange for Leather to fetch him for some 'emergency' if the dinner ran too late.

But that was tomorrow, today he had an important errand to run. Luckily, he knew where he was going and left the shipyard, heading directly to his destination rather than returning to the hotel.

He'd seen the shop that day he'd gone to the jewelry store—Madam Arlette's, right across the street. He'd taken note of Josephine's clothing and shoes the night she'd fallen asleep. He hadn't been lying when he said he enjoyed her gowns but he wanted to see her wearing clothing on her body that *he'd* chosen and purchased. For all he knew, she'd only get to use it one time, but he didn't care. He knew what he wanted to see her in but was worried he'd not be able to find what he wanted.

If his visit to the jewelry store had taken him outside his area of expertise, today's visit was taking him into a foreign country entirely.

"Bonjour, monsieur," a very bosomy woman said when he entered the feminine shop.

"Hello," he said, feeling like an awkward idiot.

She glanced around; as if he might have a woman he was hiding somewhere.

"I know what I want," he told her. "It's for somebody else," he added stupidly.

She chuckled. "That is just as well because I do not think I have anything in your size."

Stephen gave her an obligatory smile.

"Come into one of the private rooms," she said, cutting a glance at the other clerk, who was speaking to the only other customer, an older woman and what must be her daughter. The mother was looking at him through narrowed eyes.

"That would be best," he agreed.

She pulled back a heavy rose-pink velvet curtain and ushered him into a room with pale pink carpets, several pink-silk pieces of furniture, and pink walls. Stephen felt slightly bilious. Perhaps this was not the right place, after all.

"Please, sit." She went to a sideboard and poured something into a glass, which she brought back to him.

He stared at the amber liquid for a long moment before taking it, fully aware he'd now committed himself to purchasing *something*. He took a sip, pleasantly surprised by the quality of the brandy.

"Now, you want something special, I think?"

"Yes." Why the hell else would he be here?

She opened a door that was—yes—pink and fired off several sentences in what he guessed was French. Once she shut it, she came to sit on the chair beside the settee where he sat—it was the only piece of furniture he trusted to bear his weight, and that was not a certainty.

"I will have some things brought out for you."

Stephen frowned. "How do you know what I want?"

Again, she laughed, the action sending tremors through her remarkable bosom. "Aré you a businessman?"

Stephen blinked. "Yes," he said cautiously. Just what was this?

"I can see by your clothing, your shoes, your person, that you must be successful."

He said nothing, hoping that would spur her to getting to her point.

"I am a business*woman*," she said with a smug smile. "This," she waved around her, "is all mine. I am successful. I know what my customers want." She gave him a surprisingly gamine smile for a woman her age and size.

Stephen was about to open his mouth—and likely say something else stupid—when the door opened. His eyes widened.

Madame Arlette released another volley of French and the young woman—a gorgeous, long-legged, full-breasted creature with hair that cascaded over one almost naked shoulder—walked into the room. Although walked was too mundane a word for how she moved. Glided or perhaps floated, but neither of those encapsulated the sensuality of her movements. She was barely clad in a peignoir that had been cunningly composed of fine black lace interspersed with panels of something black but also sheer. Stephen stared as the girl pirouetted and posed, allowing him to see her from every angle. He began to get hard so he wrenched his eyes away from her and turned to Madame Arlette, who radiated amusement.

"You're a very good businesswoman," he conceded.

She chuckled and he turned back to the model, taking her measurements with his eyes and comparing them to Josephine's. She was perhaps a bit heavier, but she was just as tall. The gown would be slightly looser on Josephine, but it was not meant to be snug, not when it gave such tantalizing glimpses of her body when she moved and the sheer fabric shifted. The best part was that it had four slits that went almost to the crotch—it would look charmingly with the item Stephen hoped to purchase.

"I also have it in crème."

The door opened and another model came out, this one not quite as tall, wearing the same gown in a color like fresh cream. Stephen gave the canny Frenchwoman a sideways look; how did she know what kind of female body he favored?

Again she chuckled and shrugged. "You are tall and Camille and Renee have figures any man would adore."

Stephen was uneasy that she'd read him so clearly. The longer he stayed, the more certain it was she'd end up with his wallet.

"I'll take the crème gown. I also want opera gloves to match, stockings, and there's some sort of belt device that—"

"Yes," she said drily. "I am familiar with women's undergarments, monsieur."

"I'll want it delivered," he told the woman. "Put it in a pretty box."

She rolled her eyes and Stephen actually smiled.

"All right, all right," he conceded. "You know your job. But make sure it is there by nine o'clock tonight."

She nodded and said something to the girls, who left.

"Camille will bring you a pretty card for the box."

"Just write the name Josephine on it," he said. He had no intention of writing anything personal and sending it to a bloody whorehouse.

"Of course." Her expression was hopeful. "Is there anything else?"

Stephen considered her question. If he could find what he wanted today, he wouldn't want her wearing anything else tonight. But, if he couldn't, it would be nice to have something for her. "Put together a second gift—the same woman. She is built rather more like Camille."

"Would you like to look? I could—"

"I have no time. Just make it something special—you already know what I like."

"But of course."

"Have it delivered tonight. Again before nine." He stood and took out his card, handing her one. "Send the bill to the Hotel Cameron

"Very good, sir."

He then took out his wallet and extracted five pounds. "I am looking for a place that sells unusual items."

Madame Arlette was *exceptionally* skilled at her job and her intelligent eyes narrowed. "Ah, *plaisir.*"

Stephen didn't speak French, but they understood one another. "Yes."

"Go to Buchanan and Argyll and take a right. It is number 142. Tell them you are a discerning gentleman." Stephen's eyebrows shot up, but she nodded.

"Very well. It's been a pleasure doing business with you," he said as he put on his hat and buttoned his coat.

"And you as well, Monsieur Chatham."

Stephen let himself out, pausing on the steps to pull on his gloves. The day was heavy and it felt like it would rain, but it wasn't yet.

"I'm going to stretch my legs," he told his driver. "Pick me up at 142 Argyll in a half hour."

"Very good, sir."

It felt like it had been days since he'd walked. In London he worked his body hard every morning for at least an hour. He'd had no time here—what between work and his evenings.

Not to mention your newfound interest in shopping.

Stephen had to smile at that thought. He knew this wasn't love, but it was certainly infatuation, which was rare enough. If he'd learned one thing this week it was that his days of employing only whores were numbered. There was nothing to compare to a woman who chose you out of her own free will. And, clearly, some women enjoyed having adventures in the bedroom. It behooved him to—

A figure ahead of him caught his eye—was that Leather leaving that shop and climbing into a cab? But the door closed and the carriage moved off too quickly. Stephen shrugged. What did it matter? The man was allowed a life.

But as he got closer to the spot where the carriage had stopped he realized the business was 142 Argyll.: Leather had come out of the same shop?

He frowned as he studied the bland storefront which only had a window with four rather dowdy hats. The shop next door advertised watch repair. Yes, that was likely where he'd gone.

He pushed open the door and found himself in a cramped room with a handful of dusty hats displayed in a rather haphazard manner. He frowned around him.

A well-dressed young man was sitting at an elegant wooden desk— the only nice piece of furniture in the drab room—entering something in a ledger. He looked up and smiled at Stephen.

"Good afternoon, sir. Are you here for a hat?"

Stephen's face flushed slightly, but he said the words the woman had told him he'd need to say. "I'm a discerning gentleman."

The young man's smile broadened and he stood. "Right this way." He opened an overlarge door that had been painted black and bore a sign saying, *Stock* on it. "Go all the way back and take the door on the left, sir."

"Why all the secrecy?" Stephen asked. The shop he visited in London took none of these precautions.

"Such shops are susceptible to extortion and often find themselves raided if they don't pay."

"Tell me," he asked on impulse, "Was there just a gentleman in here with close cropped brown hair wearing very thick spectacles? He would have been wearing a black suit."

"I'm sorry, sir. But I'm afraid we don't give out details about our other customers."

Stephen could appreciate that. He headed through the doorway, a smile of anticipation on his lips. God willing—or not, rather—he'd find what he wanted here. He had an idea this would be one treat that Josephine had never anticipated.

Chapter Thirteen

"Are you ever coming out, Josephine?"

"Almost ready." She could hear the nervousness in her own voice: just what would he say when he saw her?

He chose this for you, you ninny.

That was true, and you could have knocked her over with a feather when he gave her the box tonight. Inside was a beautiful negligee, butter soft crème opera gloves to match, and stockings and . . .

"It is a double-ended phallus," he'd said, taking the large ivory implement in one of his huge hands. "I thought you might enjoy using this and seeing what it was like to enjoy a tandem fuck from a different perspective," he'd smiled, his eyes dark with arousal.

Jo looked at her reflection in the mirror and smiled—she looked very fine, and the gown fit her to perfection. Not only that, but the slits in the negligee were perfect to showcase her new toy. It was unfortunate she could not wear the belt and stockings, but it was too awkward with the leather harness for the phallus.

Jo stared at the big ivory cock and took a deep breath. It had almost killed her to get oil on the fine leather gloves, but she knew he wanted her to wear them tonight. They'd cost more than a maid's yearly salary, but he wouldn't even think of such things. She smiled, realizing the thought made her feel wonderfully decadent. So did the massive tool in her hands.

She placed the slick head against her entrance, gave an experimental nudge, and winced. It was big—as big around as Stephen but twice as long. Luckily it wasn't all meant to go inside her. She took a deep breath and then pushed, grunting as she tilted her hips to take the monstrous phallus inside her body.

She didn't stop pushing until the ivory scrotum rested snugly against her sex. She stared down at it, something humming inside her head as she studied her erect cock. Her breathing was too rapid and she felt dizzy. But she also felt . . . *right*. She took the shaft in one hand, sucking in a breath as she gave it a stroke, the action moving the part inside her. Jo swallowed repeatedly, unable to stop looking at it.

Good Lord, but it was bloody beautiful. All her life she'd dreamt of having a prick, although she'd never imagined herself endowed so generously. She gave it another stroke and grunted with pleasure. If she narrowed her eyes, she could almost pretend it was real.

Jo experienced a painful squeezing sensation in her chest as she stroked herself. She loved it, absolutely adored it.

She still remembered the first time her father had taken her aside with her brother Ben. She must have been only three.

"Take your pants down, Ben."

Like most little boys—most *real* little boys—he'd been eager to show off what he had.

Jo remembered even now how her hand had gone to her own flat crotch. "Why, papa?"

But her father—who'd been her god back then and for a long time after—had merely given an impatient shake of his head. "You must never take your clothes off in front of another, Joseph. Do you understand?" Her father had been her whole world, not to mention the most important person in the duke's house after the duke and duchess, and she'd wanted nothing more than to please him.

"Yes, papa."

"You're a shy boy and that's why you'll never disrobe before others." Jonathan Leather had turned to Ben. "Remember that—your younger brother is shy—terribly shy. You must look out for him, Benjamin—it's your duty as the elder."

"Yes, papa," Ben had answered automatically. Back in those days her brother had been glad to have a younger brother rather than a younger sister—not that either of them had been given a choice. Even on her birth papers it said Joseph Edward Leather.

"Josephine?"

Jo jolted, the phallus jiggled, and she gasped before answering. "Almost ready, si-Stephen." She cursed her slip. That wasn't the first time she'd almost called him *sir*. She needed to keep her wits about her. All these years she'd managed to subvert who she was beneath her carefully cultivated veneer. Even her voice was different around Stephen—not the dull, toneless valet, but her real slight brogue—all that remained of her Scottish heritage.

She'd belted down the drink Stephen handed her when she'd arrived, and it was making her feel fanciful. Jo took several deep breaths, stopping only when she was calm.

There was a knock on the door and she heard Stephen say *enter*, followed by the murmur of male voices.

"Do you want a drink, Josephine?" Stephen asked her, amusement in his voice.

"Er, no thank you." Jo adjusted the leather harness and took three deep breaths. And then she stepped out from behind the screen where she'd retired to change.

Julian saw her first and his full lips parted in surprise.

Jo grinned at him and she knew it wasn't a nice expression. "Hello Julian." She planned on enjoying herself to the hilt—pun intended—and young Julian would be her toy.

Stephen was pouring a drink and put the stopper back into the decanter before turning around.

"I thought you'd never—" His jaw sagged and his eyes bulged

Jo walked toward him, aware of how she must look: a tall, slim woman wearing a flowing peignoir with a large ivory phallus. Every step provided her with more stimulation than she really needed just now.

"Good God," he said, draining his glass and setting it down without looking, his eyes glued to her *cock*.

He came close, his big hands sliding inside the slits in the gown and tracing the belt she wore, lightly stroking over the leather, his fingers tugging the strap that was snugged between her thighs. He gave a low, guttural grunt when he felt the shaft that impaled her.

His expression was one of awe and lust. "You look bloody gorgeous." He circled her shaft and stroked, his action gently moving the double ended phallus in and out of her, even though it was secured with the harness.

Jo caught her lip and grunted.

"Feels good, hmm?" Stephen asked.

Jo nodded.

"You look beautiful," he said, releasing her with obvious reluctance, but then capturing her mouth in another of their savage kisses. His huge hand slid around the back of her head and she felt his fingers grip the laces of her mask, their teeth and tongues clashing, the metallic taste of blood flooded her mouth. Still holding her laces, he jerked her back sharply, his eyes blazing with desire.

"Tell me, Josephine, which of Julian's holes are you going to fuck first?"

She clenched around the hard shaft impaling her and shuddered.

He gave her another hard kiss before stepping back, his hand going to his collar. "Strip him while I watch," he ordered, pulling off his tie and tossing it onto a chair and then shrugging out of his coat.

Jo turned to the beautiful young whore, who was waiting for her. He wore closely tailored trousers as he'd done last night, with a tight-fitting waistcoat and an open shirt that exposed a great deal of smooth, muscular chest.

While Jo unbuttoned his waistcoat, he stared down into her eyes and she saw a genuine flare of passion—or perhaps he was just a very convincing whore. But when she removed his waistcoat and began to pull his shirt from his trousers, she saw his bulge and tell-tale wet mark, and her sex clenched yet again, sending a spasm of nearly painful pleasure through her body.

She knew he was only hard at the thought of performing in front of Stephen, but it was no less effective.

"You can have his mouth," Jo said, her eyes never leaving Julian's. "I'll take his arse."

***

Any doubts he had as to whether he was irretrievably bent disappeared when he saw her sporting a cock and balls.

Good God! Who knew such a thing could be so unspeakably erotic? And *why* for God's sake?

He didn't care. He was as hard as a pike. He'd known he would enjoy watching her fuck the arrogant young whore, but he'd never expected this much of a reaction.

Julian might be pretty, but he was also broad shouldered, tall, narrow-waisted, and—as Stephen knew from last night—well proportioned.

Stephen's heart staggered in his chest when Jo moved closer to push Julian's shirt off his shoulders and Julian's tumescent organ rubbed against Jo's much larger ivory prick.

Fuck!

He couldn't help imaging that it was Stephen she was undressing; Stephen's cock she was pressing against. Good God but he didn't know if he could keep to the evening's plans.

Stephen had wanted to have Josephine alone tonight—and now wanted it more than ever—but he could not deny he was going to get a great deal of pleasure out of fucking Julian's mouth while watching her.

As if she'd heard him, she turned, her eyes flaring when she saw he'd stripped down to only his trousers, her eyes hungrily roaming his chest. She turned back to Julian. "Oil?"

The boy's smirky lips curved. "I'll fetch it."

Julian strode gracefully across the room, making sure to pass close to Stephen's chair, his hard cock bouncing at eye-level.

When Julian returned, he handed her the bottle but she shook her head. "Oil me."

Stephen saw the man's cock jump as he hastened to comply, slathering his hand with oil and then stroking her shaft, making sure to push it hard with each down stroke. Her eyelids fluttered and she arched her back, widening her stance to take more.

Stephen swallowed a groan and his hand sought his own prick, which was straining and leaking and unbearably hard as he watched Julian stroke her to arousal.

"Enough," Stephen said, his voice heavy and thick. He pointed to the floor between his spread thighs. "You heard her—you get the pleasure of sucking me off."

Julian gave him a smoldering look that belonged on stage, sank to his hands and knees, and crawled toward him. It was an amusing performance and Stephen smiled as he spread his thighs to accommodate the man.

When he'd dreamt up this scenario he'd wondered—briefly—how he'd feel about having a man's mouth on his cock. Or whether he'd be able to fuck another man's arse. He'd worried he'd be repelled. As it turned out, the thought of fucking such a virile young buck made him ache.

Julian's fingers made short work of Stephen's trouser buttons and they both made sounds of pleasure when Julian reached in and took out his cock

Julian licked his lips, his gaze riveted to the slick, fat head.

"Suck it," Stephen said.

Julian lowered his mouth immediately and Stephen groaned. Good God, the man's mouth was *strong*, and his tongue knew exactly where to press and stroke. Stephen shifted in his chair so he could watch Julian's jaws stretch wide to take him. He had broad shoulders and his thick bicep flexed impressively as his hand moved up and down on his shaft. Yes, there was something to be said about having a muscular man kneeling between one's thighs and sucking one's prick.

He looked up from Julian's bobbing head to find Josephine consuming him with hungry eyes, her breathing labored, her hand absently stroking the long ivory shaft, her leather-sheathed fingers slick with oil. Stephen reveled in the sight, not caring if wanting her this way was beyond perverted. He'd purchased this double-headed cock because it was thick shafted and long, not dissimilar from his own prick.

Not only had he fantasized about seeing Josephine with a huge cock jutting from her slender hips, he'd also wanted her to feel powerful when she dominated the snide whore. And by God she was beautiful as she rocked back and forth, slicking her big tool.

Stephen's hand dropped to Julian's head and he stroked him the way he would pet an obedient hound. "Fuck him for me, Josephine. Fuck him hard."

She shuddered, her high, small breasts shaking enticingly as she dropped to her knees. For a moment he thought she'd just plow him without preparation and he opened his mouth to stop her—no matter what an ass Julian was, Stephen didn't want the man damaged.

But he should have known Josephine was not petty. Indeed, she reached beneath Julian's body and held Stephen's gaze as her arm pumped in a familiar rhythm. Julian's sucking became harder, faster, more frantic. Stephen thought she'd bring him off but she stopped as suddenly as she'd started.

Stephen grinned at her erotic cruelty; it would be another evening of no release for the handsome young whore.

She picked up the oil and poured more on her hand before using it to massage between Julian's cheeks, all the while staring at Stephen. He knew as he met her almost black eyes, that she wanted to do *this* to *him*. Even more shocking was his immediate physical reaction to the image of Josephine plunging into his body, fucking them both to orgasm.

God, he *wanted* her to use him that way.

Intense desire shot straight to his groin and drove him dangerously close to coming. He laid a staying hand on Julian's head, his chest heaving.

"Enough," he said hoarsely. "Suck my balls."

The exquisite suction disappeared but was quickly replaced with a different kind of pleasure when Julian took him into his hot wet mouth and massaged his aching jewels with his tongue.

Stephen watched Josephine through slitted eyes, knowing the moment she breached the whore with her finger because Julian's muscular body tensed. Her arm moved gently at first, in and out slowly, but with increasingly deep thrusts. She added more oil, preparing him with the same care Stephen had used on her last night.

He grunted at the memory and his prick jumped, his balls so bloody full they ached. Stephen shifted in his chair and spread his thighs. "Use that clever tongue to fuck my arse while Josephine takes yours," he ordered.

Julian released his sac with a soft, wet *pop* and instantly lowered his mouth to Stephen's pucker, licking and probing while making small sounds of pleasure against Stephen's sensitive flesh. Stephen knew it was all part of his act, but he couldn't help enjoying Julian's eager obedience as much as his skilled mouth.

Josephine's gaze was riveted to where Julian's head was bobbing. "I like to watch," she said in a breathy voice, her eyes never leaving Stephen's crotch. "But I wish it were me giving you such pleasure."

Stephen's cock pulsed at her words and he wanted to push Julian aside and give her that wish and more, but then she took the big phallus in one hand and began to stroke it up and down Julian's crack. The motion was mesmerizing and menacing, like a cat playing with its prey.

Julian's rhythmic tonguing barely faltered, not even when she placed the flared head against him, breaching him with exquisite slowness. Josephine's expression was almost feral as she sank deeper and deeper. She seated her not inconsiderable length and then tilted her hips before pushing into him with a sharp thrust that made Julian squeak.

Stephen smiled at her little act of cruelty, imagining how the ivory scrotum in the middle of the phallus would be pressing hard into Julian's arse while she kept him filled, grinding her hips against him.

An image of her filling and stretching and dominating *him* exploded in his mind's eye.

Jesus! Was something wrong with him that he was so aroused by the thought of a woman—*this* woman—fucking his arse?

He didn't care if he was bent.

He grabbed a handful of Julian's hair. "More," he gritted through clenched teeth, grunting when Julian's tongue probed him deeper, but still not as deeply as Stephen wanted.

Josephine's face contorted with a grimace of pain mixed with pleasure and Stephen knew she was feeling her part of the cock just as acutely as the man she was fucking. No matter how powerful the sensation, her determined expression told him that she wasn't done with the arrogant whore just yet.

She began to fuck him with slow, powerful strokes, crying out each time the phallus drove deep inside her. Her free hand slid slowly up her belly to her breasts, leaving a slick trail of oil in its wake.

Stephen watched in an erotic stupor as she pinched and tugged on her hard nipples, using the man between them for her pleasure.

It was the most arousing sight he'd ever seen. He could tell by her sweat-slickened skin and shaking body that she couldn't endure too much more.

Stephen wanted to be with her when she climaxed. He yanked up Julian's head. "Suck," he growled, not taking his eyes from Josephine.

Julian took him shockingly deep, not stopping until the head of Stephen's cock hit the back of his throat.

"God yes." He jerked into Julian's mouth as the man swallowed around him, the tight muscles of his throat massaging him. Stephen groaned and used both hands to hold Julian's head at just the perfect angle, driving into him with savage thrusts. The eager whore not only throated every inch of his cock, he submissively canted his hips to take Josephine's brutal pounding deeper.

Josephine mirrored Stephen's thrusts and they fell into a rhythm, fucking the man's willing body in tandem.

All too soon Josephine's movements became jerky, her breathing increasingly ragged.

"Stephen," she gasped. "I can't—I just—" She gave one last brutal thrust and shuddered.

Bloody hell she was gorgeous.

And that was Stephen's last conscious thought as he emptied himself in Julian's snug throat and floated off into oblivion.

***

Stephen was still sleeping when Jo carefully lowered herself into his lap.

His eyelids looked heavy and she could tell he didn't know where he was for an instant. And then he smiled: a sleepy, sated, glorious smile.

"You didn't leave," he said.

"No, I couldn't leave you without saying goodbye. But I have to go soon."

He frowned. "Is it really time?"

"Almost."

He stretched and gave a huge yawn.

"Did you have a long day?" Jo asked.

"I did." He cut her a wryly amused look. "I didn't get much sleep last night. Which reminds me," he said, pushing his messy hair off his forehead, "I might be a few minutes late tomorrow night—I'll try not to be."

Jo wanted to demand what could possibly interfere with their last night but knew she would likely find out when she waited on him in a few hours.

"Is your business trip a success?"

He snorted. "I seem to be distracted."

Jo's heart pounded in her ears. "Oh, why is that?"

He laughed and shook his head. "You're terrible, you know that?"

Jo grinned.

He traced the edge of her mask, his expression pensive. "I have to admit this—" he flicked a hand to encompass her and everything around them. "Well, this was more than I was expecting."

"Me too."

He looked up sharply, as if expecting something more. When she didn't speak, he opened his mouth, and then closed it, and then opened it again. "I know I promised not to pry, but I have to tell you something."

She swallowed noisily. "Oh?"

"I want you to know that I would help you if you decided to change your plans." His jaw worked from side to side and he stared at something over her shoulder. "I would be pleased to—well, to take care of you."

Jo was having a hard time breathing. "Are you—"

His eyes widened and she knew instantly she'd been mistaken; he wasn't asking her to marry him, he was asking something else, entirely.

"You're asking me to be your mistress." It wasn't a question.

It was the first time she'd ever seen his cheeks flush. "I don't mean to insult you, but I would be honored to set you up your own establishment. Your life would largely be your own as I would rarely be here."

Jo didn't know why her chest was so tight—why her head was pounding. She would have refused his offer of marriage, but it still hurt to be offered something . . . less.

Fortunately, she'd had a lifetime to hone her acting skills. She gave him a smile she hoped communicated regret and gratitude. "That is . . . tempting." And it was, oh God it was tempting. "But I'm afraid I must decline."

"I've offended you," he said, his expression cold and guarded, which she now knew was self-preservation.

Jo wrapped her arms around him and squeezed him tight, blinking back the tears. "You haven't offended me, Stephen. But I'm afraid my plans have already been set in motion, no matter how much I might wish to change them." She sat back and looked at him.

Was that relief she saw in his eyes?

"I'm pleased I haven't insulted you. I'm afraid my social skills are rudimentary at best. I've greatly enjoyed our time together and," he shrugged and gave a slight shake of his head, as if dislodging an unwelcome idea. "I want you to take my card and keep it. Call on me if you ever need help."

Jo could see how mortifying this conversation was to him and it was clear he genuinely cared about her.

Not enough to offer marriage.

She ignored the unwanted observation.

"Thank you, Stephen. That's a comfort. But you mustn't think I'm entering a situation that is repellent to me," she told him, wanting to erase any doubts he might have that the fictional Josephine was being sold into a life of slavery. "I'm very happy with my future plans." That much, at least was true: she would be with him, wouldn't she? At least for as long as he wanted her services and as long as Jo could bear being near him, but never touching him again. Jo forced a smile and changed the subject. "I had a lovely time tonight—thank you for your wonderful gifts."

"You're welcome."

She hesitated. "You enjoyed it, didn't you? You didn't just do it for me?"

He chuckled tiredly. "I enjoyed it *and* I did it for you."

"I know most men might not think—well, I know it is unusual."

His lips curved into a wicked grin, which she never would have expected to see in a thousand years. "Since it was my idea, I guess that means I'm too debauched to save."

Jo's heart was so full of emotion—of *love*—that she felt like she might explode.

Only one more night, her relentless inner voice reminded her.

"Stephen?"

"Hmm?"

"I was thinking—can it be just the two of us tomorrow night?"

His pupils flared and he pulled her down to kiss her. "You read my mind, Josephine."

Who was this man? And why did he have to be so loving? Why did he have to gut her like this? Why couldn't he be the way he'd always been with the women he'd bedded? Why did he have to inject something more into a situation that could never lead anywhere?

"Stephen?" she said again, a dangerous warble in her voice as he trailed kisses along her jaw, his hand idly stroking her thigh in a way that was already waking up her exhausted body.

"Yes?"

I love you, Stephen.
But instead she said, "I have to go."

Chapter Fourteen

Night Five

Stephen knew things were bad when he realized the most enjoyable part of last night hadn't been getting his knob polished, or even watching a beautiful woman fuck herself while sodomizing a man. No, it had been the few minutes he and Josephine had sat together afterward.

But then he recalled his clumsy probing and insulting offer.

He closed his eyes and groaned.

"You all right, Mr. Chatham?"

Stephen looked up; he'd forgotten the shipyard overseer was at another desk. "I'm fine."

"Want some more tea?"

"No thank you." Good God, one cup their lousy tea had almost killed him. He glanced at his watch: four o'clock and another day in which he did shockingly little.

Well, once he no longer had his evenings to look forward to, he'd welcome the opportunity to bury himself in work.

"Did you get through everything, sir?"

Stephen sighed heavily as he stared down at the thick folder. "Not quite, but tomorrow I'd like to see the next one, anyhow—the one in dry dock number five."

"Very good, sir. We'll be ready."

Stephen glanced at his watch again: it was still four.

"Er, are you finished for the day, sir?"

He'd better; he was meeting MacDonald at six-thirty. That would barely leave him time to bathe, have a brief rest, and get downstairs to dinner.

"Mr. Chatham?"

Stephen realized the man was waiting on an answer.

"Yes, I'm finished for today."

"I'll go summon your driver and carriage, sir."

Stephen straightened the pile of papers and put them in his satchel. What he really wanted was a cup of Leather's tea. Yes, that was what he needed to wake up and shake the cobwebs from his head.

This was it. Tonight was it.

He sighed, exhausted by the constant chaos in his head.

As Stephen left the dingy shipyard office and climbed into the carriage, he knew he'd behaved selfishly to agree to just the two of them on their last night. Hadn't he promised her exciting times and adventures? Instead she was getting *him*.

Still, he told himself, it had been Josephine who'd suggested it.

Even after you asked the woman to be your mistress, a sarcastic voice pointed out.

What a fool he was. How he wished he could go back in time and undo that mortifying scene. How could he have thought she would agree to be his mistress when she'd been married once and was getting married again? For all that she'd been sexually adventurous she'd never given him the impression she'd been promiscuous. He was a bloody idiot.

What was done was done. All he could do was go tonight and make their last evening as pleasurable as possible. He thought about the second gift he'd bought for her. Would she wear it tonight?

Stephen suddenly realized he didn't care what she wore or what they did. He just wanted to see her. And why was that so bad? Because he'd once been betrothed to a woman who'd lied to him from start to finish? A woman who'd only wanted a rich man who could take care of her—*and* her lover.

He'd been behaving like a scared little boy for fifteen years because one woman had betrayed him. Because of something Louise had done to him all those years ago, he'd insulted the first woman whose company he'd enjoyed in ages.

"Good God."

You could fix that.

Stephen blinked at the sudden thought.

Marry her, you idiot.

His breathing became stilted. *What?*

The realization dawned on him like a creeping winter sunrise. Marry her? He was wheezing now, like some old man who'd run up a flight of stairs. *Marry her?*

Why not?

Stephen swallowed and swallowed, but still the lump wouldn't go away. Why hadn't he thought of that? She was the sort of woman one married, not the sort to set up as a mistress.

But to marry somebody on only four days'—*nights'*—acquaintance? Wasn't that mad?

But to lose her because he was afraid to take the risk was even madder, wasn't it?

He'd *almost* lost her last night and it had left him sick with regret and remorse.

Yes, he thought—serene for the first time in days, perhaps years— this made absolute sense.

Stephen smiled to himself as he looked out the window at the black thunderclouds that threatened. Tonight he would ask Josephine to marry him.

***

Jo was giddy and half-mad with excitement about their last night together. Unfortunately, Mr. Chatham was driving the sane half of her brain mad as well.

He'd come back to the hotel a bundle of nerves: an irritable bundle.

He'd taken another shower bath even though he'd had one that morning. He'd always been an excessive bather and it was a wonder he had any skin left.

There was no mouth-watering erection for her to work around while she dried his body. Indeed, he seemed the farthest thing from amorous.

He twitched so much while she was shaving him that she almost snapped at him—out of fear—when he whipped around and she just about sliced off his ear.

There was no time for a massage this evening, and it was one of those times when he truly could have used it.

"Please just let me work your shoulder for a few minutes, sir." Jo all but begged—for altruistic rather than lascivious reasons—when he winced putting his shirt on. "It will only get worse without any attention."

He hesitated, his jaw flexing. "Fine," he said, pulling off his shirt and flinging it to the ground. "Don't dawdle. I've got thirty minutes to read something about the bloody man's shipyard and get down there." He sat back down in shaving chair. "And don't forget to come down for me no later than nine o'clock."

"Yes, sir." That was the fourth time he'd reminded Jo. She knew she should be flattered since it was *her* he was so excited to see, but he could be irascible and insistent when he was in a state. She found the spot on his shoulder that always ached.

Stephen yelped. "Bloody hell, that *hurt*, Leather."

He was behaving like a baby. "I'm sorry, sir. You've got quite a knot in here. If I could just," she pressed her thumb down and he leapt out of the chair.

"Enough! Not tonight. Fetch me another shirt," he toed the one he'd thrown down mere moments earlier. "This one is wrinkled." He frowned when Jo bent to collect the shirt. "You can attend to that later. I need to get going."

Jo forbore pointing out he had at least a half-hour before he needed to meet for dinner and did as she was bade.

"No, not that one," he said when Jo returned with his standard black four-in-hand. "Don't I have something," he shook his head, his face creased in lines of irritation. "I don't know. Don't I have something less *grim?*"

Jo was glad he was looking at his reflection rather than her. Grim? Mr. Chatham was concerned about appearing *grim?* Grim could have been his middle name, at least when it came to his clothing.

"You have a dove gray, sir."

He lifted his lip in a slight sneer and then shrugged. "Fine, that will do."

Jo fetched the tie and, on a whim, took his pearl stickpin from the small cask of valuables she kept for him. Once he was suitably tied, she offered him the pin.

He grunted and then stuck it into the gray silk, eyeing his reflection pensively before making a dismissive noise and turning away. "Fetch me a brandy," he ordered.

Jo watched him stalk toward his desk, which was uncharacteristically messy, piled high with stacks of paper, and felt a twinge of remorse that he was so tightly wound tonight. And all because of her.

She poured his drink and delivered to his desk, where he was staring at a sheet of paper covered with incomprehensible figures. He didn't appear to see her, so she set the glass down and retreated to his bedchamber, where she could watch him through the door while appearing busy.

His usually indecipherable mien was perturbed and troubled. What could he be thinking to cause such distress?

Perhaps it wasn't her at all, but something that had happened at the shipyard today. After all, he'd invited one of the shipbuilders to dine with him at the last minute. He was a man who despised socializing and rarely even dined with his own business partners.

Well, there was nothing she could do to help him with that. All she could do was ensure he was finished with his meal early enough to get to Frau Meisen's.

Jo felt her lips curve into a smile as she allowed her thoughts to wander to this evening. What would he have planned for tonight? Anything out of the ordinary?

Jo realized, as she absently studied a scuff mark on one of his shoes, that she hoped they would make love, eat and drink and talk, and make love some more. Tonight she would have to make sure she left him while he slept. She could not bear a painful leave-taking.

***

"My man said you quite liked the looks of *The Pelican* and *Lady Dorcas*," the Scotsman said—not for the first time this evening.

Stephen nodded, wishing he could look at his watch but aware he'd already done so only a few minutes earlier. "Yes, that's true. But I've still got several prospects to look at."

Kyle MacDonald gave a hearty laugh that put Stephen's hackles up. The man was a bloody highwayman masquerading as somebody's roll-poly grandfather. "Ach, you're thinking of Angus Cooper's pitiful tubs, I know. The man has nothing but rubbish."

That was rich coming from MacDonald, who was currently trying to sell—for an extortionate amount—two ships that were probably around during Sir Walter Raleigh's time.

Stephen tried to smile but doubted he was successful judging by the other man's expression. "I shall certainly keep you in mind, sir."

MacDonald put his pudgy elbows on the table and leaned across it. "I tell you what. I can offer you—"

"I'm sorry, sir."

Stephen looked up at the voice. It was their waiter. "Yes?"

"I've got a telegram for you, Mr. Chatham. I would have waited until after you'd finished, but I was told it was quite urgent."

Stephen almost smiled—this time a genuine one. Leather was certainly clever—why hadn't Stephen thought about having a telegram sent? He took the paper from the man and handed him a coin. Once he'd left Stephen turned to MacDonald, who was frowning and chewing on his cigar as if it were a cob of corn.

"I'm so sorry, Mr. MacDonald, but I'd better look at this."

MacDonald's smile reminded Stephen of a shark. "Of course, you must.   Please,   go   ahead." The telegram was brief, and it was *not* from Leather:

"Need any information you've gathered IMMEDIATELY. *Fanshawe needs by morning. Send all. Clerk will await at St. Vincent Place. Smith."*

Stephen glared at the paper. All of it? Smith wanted *all* the information he'd gathered? Was the man bloody mad? It would take at least an hour to send and would cost a bloody fortune. Stephen was just about to reach for his watch when a familiar voice stopped him.

"I'm terribly sorry, sir, but I've received a rather pressing message."

He looked up to find Leather hovering beside the table and held up a staying hand before turning back to MacDonald, who looked positively thunderous.

"I'm sorry, Mr. MacDonald but this message is from my partners." *And they have a deal that might make you irrelevant, kind sir.* "I'm afraid I need to dash." He gestured toward their waiter who hurried back to their table. "Please see that Mr. MacDonald gets anything he wants and don't let him pay for anything." *Ha! Fat chance of that—the man was notoriously clutch-fisted.*

MacDonald looked slightly appeased by the generous offer. He should do, after all, he was the one trying to sell the bloody broken-down hulks; he should by buying *Stephen* expensive scotches and cigars.

"I understand," he said to Stephen, magnanimous as his eyes spotted the desert cart the waiter had rushed off to fetch. "I suppose I'll see you next Monday, after I get back from the country."

Stephen stood. "Yes, that will suit admirably. Thank you for your time, sir. Have a pleasant holiday with your family."

He motioned to Leather, who'd gone to stand behind a nearby potted palm. "Come along," he said, striding toward the hotel lobby. "I've got a real task now—not an imaginary one. I'm going to want you to—"

"Mr. Leather?"

Stephen and his valet stopped at the sound of the tentative voice and turned.

"It *is* you." A mousy looking woman was staring at Leather as if she'd seen a ghost.

For his part, Leather was looking rather ghostlike. "I'm sorry, do I know you?"

"It's me, Miss Bindon—Her Grace's cousin," her stunned expression shot through with a certain amount of stiff reproof. She frowned. "It *is* Mr. Joseph—not Mr. Benjamin Leather?"

Leather bowed. "Er, Miss Bindon. What a surprise."

Miss Bindon—whom Stephen now recalled he'd seen trailing after the Duchess of Tarland the day of the rainstorm—was frowning at Leather.

What was this? One of Leather's former loves? And one he'd treated cruelly by the look of it. Whoever she was, Stephen didn't have time for this right now. He gave the woman a curt nod and said, "I do hope you'll excuse me, ma'am, but I'm afraid we're rather in a hurry."

"Of course, of course," she said, no longer judgmental but flustered as she looked up at Stephen, quailing under his severe stare.

"Good evening, ma'am." Stephen turned to his silent valet. "We must go."

Leather had recovered from any surprise and nodded coolly at the woman. "It was a pleasure to see you again, Miss Bindon."

They bowed and made their way toward the stairs.

Stephen put the woman out of his mind. "I've got something for you to do tonight, Leather," he said when they reached the first landing.

"Yes, sir, of course," Leather trotted behind him, sounding rather winded.

"I need to send information to London and I need to do it quickly. I've got it all laid out in a ledger, so it is easy to read. But it shall take some time and I'm afraid I have none to spare this evening." That was a bloody understatement.

"I want you to go to the telegraph office at St. Vincent Place. You'll have to send a series of messages." Stephen thought about the vast amount of information Smith had requested and shook his head; it would take all bloody night. But, still, if Fanshawe was asking then he must have something better than what Stephen was looking at.

Leather hurried around him to open the door to the room. Out of habit, he pulled out his watch: it was ten after nine. By the time he assembled the requisite information and told Leather what to do it would be close to ten. Bloody hell!

Stephen tossed his gloves into his hat and dropped both into a nearby chair. "Come into the study with me, I'll show you what you need to do. We've not got much time."

***

Jo stared at the telegrapher's bent head and screamed inside.

The information she had to send was an outrageous amount and she speculated it would run well over a hundred pounds. She looked at her watch: it was eleven-thirty and she had to find some way of getting a message to Mr. Chatham.

She glanced down at the brief letter she'd written, chewing her lip. Was it too little? Too much? Her head pounded from wondering what to say. If she didn't send it soon, he might simply leave.

Jo heaved a sigh and folded it before tucking it into the envelope she'd taken from the hotel when she'd known she wasn't going to see him tonight.

"I need to send a message to somebody," she told the clerk. "Can I leave for a quarter of an hour?"

"This will keep me busy for twice as long," the clerk said absently, not looking up from the columns of numbers and words.

"If I'm not back you can start on the top page of that stack. You'll need to do all of them."

"Yes," he said drily, "You mentioned that already. A few times. I know what to do, this is my job."

Jo stepped out into the cold, clear night and walked toward Hanover Street rather than Buchanan, even though there would be far more cabs on the busier street. But she needed a little time to clear her head and make sure this letter was the best decision.

She tried to imagine what he must be thinking right now. He would be worried—wondering if something had happened—she knew that.

Why tonight of all nights? *Why?*

Jo tried to console herself that it would have come to an end in a few hours, anyhow, but that was cold comfort.

All too quickly she reached Hanover, where several carriages were lined up, waiting.

The drivers were standing together off to the side, smoking and laughing. They broke up when they saw her and one of the men came toward her.

"Need a lift, sir?"

"I need you to deliver this message for me." Jo held up the envelope. "I'll give you this," she put a crown in his grubby palm, "to deliver it to the name and address on the front. I'll give you this," she held up two more, "when you bring me back a note saying the message was received. Understand?"

His eyeballs threatened to roll out of his head, as well they should. "Aye, sir. Nay bother. Will ye be here?"

"No, come to the telegraph office on St. Vincent's Place. I'll be there for the next several hours."

Jo watched him head off at a rather reckless pace and questioned the wisdom of getting him so excited. What if he got into a wreck before ever getting there?

But if she hadn't, there would have been nothing to stop him from throwing away the message once his carriage turned the corner.

Anyhow, it was done. In every sense of the word.

Jo took a deep breath and headed back.

Chapter Fifteen

*S*tephen spun around so quickly at the knock that he sent amber liquid sloshing over the lip of his glass.

Not until he was facing the door did he recall that Josephine didn't knock, she just entered.

"Come," he said, throwing back the contents of his glass.

It was Julian.

"What do you want?" Stephen snapped, setting his empty glass down with a thump.

"I've got a message for you, sir." He stood hesitantly in the threshold.

"What are you waiting for—bring it here." Stephen was already moving toward him, his hand out.

It was just a plain white envelope with Frau Meisen's name and address on the front. The handwriting was not one he recognized.

"When did this come?"

"Just a few moments ago, sir."

"Did you see who delivered it?"

"A cab driver."

"Is he waiting for an answer?"

"I'm afraid not, sir."

Stephen recognized the avid glint in the other man's eyes: he thought he was going to earn some money tonight.

"You may go."

Julian's face fell. "Yes, of course, sir. Please ring if you have need of . . . anything."

Stephen turned his back and slid his thumb beneath the flap of the envelope.

He sat down before unfolding the single sheet.

Dear Stephen,

By now you will know I'm not coming tonight.

"Goddammit," he hissed under his breath. He *had* known it, but he'd not wanted to believe it.

I regret that I'm unable to be with you on our last night, but I'm afraid something came up I could not ignore. Never fear, I'm not injured, I'm just not my own mistress tonight.

I want you to know that the past four days—or nights, rather—have been the best in my life. Some might see that admission as a sad commentary on my life! Not only was I able to experience many of the things I've only ever fantasized about, but I was able to experience them with you. I will think of you often in the years to come.

I wish you the best in your life.

Yours,

Josephine

Stephen turned the page over, as if there might be more. There wasn't.

He gave a bitter laugh and crumpled up the page. That was it, was it? He flung the letter to the floor and stood, refilling his glass yet again. When he lifted the glass to his mouth he realized he'd lost track of how many he'd had. Two at dinner, two here, this would make five.

He ground his teeth. "Dammit."

Stephen thumped the glass down without even taking a sip. She'd turned him into a foolish wreck, he would not allow her to make him into a drunk.

Instead of drinking, he paced. It occurred to him he could simply leave—go back to the hotel. After all, there was nothing here for him, was there?

He could go find Leather and see to the telegrams, which were really his affair, not his valet's.

Stephen knew it wasn't true that she'd made a fool of him; he'd made a fool of himself—*he'd* been the one foolishly thinking of marriage, not her.

All week long he'd felt it, that lurching sensation in his stomach— the feeling you have when you step on a patch of ice and slide, knowing that a painful fall will be the only way of stopping.

So, he'd fallen. Was it painful? Marginally.

Liar, liar, liar.

Yes, it was bloody painful—and mortifying as well. After all, he hardly knew the woman. But his inner, mocking voice was right: he was a liar. The fall was incredibly painful and made more so because he'd allowed himself to have expectations. He'd not come here tonight to bid her goodbye; he'd come to offer her marriage.

He should be relieved and grateful. After all, he'd been about to offer marriage to a woman whose hastily scrawled regrets were no deeper than those of an acquaintance writing to apologize for missing a dinner party.

That's all he was, wasn't he? Her acquaintance. Just when had he begun to believe he was more? She'd never led him to believe anything other than what was in her letter. If anyone was to blame here, it was Stephen.

Why did that just make him feel angrier at her? She'd done *nothing* to him.

Including not caring for you.

Stephen closed his eyes and pressed his fingertips against his pounding temples, as if he could manhandle the pain away.

The pain of not being loved. Just like Louise never loved you. Just like your parents. Just like—

"Enough!" he roared, appalled to realize that prickling feeling behind his eyes heralded actual bloody tears.

When would he finally be able to forget things that had happened another lifetime ago? Was this to be his life? Condemned to constantly repeat his mistakes? Destined to become an old man still paying women? A man who loathed his own past but could still never manage to escape it?

He was breathing so hard he barely heard the soft scratching on the door.

"Goddammit! What the hell is it?" he yelled.

The door opened hesitantly and Julian's face appeared in the crack.

"I'm sorry to interrupt, sir, but—"

"Get in here and shut that door."

Julian obeyed quickly.

"Come here."

The younger man stopped in front of him, his hands behind his back, his eyes downcast.

"Look at me."

Julian's blue eyes flared when they met Stephen's: this man *wanted* him, and not just because he would get paid for it. Like the degenerate Stephen was, the realization penetrated his fog of anger and despair and stirred him. He couldn't have Josephine, but he knew the man's eager, skilled mouth would remind him of watching Josephine. He could relive her in that small way . . .

He really was no better than a dog.

"I need you to get a carriage for me—I'll also need to settle with Frau Meisen."

"I—I wish you wouldn't go."

Stephen snorted. "Quite the salesman, aren't you?" He reached into his coat and took out his wallet. He'd purchased the younger man's services these past two nights and knew what he cost. He handed him enough for a week, hating himself even more than ever. "What do you know about the woman from the last two nights—Josephine?"

Julian held the money in the palm of his hand and stared down at it for a long moment before shaking his head. He met Stephen's eyes. "Nothing. Frau Meisen always dealt with her manservant."

Stephen's eyebrows shot up. "A servant made her arrangements?"

Julian nodded, his eyes slipping back to the money again.

"What did he look like?"

"I don't know—I only saw him leaving. He was dressed like a butler, all in black, a bowler." He shrugged.

Stephen considered that rather surprising information. Somehow he'd gotten the impression that she was too poor. Even if she wasn't, who trusted a servant to arrange such an affair?

I trust Leather to manage such matters.

Yes, but that was Leather, and there were few enough servants like him.

"How much money would it take to get Frau Meisen to tell me her real name?" he asked.

Julian was shaking his head before Stephen even finished. "I don't think she would take any amount, sir."

"I find that difficult to believe."

Julian opened his mouth, glanced at Stephen's wallet, and then closed it again.

Stephen heaved a sigh and took out more money, slapping it down in Julian's palm.

"She used to do this same thing someplace in Prussia—her, well, her last partner, Gerhardt, told me this." He gave Stephen a coy smile. "He was with Frau Meisen but he wasn't *with* her, if you know what I mean."

"Yes, yes, he was fucking *you*. Get on with it."

"The place she had over there was like this one. She took money to give out the identity of one of her clients and it turned out the man was a prince or duke or something. When he learned it was Frau Meisen, he had her thrown in jail. She lost everything—she almost lost her life, but Gerhardt was able to bribe a guard to get her out. She's terrified of such information getting out here and ruining her life a second time. She manages all of the sensitive clients herself so none of us know anything."

Well, that answered that.

"You can go." Stephen put the rest of the money in his hand and closed his wallet.

When the other man didn't move Stephen glared at him. "Just go."

"I'd rather stay."

Stephen frowned. "You don't understand—I'm not paying you to stay."

"You've already paid." His full lips curved into a smile that meant only one thing and he lowered himself to his knees as gracefully as only somebody twenty years old could do. He stared up at Stephen his full lips parted. "Please."

Stephen snorted. Had anyone ever begged to suck his cock before? Not that he could recall. "I won't be gentle."

Julian's chest began to move faster. "I don't want you to be."

Stephen felt himself becoming hard; apparently he would fuck anyone. Wasn't that what he'd accused Gideon of? Fucking a knothole in the fence?

So what? Who cared what he did except him? Nobody. And who cared that Josephine had buggered off with little more than a by-your-leave? Not him, apparently: he was as hard as iron, primed, and ready. He didn't need her. Hell, he didn't even need a *woman*.

He'd come all this way; he might as well get some pleasure out of this miserable fucking night.

Stephen began unbuttoning his trousers, his cock straining at the eager lust on Julian's face. "I'm going to fuck your mouth hard," he said in a conversational tone as he took out his prick and slowly pumped it.

"*Irrumare,*" Julian murmured, his eyelids heavy, his pink tongue moistening his full lower lip.

"What?" Stephen asked.

"It's Latin and it means to force to fellate."

Stephen's lips twisted but he knew it wasn't a smile. "Where I come from, we just called it face fucking," he said, aiming the slick crown of his cock toward Julian's mouth. "Open wide."

Julian opened all the way, taking him deep into his throat, his pupils huge as he kept taking more, even after Stephen stopped pushing, until his lips rested in the nest of hair at the base of Stephen's cock, his eyes straining to look up at him.

Well, *that* was certainly impressive; he didn't recall anyone taking all of him, before.

Stephen slid both hands under his wide-open jaws and thumbed his stretched lips, the light stroking causing Julian's entire body to shiver with pleasure. Stephen smiled and held him firm while he tilted his pelvis and then flexed his hips, rubbing his throat with his sensitive head.

Julian's eyes widened and his body tightened in terror for one exquisite instant before he became pliant.

"Good boy, now suck," Stephen growled.

And Julian began to work his magic, his tight, wet throat massaging his shaft and head as he swallowed.

He slid his hands around Julian's skull and proceeded to give him every bit of what he'd asked for.

Stephen closed his eyes as he began to thrust, not surprised when Josephine's image materialized behind his eyelids. He didn't care; he'd take whatever little part of her he could get, even if it wasn't real.

Chapter Sixteen

Jo was pacing and had been for some time. It was just after one when she'd finished the bloody telegrams and returned to the Cameron. For a mad moment she'd considered dashing to the Royal Scotsman Hotel, changing, and then charging over to Frau Meisen's. After all, even an hour was better than none.

What had stopped her?

Fear. Fear that he wouldn't be there—or fear that he was with somebody else. She was such an idiot. She should have gone—even thirty minutes of him would have been better than none.

As it turned out, she was lucky that she'd resisted the impulse because Mr. Chatham returned to the hotel at a quarter to two.

"Good evening, sir." Jo went to assist him when he entered.

"I'll see to myself." He paused in the act of removing his coat. "How did everything go?"

"Everything went as planned. We received a confirmation after the last of the telegrams." Jo took it out of her breast pocket and handed it to him.

Mr. Chatham scanned it briefly and then nodded. "Any other messages?"

"No, sir."

"Go to bed and get a few hours' sleep. I'll want you at five-thirty."

"Very good, sir."

Jo went back to her room but was too anxious to sleep. Instead she sat on her bed and wondered where he'd been until then. Had he stayed at the brothel even after learning she wasn't coming? What had he done for so long? The thought shook her to her marrow.

Or, what if he'd not received her letter? He must have—she'd sent it a good two hours before he'd returned. But what if he'd not stayed at the brothel but had gone somewhere else?

The cab driver had brought Jo a card with Frau Meisen's name scrawled on it. But what if somebody else had signed her name? Perhaps the message was still sitting on a salver somewhere? Never to be delivered?

Her mind raced around and around and around. She tried to close her eyes, but they'd just pop open again.

When she heard movement next door, she looked at the clock: it was five thirty. She'd spent almost four hours in a stupor.

"Good morning, sir," she said when she entered his chambers.

"I'll bathe before you shave me," he said, already up and seated at his desk, sorting through his papers. He didn't even look up at her.

He hardly said a word to her over the next two hours, staring at nothing while she shaved him, staring at more nothing as she dressed him, and then eating his breakfast while staring at the same page of the paper.

"Shall you be home at six, sir?" she asked as she helped him into his overcoat.

"I don't know." He pulled on his gloves and then took up his hat, cane, and satchel, leaving without another word.

Once the door closed she collapsed on the settee, exhausted. She knew she should get some rest, but she couldn't. Somewhere during all her dithering this morning she'd decided to call on Meisen's one last time to make sure he'd received the message.

She glanced at the clock and grimaced: it was only seven-thirty. Could she go now? Or should she wait? Would she be of any use if she waited? And what would she do if the message hadn't reached him? Sent another to him? At this hotel? Or to London?

"Oh God, please, let him have received the message," she whispered, knowing God was unlikely to go out of his way to aid a conscienceless fornicator.

Jo took a deep breath and exhaled slowly. And then did it again.

She'd finish her chores and *then* visit Meisen's around noon. Lord knowns she'd paid the madam enough to get a few answers.

Heartened by this thought, she pulled on her polishing gloves and started on Mr. Chatham's shoes.

***

Jo had never seen Mr. Chatham intoxicated before, but tonight he was as drunk as a wheelbarrow.

She'd known something was wrong the moment he'd blown into the hotel, heading straight for the decanter, his bag still in his hand.

Unlike most people who became drunk, Mr. Chatham didn't act silly or uncoordinated. No, he just became increasingly morose, which was saying something.

He barely ate anything, pushing his dinner around until it got cold.

"Would you care for something else, sir?" she asked as she cleared away the nearly full plates. "I could—"

"No." He stood up and poured another drink from the brandy decanter before going to sit down with a stack of documents.

Jo pretended to be busy in the bedchamber while spying on him. He did not turn a single sheet of paper. Either he was the world's slowest reader, he'd fallen asleep, or his mind was in chaos.

Jo looked at his broad powerful shoulders—now slumped—and ached for him. It was like seeing a big, majestic animal brought low—like watching bear baiting or witnessing a tiger that was forced to beg for scraps.

He needed something to get his mind off things. Even though it would torture her, he should go back to Frau Meisen's—or perhaps somewhere else—and at least indulge in some physical pleasure. Sitting here in his room and thinking about the past five days was almost killing her and she knew it would probably be worse for him. At least she was still with him; he was only with his valet: dry, boring, dependable old Leather.

Whatever he'd felt for her, it had hit him hard. He needed release. She would suffer agonies of jealousy, but it was better for him to get sexual satisfaction than to drink himself into a stupor.

When it reached ten o'clock and Jo had taken as much as she could stand, she steeled herself and marched up to his desk.

"I beg your pardon, Mr. Chatham?"

He looked up slowly, his mind a thousand miles away. It took a moment before his eyes focused on her. "What is it?"

"You don't have an appointment tonight, sir?"

He hesitated at the question and for an infinitesimal moment she knew he was entertaining the idea. But then his gray eyes blazed and he sat up, looking once again like the proud, cold, arrogant Mr. Chatham she knew and loved. "No, I'm finished with that. Go run me a bath and then you can give me a massage."

Jo bowed her head, torn by emotions. On the one hand, she worried about his mental state if he stayed here alone. It would be better for him to go engage in physical pleasure that would likely make him forget Josephine. After all, it was unlikely the care of his valet—no matter how sedulous—would be enough to get him through this period.

Still, she couldn't help thinking, as she placed the bottle of oil on Mr. Chatham's nightstand, that if he was going to be miserable anywhere, he might as well be miserable and naked under her hands.

Her face heated at the selfish feeling. How could she take any enjoyment in his company when she was the reason for his suffering?

No matter how much she chided herself, it did nothing to stop her body's reaction.

Jo was, she knew, a bad, bad person.

***

Stephen stood beneath the stinging hot water long after it felt good, his skin bright red.

Poor Leather had no idea what was going on and had already checked on him twice while he turned into a prune. But Stephen didn't want to come out of the shower-bath until he was sure he wouldn't make a fool of himself and run like a frantic chicken to Frau Meisen's.

He *knew* he could pay the greedy Madam enough to give him the information he wanted. He knew it. But he'd given his word to Josephine to respect her privacy. Already he'd broken that word by paying Julian and pumping him for information.

He sighed and turned off the water, standing in the swirling steam before finally getting up enough energy to shove back the curtain and step out. Leather was waiting.

"What time is it?" he asked.

"After eleven, sir."

Stephen grunted. No wonder he was painfully sober, he'd been standing in the bloody bathtub, crouching under the shower head, for almost an hour.

He didn't even bother to dry the front of his body, but just stood there like the pitiful lump he was.

170

Leather did his usual efficient job and then came around to the front of his body and began drying him without saying anything. It was such a kind, considerate gesture that Stephen wanted to weep. That was when he realized that he must *still* be drunk, but not drunk enough.

"I want another brandy," he told Leather once he'd finished toweling him until his skin was warm and rosy.

"Of course, sir."

Stephen didn't bother to wrap a towel around himself as he made his way—yes, a trifle unsteadily—toward the bed, where he sat down, his mind lurching back onto the same track, like a train that had only one destination.

Stephen knew, although he wouldn't admit it to himself, that he would go back to Frau Mesien's before he left Glasgow. He had to. He would do anything to learn more about Josephine. It wasn't as if he would stalk her or approach her, but he wanted to assure himself that she was all right—that she'd made the right decision for herself. That she hadn't changed her mind and needed help.

"You fool," he accused himself out loud. She knew his name—it would be simple to find him, if she wanted to. He lifted his arm to shove his wet hair off his forehead a sharp pain shot out from his shoulder. "Blast and damn,"

"Ready, sir?"

He looked up and found Leather rubbing oil on his hands. "I'm beyond ready," he muttered, flopping face down on the bed. He closed his eyes and tried not to think about how badly he'd been struck by all this.

Leather's magic fingers helped to forget, sending him into a pleasurable fog. It wasn't until Leather was half-way down his back that Stephen realized the man hadn't brought him another drink.

He thought about that for a moment, wondering if he was pleased or displeased by his disobedience? He finally decided it was just as well. No, it wasn't just as well—it was yet another example of the way the man took care of him. He felt an unexpected wave of gratitude toward his loyal valet. Leather was kind—beyond kind. Why did Stephen insist on holding him at arm's length? Why did he hold *everyone* at arm's length?

Louise.

"Oh bugger off."

Leather's hands paused. "I'm sorry, sir?"

God, he needed to think about something else. Anything else.

"I know you said your father died, Leather, do you have any other family?"

Even in Stephen's tipsy state he could tell the difference in Leather's hands on his body. He'd shocked the man. Well, of course he had. He opened his mouth to tell him to forget it, but Leather spoke.

"I have one brother, two years older than me."

Stephen thought the other man sounded not at all like his usual self. Of course that was more likely to be Stephen's intoxicated hearing rather than Leather's voice. And perhaps he'd been mortified by Stephen's personal question? He'd crossed the line between them, hadn't he?

Well, now that he was across, he might as well keep going.

You're a lonely, pathetic lump who has nobody to talk to except your servant. All the people who spend any time with you are paid to do so.

So what? Stephen snapped—thankfully inside his head. So. Bloody. What. He'd do anything to stop thinking of Josephine, even for just a few moments.

"Does he live in London? Your brother?"

Again, a slight hesitation and then, "He did until six months ago. He is a valet with a member of the diplomatic corps and went with his master to a post on the Continent."

"Another valet?" Stephen said, his mouth taking over and dismissing his brain or good sense. "Is everyone in your family a valet?"

He heard something he'd never heard before: Leather laugh. And it reminded him of somebody? Some other laughter. The room shifted oddly, his head spinning. He closed his eyes tightly—he was drunker than he'd thought and now he was paying the price. *This* was why he always, well *usually*, avoided drink.

"My mother was not a valet," Leather said, traces of his laughter still in his voice. "But, yes, my brother, father, and I all followed the same path."

Leather's hands kneaded a muscle in the back of his leg that was exceedingly sore and he groaned.

The hands froze. "I'm terribly sorry, sir, did I—"

"Do that again," Stephen ordered, even though the pressure had almost brought tears to his eyes.

"Right here?"

"Ahhhh, yes. There. God, it hurts, but it feels bloody good." The odd pleasure-pain from his leg robbed him off all thoughts and words, even Josephine and his current misery.

He must have drifted into sleep because he next felt Leather's strong thumbs rubbing the soles of his feet. He had no sense of the time.

"What time is it?" Stephen asked, his voice groggy and slurred.

Leather's hands froze. "It is a quarter to midnight, sir."

Stephen blinked. A quarter to midnight? Hadn't he laid down here at eleven? No, that was not possible. Or had Leather really spent three-quarters of an hour working on him?

"Do you wish to continue, sir? Or would you rather have some tea? Or perhaps go to sleep?"

The last thing he needed was to go to bed and toss and turn.

"I'll have a cup of tea after you finish," he said, rolling onto his back. "Oh, and Leather, thank you for *forgetting* to bring me my drink." Because Stephen had his eyes open and Leather was working his shoulders he caught the miniscule smile.

"I'd hoped you'd not noticed, sir."

"I did. While I'm not entirely appreciative of your efforts now, I know I will be in the morning." He hesitated and then said what he'd only be able to say when he'd had a few drinks in him. "I also appreciate you tolerating my personal questions." Leather's hands stuttered slightly.

"It's my pleasure, sir."

"What else is your pleasure?" Stephen asked, unable to believe the words came out of his mouth but recognizing his voice.

His valet paused and met Stephen's eyes. As ever, he was cool and unreadable. "It is my pleasure to serve you in any way you desire, sir."

Stephen inhaled sharply, his nostrils flaring and stomach tightening at this undeniable invitation. Part of his mind, the sober, analytical part, knew he would *most heartily* regret his actions later.

Why not? his evil imp demanded. *You're no stranger to a man's touch— you used Julian yesterday and suffered no qualms.*

Stephen grimaced; that wasn't quite true.

You certainly didn't let any such qualms hold you back ...

Fine, so that was true. *I enjoyed every second of fucking his face. There, are you happy?*

The imp laughed.

But this was his servant. His valet.

Your valet who lives to serve you.

Stephen tried to ignore the smug voice, but right now, the sensual part of his brain—on which he generally kept such a tight leash—reveled in the man's submission.

"Right now what I desire is release," Stephen said, feeling like a spectator in his own body, listening to his mouth say things his brain had not approved.

There was not even a flicker of emotion on Leather's face. "I understand, sir, and it would be my pleasure."

His cock jumped at the other man's words, but neither of them broke their locked gaze.

"Nothing will change if you say no; your job is secure." He gave Leather a hard look; he needed to know that Stephen wanted nothing that was not freely given. "You know I speak the truth on that."

"You've never lied to me, sir." Leather said. He hesitated and then asked, "Will anything change if I said I *would* rather, sir?"

Stephen stared, his body throbbing.

Leather didn't blink or color or turn away, he merely peered down at Stephen through his impossibly thick lenses.

Stephen considered what he meant but decided he didn't bloody care. He just wanted to come by somebody's hand other than his own tonight.

"Nothing will change, either way."

Leather nodded and then reached for the oil on the nightstand and slicked his hands, his expression the same as if he were about to rub Stephen's feet rather than his cock.

Stephen's prick wept harder and jumped with excitement; why was he finding this plain, dull, disinterested man's offer to frig him so erotic?

You enjoy the thought of owning him, controlling him so completely he would serve you in any way. You like thinking of him as your slave.

That was sick, but also true: it made him incredibly hard wondering just how far this man would go to please him.

Leather lowered his slick hands to Stephen's hips. One went to his shaft while the other slid between his already spread thighs and began to massage his aching balls.

"*Fuck* that feels good," he ground out as Leather's slim, smooth hand pumped him with firm, competent strokes, his thumb rubbing the sensitive underside of his crown with each pass.

He stared at Leather, his jaws clenched as he struggled for control. His valet focused his attention on what he was doing, only the slightest sprinkling of color over his sharp, high cheekbones. Stephen glanced down to Leather's hips to see if his work was arousing him. Leather's trousers were lifeless and flat. So, this really *was* commitment to his work rather than desire.

Stephen didn't know whether that was better or worse, and then decided he didn't care. Leather was working him with more skill than any whore he could recall, stretching the sensitive skin of his sac, one oiled finger brushing the area below it by accident. And then brushing it again.

So, not by accident.

Leather's fist tightened and the pumping quickened. The oiled finger between his thighs quested down and down and then stopped. Stephen spread wider; his invitation clear.

A soft, slick pad probed his hole and he grunted with animal pleasure, his hands bunching the bedding on either side of his body as the orgasm began to build.

Stephen forced his eyes open, twisted curiosity making him want to see his servant's impassive face when he brought him to climax.

Just as he did in every other way, Leather knew exactly what he wanted and Stephen moaned as a slick finger stretched the tight ring of muscle.

Leather stroked him harder and faster while his finger began to fuck him. Stephen's hips pulsed with sharp jerks to meet Leather's fist and to bring his finger deeper. The pressure had built so slowly that he wasn't ready when his throbbing balls tightened.

"Yes," he ground out between clenched jaws as he drove his cock into Leather's hand, fucking his fist. "*Harder.*"

Leather's finger rammed him with deep, rhythmic thrusts. His narrow face was hard, his jaw tight as his arm pumped, his nostrils flared with the force of his labor. And then he hit that spot that was like heaven on earth and Stephen yelled something and jerked into the other man's hands twice more before thrusting off the bed, his back arched as he fucked the sky.

The last thing Stephen saw before his eyelids slid shut was Leather's flushed face and the way his lips almost curved into a smile.

Chapter Seventeen

For the second night in a row Jo couldn't sleep.

Mr. Chatham had fallen into a deep sleep after his orgasm, not even twitching when Jo bent and licked the soft head of his cock clean, reveling in the taste of his spend. She'd been tempted to use her tongue on the delicious ridges of his abdomen but came to her senses. Still, he'd not moved when Jo brought a warm cloth and tenderly bathed every part of him. Nor did he stir when she took a pillow and placed it beneath his head.

She'd pulled the bedding over his naked body, tucking the ends beneath him so that the chill could not seep in.

And then she'd gone to her room and given herself one explosive orgasm after another, her mind's eye full of Stephen, his hard, muscular body slick with oil and rosy from both the massage and arousal. His thighs spread wide—sprawled and exposed, his hips pumping while she fucked him with one hand and stroked his magnificent cock with the other. It had been even more erotic to see her hands on his body when her own body was fully clothed—clothed as Leather, not Josephine.

Jo had felt his eyes on her, and it had made her wetter. For whatever reason, he wasn't trying to imagine she was somebody else, he'd *wanted* to see her face when he climaxed.

And what an orgasm it had been: he'd come so hard it spattered his chin, his beautiful cock pulsing, the thick blue vein throbbing with each spasm.

All types of thoughts had crossed her mind while she'd worked him. What would he have done if she'd taken him in her mouth at the moment of orgasm and milked him until he screamed?

Only years and years and years—a lifetime—of self-control had stopped her. She was his valet, not Josephine. She was the man who cleaned his boots and shaved his face and mended his clothing. And now she was the man lucky enough to give him release when he couldn't be bothered to seek it someplace else.

"God. Let that be often," she muttered, her finger sliding up and down her slick, swollen slit, wondering if she should give herself just one more.

Jo had to admit the sorry truth: that part of tonight had been so much better than the four nights with him because he'd ejaculated while looking at the *real* her—not the invented person, Josephine—but Joseph Edward Leather: *Jo.*

She hadn't needed to wear a mask or fake long hair or dress in clothing that wasn't comfortable. She'd given him pleasure dressed like herself, and she'd been able to *see* him for the first time because she'd been wearing her bloody glasses!

Every time she was Josephine, he'd been muted, fuzzy, unclear. Not tonight. Tonight he'd been as clear as a diamond. It had been a feeling unlike any other, and she would do anything to experience again.

No matter how unlikely that actually was.

Jo knew she should enjoy tonight, because it was likely the first and last time. Not that he'd fire her, no, he'd given his word and he didn't lie. But he'd not been himself: he'd been drunk.

She'd taken advantage of that, and she didn't care. She'd do it again in a heartbeat.

But it was entirely possible that tomorrow he would decide one time was plenty—that being fisted by his valet wasn't worth the possible complications. It wasn't beyond comprehension that he would worry Leather was a sod and would develop a fixation on him.

Jo snorted. If only he knew.

He would be on edge—one way or another. And that meant Jo needed to behave as if *absolutely* nothing was amiss when she went to wake him in only—she glanced at the bedside clock and groaned—less than an hour.

***

It had been a bloody long day and Stephen didn't arrive back at the hotel until sometime after eight o'clock. Just like always, Leather was waiting for him.

"Good afternoon, sir," he said, taking his satchel and hat and waiting for his gloves. "There are two messages for you on the salver."

Stephen grunted—just like he always did—and began unbuttoning his greatcoat. There was something not quite real about the way he and his valet were going on with each other.

It wasn't awkward, startling the reverse, actually. He'd arrived at Stephen's bedside this morning at five-thirty with the same bland expression as always and had proceeded to shave, bathe—complete with vigorous all-over toweling—and dress Stephen like always.

While Stephen was grateful that he was so unflappable, he couldn't quite get his mind around the fact there was absolutely no sign of the man who'd fisted and finger-fucked him not even twenty-four hours ago.

Both of which he'd done quite willingly—not to mention deliciously—and which you can enjoy again tonight—and every other night, if you so choose, an insidious, selfish, amoral voice whispered inside his head.

The twinge in his groin at that thought made Stephen feel more than a little concerned.

"Shall I order dinner up for you, sir?" Leather asked after he'd helped him off with his overcoat.

Stephen pushed aside his erotic quandary and considered the man's question. Should he eat here? Or should he go to Meisen's and order a dinner and a couple deserts?

Or perhaps you might just stay in and enjoy a massage . . .

"No, I don't think so," he said. He needed to get out of this room—but he didn't need to go to a whorehouse. If he wasn't careful, he'd turn into Gideon Banks. He'd always liked sex, but he'd had more—and of greater variety—over the past few days than was probably good for his sanity. And the last thing he needed to do was make a habit of using his valet like a bloody prostitute. No matter how much the notion made him throb.

Which was, in itself, more than a little unnerving.

"I believe I'll go down for dinner tonight."

"Very good, sir. Would you like me to pour you a drink?" he asked, holding Stephen's coat and looking up at him with the same expressionless face.

Stephen tried to see beyond the thick glass that seemed to insulate the other man from the world. Leather met his eyes directly, not coloring or flinching or looking away.

Stephen exhaled slowly. He had to admit his valet was one-of-a-kind in more ways than one. He'd never encountered such an unreadable face.

"Make me some tea and bring it to the study." He turned to the salver and removed the two messages before catching up his satchel.

He dropped into the chair closest to the fire, tossed his bag down beside it, and looked at the two messages: one was a telegram and one something hand-delivered. He opened the telegram first: it was from Smith, who'd written to inform him Fanshawe had used the information he'd sent to leverage a deal in Bristol—he'd purchased two ships and Stephen could come home.

Stephen tried not to feel annoyed that all his work had been useless, because it hadn't. Just because they hadn't bought any of the ships he'd looked at didn't mean his information hadn't been critical.

He could go home, but he should finish out the last of the boats, just in case. After all, if things fell through down in Bristol they'd be glad for all the information.

Stephen frowned; why was his deceitful brain trying to come up with reasons to stay?

He knew exactly why.

But staying in Glasgow did not get him any closer to Josephine; at least not beyond geographic closeness. She had his card, if she wanted to reach him, she knew how.

"Leather!"

Stephen heard the sound of hurrying feet and his valet appeared in the doorway. "Yes, sir?"

"We're leaving tomorrow."

"Leaving."

It wasn't a question and Stephen wouldn't have answered it if it was. Leather could fist him from now to next year but Stephen would be damned if he answered a servant's bloody questions.

"You'd best get packing," he said, turning to the second message, the hand-delivered one.

"Very good, sir."

Stephen didn't bother responding. He unfolded the single sheet, his eyes dropping to the bottom, first. He sat up straight; it was from Julian.

Mr. Chatham,

I hope it isn't too forward of me to send you this message, but I have some information about your lady friend and felt that you'd want to know.

Stephen gave an unamused bark of laughter. No, what he'd *felt* was that Stephen would pay a great deal such information.

"I would have sent you this earlier, but I only found out today because yesterday was my one day off. I hope you don't mind, sir, but I took the liberty of telling the lads who watch the doors to keep an eye out for either of them."

"You enterprising little weasel," he said under his breath, not without a little admiration.

"I'm sorry, sir?"

Stephen looked up to find Leather holding a tea tray. "Nothing," he said. "Just put it down, I'll serve myself."

He waited until Leather left before turning back to the message.

"Charles, the tall blond footman, said your lady's servant was by again yesterday."

Stephen's heartbeat quickened and he deliberately turned the letter face down and sat back in his chair, glancing at the crackling fire. He should throw this into the hearth *now*. He swallowed and glanced at the steam coming from the nearby teapot. He noticed his hand was shaking when he went to pour a cup and set the pot down with a *thump*.

This was ridiculous.

He flipped over the page.

Since Charles knew how important it was, he paid the driver of the hackney that brought the servant and waited for him, to come back to Meisen's after he'd dropped him off. I know you will want to know this information and I will be available tonight if you should want to make an appointment.

Respectfully,

Julian Clark

"Why you little shit," he gritted, crumpling up the paper and shooting it into the fire. "Leather," he called, pushing to his feet.

His valet must have been in the next room because he appeared instantly in the doorway. "Yes, sir?"

"When did that message come today?"

"Which one, sir?"

"The hand-delivered one."

"Just after noon, sir."

Blast and damn! Stephen supposed the clever little bastard had probably already been reserved by now. Well, there was only one way of finding out.

He saw Leather was still waiting. "Fetch my coat and hat, I'm going out," he said, already moving toward him.

Leather hesitated only a fraction of a second before scurrying away to get both.

Stephen tapped his foot impatiently as the other man helped him into his coat, and then he snatched up his hat.

"Your muffler, sir?" Leather ran after him as he strode down the hall and Stephen snatched it from him.

"Will you be back soon, sir?"

He ignored the question, telling himself he was being a fool. What was he going to do if he discovered her identity? Storm to her house, kidnap her, and carry her away on a white charger?

Stephen snorted; he'd better learn to ride a horse before he attempted that.

He slowed his pace when he reached the ground floor, having to turn sideways to get around a porter with more luggage than Stephen had ever seen.

Why was he doing this? Why couldn't he—

"Sir? *Sir?*" Stephen felt a tug on his overcoat and turned.

A thin, mousy woman with a pinched expression looked up at him. "May I help you?" Stephen asked, not bothering to hide his impatience.

"You don't remember me?"

Stephen squinted at her, distantly aware that she colored under his rude inspection.

"We met the other day?" she said. "You were with Mr. Leather. Mr. *Joseph* Leather."

Comprehension dawned. "Ah, yes. You knew him from the Duke of—" he paused, scrambling.

"Tarland, sir." She stood up straight, as if *she* were the duchess, not just a menial.

He frowned and said. "If you are looking for Leather, he's not with me at the moment."

She glanced around in an overly dramatic fashion and then shook her head. "No, it was *you* I wanted to talk to, sir."

He raised his eyebrows, only just stopping his hand from going to his watch. "Yes?"

She swallowed hard, her eyes darting around again.

Stephen sighed and snapped his fingers at a hovering lackey. "Is there a place we might have a few moments of private conversation?" He pulled out a coin and the man nodded vigorously.

"Yes, sir, this door right here leads to one of the small parlors."

He moved toward it and Stephen said, "Don't bother, I'll get the door." He turned to the hovering woman. "Ma'am?" he said gesturing ahead of him.

She hesitated, her face puckering. "I'm not sure that would be quite proper. I—"

It was all he could do not to roll his eyes. "If you want privacy, those are our options. If not," now he *did* take out his watch. "I'm running late for an appointment."

She nodded reluctantly and clutched her small bag to her sunken chest, as if Stephen might wrest it from her hands.

He opened the door and followed her inside, waiting for her to take a seat before lowering himself across from her and waiting.

She shifted in her seat, cleared her throat, placed her bag on the table beside her chair, and then put it back on her lap.

Stephen cleared his throat and she jumped.

"Ah, yes. Well, it's about Mr. Leather."

"What about him?"

She pursed her lips and moved them side to side. "You seem like a nice young man and I just thought you should know about him."

For the first time, Stephen felt a pang of . . . *something*. Instead of hurrying her along, he forced himself to be patient.

"I knew him and his brother since they were just little boys. Their father, Mr. Jonathan Leather, was the duke's man." For the first time, she smiled. "He was cut from good cloth—a true servant, through and through. I know it broke His Grace's heart that he was the last of his line to serve the family. Jonathan Leather was the sixth Leather to valet a Duke of Tarland. His older son, Benjamin, should have valeted the young master, but he was a willful boy who insisted on breaking a tradition of hundreds of years and seeking work elsewhere. Why, there have been Leathers at Tarland's End almost as long as the family itself. Of course nobody expected much better out of either of the boys given the mother they had." For a moment it looked as if she was going to turn her head and spit. "Rosa Leather was no better than she should have been. Poor Jonathan got taken in by her pretty face and paid the price for it, didn't he?"

Stephen lost the small bit of interest he'd developed. "I'm sorry ma'am, but—"

"But it wasn't Benjamin who was responsible for what happened. It was that younger son of his—Joseph—he just broke his father's heart. Poor Jonathan died less than a year after Joseph was banished. Yes, it killed him, it did."

"Banished?" Stephen asked, not bothering to keep the skepticism from his voice.

Her mouth pursed and she glanced around again, scooting closer to the end of her seat, until her boney arse was barely touching it. "I only tell you because Joseph is valeting you, is he not?"

"Yes."

"This is just between us, sir, it was only by mistake I heard even a tiny snippet about it." Her cheeks colored and Stephen could picture her with her ear to a keyhole. "Mr. Joseph was sent off for," she made a choking sound. "Well, he was valeting the young master—His Grace now, but back then just a lad of seventeen, Marquess of Staunton he was called." She swallowed several times, her face becoming alarmingly red, and then hissed, "Joseph tried unnatural acts with his master."

Stephen blinked. "I'm sorry?"

"I'm not saying it twice!" she snapped.

Stephen almost laughed, but wisely repressed it. "I see," he said, thinking that he just might. "So this happened and the duke turned him off. Yet I saw a letter of recommendation from His Grace—the current duke's father. That seems rather odd if what you say is true." He gave her a hard look. "Perhaps you misunderstood?"

What Stephen really wanted to say was: *Perhaps what you heard is that the young master and his valet were going at it like rabbits and were caught, a much more likely scenario than bland, boring Leather physically attacking his employer. Perhaps* <u>that's</u> *what you heard, you spiteful old cat.*

But of course he didn't.

She frowned, as if she could see his thoughts on his face, which was likely. Stephen disliked moralizing gossips.

She sniffed and shrugged. "Yes, well, I don't know about that. I just thought you should know." She gave him a nauseatingly virtuous look. "It's my Christian duty to protect against such ungodliness."

Stephen stood. "Thank you Missus—?"

She clutched her bag to her chest and shot to her feet. "It's *Miss*, Miss Bindon."

"Thank you, Miss Bindon, your duty is done. Now, if you'll excuse me?"

He didn't wait for an answer but rudely strode out, leaving the door open behind him, fuming that he'd wasted his time on such a mean-spirited bitch. Only an idiot would believe what she was intimating. Stephen already knew how amenable Leather was, and it sounded like he'd always been that way. No doubt the old duke had looked askance on his son's valet fisting him. Stephen's lips twitched at the image of an eighteen-year-old Leather. The man was skin and bones now, he'd probably been a bloody waif ten years ago. He would have been the one punished, not the duke's get—no matter that his master had taken part, as well.

That was the way of the world, as he knew all too well from the first fifteen years of his life. At least the duke had given Leather a positive letter of reference, that was unexpectedly generous when the man just as easily could have squashed him like a bug.

Stephen shook his head, dismissing the matter from his mind. The concierge saw him and almost came vaulting over the desk. "Mr. Chatham, how can I—"

"I want a carriage, immediately." He paused, considered the evening ahead, and then added, "I'll take it for the rest of the night."

Chapter Eighteen

Jo only waited until Mr. Chatman disappeared down the stairs before running back to the room, catching up her hat, coat, and stick, and darting down the servant stairs.

She walked several streets over before flagging a cab. "The Royal Scot Hotel," she told the driver, her heart racing a million miles a minute and not from physical exertion.

It if had just been the clothing at the hotel, she would have left it. But the bracelet Stephen gave her was there. She *had* to take that with her.

As the carriage rumbled along, she couldn't help wondering what had happened to cut his trip so short. Was it really a business matter? Or was he so distraught he could no longer bear being in the city?

Well, it didn't matter, did it? They were going, and it was just as well. Her visit to Meisen's yesterday had been rewarding in the sense she'd discovered Mr. Chatham *had* received the message. Still, it had hurt to be in that place without him and without any expectation of ever being with him again. Oh, she could serve him, be near him, and maybe even do what she'd done last night again. But they could not be together as lovers.

The carriage jolted to a halt and Jo jumped out before the driver had to open the hatch.

She nodded to the desk clerk, the same fellow who'd been here most evenings.

"Good evening, Mr. Brown," the young man said cheerfully. "I hope everything is up to standard for you and Mrs. Brown?"

"Yes, thank you. But I'm afraid I'll be leaving early—tomorrow in fact."

"Oh, nothing bad, I hope?"

"No, nothing bad. Mrs. Brown has gone on ahead, but I'm going to fetch my things and when I come down perhaps you would have my bill ready?"

"Of course, of course."

Jo left him looking rather perplexed and she knew he found it odd that his wife had left without him.

Her room was on the third floor and not much bigger than the tiny room she had at the Cameron. She'd been in a hurry the last time she left so it took a few moments to gather everything up and pack it into the locking suitcase.

She took one last look around to assure herself she'd not left anything, and then closed the door.

Jo couldn't help feeling sad as she descended the steps. Once she left this hotel, her adventure was officially over. While it was true that she'd not had her final night as planned, the experience had been well worth the money.

But, as good as the memories were, she couldn't help wondering if they'd be enough to sustain her for the rest of her life.

***

Stephen simply couldn't believe his eyes. It was Leather, bloody Leather walking out of the Royal Scot Hotel with a suitcase in his hand.

Stephen had just started to open his door and step out when he saw Leather leave the rather ratty looking little building and go to the street. He waved down a hackney without any waiting, climbed in, and drove away.

The vent opened. "Is this not the right place, sir?" the driver asked.

"No," Stephen said, still stunned. "It's definitely the right place. Just wait here for me."

The driver nodded, hesitated, and then closed the panel.

Stephen had to catch his breath—he felt dizzy. Either from shock or anger or dread—he didn't know.

You never should have opened that message.

No, he bloody well shouldn't have. He didn't even want to consider just what the hell was going on.

Julian *had* been engaged when Stephen showed up at the brothel, but that turned out to be a good thing. The tall blond footman knew who he was right away.

"Julian said you might be coming by, sir."

Stephen had given the man a stare that usually left people a quivering mass. He rarely used the advantage of his height to bully people, but he stepped close to the younger man and *towered*.

Charles swallowed noisily. "Er, you'll be wanting the name of that hotel."

Stephen smiled and could tell by the way Charles's face blanched it was not a nice smile. "Among other things."

"It's the Royal Scot Hotel, sir." His eyes shifted to Stephen's hand, which was reaching into his coat to extract his wallet.

"What did this servant look like?"

Charles shrugged. "He wasn't much to look at—the sort of bloke you'd never notice but for his glasses. Thickest things I've ever seen."

Stephen had felt sick inside after he'd handed the young man the money and climbed back into the waiting carriage.

"Back to the hotel, sir?"

He'd been bloody tempted. But it was too late for that now. He had to see this thing through. "No, to the Royal Scot."

And there was Leather, as bold as you please.

Stephen took a deep breath and opened the door. A young clerk stood at the front desk. "Good evening, sir," he said, his eyes widening as he looked up and up to meet Stephen's eyes. "Do you have a room with us?"

"No. I'm here for information." Stephen took out a five-pound note and the young man gaped, his eyes bulging like a frog's.

"Tell me everything you know about the gentleman who just left— the one with the thick glasses."

The boy gulped, his eyes still on the money—a fortune to him and *nothing* to Stephen. He almost felt bad about how easy it was going to be to get what he wanted. Almost.

"That's Mr. Brown," the boy said, his flushed cheeks saying this did not sit easily, but how could a man possibly resist?"

"I see. And how long has he been staying here?"

The boy flipped through his ledger. "He was scheduled to stay another five days, but he checked out tonight—so . . . that's a week he's been here."

"Did he give an address to make his booking?"

The clerk's jaw moved from side to side in uneasy deliberation before he finally answered. "Number twenty-seven Dunn Street, London."

Stephen didn't immediately recognize the number, but something about Dunn Street tickled his memory. He shrugged it off and slid the bill across the counter.

He was almost to the door when the clerk said, "Sir?"

Stephen stopped and turned.

"He's not in trouble with the authorities, or anything?" He looked guilty now that he had the filthy lucre in his hands.

"No, he's not in trouble with the law." *Not yet.*

"I'm relieved to hear it," the clerk said. "Because he and Mrs. Brown were such nice people."

Chapter Nineteen

Mr. Chatham buried himself in reports and papers the moment they boarded his private railcar and had only barked at Jo twice—once for tea and a second time for his luncheon.

Jo had very little to do aside from cooking, cleaning up after, and waiting until Mr. Chatham wanted to go to bed. She was curious why Mr. Chatham hadn't waited until later, when the direct train ran, but it wasn't her place to question him.

As a result of all the stops, the journey was almost six hours longer.

Most were rather brief, but there was one coming up at five o'clock that was almost an hour.

Jo was glad she'd purchased a book in Glasgow, Mr. Blackmore's latest, *Lorna Doone,* because she was getting plenty of time for reading.

But as good as the story was, it couldn't hold her attention.

She felt uneasy and had done since Mr. Chatham had returned last night—frighteningly close on her heels.

He'd had her undress him, told her when he wanted to be woken in the morning, and gone straight to bed. He'd even decline her offer of a tea tray, so she assumed he'd had a late dinner.

He'd let her dry his body this morning, but there'd been no more massages. And Jo was *not* going to be the one to broach that subject.

"Leather."

Her head snapped up at the sound of his voice and she immediately stood, her heart in her throat at his abrupt tone. "Yes, sir?"

He was giving her a speculative look, his reading spectacles sitting down his nose so his eyes were not obscured. "We're going to have a stop in Lancaster—almost an hour. I want you to fetch a few things for me while we're there."

"Of course, sir."

It felt like he held her gaze for a long time before he turned to his work.

Jo sank back onto the black leather settee, her legs wobbly. What was *wrong* with her? Indeed—what was wrong with him? Because he was not behaving normally.

Jo gritted her teeth at her idiotic dithering and picked up her book, reading the same page for the hundredth time.

***

Stephen pretended to stare at his work but really watched Leather disembark and walk across the platform, his black-clothed, slender figure walking with rather more haste than normal. Stephen knew Leather hadn't liked the idea of going so far from the station. He'd also not liked the fact the items Stephen asked for—brandy, cigars, and a bottle of blue ink—were already on the train.

"Yes, I'm aware we have brandy, but I want something different," Stephen had said when Leather made that point.

He could see the other man was rather flustered, but he didn't give a damn. The moment his back disappeared Stephen locked the doors to the rail car and went to where his valet slept. It took him longer than it should have done before he found what he was looking for: the small case he'd seen Leather carrying away from the Royal Scot Hotel.

It was tucked behind a mop, dust bin, and large bucket of cleaning cloth. Why the devil would a person put their luggage in such a place unless they had something to hide? Because he *did* have something to hide.

It was too bad the bloody thing was locked—and a sizeable lock, as well.

Stephen sat with the case on his lap, staring at it, as if he could open it by pure will. He *should* have been able to—because he had a bloody lot of *will* to learn what the hell was going on.

But his will failed him and the case remained locked and closed, its secrets secure inside.

Stephen stood and put the case back in place, covering it with the other items as nearly as he could remember. Knowing Leather, there had probably been a bloody hair on it and he'd immediately know it had been moved when he came back.

He snorted, amused, angry, and embarrassed by his behavior. He should have confronted the man last night when he'd come back. He'd *meant* to confront him. But the more he thought about it, the more he realized Leather had utterly and completely fooled him for almost two years. The last person to deceive him—Louisa—had only managed to pull the wool over his eyes for a mere eight months.

If not for Julian's competitive greed, Leather's and Josephine's little ruse—whatever the hell they were up to—would have gone undetected.

It had been easy to get the hotel clerk to describe Josephine once Stephen had learned that Leather hadn't been at the Royal Scot alone.

Stephen couldn't describe her face well as he'd only seen from beneath her nose to her chin, but that had turned out to be unnecessary.

The younger man had a vivid recollection of a glimpse of her red gown—Stephen just bet he'd recalled that—and of course there was the fact she was always hatted and veiled. And she'd worn a particularly stunning bracelet on one leather-clad arm.

That was perhaps the worst moment so far: hearing some stranger describe the gift he'd bought a woman that he'd—well, to be honest—a woman he'd come to adore. He could recall his idiot description of her in the jeweler's like it was yesterday. Had Leather and Josephine laughed together about that? As they'd lain naked and entwine and sweating and—

"Christ!" he muttered dropping his head to the wall behind him.

Stephen had believed his mind was a morass of confusion while he'd been anticipating his nightly visits with Josephine. Lord had *he* been wrong!

He simply could not seem to find an end in this basket of tangled yarn that was Leather and Josephine's machinations. Were they going to blackmail him? Was that it? Were they hoping to accuse him of sodomy?

His lips curved into an unpleasant smile and he raised his head, staring blankly at the table full of papers. The problem with accusing another man of homosexuality was that one could easily find one's own neck on the line.

And if that was the case, why hadn't Leather simply managed the affair alone? Why bring in Josephine?

Were they hoping she would become pregnant with Stephen's child? Or was she already pregnant by Leather and the two of them had conceived of this plan as a way to feather their nest?

It seemed like a bloody lot of work to make a small amount of money.

Stephen's eyes widened as something occurred to him. Perhaps the plan had been to lure him to offer marriage.

If that was the case, then how very, very close he'd come to trapping himself into marriage with that woman.

Stephen stared at the cupboard where Leather's mysterious suitcase was hidden. He *needed* to get into that case and he *wanted* to do it without letting Leather know that he was onto to him.

Why not just have him thrown in jail for some infraction or, barring that, have him disappear forever beneath the murky waters of the Thames?

Because Stephen didn't need anyone else's help dealing with this matter.

Then why sneak around? Why not just get the truth out of the man?

His lips twitched into a smile. Beating the truth out of Leather—which he thought about every half hour—would offer some satisfaction but resorting to force would mean the man had been cleverer than Stephen. As much as he hated liars, he hated losing battles of wits even more.

His wits were all he'd had for a very, very long time—they were what first brought him to the attention of Edward Fanshawe and his partner, Mr. Smith, so many years ago.

At the time, Stephen had been nothing but a drudge who worked in the counting department of a manufactory that built farm machinery. He'd been with the company for eleven years. In all those years, he'd only been given a few small raises in pay, although he'd gradually taken on more and more of the work, until he was doing all the chief accountant's work except for his embezzling.

Stephen had been aware of the chief accountant's thieving for years, but the other man was the owner's brother-in-law, so he'd also known who his employer would believe if he ever came forward.

Indeed, Stephen had been remarkably fortunate that the owner of the manufactory had ever hired him. At seventeen, which is when Stephen had begun working there, he'd still stammered. Although the affliction hadn't been as debilitating as it once was, he rarely spoke, and when he did, he did so very slowly.

He'd learned over the years that people equated stammering, or even slowness of speech, with stupidity.

It hadn't been until two men his age—Edward Fanshawe and Mr. Smith—had purchased the company that he'd finally come forward with proof of over a decade's worth of embezzlement.

Fanshawe and Smith had thanked him, gone on a sacking frenzy, and promoted him to head of the accounting department. Six months later they'd offered him an investment opportunity. A few months after that, they'd offered him a partnership in their syndicate.

Clearly, somewhere along the line, his wits had become flabby because Joseph Leather and his little tart of a wife had played him like he was a bloody instrument and they were virtuoso musicians.

There was a knock on the door and Stephen looked up to find Leather's familiar, emotionless face. He was patiently waiting for Stephen to unlock the door.

They locked eyes and that was when blinding inspiration struck him.

Stephen smiled, and even from across the length of the railcar he saw Leather recoil from his expression.

Oh, Mr. Joseph Leather, he thought with an evil chuckle, *how I'm going to enjoy sharpening my wits using you as my stone.*

***

Jo had prepared Mr. Chatham a simple meal of fresh bread, roast game bird, herbed potatoes, and a custard. She enjoyed cooking and the railcar's kitchen was small but cunningly designed. Besides, cooking gave her something to do other than sit and stare at her employer.

"That was an excellent meal, Leather," he said once he'd eaten a second helping of custard.

"It's my pleasure, sir." Jo's face heated at his praise. She could control her expression without ever slipping, but she'd not yet learned to control her skin.

Stephen—*Mister Chatham,* she mentally corrected knowing full well that it would be a mistake to think of him in such casual terms even in her mind—sat back in his chair, his long body relaxed and sprawled. Most of the furniture had been built to accommodate his size, although he'd seen to it that there were "lady-sized" seats available, as well.

194

Jo cleared away the dishes as he watched her. Such behavior was singular—he rarely just sat doing nothing. And he'd *never* just sat looking at her. It gave her a tingling feeling in her sex but a less pleasurable sensation in her chest.

When she returned from the galley, she saw that he'd refreshed his glass of whiskey. It was not the bottle he'd sent her out to buy. She was perplexed about that whole episode but knew employers could be as willful as cats at times.

"I believe I'll have a bath." He looked up at her from beneath his heavier than usual eyelids and *smiled.*

Jo's breathing stuttered at the oh-so-rare expression. "Very good, sir. When would—"

"Go run it now," he said, his face relaxed, but no longer wearing that shocking smile. "I think I'm going to need a thorough massage tonight."

"Right away, sir." Jo turned, her walk wooden thanks to the distracting swelling between her thighs.

Good. God. What was going on?

Was he developing a *tendre* for his valet—for *her?*

Jo's heart leapt like a deer at the wonderful thought and then just as quickly crashed to earth.

Lord, what if Mr. Chatham wanted more than Jo's fist? She throbbed at the thought of him wanting her mouth, but what if he wanted to fuck her arse? Her body shivered with joy.

"You idiot," she hissed under her breath, trying to breathe steadily and keep her hands from shaking as she turned the various dials and levers that diverted the water to the long tub.

No matter how badly she wanted his cock inside her again, the minute she dropped her drawers everything would be over.

You can always say no, an annoying sing-song voice taunted in her head.

She groaned. Wouldn't that be just retribution for being such a horrid lying degenerate?

But he *had* said she could demur and it would not jeopardize her job—surely that was still true?

It was like a punch in the gut thinking about him wanting her and Jo not being able to do a damned thing about it for fear of exposing her identity.

Jo stared at the steaming water as it filled the tub, her mind and body at war.

"Is aught amiss, Leather?"

Jo gave a high-pitched yelp, spun around, and gasped.

It was Mr. Chatham, and he was as naked as the day he was born. With an enormous erection.

He cocked his head at her, his frown one of concern. "Are you all right?" he asked while leaning against the door frame, his arms crossed casually over his chest, his prick jutting out a good eight inches in front of him.

Jo swallowed and pushed up her glasses. "I'm terribly sorry, sir. I'm afraid you startled me."

"Ah."

She couldn't seem to stop swallowing; her mouth was producing enough moisture for ten mouths.

"You might have noticed this," Mr. Chatham gestured to his erection, which meant Jo was free to look at what she'd been trying so hard not to look at.

"Er, yes sir." She wrenched her head up and met his gaze.

His mouth pulled up on one side into a smile the likes of which she'd never seen. It looked almost . . . *puckish*.

"I thought you might take care of this for me." His cock jumped, as if to exhibit agreement with his words. "But remember you are free to say no, things haven't changed."

Jo felt as if she'd walked into one of her fantasies, but wide-awake.

"Of course, sir. I understand." She was relieved there was only the slightest warble in her voice.

Get hold of yourself and do your job!

It was her father's voice, and it acted on her the way it always had: she was a gentleman's gentleman first; everything else was irrelevant.

"Would you like to lie in the bath, Mr. Chatham?"

She saw a flicker of surprise in his grey eyes at her cool acceptance. "I decided I'd like your mouth this time, Leather."

Her vision blurred with the effort of staying upright.

"Again, you may always decline." His voice sounded like it was coming from somewhere far, far away.

"I understand, sir." Her voice didn't sound quite normal, either.

"Good." He pointed to the floor in front of him. "Kneel there."

Her body jolted, but she immediately obeyed.

"You'd better use a towel." His voice stopped her and the slight smile on his lips made her chest ache. "The floor is hard."

Jo's hand shook as she took a towel off the stack without taking her eyes from his. She tossed it on the floor in front of him.

And then she dropped to her knees.

Chapter Twenty

Part of Stephen wanted the man to stop this farce, even if he didn't confess to anything.

Part of him—well, two parts, actually—wanted to humiliate him by shoving his cock down his throat. And yes, he knew it would be a humiliation because the placket of Leather's well-cut trousers were as flat as a bloody desktop: the man did not find the thought of servicing him arousing. Indeed, it was likely that Leather was actively repelled.

Just how far would Leather go with this farce? And what was the point of all this? Why couldn't Stephen see the angle these two were working?

He had stopped caring about those things when Leather dropped to his knees, his movements as obedient, efficient, and emotionless as ever.

Stephen looked down at the kneeling man, his prick as hard as the plumbing pipe that brought water to his bathtub. Oh, there was definitely something wrong with him to be enjoying a sick and twisted situation like this. Somebody should stop it, but it wasn't going to be him.

Instead, Stephen rested his fists on his hips and lifted an eyebrow when Leather looked up at him.

"Mr. Chatham?"

"Hmm?" Stephen childishly amused himself by flexing his cock, making it jump only inches from Leather's surprisingly plump lips, his magnified eyes following it.

"I'm not—well, that's to say—er, this is not an area in which I am very skilled, sir." His distorted eyes blinked rather rapidly.

"Ah, I see. Well, I suppose there is only one way to *get* more skilled, isn't there?"

Leather's jaw dropped and Stephen almost choked on his laughter. Surely the man would stop him. Surely—

But Leather opened his mouth wider and then lowered it over Stephen's weeping prick.

He hissed in a sharp lungful of air, spreading his feet to steady himself as well as bring himself closer to Leather's level.

Stephen could tell by his clumsy tongue and the noisy sucking sounds that the man hadn't been lying.

"Careful," he snapped when teeth grazed the most sensitive part of his cock, that area just beneath the crown. So, face fucking was off the table, unless Stephen wanted to visit a physician at the next stop.

"Suck only the end and stroke my shaft with your hand."

Leather immediately complied, his hot mouth clumsy, but eager.

Stephen had to admit the man was an excellent actor—at least his face was—because he never would have guessed that he was disgusted.

"Use your tongue to massage below my crown—urgh, yes," he hissed, closing his eyes as Leather obeyed his instructions.

The man was a remarkably fast learner, and soon he was using his tongue and lips to swirl and suck like he'd been at it for years. It wasn't really surprising—Leather had a cock of his own, after all, and would know what felt good. Surely his wife—

Stephen's eyes flickered open at the unwanted thought of Josephine kneeling for this man and servicing his prick.

He suddenly recalled that she'd not been particularly skilled, so perhaps—

Stephen blinked away the unwanted thoughts of Josephine and looked down at Leather's closely-cropped hair, anger mixing with lust. He reminded himself that this wasn't about getting sucked off. At least not entirely.

"Tongue my slit," he ordered gruffly, his hips bucking as the point of the other man's tongue probed and laved. Stephen groaned with pleasure when a second hand began to play with his full, aching balls. He wanted to keep the deceitful bastard on his knees until they pulled into Paddington Station four hours from now, but he wanted to come down his throat even more. His lips curved at the thought of how much Leather would likely hate such a thing.

"Stroke me harder, faster," he ordered, letting his shoulders fall back against the cool tile wall. He closed his eyes and realized that one mouth felt just like another. He could easily imagine it was Josephine, rather than her lover, that he was about to fill.

Stephen grunted as the pressure in his balls began to overwhelm his control. He wasn't so far gone with lust that he forgot he couldn't fuck the other man's mouth without endangering his prick, but he couldn't help thrusting deep and holding Leather's skull immobile as he jerked and spent.

A last thought assaulted him as he plummeted toward oblivious bliss: Leather wasn't trying to pull away. Instead, his lips were wrapped tight, and he was milking each jet as it came.

***

It wasn't the first time Jo had orgasmed without touching herself, but it was one of the most powerful climaxes she could remember. She was so deep within her own pleasure that she was still sucking when he shoved her head away.

"Enough," he said, the word sounding more like a groan.

Jo wiped her mouth and swallowed several times, wishing she could savor the taste of him, but knowing that was impossible. Mr. Chatham was still slumped back against the wall, his hips at a provocative angle, his big shaft softening.

He blinked down at Jo when she pushed to her feet and then seemed to shake himself, a huge yawn distorting his face as he stood up straight and stretched out his magnificent body. It reminded Jo of the time she'd seen a tiger stretch at the zoo.

When he lowered his arms and opened his eyes, he frowned at her, as if he were wondering who she was and why she was standing there.

"I'll have tea while I soak," he said, absently rubbing one huge hand over his tautly muscled abdomen in an unconsciously sensual gesture that immediately had her clenching for more. "And then you can give me my massage."

"Of course, sir." Her voice was rough and harsh, but she supposed that was acceptable after having one's employer's cock—at least part of it—in one's throat.

The familiar ritual of making tea helped bring her pulse rate back into the human range.

Jo's mind spun like a stripped cog as she tried to understand what this meant. Or did it mean nothing other than she was a convenient form of release?

She slammed the cupboard door that held the tea, flinching at the loud bang it made. Of course that was what it bloody meant—she was *convenient*. Did she really believe Mr. Stephen Chatham had suddenly taken a fancy to his valet?

This was like her worst nightmare meeting her most beloved dream: he was allowing her to touch his body, to pleasure him, but there wasn't a damned thing on his side other than physical release.

Jo groaned and leaned against the counter and waited for the water to boil. What was wrong with her?

She knew better, and yet she'd just broken her father's most important rule: A gentleman's gentleman has no needs beyond serving his master.

He'd told her that a thousand times, but Jo still recalled the first time she'd hear it. It had been Christmas morning and Jo had wanted to open the gifts that sat in the middle of their small table, but her father had work to do first. She'd been five or six at the time, impatient and kicking the rungs of her chair while watching him clean and mend one of His Grace's riding boots.

"A lesser valet would send this out to a cobbler," he said, gritting his teeth as he'd shoved the awl through four layers of leather. "But an exemplary valet will know how to repair all his master's clothing and footwear so he will never be at the mercy of capricious tradesmen."

All Jo had been able to think about was what was in the package with her name on it. She hoped it was more soldiers so her army would be as good as Ben's.

"A lesser valet would have a footman handle such a job on a day like today," her father had continued, painstakingly sewing the boot, stitch by stitch. "But an exemplary valet will always see to his master's needs before his own."

That had been her father in a nutshell: every holiday or free day Ben and Jo would wait for the moment when His Grace needed something and only her father could do/make/fetch it.

As Jo stared at the steam coming out of the kettle she recalled the first time that she'd learned just how far her father would go to please his master.

The duke's estate was vast and there was a veritable army of children who lived in and around the castle. Like any group of children, there were squabbles and struggles for power. When her brother Ben had inherited the old croquet set from the duke's steward, it had caused petty jealousies to flare that had long been dormant.

"You only got it because your mother was a whore who used to spread her legs for old Ducky," Bobby Jenkins had hissed in her ear after he and his brother Marty had beat up Jo and Ben and then broke the mallets and tossed the beautiful colored balls into the lake.

Jo hadn't known what had shocked her more, the information about her long-dead mother, or that anyone was brave enough, or foolish enough, to mock the godlike Duke of Tarland.

That had been the first time, but there'd been more digs with each year that passed. It irked the other servants to see Jo and Ben move up so quickly. And when Jo was given to the young master—the Marquess of Staunton—at the mere age of seventeen, the envy had become a poisonous stew.

Jo lifted the kettle off the tiny stove and poured steaming water over the tea in the pot as she recalled her unexpected promotion.

She'd been proud and arrogant when she'd learned she was to valet the marquess. Although he wasn't well-liked around the estate, he would one day be master.

The only person more pleased than Jo had been her father; he'd been ecstatic. "You'll grow with him, Joseph, like a vine to his trellis. He may seem a difficult master at first, but remember conflict is only possible if you believe you have the right to pit your will against his. Your will *is* his, Joseph—you are an extension of him and that is a position you should cherish. Obey him as you should, and he'll take care of you."

Jo snorted at the distant memory and placed five of the shortbread biscuits she'd earlier made in the tiny oven on a small plate, presenting them in a fan. She took one last look at the tray: a vase with a fresh flower, cream although her master took none, and sugar. *Always be prepared for what he might want, Joseph, and know what he wants before he wants it himself.*

Mr. Chatham was reclining with his eyes closed when Jo entered the bathroom. She stood for a moment, considering whether to back away and let him sleep.

"Fix me a cup," he said, without opening his eyes.

"Yes, Mr. Chatham."

Her master's tea was simple: he took it black and strong with only the tiniest hint of sugar. Jo went to stand beside the tub with the cup and saucer.

He didn't open his eyes or move or otherwise acknowledge her presence. That was fine with her, she spent the time examining him as closely as a horologist examined a watch. His nipples had hardened and she knew the water would have cooled. Her mouth watered as she stared at them and she wished she'd taken the opportunity to suck them when she'd had the chance at Frau Meisen's.

His eyes opened, as if he'd heard her thoughts, and she could tell by the slight curve of his thin lips that he'd known she was standing here. He took only the cup, meaning she should stand and hold the saucer. He sipped and sighed.

Jo *consumed* him, praying that her expression didn't show the ecstasy she was experiencing just to be his human side table.

He took another drink and then looked up at her. "You dispatched my need adequately, Leather, but you lack finesse. That tells me these particular services are not ones you've offered to your masters in the past?"

Jo was reeling from the words *adequately* and *lack*, her misery thicker in her throat than his cock had been. She had to swallow several times before she could speak. "I apologize, sir. You're correct, this is a new area of service for me."

He took a sip of tea without commenting.

Jo flung caution to the winds. "I will become more proficient if offered more opportunities to hone my skills."

His eyebrows rose and he set the half-empty cup into the saucer and began to push himself up. Jo hastened to move the tray and be ready with a towel when he stepped onto the floor. He stood still as she dried him. *All* of him, this time. He gave a soft grunt when she toweled between his muscular buttocks and carefully dried his sac.

When she'd finished, he strode from the room without waiting for his robe.

There were two bedrooms in the railcar, but the master was three times the size of the other. It was a room made for pleasure and Jo had noticed the metal rings immediately. The bedding was supple black leather, the feather quilt sinfully soft.

Mr. Chatham lowered himself to the mattress with a sensual groan, his long, powerful body strikingly pale against the black. Jo looked at the small bottle of oil she'd placed on the side table and then at the fine leather bedding. She hesitated.

"It's all here to be used and enjoyed. And I like your hands oiled," he said, his face turned away from her.

It unnerved her that he could read her without even looking at her, but then she supposed every valet of any worth railed against ruining fine bedding or garments.

Jo oiled her hands and proceeded to do her now second-favorite part of the job.

"Yes, that feels good," he said with a moan as she kneaded the smooth muscles of his shoulders.

Jo tried not to preen at his words, instead making herself recall his comment from only a few moments ago: adequate and lack. Failure of that sort would eat at her and shame her. But she didn't give up easily; she'd work until she could please him perfectly.

That was what her father had told her that first time she'd come to him, her eyes glittering with tears she'd had to hold inside for *hours* before she could shed them.

The Marquess of Staunton had struck her face, one blow on each side, when he'd found a dull streak on the toe of his boot.

"It wasn't me, Papa—it was from his other boot after he put them on."

"*Tsk, tsk,* Joseph—I'm ashamed at you! Trying to blame your own shortcoming on your master."

Jo had gritted her teeth at the unfair accusation, but kept her mouth shut.

"Next time you'll be more careful and do a better job. A perfect job," her father had said, patting her awkwardly on the shoulder. "Instead of coming to me and crying, you should go to your master's dressing room and inspect each and every piece of footwear and clothing."

Jo's jaw had ached from the brutal blows. His lordship had not struck her open-handed, but with a fist. Jo hadn't told her father that she suspected the real reason for the punishment hadn't been the boot, it had been what she'd caught her master doing with—or to, rather—one of the footmen.

Jo had returned to his chambers from laundering and pressing his neck cloths and had stopped on the threshold, her mouth open.

Lord Staunton stood with his hands on his hips, the placket of his buckskins open. Kneeling between his thighs was the new footman—an exceedingly young man—too young, her father claimed—but big and brawny and handsome. And there he was, his lips wrapped around her master's cockstand while the marquess held the boy's hair and thrust viciously into his mouth. Jo had backed away, but the marquess had looked up and seen her. Rather than stop, he'd smiled and fucked the young footman's mouth all the harder.

Since that day, the marquess had been watching her. At first, she thought he'd try to use her mouth the same way. He hadn't—not immediately. Instead he'd begun to demand more and more intimate service.

"A gentleman's gentleman never neglects his master's needs," her father had said when she'd come to him to tell him that his lordship expected her to wash *every* part of his body in his bath, even his organ when it was erect.

Her father had said the same thing when Jo told him about another episode.

His lordship had made Jo sit in the dressing room with the door open a crack. He'd then summoned a chambermaid, a very pretty ginger girl of four and ten, who'd made shy, worshipful eyes at Jo more than a few times.

When his lordship had told her to lift her skirts and bend over his bed, the girl had done it, although she'd been weeping quietly. Lord

Staunton had proceeded to ride her brutally, pressing her face down into the bed when she'd cried out.

Jo had seen the blood on the girl's thighs when her master was done.

Jo's father had procured a medical text for Jo to read when she'd turned twelve—to prepare her for her courses, she supposed—so Jo had known the blood meant Lord Staunton had broken the girl's hymen: she'd been a virgin.

When Jo told her father, he'd frozen for the briefest of moments but then quickly adjusted his mask. "I daresay the girl was flaunting herself in front of him—you know how those village lasses can be— and is proud to give her maidenhood to a man who'll one day be her master. She's probably boasting of her conquest even as we speak. Take my word, Joseph, the girl got exactly what she wanted. You mustn't think harshly of him, Joseph, he is little more than a boy. Besides, always remember that he is your master and whatever he does is right. It is never *your* place to judge *him*."

The marquess had been a year older than Jo, but she'd known better than to point that out to her father. Indeed, that had been the last time she'd gone to him with anything. Well, until her last day at Tarland Castle.

"Should I turn over Leather?"

Jo looked down and saw that her hands had reached his feet. "Ah, yes, sir, of course."

He rolled over and Jo's eyes couldn't help but go to his hips. He wasn't yet fully hard, but he was on the way.

He was waiting for her when she looked back up, his mouth twisted into that odd smile. "It seems you are fortunate, Leather: an opportunity for practice has presented itself sooner, rather than later."

Chapter Twenty-One

The day after he returned from Glasgow, Stephen paid his first ever call on Smith at his house.

"What an unexpected pleasure," Smith said after seating Stephen in his study, which was remarkably black: black wood floor, black drapes, black leather furniture.

"Sorry to surprise you," Stephen said.

"But it is a pleasant surprise." Smith pulled the *black* velvet cord and a servant appeared so quickly you would have thought the bell was outside the study door rather than in the bowels of the house somewhere.

"Bring us some tea," he told the servant—a man dressed in, yes, black.

All the servants in his house were male—Stephen had heard all that from Gideon, who found Smith's domestic arrangement a subject of endless fascination. Personally, Stephen didn't give a damn *who* Smith employed.

"I'd like you to teach me how to pick a lock," he said once the door closed.

Smith sighed. "If you need something, it would be better to allow an expert to handle it."

"Like you?" Stephen asked. "Just show me how," he ordered, since it looked like Smith was digging in to lecture him.

Again, Smith sighed, and then he reached into the exquisitely tailored coat he was wearing and extracted a small set of tools from his pocket.

"B-bloody hell," Stephen exclaimed, so surprised he stammered for the first time in ages. "Do you always carry that on you?" he asked, once again employing the slow, measured speech that might make him sound like a dunce but kept him from embarrassing himself.

Smith didn't answer his question. Instead, he proceeded to show him how to use the simple, but clever, tools.

"Practice on the locks at your house," Smith advised him half an hour later, after they'd picked the lock to Smith's desk, his door, and anything else they could find. "Try it on that lock to your wine cellar. Perhaps you'll see why it needs replacing."

Stephen laughed. Fucking Smith.

He practiced for a few days, until he was proficient, if not exactly speedy.

Then he sent Leather out on some pointless errand and ransacked his room.

Nothing.

Well, nothing other than a boring wardrobe, bathroom kit, two pairs of impeccably polished shoes, a few books, a portable shoe repair box, some sewing supplies, and a cloth bag that was empty.

What the devil had he done with the case Stephen had seen him carrying?

Whatever he'd done, it was clear Stephen would be finding no answers in that quarter.

Undeterred, he'd gone back to the drawing board.

And he'd been at that drawing board for eight bloody days.

Stephen decided he was being driven mad—and he was quite certain that he was the one doing the driving.

He'd come to the conclusion that he was engaging in a game with a man whose mask *never* slipped. And it was not because of a lack of effort on his part. Indeed, Stephen had become a right bloody bastard in the process of trying to get a peek beneath Leather's mask.

Thus far, he'd received nothing from his labors.

Well, that was hardly true—he'd received some of the most powerful orgasms of his life, but he'd learned not one single tiny thing about the man who not only willingly, but *eagerly*, serviced his every demand.

Stephen had worked Leather relentlessly, hoping to force him into becoming angry, if nothing else. He'd not just worked the man's body—which he used daily and with increasing brutality—but his mind.

He was working his own nerves in the process. If he continued selfishly taking his pleasure and behaving like a beast, he would eventually turn into one.

But he'd decided it was either become a beast or go mad—or perhaps both—because he was beginning to believe he'd imagined the whole bloody mess in Glasgow.

If Stephen was being driven mad, he'd make damned sure he had some company on his journey.

The only thing he knew for certain about Leather after all his efforts was that the man thrived on his job and was obsessed with perfection. Why else would he submit to Stephen's daily savagery?

So, Stephen had begun to ever so slowly . . . *criticize*. Nothing overt, just small comments here and there. It had taken only a few days before he'd noticed that Leather was fraying a little at the edges. It was astonishing, really. The comments Stephen made were so very insignificant, and yet they worked as well as the sharpest sword.

"This bath water is far too hot, Leather." Or, "My shoe had a hideous scratch on it when I went out—have you had one of the footmen polishing them?" Or, "Make another pot of tea—this one is bitter." And then there was Stephen's favorite, "You were correct about needing practice, Leather, you're slowly gaining some proficiency."

That last comment was something he'd said just moments after Leather had sucked and throated Stephen's cock for a good half hour, giving him an explosive orgasm—one of the best he'd ever had.

But as skilled as the man was, even sexual pleasure was beginning to leave a sour taste in Stephen's mouth. He'd worked on Leather for ten days, but all the while he was working on Leather, Stephen was working on himself, and it was taking its toll.

He was supposed to be running through the accounts on their newest investment—an immensely profitable company that made hollow needles for medical uses—rather than staring at the fireplace in his room obsessing about his valet.

But obsessing was what he was doing. He just *knew* there had to be something—something small and insignificant that he'd missed.

He'd gone back to Leather's rooms twice more, but there was nothing.

There was no evidence that Leather communicated with his partner in crime, he'd certainly found no letters or messages.

The address Leather had given to the hotel desk clerk at the Royal Scot was for a ten-room hotel in a part of London that catered to upper servants or small businessmen. Stephen had no idea why the address had seemed familiar.

He'd spent far too much time investigating the hotel and its inhabitants—even its employees, for Christ's sake! And he'd found nothing.

He needed to impose a deadline on this madness—just as he would with any other project—and he knew exactly what it was: Leather's upcoming Monday off. That *had* to be when the man did all his nefarious business.

But that Monday was over a week away and Stephen wasn't sure he'd still be sane by then.

***

For the first time since she'd begun working for Mr. Chatham, Jo was eagerly looking forward to next week and her Monday off.

Her employer, she hated to admit, had become a veritable monster since returning from Glasgow.

It wasn't his almost maniacal need for physical gratification—no, those needs she was rather enjoying—but he seemed to find fault with seemingly miniscule, indeed, non-existent, issues.

For example, he'd said that Jo had given him a torn shirt to wear, that Jo had used a dull razor on him, and a dozen other accusations.

Each time he criticized her she could hear her father's voice, chiding and disapproving.

Quite honestly, she was bloody exhausted.

The only thing that kept her going was her master's sexual demands.

Jo knew there was something wrong with her to find his cruel—yes, savage—behavior arousing, but she *adored* it.

Jo smiled as she recalled this morning. As usual, he'd done his hour and a half of physical exercise. He'd returned sweaty and had stripped, handing her his soiled clothing, piece by piece.

His slick naked body was always breathtaking, but he'd appeared even more impressive this morning. Jo knew it was because he'd recently lost weight—something that concerned her greatly. But as

210

much as she worried about his drop in appetite, she had to admit the loss of even a few pounds had left his already glorious body even more stunning. He resembled a sculpture, his pale skin stretched tight over muscles that were hard and engorged from his vigorous exercise.

And then there was the engorged part that jutted proudly from his hips.

Jo set aside his clothing and turned back to him: he'd taken his heavy prick in his fist and was casually pumping it while looking down at her.

"Your mouth, Leather."

Jo's mouth had already been flooded from looking at him and his words drove her willingly—joyfully—to her knees

"I want to fuck your throat."

Her cunt clenched so hard she had to squeeze her thighs together; that didn't help matters.

"Yes, sir," she croaked.

He stared down at her, his lips curved in a cruelly amused smile. "Will you be able to manage it, or shall I end up shredded?"

Decades of practice allowed her not to exhibit the hurt she felt at his criticism, but still she felt it.

Feelings are an indulgence you're not entitled to, Joseph. You're nothing more than an extension of your master.

"I'll take care, sir."

"See that you do."

He was sweaty from his exertions and his crown was deliciously slick and musky when he pressed it against her lips. Jo opened wide, taking him all the way, not stopping until he blocked her airway.

"Ahh," Mr. Chatham murmured, rocking into her while one hand slid around her head and cupped her skull. "Swallow," his voice was raspy and he groaned when she complied.

Her entire body thrilled at his nonverbal praise and she tamped down the hysteria that had been building since the moment his cock deprived her of breath. She'd been practicing holding her breath for exactly this purpose: she could easily go a minute and five seconds.

He tightened his grip and flexed his hips, forcing his thick rod impossibly deeper. "God, yes." He kept her filled until she began to get dizzy, and then he slowly pulled out.

Jo managed half a gasp before he rammed back in. She also remembered to swallow—to massage him—before being told.

He gave a breathy chuckle and then proceeded to fuck her with a savagery that left her drawers soaked.

And then, suddenly, Mr. Chatham did something terrifying: he looked down at Jo and plucked her spectacles from her face.

She tried to gasp, but her throat was full of cock. Panic clouded her vision and she swallowed convulsively.

He jerked into her, hard. "Again," he murmured above her, and then grunted when she complied. "Bloody amazing."

His words were like a slap that dashed away her incipient hysteria and Jo blinked to clear away the tears, until she could see his blurry image.

He was turning her spectacles slowly, examining them.

He removed his other hand from her head. "Stay," he ordered when she tried to pull away to ask him what was wrong.

The single word instantly halted her progress and she watched with mounting concern as he placed the glasses on the shaving tray beside him before looking down at her.

His hips began pulsing lightly, but he allowed her to breathe.

"I'm going to use you hard, and I wouldn't want these to break."

Jo thought he smiled but couldn't see him clearly enough to know for certain. She dropped her eyes, her heart thudding loudly and no longer just from arousal.

"Massage me with your throat again," he said. "God, yes, that's the way." His hands imprisoned her skull, holding her immobile as he thrust into her. "I want you to make this last, Leather."

His words were music to her ears and the matter of the spectacles was forgotten: if he wanted this to go on longer, that meant she must be pleasing him at least a little.

Didn't it?

The relief she felt turned her bones to water, and she opened wider.

"Yes," he muttered, his hand relaxing its grip when Jo's body became more pliable.

Jo pushed away every thought that cluttered her head, all but one: *Perfect, this must be perfect,* she reminded herself.

His thrusts were slow but deep and her eyes teared and her fingers twitched to grasp his hips, to caress him and feel the power of his flexing muscles under her fingers.

She began to reach but then stopped, placing her hands back on her spread thighs for balance.

It would be madness to touch him like that—not unless he ordered her to. She was not his lover, she was his servant.

Not just any servant, but the perfect valet—an extension of her master.

And she was going to give him the most powerful orgasm of his life.

She throated and tongued and sucked until he became impossibly rigid, but never enough to bring him over the edge. She worked him until he was sweating and taut and shaking with need. Over and over she brought him to the point of climax and then denied him.

"Fuck," he ground out savagely as she began to tease him along a fourth time. "Enough," he said, fucking her harder, deeper. "Take my come now."

Her climax, which she'd controlled as brutally as his, began to unfurl. Powerful, exquisite contractions struck her in waves and she began her slide toward oblivion—

Recall who you are, where you are, and what you are, Joseph.

The words were like the crack of a whip, driving her back to awareness.

Jo was his servant, an extension of his will. His needs and wants were paramount. Perfect, she must be perfect.

She crushed the paroxysm that threatened to seize her body and wits and gave herself up utterly and completely to his pleasure, massaging his pulsing shaft with her mouth, tongue, and throat.

A guttural, primitive cry tore out of his chest, his fingers spasming painfully on her skull as he shuddered, his beautiful cock filling her.

Jo had only one thought as she milked him of every last drop.

Perfect. She'd been perfect.

***

Stephen was in the middle of one of those dreams when you know you are in a dream. It was a pleasant dream, so he did nothing to shake himself out of it.

He was hard and Josephine was kneeling before him. Her mouth was a silken vise and she sucked so hard it hurt.

"Yes," he said in the dream, "Like that—suck me just like that." When he looked down at her, he realized it was Leather's eyes that met his.

"Hello, Stephen," his valet somehow said, his full lips curving into a smile.

Stephen jolted upright so fast his head spun.

He blinked into the darkness, the usual questions one always had on first waking bouncing around in his head: *Where am I? What is happening?*

He was home, in his bed.

The realization sent him falling back onto his pillows. Home, not at Meisen's with Josephine.

Home.

The dream, so vivid only a few seconds earlier, refused to be pinned down. The images eluding him. He squeezed his eyes shut and concentrated, as if that would help.

But there was nothing.

All he could recall was that it had featured both Leather and Josephine.

Leather and Josephine and Leather and Josephine and Leather and Josephine—

Snippets assaulted him: full, red, ripe lips, blue eyes that were black. Blue eyes distorted by lenses. Blue eyes.

A sky after a storm.

Stephen's eyes flew open and he stared into the darkness overhead. "Bloody. Fucking. Hell," he whispered.

All he could hear was the pounding of blood in his ears, his mind spinning and spinning and spinning.

Leather and Josephine.

He shook his head. "*No.*"

It was impossible.

Except, it wasn't.

Chapter Twenty-Two

emarkably, Jo felt even worse after her Monday off than she'd felt before it.

That was saying something because those last few days with Mr. Chatham—not long after she'd given what she'd believed to be the perfect mouth-fuck—had been more miserable than the summer she'd served the Marquess of Staunton. But for entirely different reasons.

The five days leading up to her day off had not been terrible because Mr. Chatham had continued his criticism. No, he'd not said another critical word to her about anything.

In fact, he'd hardly said a word to her at all.

In the blink of an eye, Jo's life had gone from a delicious flood of physical contact with him to nothing.

It all began the day after she'd given him such blissful service—or so she'd thought.

She'd gone to wake him at his usual time, only to find that he'd already bathed, shaved, dressed himself, and was gone. He'd never done that before.

He'd not returned until almost two o'clock that night, even though she knew it was not the night of his weekly meeting.

"I don't need you," he'd said when he found her awake and waiting.

When Jo had hesitated, her mouth partway open, he'd merely turned his back and disappeared into his dressing room.

She'd been awake and waiting an hour earlier the next morning.

But when he returned from his exercise he'd said, "Lay out my clothing for me." And then he'd gone into the bathroom and shut the door.

The next day had been the same.

Every time Jo worked up her courage to ask if she'd displeased him, she heard her father's voice: *It is not a valet's place to question his master.*

So, she'd remained silent as Mr. Chatham had gone about his life without her.

Jo hadn't been able to force down more than a mouthful of food for days. The Saturday and Sunday before her day off had been so awful that she hadn't been sure she would make it until Monday.

And when Monday had finally rolled around, she'd headed to Bernina's: only to find Cecile gone.

"Gone?" she'd stupidly asked the footman, Daniel.

He'd smiled at her plaintive, forlorn, tone. "Yes, gone to take care of family business. But she'll be back next week—she's not gone forever."

She hadn't told him it might as well be forever. She had *so* looked forward to seeing Cecile and asking the sage woman's advice. But that was not to be.

"Marie is ready and waiting for you," Daniel had said.

So, she'd gone to Marie. But the usually pleasurable experience had been so miserable that Jo had paid her and left early, wandering the streets aimlessly for hours rather than return to Mr. Chatham's.

For the first time in almost two years she was not looking forward to going back to her job. Whatever had happened, one thing was clear, Mr. Chatham no longer felt comfortable having Jo wait on him. Period.

By the time six o'clock came around, she'd walked miles but was no closer to understanding her situation.

Jo stopped in the kitchen to let the housekeeper know that she'd returned early from her day off.

"Very good, Mr. Leather," the older woman said. And then her brow had creased with concern. "Are you not feeling well? You look a little peaked. And have you lost weight?"

Jo smiled slightly, but repressively, not interested in talking about her health with a fellow servant. "I'm well but thank you for asking." She nodded to the others milling around the kitchen and left, taking a detour to the laundry to collect a basket of fresh linens for Mr. Chatham's bed—which she always took care of herself— before trudging slowly up the servant stairs.

Jo set down her basket and then fished her key from her pocket. When she inserted the key in the lock, the door swung inward.

Jo's brain froze but her blood thundered in her ears. She didn't want to, but she had to. She reached out and pushed the door the rest of the way open.

Mr. Chatham was reclining in the room's only chair. Beside him, on the end table, was Jo's case, open.

His smile was chilling. "Come in, Mr. Leather. I've been waiting for you."

Chapter Twenty-Three

*I*n the end, it was the hair.

Stephen could not believe it had taken him so long to put it all together, and it was all because of the hair.

He stared as the familiar, bland face of his valet and wavered and shifted into another face.

"Shut the door," Stephen ordered.

Leather did so, and then stood before him, hands behind his—no, *her*—back.

"Take off your hat and glasses."

She did so, holding both in her hands—hands he now realized were not just slender, but *femininely* slender.

Stephen couldn't help it, he laughed. But not with amusement.

Leather stiffened at the sound, looking like a deer poised for flight.

"What's your real name?"

She cleared her throat. "Joseph Edward Leather."

The anger he'd been holding in check flared. "Don't toy with me," he snapped.

For the first time ever, he saw an emotion on that utterly emotionless face. "I am *not* toying with you, *sir*." She looked stunned— as if startled by her own belligerence. "That is the name on my birth certificate. That is the name I've been known by all my life."

Stephen's head pulsed with fury. "But you're a *w-woman*." His entire body heated, both at the stupid words and the slight stammer. He needed to calm down or he'd make a fool of himself in front of this— this duplicitous *bitch*.

"Yes, sir," she answered coolly.

He snorted, almost amused by the typical emotionless valet routine. But then he caught a glimpse of the open case beside him.

Stephen had felt like a bloody idiot when he finally thought to look where his own empty luggage was stored. Of course! What could be more humiliating than to hide the truth in plain sight? Why not make even a bigger arse of her dull-witted, infatuated employer?

He picked up the mask and tossed it to her, childishly pleased when she fumbled with the hat and glasses she still held, and it fell to her feet. She looked up at him and, once again, he felt the anger beneath her bland expression. So, the mask was slipping now, was it?

"May I put on my spectacles, sir?"

"Suit yourself."

She replaced her glasses and then picked up the mask.

"So, tell me about that," he said.

Her collar was too high to see her lack of Adam's apple, but he heard her swallow. "I just wanted—"

"To make a fool out of me?" he suggested with barely suppressed violence.

Her head whipped up and there she was: Josephine, but with no hair and wearing glasses. The room seemed to shrink and then swell. By God. It really *was* true—he'd known it was, but still . . .

Her eyes were huge, dark, and beseeching. "I wanted to be with you," the words were hoarse, but audible, and they were like a mule-kick to his gut.

Stephen's mouth refused to work.

"I knew it was wrong—deceptive," shame flitted across her face. "But I'm afraid that is my entire life, sir: deception." Her chest rose and fell rapidly. "When I heard about Meisen's I knew that would be my chance to finally be with you," the words tumbled over one another, as if she wanted to get it all out. "I just—"

"Look at me," he ordered.

Her head immediately came up. He hated that her instant, unquestioning obedience did what it always did to him: stirred his blood.

"I assume you learned about Meisen's place at Bernina's?"

Her jaw dropped and he enjoyed her surprise more than he should have.

"Yes, I followed you. I saw where you went—it wasn't difficult to bribe an employee and learn about you." And Lord the things he'd learned. His cock, which had only been twitching before, hardened fully—just as it had done every time he thought of her fucking another woman. He was a man, after all.

No wonder she'd seemed so skilled yet innocent; she'd never employed men at Bernina's, but it appeared she'd been with plenty of women.

"Emma?"

He frowned, not comprehending what she meant.

"The whore who told you about me was Emma—small, slight, pale … pierced?

"I couldn't say about the last, but yes, that sounds like her." He could see his words surprised her—she would have believed he'd fucked the woman. Good. He didn't want her to know just how bloody confused and tied up in knots he'd been since the night he'd had that dream: the night he began to understand what was going on. Not that he understood much—not even now.

How could he find her so bloody alluring wearing a suit and those laughable spectacles? What was wrong with him to want her more than ever?

Stephen was frightened by the intensity of the desire he felt—terrified. He needed to gain some measure of control. *Immediately.*

"Tell me, what do you think I should do?" he asked, genuinely curious although he already knew exactly what he was *going* to do.

"You've not paid me for this quarter. I can go—leave without the pay and—"

Stephen laughed, genuinely amused. "You think a paltry sum is going to be just compensation for what you've done?"

She bristled. "It isn't paltry to me, Mr. Chatham."

"Well it is to me, *Mr. Leather,*" he retorted, coming out of his chair, unable to restrain either his fury or lust any longer. She stood rigid as he stalked toward her and Stephen didn't stop until their bodies were touching. He looked down at her, wanting her to feel small, weak, vulnerable. "You've lied and manipulated me for one year, ten months, and eight days—according to my records. I think I will want that amount of time back."

She blinked, and he relished her stunned look.

"I'm sorry, sir?

His eyes flickered over her face; he simply could not believe the evidence of his eyes.

"Are you even capable of answering a question honestly?" he asked, unable to keep the bitterness from his tone, hoping she couldn't hear the pain and confusion below it.

She hesitated a telling second, her gaze flickering behind the thick glass.

Stephen shook his head. "Never mind. I've decided I don't care what your answer would have been," he lied. "I've decided I shall just please myself, no matter what you might think or want—the way you've been doing since you deceived me into hiring you."

Her face heated at his accusation and she had the decency not to deny his words. She'd done what she wanted—spied and lied—for herself, not caring enough about his right not to be spied on or lied to. And now it was time to pay the price.

"It must have been expensive to purchase five nights at Meisen's?"

She blinked, confused by the sudden twist in subject.

"Wasn't it?" he repeated in a menacing tone.

"Yes, it was." She held his gaze with a look that just about drove him mad and filled his mind with a malignant stew of lust, hurt, confusion, and fury.

"You must have expected to earn a great deal from me. Tell me, what was the plan? You can tell me now that it's over."

***

Jo could not believe what he was saying. "No," she said, shaking her head, as if that would make her unhear it. "No, I did it so I could be with you."

He threw back his head and laughed, sounding genuinely amused. But when he looked down, his eyes were hard. "My God! You just don't give up, do you? Your little game is over, *Joseph*." His eyes dropped down her body, an insulting sneer twisting his lips. "Are you pregnant? Is that it? You thought you could blackmail money out of me with a child? Go ahead, tell me. Because it doesn't matter any longer— you won't get whatever it is you wanted."

"I—I don't understand," she said, wondering if he'd gone mad. "Why would you—"

"Enough!" His voice was thunderous and it shook the glass in the windows and left Jo breathless. He pushed his body against hers and Jo took a step back, but he just kept on coming, backing her into the door behind her and pinning her against it.

"You must think I'm the stupidest, most pathetic man on the planet."

Jo opened her mouth and his eyes narrowed dangerously. "Don't. Don't open your mouth again until I tell you. You had your chance, and all you did was lie. Again. Now it's my turn to talk. I started to wonder about you in Glasgow—when I saw you leaving the Royal Scot." He nodded. "Yes, I saw that—I spoke to the clerk. Of course, back then I thought there were two of you." He snorted. "Go ahead and laugh— you should, your pitiful disguise took me in hook, line, and sinker. It was the hair," he said in a confiding tone. "That was a stroke of brilliance. Anyhow, I assumed that constantly demanding sexual favors from my valet would eventually drive him to do something foolish—to contact his female partner. I admit I was becoming a bit frazzled. I knew whatever was in that suitcase you were carrying would give me answers, but I couldn't find the damned thing." He laughed, shaking his head.

"But then I remembered something—a conversation I had with your friend Miss Bindon the night before we left Glasgow." He smiled at the horror on her face and nodded. "Oh yes, she didn't like you. Not at all. At the time, I thought she was just a jealous, spiteful old cat who—"

"She is," Jo blurted and then shrank back—or at least tried to but the door was behind her.

He frowned. "I thought I told you not to speak?"

She swallowed at his icy tone. "I'm sorry, sir."

"Now, where was I? Ah, yes, Miss Bindon. I didn't pay her words any mind until I was back in London a few days. I'll admit I was grasping at straws. So here's what I did—I sent a man up to the duke's castle—what's it called, again?"

"Tarland Castle," Jo whispered.

"This man can find a proverbial needle in a haystack, so finding information about a young man who'd once valeted the heir—the

Marquess of Staunton, I believe his name was—wasn't very challenging."

Jo shivered at hearing the name out loud.

"Ah, yes. I see you recognize the name. It turns out there were plenty of people willing to discuss not only this young man, but his fascinating family—all valets. Well," he gave Jo a look that burnt right through her. "All except their mother—but then you told me that, yourself, didn't you Leather?" He didn't wait for an answer. "But it seemed that Mrs. Leather had a very special position in the duke's household." He paused, his smile cruel. "Now what was that position again," he mused.

"She was the duke's whore," Jo ground out.

Mr. Chatham smiled evilly. "You'd like to hurt me, wouldn't you?"

Jo didn't deny it.

"Yes, Marie Leather was the duke's whore." He paused, his gray eyes like rapiers. "I don't want to have to finish this story, Leather. Why don't you tell me what you had planned for me? Tell me how you were going to fleece me and I'll stop this painful tale right now."

"I wouldn't dream of cheating you out of such pleasure."

His eyes widened at her bitter tone, but then he nodded. "Very well. My investigator learned that almost everyone, including Marie's husband, an older man by the name of Jonathan Leather—the duke's valet—knew that her children had been fathered by the duke. My man learned that Marie had given the valet two sons before she died, but that she'd also had *four* miscarriages." This time Chatham looked more than a little sickened as he stared at her.

It was a look Jo had been accustomed to receiving—at least for the first eighteen years of her life—and no longer bothered her. Or so she'd believed.

"Six children she carried for the duke. The servants who remembered the old valet claim he not only knew what the duke did with his wife—but that he was *proud* to let his master use her as his broodmare." He voice was thick with amazed revulsion.

Jo was breathing hard, but she was still unable to get enough air. "I take it there's a point to this story, *sir.*" She let all the fury she felt at that moment show.

He stared down at her with dark, unreadable eyes. "There is. And I am almost there. It seems Marie Leather was not so proud as her husband to be the duke's whore. After giving birth to her second son— her sixth pregnancy— she killed herself. The valet never re-married and the duke never acknowledged his bastard sons. Indeed, he allowed his willing and eager valet to train them so that one day they could serve at the pleasure of his legitimate son." He paused, his eyes narrow as he lowered his mouth to her ear. "We both know what happens, don't we, Leather?" he whispered. "You can make it stop—you won't have to hear the rest of this sordid little tale— if you'll only tell me what nasty little trap you set for me in Glasgow."

Jo just stared.

Chatham's jaw flexed and she saw the spark of anger in his eyes.

He nodded. "Very well, I'll go on. It seems the valet's two sons were not the same caliber as their father. The eldest, Benjamin, was in service to Lord Staunton when he disgraced himself by getting a chambermaid pregnant. He was dismissed, but his father—not his *real* father— managed to beg the duke to give Benjamin—his own flesh and blood, after all—a letter of reference. Benjamin left the duke's service and the old valet's second son took over the very honorable position his brother vacated."

Mr. Chatham grinned down at Jo. "Now this is my favorite part of the story—are you ready?"

She didn't move so much as a hair.

"Joseph, it seems, had other plans for the duke's son— his new master. Who knows how long Joseph had to plan and plot, but the night came when it all paid off. There was Lord Staunton, buck naked in his large, four poster bed. And there was his young valet, kneeling between his half-brother's thighs and servicing him." Chatham laughed and shook his head, a hard gleam of appreciation in his eyes. "Somehow the butler had been summoned to his master's room— nobody knew who arranged that—and it was this august personage who walked in on the show."

He cocked his head at Jo. "It's like one of those melodramas that are so popular, isn't it? Well, it was the same thing all over again—scandal and dismissal. But Joseph had something on his side that Benjamin had not—a weapon, two weapons, actually: incest and sodomy. And so it was that young Joseph ended up with a fine recommendation, a pleasant little seaside cottage in his name, and an order never to return to Tarland Castle."

Jo was so cold inside she was surprised frost hadn't formed on her skin. "Well, I guess you learned everything, didn't you, sir?"

Mr. Chatham recoiled from whatever he saw in her eyes, but he came about quickly. "No, I didn't learn it all—I still don't know what you had planned for me, although I can now make an educated guess." He placed his hands on the wall on either side of Jo, caging her. "But I *did* learn enough to help me decide what I should do with *you.*"

Jo could only shake her head; how could he believe this of her?

As soon as she thought the question, she knew the answer: it was *her* fault he believed the worst of her. Who would ever believe the truth? A truth so bizarre it defied logic. As for what he'd learned about Staunton? Well, there were only two people alive who knew the truth about that: one of them was a duke, the other a valet. Who would people believe?

"I'm not going to turn you over to the authorities, nor am I going to sack you."

Jo wasn't fast enough to hide the joy that leapt inside her. He would keep her on? That was impossible. Why would he—

"Tell me what I just said?" Mr. Chatham stared at her, arrested.

"I'm sorry, sir?"

"Tell me what you heard me say," he repeated in a slow, hostile tone.

"You said you wouldn't turn me over to the constables and that I would continue on as your valet."

He barked a laugh. "You got part of it right—I won't have you thrown in jail. Nor will I sack you—because I'm not going to admit that I ever *hired* you—but you sure as hell aren't continuing in my house in *any* bloody capacity. I wouldn't employ you to be my fucking charwoman. As far as I'm concerned, you don't exist—a figment of my imagination. Good luck finding a job with some other poor dumb bastard with two years of *nothing* on your work history."

Jo opened her mouth, but nothing came out.

"Pack your things." He turned and strode toward the door that connected his room to hers and opened it. He paused but did not turn.

"My secretary will have your final pay at the front door. See that you are out of my house in a quarter of an hour. And if I ever see you again, you will discover yourself in the deepest darkest cell in Christendom." He left, not closing the door behind him.

Chapter Twenty-Four

It took Jo five minutes to pack, which gave her ten minutes to contemplate her future before she would be out on the street with all her worldly possessions.

She couldn't go to Ben, because he was still in Europe somewhere—or so she thought. She might have gone to Cecile—to ask her for help finding a position—but she was gone.

Luckily, Jo still had a little money on her person and could always dip into her savings, if necessary.

But, first, she would find a cheap room where she could sit and think.

Jo picked up her bag and took the main stairs to the foyer, where Mr. Chatham had said her pay would be waiting. Part of her wanted to leave it behind, but that would be a costly message on her part, and one he'd likely never even know about since his secretary handled household matters and would not bother his master with such a pittance.

The foyer was empty and she realized that she'd beat Mr. Chatham's orders she'd packed so fast.

There was a rap on the door and no footman nearby, so she opened it.

It was Mr. Smith. "Ah, Leather, how are you? On door duty today?"

Jo returned his smile, flattered that he'd remembered her name.

"Good afternoon, Mr. Smith. Please come in. Let me ring—"

"Nonsense, I know my way to Chatham's study." He looked at the bag she held. "Are you off on a holiday?" Jo hesitated and Mr. Smith raised a hand. "I beg your pardon—that really isn't my concern."

Something about his open, curious expression—or maybe just her current state of anguish made her do something she rarely did: volunteer information.

"As it happens, I'm leaving Mr. Chatham's employ, sir."

Mr. Smith didn't appear surprised. "Ah, I see. Well," he reached into his exquisitely cut coat and extracted a silver case with a strange symbol on the front. "Here's my card. It just so happens my own valet recently took off to pursue his future in the gold-fields of Australia." He smiled in a way that let her know the man had left without hard feelings. "Come see me tomorrow at noon," he paused, "that is if you don't already have a position?"

"Er—" Movement on the stairs drew her eyes: it was Mr. Chatham, and he was descending faster than his usual pace.

"Smith," he barked, his sharp eyes moving between Jo and his business partner. "What are you doing here?" he demanded rudely.

Smith chuckled, apparently used to such behavior. "I came to see you about that work you were doing on the Midland project. Fanshawe wants to take a trip up there and I told him I'd take a look at what you had to determine if it was worth the time."

Mr. Chatham hadn't taken his eyes off Jo as his partner spoke and Jo wasn't sure he'd even heard Mr. Smith. Before anyone could say anything, Mr. Chatham's secretary came around the corner and stopped when he saw there was not just a sacked valet awaiting him, but also his employer and wealthy business partner.

"Oh, I say," he said, his eyes bouncing among them.

"Thank you, Mr. Knowles," Jo said, taking advantage of the brief moment of confusion to get the hell out of Mr. Chatham's house before fifteen minutes passed and he changed his mind about the matter of jail.

She bowed to the other two men. "Mr. Chatham, Mr. Smith."

"Good luck to you, Mr. Leather," Mr. Smith said.

Jo knew better than to expect anything from Mr. Chatham.

She turned and walked out the door, and out of his life.

***

Stephen didn't say anything until they were inside his study and he'd shut the door. And then he turned to Smith, who was smiling genially up at him.

Smith was one of the most charming men Stephen knew. He was also the most dangerous. Stephen believed his charm was directly linked to his danger. He likely lured his enemies into a false sense of security and they never saw him coming.

"What are you *really* doing here?" Stephen snapped.

Smith gestured to the small collection of decanters. "May I?"

Stephen heaved an irritated sigh and strode over to the bottles, pouring two fingers out of the first bottle he grabbed. And then he strode back to Smith and shoved the glass into his hand.

"Thank you, Stephen." Smith held up the glass, as if by visually inspecting it he could discern its contents. "Brandy?"

Stephen shrugged.

"Aren't you having one?" Smith asked mildly.

"No."

Smith's lips curved into a smile of genuine amusement. "I think you are the rudest man I know, Stephen. You even make Edward seem gracious."

Surprisingly, his words got through. Stephen gritted his teeth and forced a smile. "I'm sorry for my rudeness," he lied. "Have a seat." Stephen turned toward the fireplace.

Once they were both seated, Smith took a sip. "Ah, yes—exquisite brandy. I was serious about Edward wanting that information, by the way. But I was also curious about your lock picking adventure."

"You were correct about the cellar lock. I've already replaced it."

Smith grinned.

Stephen sighed and shook his head. "But you already knew that, didn't you?"

Smith ignored his question—which he did irritatingly often. The man reminded him of a bloody cat in human form.

"I see you've discharged your valet."

"What of it?" Stephen demanded.

"Nothing. I was just in the market for a new valet since Nash left."

Stephen ground his teeth. What were the chances that Smith would *happen* to be in his fucking foyer at *exactly the same moment* Leather was leaving? Nothing was a coincidence when it came to this man.

"I thought you were satisfied with Leather," Smith said.

"Clearly I'm not anymore."

"Ah. Have any objections if I speak to him?"

"Would it matter if I did?"

Smith smiled.

Stephen simply couldn't stand it. "You should know that Leather is not a man," he blurted, feeling like a regular tittle-tattling arsehole before the sentence was even out of his mouth.

"Yes, I know."

Stephen goggled.

"Lord. You're not telling me you only just found out?" Smith asked.

"How in the hell—" Stephen held up one hand. "Never mind, it doesn't matter. Hire him or her or whatever and do what the hell you want. You will anyhow."

"So, you're done with Leather, then?" Smith was smiling pleasantly, swirling the slight bit of liquid left in his glass.

No matter how deeply he breathed, Stephen's lungs didn't seem to fill with enough air. "Yes," he grated with insulting deliberation. "I'm most certainly done with Leather."

"Thank you, Stephen."

Whatever the bloody fucking hell *that* meant.

But Stephen refused to allow even a hint of curiosity to pollute his mind. What Smith did and whom he did it with was his own business. But he wasn't finished with him yet.

"There's one more thing." Stephen pointed an index finger at him, a consciously obnoxious gesture that made Smith's pupils shrink dangerously. "I want *you* to quit snooping in my bloody house. Do you understand that?"

"All right."

Stephen blinked. "That's it—*all right?*"

"Yes, of course it is."

"Then why didn't you stop before?"

Smith shrugged. "Because you never asked."

Stephen shook his head.

"What?"

"You."

"Yes? What about me?"

"Never mind." Smith had only been here five minutes and already Stephen had a raging headache. "Let me get you the work I've done on the needle factory."

***

230

Jo found a cheap but clean men's hotel off Broad Street and settled her few possessions in the room's one cupboard before lowering herself onto the narrow bed.

It was after nine o'clock and she was famished, but too exhausted to bother hunting for food at such an hour.

She stared at the plaster ceiling, which was crazed with cracks but freshly painted, and considered what she would do. It wasn't as if she had too many options. She could head up to Scotland, to the cottage, but that was a place she'd avoided for almost ten years because there were no good memories there.

She could always sell it and live on the proceeds—or buy another cottage—but then what would she do with her days? She enjoyed working and always had—even when she hadn't worked for a man she loved.

Jo chewed the inside of her cheek. A two-year gap in her work history would present a host of problems. Every prospective employer would want to know what she'd been doing. She could claim an illness—two years convalescing in Scotland—but many employers would not want to take a risk on a sickly servant, especially not for such a rigorous position as valet.

She could say she'd travelled with her last employer, who'd decided to stay in France. Jo knew French, and a little Italian and Spanish, thanks to her father. He'd been correct, as usual, to task both her and Ben with such onerous studies in addition to their work. Although her father had not traveled with the duke, he'd trained both her and Ben to be prepared for such an eventuality.

The problem with claiming either illness or foreign travel is that it would involve more lying. And look where lying had landed her?

She glanced around her grim room, as if she needed reminding.

Don't forget about Mr. Smith, her sly inner companion whispered.

Jo reached into her vest pocket, where she'd carefully tucked his card: 12 Russell Square. That was a nice address, not in the poshest part of town, but certainly respectable.

Had he been serious? And had he told Mr. Chatham that he'd given her his card? If he had, Jo couldn't imagine Mr. Smith would see her tomorrow if she *did* show up at his door.

Still, he seemed like a good master to work for; she recalled that Nash had appeared happy. But if that was the case, why had he left Mr. Smith's service?

Had he? Or was *"going to seek his fortune"* a euphemism for something sinister?

That thought gave Jo pause; she'd never understood why she felt Mr. Smith was a dangerous man—or a sinister one. He was pleasant and charming, but his eyes, she'd noticed—both today and during those weeks when she'd been exposed to his company—were oddly unnerving.

He was attractive—almost too attractive.

What would it be like to work for him? Would she end up as infatuated with him as she was with Mr. Chatham?

Infatuated? You're in love with him.

For the first time since she'd left his house—or been tossed out, rather—Jo allowed her mind to wander back to her bedroom and those few moments with Mr. Chatham.

The ease with which he'd thrown her out of his life had been crushing.

Jo knew that his behavior—as harsh as it felt—wasn't undeserved.

From Mr. Chatham's point of view, Jo was a woman who'd lied to gain entrance to the most intimate part of his life—and continued lying for almost two years. In his mind, she was a woman masquerading as a man. He couldn't know—didn't *want* to know—that those four nights with him had been the only time in her life she'd dressed and behaved like a female. He couldn't believe that she'd pretended to be a woman because it had been the only way she could be with him.

As much as she'd enjoyed being a woman with him in the bedchamber, the clothing had made her feel like an imposter.

It had also made her realize that, after almost twenty-eight years, she didn't know how to be a woman, at least not *that* kind.

More importantly, it made her realize that she didn't *want* to change who she was. Other than the frustration of falling in love with Stephen, she'd *liked* being Joseph Leather.

Jo had never contemplated having a "normal" marriage, but, if she had, that dream would have been dashed to bits after meeting and falling in love with Stephen. Not until him did she understand just how much *who* she was, was tangled up with *what* she was.

She knew the truth—that she enjoyed her warped, sexually charged, and submissive position with Stephen—should have left her horrified, but it didn't. She *adored* serving his every need and submitting to him in every way. For good or for ill, that was who she was: a valet who lived to serve her master.

She wasn't stupid, she knew a person like her could only be the result of a deeply abnormal childhood. But knowing that wouldn't change anything.

Nothing she did—no position she took—would ever allow her to remove the cloak of deception she wore like a second suit of clothing.

There were no good—or at least easy—choices open to her.

However, in the unlikely event that Mr. Smith decided to engage her, it would mean she might sometimes see Mr. Chatham—*Stephen*, she allowed herself this one last time to use his name. That meant she wouldn't be entirely cast out of his life.

It also meant the gaping wound in her chest would never heal.

***

Jo was five minutes early for her appointment with Mr. Smith.

"Ah, Mr. Leather, Mr. Smith is expecting you." The man who opened the servant door was middle-aged and dressed in a well-made black suit—*all* black, from his linen to his cravat to the tips of his boots. Jo recalled Nash had dressed the same way.

Interesting.

"Please, let me take your coat and hat."

Jo blinked with surprise, but said, "Thank you." As a servant coming to interview for a position, she was accustomed to standing before her prospective employer's desk, coated, with hat in hand.

Once the man had divested her of her things he said. "This way, please. We'll use the main stairs as Mr. Smith requires only service or delivery workers to use the back stairs. I'm Mr. Bevin, by the way, Mr. Smith's house steward," he said as he escorted her up a magnificent black marble staircase to the first floor.

The corridor had dark wood floors with a black and gray runner. The walls were a dove gray and the few pieces of artwork were stunning.

233

"Several of these were done by Natalie Hartwicke."

"Ah," she said with dawning comprehension. "I know of her but have never seen her work. These are lovely." Jo recognized one of the landscapes as Hyde Park.

"Here we are," Mr. Bevin stopped in front of heavy double doors and knocked. A voice called out to enter.

Mr. Smith was sitting behind an enormous desk, the surface of which was almost completely clear. "Ah, Bevin, thank you. Will you send tea, please?"

Bevin bowed. "Of course, sir."

Everything that could be black in the room was. Jo had never seen anything like it.

She stood in the center of a medallion pattern on the carpet—and it occurred to her it had the same symbol as his card carrier. She clasped her hands behind her back and raised her eyes.

He was smiling. "There are several chairs—no reason for you to stand."

"Oh. Thank you, sir." Jo had no idea what to make of him; he was treating her like a guest.

He leaned back in his chair. "Tell me something about yourself, Leather."

Jo reached into her coat for her letters.

Smith waved a dismissive hand. "I already know your work history. You started at the Duke of Tarland's as a page, worked your way to valet over time, served the Marquess of Staunton briefly, and had two other masters before Stephen Chatham. Anything I missed?" His expressive mouth curled up at the corners.

"No sir." She cleared her throat. "I don't know if you're aware, but I have no letter from Mr. Chatham."

"Yes, I know. Do you wish to tell me what happened? The choice is entirely up to you."

Jo couldn't help it; she gaped.

He chuckled. "Oh, Leather—you've mistaken me for an inquisitor and my home for a prison."

"I'm just surprised, sir. I would've thought Mr. Chatham would have told you everything."

"No, he didn't tell me everything." His careful wording indicated that Mr. Chatham had told him *something*.

"I see, sir." But she didn't.

"I had Nash for fourteen years." Jo's eyebrows rose and Mr. Smith nodded. "Yes, it was a long time—longer than I've known almost anyone. But Mr. Nash decided to chase his dream before he was too aged and infirm." He shrugged. "It is his one life, to do with as he pleases and I admire his choice." He cocked his head and gave her a self-mocking smile. "Be that as it may, it has left me without a manservant for more than three months. I've been putting off the hiring process because I find a valet a particularly difficult position to fill as it is so very . . . intimate." He paused, his lips still curved. His eyes were dark, the pupil and iris too similarly colored to distinguish. "Would you agree with that characterization?"

Jo felt the vein at the base of her neck pulsing and was grateful he could not see it. Why did she feel like his words had some other, deeper, meaning?

"Yes, sir. I would agree with that."

"I'm pleased to hear it." And he *looked* pleased—genuinely so. Predictably, Jo's face heated, the same way it always did when she received even the slightest bit of praise from an employer.

He did not appear to notice her sudden flush—or at least he gave no sign of it. "My household is unusual and not everyone is suited to it. I employ twenty four servants and all of them—from my scullery maid to my chambermaids to my house steward—are men."

Jo blinked.

"I can see you are surprised," he said with a faint smile.

"It is an unusual arrangement," she admitted.

"It isn't that I don't *like* women, or believe they make good servants, but an entirely male household suits my needs."

Jo had no idea what he was getting at, but clearly this was not a position for her. The dejection she experienced at that though was surprising. Before she could apologize for wasting his time and leave, he continued.

"I've chosen the men who work for me carefully. They are men who share my sexual tastes."

Jo's breath caught; did he really just say that out loud?

"Not only does that make it less likely that they will be repulsed by my behavior, but they will also be unlikely to do anything foolish as it would jeopardize their own situation."

Jo knew that "anything foolish" translated to blackmail.

"I, see."

"Do you think you could work in such an environment?"

Jo stared at him for a long, uncomfortable moment as a struggle occurred inside her: a sudden, almost passionate, desire to work for him, versus the knowledge that this was not a man one should ever lie to.

"I'd like to work here, but I'm afraid I don't fit your criterion."

"I think you do."

Jo sighed and then stood. "I'm honored by your offer, sir, but I must decline."

Just then there was a knock on the door.

"Will you stay for tea?" Smith said, his tone polite, unoffended.

She hesitated, and then said, "Thank you, sir."

"Enter," Smith called out.

Two men, clothed in black suits identical to the house steward, entered and proceeded to set out the tea and a remarkable selection of biscuits and cakes.

Mr. Smith gave a sheepish shrug at Jo's stunned expression. "I'm afraid I possess a severe sweet-tooth."

She couldn't see any sign of that by looking at his lithe, muscular body.

Once the food had been set out the servants stood. "Will that be all, sir?"

"This is Mr. Leather, he's here about the valet opening. Mr. Leather, this is Thomas and Malcolm."

Jo stared at the saturnine-looking Smith, more than a little confused by this introduction. But courtesy was bred deeply into her, so she instinctively turned to the two men and then froze.

"A pleasure," Thomas murmured. He was a handsome man, perhaps Jo's own age.

But it was Malcolm Jo was staring at.

"A pleasure to meet you," Malcolm said in a high, fluty voice, blue eyes crinkling in a genuine smile.

Malcolm's collar was not high enough to hide his throat and Jo gulped and nodded, only then recalled her manners.

"A pleasure," she said hoarsely, bowing her head.

Jo watched them leave the room, her eyes fastened on Malcolm's short, slender form and narrow shoulders.

She turned to find Smith watching her, his expression so very knowing.

"Would you do the honors, Leather? I like my tea strong and black."

Chapter Twenty-Five

Mr. Smith

Smith watched the tall, slim valet leave his study, and then turned back to the single sheet of paper that lay before him on his desk: a report on Joseph Edward Leather.

He never engaged any servant or did business with anyone or fucked anyone without gathering information on them, first. It was something of an obsession of his—knowing everything about everyone—and did not make it easy for him to become close to people. Indeed, he generally found out things he wished he'd never discovered.

An image of his last lover, Charles, coalesced in his mind. Smith knew there was no use trying to thrust Charles away—even from his thoughts—so he let him linger, drinking his fill of the remarkably clear picture his mind's eye presented for his delectation. For his punishment. When the phantom image began to waver and dissolve at the edges, Smith let it go—just as he'd released the real man: without a struggle.

He glanced down at the page of tightly written handwriting while he thought about the man who just left.

Poor misguided Leather believing Smith when he said he'd not looked into him. Not that the younger man could be blamed for believing him; Smith was such a good bloody liar that sometimes even *he* wasn't certain when he was telling the truth.

Smith not only excelled at lying, he enjoyed it. Reveled in it, in fact.

Did that make him a bad person?

Absolutely.

But then he'd broken all the other nine Commandments—several times over—so what did one more lie matter?

He'd been breaking the tenth Commandment on and off ever since the first time he'd met Chatham's mysterious, reserved, and rather delectable servant. He'd coveted, but not acted, of course. Smith might be a liar, but he was not a poacher. If he wanted somebody—man or woman—they would come to him of their own volition.

Smith had patience in abundance and yesterday eight months of waiting—give or take—had given him a chance at what he'd long wanted: Joseph Leather.

He'd only ever met one person as naturally and utterly as submissive as Leather and that was Nora Fanshawe. Nora was a treasure he'd come upon too late to have for himself as she'd already been deeply in love with Edward Fanshawe.

Smith had known Leather was not what he was claiming to be since the first time he saw him on that trip to Brighton.

Or, to be more accurate, Smith knew that Leather was not *society's* definition of a man.

But he also knew that the person who occupied Leather's body was as much a man as Smith was, no matter what the external equipment.

Leather was not the first person of his type Smith had met—and he *did* think of Leather as a 'he' because he'd clearly embraced living his life as a man. Not that his father had given him many choices.

Smith would have asked Leather his preference today—and likely would do, when his valet became more comfortable with him—but the wall of reserve around Leather was tangible, and he was particularly vulnerable now that Chatham had sacked him.

Smith thought the young valet might very well be the loneliest and most alone person he'd ever met. It poured off him in waves and was almost suffocating. Leather's emotional isolation had tugged at Smith's conscience—a part of himself he'd not heard from in years—the ver first time he'd met the younger man.

Even back then Smith had suspected the almost pathologically reserved valet carried a torch for his oblivious employer. Smith had felt a sharp and unexpected pang of sympathy for Leather. Because even if the impossible happened and Chatham—one, learned his valet had the body of a woman; and—two, didn't kill Leather or have him thrown in jail; and then—three, actually reciprocated Leather's feelings, there would always be the problem of how they could ever be together and be happy.

Joseph Leather would not be happy in dresses and jewels and Smith suspected that Stephen Chatham was not the sort of man to have a lover who dressed in men's clothing.

Smith had guessed that Chatham hadn't known what his valet hid beneath his clothing. Not because Chatham was stupid, but because he was not the sort of person to be troubled by questions of sexuality. In Chatham's mind there were women and there were men. And that was that.

Smith knew from his investigations into Chatham's affairs that his towering business partner's only forays into homosexual activity had been those which would not threaten his masculinity, i.e. getting sucked, tossed off, or fucking another man.

Smith had met a great many men who held similar views; he'd even offered up his arse and mouth to some of them. Taking a cock had never made him doubt his masculinity—quite the reverse; he never felt more like a man than when he had a big fat prick deep inside him. But he was aware that his was not the majority opinion.

He stood and went to his collection of decanters, selecting an Armagnac from 1799, and pouring himself a small glass. He then took an H. Upmann from the small Spanish cedar chest where he kept the expensive and delicate cigars and went back to his desk. He took a few moments to start his cigar, puffing until the velvety smoke plumed, and then he looked at Joseph Leather's life.

He'd actually collected the information a while back, after he'd seen Chatham's valet at Bernina's one day.

Smith had been too engrossed by a particularly talented American man that night to do any snooping, but the next time he'd gone to Bernina's he'd engaged a woman named Emma, whom he'd used once or twice before and had quite enjoyed. While Emma was his preferred physical type of female—which was to say she was in that fascinating gray zone between the masculine and feminine—he'd really chosen her because she was also an inveterate gossip.

That was fine with Smith because gossip was one of the two things he'd wanted from her that night, the other being her remarkably skilled throat around his cock.

He'd learned Leather came to the brothel only once a month and always engaged women—two on occasion—but never men. Emma had relished disclosing the truth about Leather's gender, without Smith even asking.

While Smith had no issue with gossip, in general, he'd been disgusted by the whore's willingness to release such dangerous and private information. It was the sort of information that could—if it ended up in the wrong hands— ruin a man or woman.

Smith knew that Emma would deliver information about *him* just as willingly to anyone who asked, but he didn't care; he was wealthy enough and powerful enough to protect himself against dangerous gossip, a valet was not.

Smith had let Cecile, the owner of Bernina's, know about her lethally indiscrete employee. Not only did Emma's indiscretion threaten the patrons, it threatened the establishment.

Smith studied the information on the page as his sipped his Armagnac.

He had a pretty fair idea why Mr. Jonathan Leather had raised his daughter as a man. As compliant as the old valet had apparently been about the duke repeatedly impregnating his wife, the man had apparently taken a stand when it came to his child—even if Joseph Leather was not really his.

It didn't surprise Smith that Leather senior had never confronted the duke about his wife; Jonathan was the fifth of the Leather line to valet a Duke of Tarland; the man knew nothing else. Just like his forbearers, he'd lived out his entire life on the duke's vast holding.

It didn't matter that it was 1870, some of these rural peers still ran their estates like private fiefdoms.

For once in his life Jonathan Leather had decided to thwart his master, and it seemed he'd done so. But he'd not been able to protect his second son from the next duke, Leather's own half-brother.

Smith didn't believe the story that was bandied about—about Joseph being the culpable party. The little he'd learned about Staunton—now Duke of Tarland—had been less than propitious.

He suspected that the only people who really knew the truth were Leather and Staunton, and he didn't see the valet ever disclosing what had happened.

Although Leather had accepted the valet position, Smith knew he was not the sort of man who gave much away, especially not about a subject so personal.

Still, Smith intended to get to know his valet better than the man expected.

He smiled with both amusement and anticipation as he blew out a plume of smoke.

How long would Chatham be able to bear having Leather work for him—and why would it bother the man so much? Was it because Stephen *loved* his valet? Or was it just spite—a dog in the manger attitude: Stephen didn't want him, but he didn't want anyone else to have him, either?

It amazed him how blinded by anger Chatham was. How the hell couldn't the man see that his valet wasn't working up some sophisticated blackmail scheme but was head over heels in love with him?

The interesting question was—at least to Smith—whether Leather was the type of man to wear the willow for his former master? Or would he be able to move on and perhaps give himself to another lover?

Chapter Twenty-Six

Jo couldn't believe how quickly she'd been welcomed by Mr. Smith's household. Actually, embraced would be a more accurate word to express the way she felt.

She'd moved in the very day Mr. Smith had engaged her.

"I'm afraid you're in for rather a mess in my dressing room," Smith warned her once they'd finished their odd conversation and delicious tea. "I hope you don't go running off screaming when you see it."

Jo had known that was not likely just by looking at her new master's impeccable attire and grooming. His study had been spare and organized and uncluttered—almost *too* tidy for a place where he likely spent so much of his time. There were no personal items—no photographs or bric-a-brac of the sort a person collected in his or her life—well, except for Jo, but then she didn't have a big house with pots of money. Neither did she have much of a personal life.

"Do you have a lot of possessions to pack?" Smith had asked her as he'd escorted her to the door of the study.

"Only what you saw me holding yesterday, sir."

"Ah, excellent, a man who travels light. My carriage will take you and bring you back," Smith said as she was leaving. "You will find it waiting out front."

"Oh, that's not necessary, sir."

"I know." He'd smiled, but Jo had seen right then and there that her new master was a man who liked to give an order one time and have it obeyed without question. Duly noted.

"Thank you, sir."

Jo had gone back to her pitiful lodgings, packed her pitiful bag, and climbed back in the gloriously luxurious carriage.

Malcolm, the servant who'd served tea earlier, met her at the door and took her bag.

"I'm to show you to your room and then give you a brief tour of the house."

"Thank you." Jo couldn't stop staring at her. Or him, rather.

"Here you are," Malcolm said once they reached the third floor. "This is the master's suite."

Jo's jaw dropped.

Malcolm chuckled. "Quite something, isn't it?"

"It is." It was huge, the ceiling high and strikingly coved, it was white and seemed to float above the black silk-covered walls.

Malcolm opened a door off the sitting room. "Through here is the bedchamber."

Jo gasped: it was the biggest, blackest four-poster bed she'd ever seen, but that was not what shocked her.

"That is the master and Charles." There was a hint of sadness in Malcolm's voice. "Charles was here for almost a year. We all thought—" he shook his head, as if realizing what he was saying. "Anyhow, that was painted by Natalie Hartwicke."

Jo couldn't stop staring, and knew her face would be red; it was the most erotic thing she'd *ever* seen—not that she had oodles of experience in erotic art, but . . . *Blimey!* It was bloody gorgeous. And it was making her wet.

The painting was horizontal and full length. Both men were lying on a chaise lounge, Charles in front of Mr. Smith. And his *penis*—Well, Jo had never seen anything like it.

"Lovely, isn't it?" Malcolm asked. Jo knew, somehow, that he was referring to the thick silver ring in the crown of the younger man's cock. It *was* gorgeous.

Mr. Smith had one arm over Charles's torso, resting so close to his nipple that Jo could almost *feel* his hand on her own breast. Mr. Smith was clearly naked, but most of his body—except for his arms, shoulder, and bit of chest—was, unfortunately, hidden. The artist had captured an expression she'd never seen—and she realized it was joy.

"So," Malcolm said, obviously ready to move along. "You're lucky that you'll get to look at *that* every day."

"Yes," Jo said. "That is an unexpected benefit."

Malcolm laughed.

"Mr. Smith likes black," Jo said rather stupidly, her gaze flickering from the black bedding—silk, also matte—to the thick carpets underfoot.

"He does. And tomorrow the tailor will come and take your measurements and get you attired in appropriate clothing." Malcolm hesitated and then added rather carefully. "Mr. Smith is the most wonderful employer I've ever had the pleasure of working for. Our quarters are beautiful, the salary—as you know—is unmatched, and we have more free time than we know what to do with. He feeds us as well as he eats and makes sure we have lots of time for entertainments. But he is a bit of a stickler on a few points. For example, he requires uniformity when it comes to servant clothing; we all dress the same—there is no deviation. His rooms are to be kept *exactly* the way he leaves things. *Exactly.* That is the quickest way to lose your job—move his things around. Don't put flowers on his breakfast tray or change the order of his books. Don't buy a different soap or go to a different linen draper. Those things will be written down and are easy to follow. I'll show you an example of what I mean." He led Jo through a wide arched doorway into a second room—a *massive* dressing room with every convenience imaginable, including a giant bathtub shaped like a seashell in front of a fireplace that could have held an ox.

There were several large alcoves off the main dressing room and one of them had four of the biggest armoires Jo had ever seen. They were identical, two each on opposite walls, a wide walkway between. Malcom opened the first of them and Jo's mouth opened in awe.

Long wooden dowels protruded from the back wall at even intervals. An identical pair of trousers was draped over each. The cuffs and waist hung at the same level, as if it the length had been measured with a ruler.

"You should carry one of these with you at all times," Malcolm held up a cunningly hinged ruler. "And you should use it."

Jo just nodded.

"Here, you can have this one," Malcolm handed it to her. "I've got a dozen of them, just so I'm never without one." The implication being that Jo should do the same. "His rooms will be your sole responsibility. He doesn't like having a bunch of servants mucking about in his private area. Cleaning his rooms is work some valets feel beneath them—"

"I'd rather take care of his environment, all of it." Jo had always disliked having other servants do for her masters. This would be perfect.

Malcolm showed her the rest of the master quarters, every inch of which was as impeccably tidy as the dressing room.

"And this is your room," Malcolm went through a door that exposed a spacious linen closet—built more like a hallway—and then opened a door on the other end, which led to a large bedroom.

"All this is *mine?*" Jo asked, staring around at a room at least five times larger than any she'd ever had.

"Yes, and your own bathroom is through there." He pointed to yet another door. "Complete with shower bath."

Malcolm laid Jo's bag on the floor beside a single armoire. Her battered suitcase looked forlorn and ragged in this pristine, black, gray, and white environment.

"Come down to the kitchen for a cuppa," Malcolm said.

"But I should go see to Mr. Smith's—"

"He left instructions for you to settle in. He won't be back until tomorrow morning at five. Come on, I want to introduce you to everyone."

Jo followed because to do otherwise seemed ungrateful and standoffish. But she couldn't help feeling alarmed at so much— *friendship.*

Clearly things were going to be different.

***

Stephen's cock was aching and hard. Again.

But he didn't want to go to a brothel and he didn't want a whore at his house. He didn't want a whore anywhere, when it came down to it.

You know what you want.

"Fuck off," he muttered.

"I'm sorry, sir?"

Stephen looked up to find his new valet—a footman named Charles, who'd waited on him in the past—poking his head out of the dressing room.

"I'm going to sleep shortly." That was his way of telling the other man to get the hell out of his room.

"Very good sir, good night, Mr. Chatham."

246

Stephen waited until the door shut behind him and then pushed back the blankets and got out of bed. He went to his writing desk and pulled out the report from Dawkins. He'd read it a good dozen times already, but he just wanted to read it again before he did something rash. Not that he was prone to rash actions.

Except with Leather, of course.

Stephen had given up arguing with his conscience—or whatever the nagging insistent voice was—because it was usually right.

He *had* been hasty to kick out Leather. He'd found the suitcase, followed Leather to the brothel, and then confronted her all on the same day. Almost like he was afraid of what decision he would make if he gave the matter some thought.

And so Leather was gone.

There was no denying he missed her. Sorely. Charles was a fine valet and his clothes and rooms were in perfect order. He was cheerful but not talkative, intelligent but not bossy. He was an excellent valet.

Except Stephen never got hard around him. Never wanted to make that *look* come into his eyes—the one that said he would do *anything* to please his master—to please Stephen.

Part of him was glad—at least he wasn't a sod, which he'd wondered more than a few hundred times those last few weeks with Leather, when he'd not been able to keep his cock out of his—*her*—mouth.

But was Stephen *really* not a sod if he'd still wanted Leather—even when he'd believed he was a man?

Ah, Christ. Who bloody cared? Leather was gone. And to that bastard Smith's house.

"Do you know something I don't know?" Stephen had asked Smith earlier this evening when they'd run into each other at Number 14. It wasn't a meeting night, but Smith had been playing at one of the tables—something he did often now.

For a while—a year or so ago—Chatham knew Smith had had somebody, a lover, and he'd not been around so much. But things must have gone off because now he was often at the club.

"I know a lot of things that you don't know, Chatham. Can you be more specific?"

Smith had just cleaned out three players, men who'd been taking a beating from him for a while— judging by their harried, wild-eyed expressions—so now it was just Smith and Stephen, sitting at the baize covered table, drinking the special brandy the club kept exclusively for them.

Stephen gritted his teeth. "You know damned well what I mean—about Leather."

"Ah. Well, if what you're asking me is if I've gathered information on her, the answer is no."

Stephen knew he was lying; Smith was the only man he'd ever met who was more obsessed with gathering information than he was. "Then why are you so bloody sure she won't turn on you? Blackmail you?"

Smith smiled. "I just am."

"That's a bloody worthless answer. What would you say if I told you she'd already blackmailed one of her employers?"

"I'd say you were mistaken."

"And how the hell are you so sure of that?"

Smith shrugged, unruffled by his abrasive tone. "What do you know of the alleged blackmail victim?"

Stephen paused as he thought about the current Duke of Tarland.

"Ah, nothing," Smith said.

Stephen's hands clenched at his superior tone. Honestly, Smith was lucky he was a dangerous bastard or somebody would have strangled him and left him in a ditch by now. Quite possibly Stephen, in fact.

But the man had a damnably good point: Stephen knew nothing about the current duke. All he knew about Leather's dealings with the duke were the rumors Dawkins had collected.

Stephen silently cursed his idiocy; why hadn't he had Dawkins look into the duke when he'd looked into Leather?

Because you were intent on a vendetta.

"Christ."

"I beg your pardon?" Smith asked.

"I know the man is a duke."

"Come again?" Smith asked.

"Her blackmail victim—he's a duke."

"I see," Smith said, his words pregnant with sarcasm. "And we all know a duke would never lie."

Stephen grimaced but knew that was a damned good point: aristocrats were often as bent as a dog's hind leg.

Take their partner Gideon Banks, for example. He'd recently learned that he was heir to an earldom. Clearly there was no quality control when it came to filling up the House of Lords.

"Are you fucking her?" Stephen closed his eyes briefly. He wanted to howl—or tear out his own tongue. Or howl *and* tear out his own tongue. Where the bloody fucking hell had *that* come from?

"Define *fucking.*" Smith smirked.

"You *bastard.*" Stephen couldn't manage more than that; his head was throbbing and buzzing and his body was impossibly hot.

Smith's eyelids lowered, as if he needed to hide what were already the most guarded eyes in all Britain. "Leather is the best trained valet I've ever had," he said mildly.

Stephen stared.

And then the bastard chuckled. "I must say that you seem rather interested in his doings for a man who gave him the sack. And no letter of reference. A bit punitive."

"*Him?*" Stephen snorted.

"That is the way Leather has chosen to live his life, Stephen."

"No," he ground out, "That is what her father imposed on her."

"He is an adult and has been for many years. The choice is his, whether you like it, or not. And it has nothing to do with his valeting skills."

"Oh, look at you—so broad minded. I wonder if you'll feel as accepting when you find yourself the victim of one of her schemes."

"And *I* wonder if you're this upset because you found yourself lusting after a man."

Stephen's face had burned at the other man's words and he'd stood, towering over him. "You'd do well to watch what you say."

Rather than look intimidated, Smith had smiled up at him. "I'm sorry, you're right and I was terribly wrong—please forget what I said."

Stephen had wanted to punch him in the face so badly he'd left the man sitting there.

Leather had been working for Smith for two weeks. That was fourteen days she'd been in his house. Smith was one of the most— scratch that, *the* most—devious, dark, mysterious, untruthful, manipulative, unpredictable, and treacherous men Stephen had ever met. And for some strange reason, Smith wanted Joseph Leather. And that knowledge was slowly swallowing Stephen whole, like one of those enormous snakes they'd discovered in the jungles of South America.

Smith *was* a bloody snake.

Stephen was an idiot to ask the man questions—even Smith didn't know when he was lying and when he was telling the truth.

The other man was so bloody tightly wrapped Stephen always felt anxious just being around him—not dissimilar to the feeling he'd experienced when he'd once gone too close to an electrical transformer, the hairs on his body standing on end.

While Smith wasn't as flagrant about his fucking as Banks, Stephen had heard enough things over the years—such as the fact that Smith's last lover had been a man.

So why would he want Leather if he was a sod? He must just want him—*her* dammit—because she was a bloody good valet. That thought made him slightly less crazy, but not much, because Stephen had fucked men before—and not just Leather when he'd believed her to be male— so being with a man didn't mean Smith couldn't also enjoy women.

Still, Smith had lived with a male lover while Stephen had merely emptied his balls in a few men—certainly not an action that made a man a sod.

Stephen suspected the line between what Smith would do and whom he would do it with was indistinct. Hell, where Smith was concerned there probably weren't any damned lines.

As much as Smith was infuriating Stephen at the moment, the man had made an excellent point about Tarland. What *did* Stephen know about the duke? Because now that his head wasn't on the brink of exploding with betrayal and anger, he had to admit Leather had not behaved duplicitously. Well, other than claiming to be a man and then paying a lot of money to have five nights with *him*.

Stephen had asked himself over and over again what he would have done if *Jo* had shown up that fifth night.

He now knew that *Stephen* himself was the reason she'd not come to Meisen's.

He snorted; what bloody irony.

If he'd asked her to marry him, what would she have said? Would she have told him the truth—would she have said *yes?*

Marriage? Stephen just couldn't *see* that in his mind; Leather had lived as a man all her bloody life. Just what did that do to a person?

What would he do if he could do it all over?

Stephen wasn't sure he could face the real answer to that question.

Chapter Twenty-Seven

Jo had been working for Mr. Smith a month now and had to admit that—with the exception of one thing—it was the best job she'd ever had.

It couldn't compare to being around Mr. Chatham every day, but for the first time in her life Jo had *friends*. She was enjoying her burgeoning social life so much that she almost felt bad for not missing Mr. Chatham more. Did that mean she was fickle? Shallow? Or perhaps what she'd felt had merely been an infatuation? After all, he'd been the first man she desired. Jo had believed he would be the *only* one, but she couldn't deny she was already feeling more than a little attraction for her current master.

Perhaps she was just making up for years of not even wanting to *think* of being with a man—thanks to what Staunton had done to her—because now she couldn't seem to get two men out of her mind.

Mr. Smith was the most inscrutable human being she'd ever met. He was also one of the most appealing. Not so much because of his person—although he was well-formed and handsome—but because of the individual who inhabited that attractive body.

Jo knew she wasn't the only one to find him so fascinating.

Mr. Smith's servants were given unheard of freedom to enjoy themselves, which included having a barrel of ale always ready and tapped in the cold room.

"Don't try to understand him, Jo," Donovan, one of the grooms had said one night when she'd stayed after supper to socialize. That was another thing she loved about the house, there was a hierarchy, of course, but all the servants called each other by their Christian names, it promoted a sense of camaraderie.

"Donovan has the right of it," Bevin said. "The master is a puzzle that doesn't want solving and it will drive you crazy. Besides, as pleasant and polite as he is, you do *not* want him to catch you prying. Trust me, you don't want to see the man angry."

The room had gone quiet for a moment as they all contemplated such a terrifying eventuality.

"I've been working for him as long as anyone now. Only Nash was with him longer—fourteen years—and he said that he left the house knowing as much about Mr. Smith as he did his second week on the job," this from one of the Thomases.

There were four Thomases on Mr. Smith's staff. These were men who'd really been named Thomas—not just called Thomas because the master of the house couldn't be bothered to remember their names, which is how it had been in the duke's house.

The servants referred to the Thomases as One through Four.

The Thomas who'd just spoken was Two, who was one of the chambermaids.

Jo knew, although nobody had come out and said as much, that Nash had warmed the master's bed for at least several of those years.

To Jo that sounded like a dream—heaven. She'd never even dared to imagine Mr. Chatham taking her into his bed. She would been content to go along for the rest of her life as they'd been going since Glasgow. Well, minus the subtle, cutting, and—she believed—unfair criticisms.

"Nash was good for the master," Two said. The rest of the servants nodded. "Gave him a reason to come home more often."

"I thought Charles might—" Gerald stopped, his mouth snapping shut. This happened often when the subject of Charles came up and Jo felt sorry for the young footman, a gorgeous man who couldn't have been more than twenty and was Four's lover.

That was another thing; Mr. Smith didn't frown on servant fraternizing as long as there was never any squabbling.

"If you're going to squabble," Bevin, the house steward, who also happened to be Donovan's lover, said, "Go do it somewhere far away from here. I don't like to think what the rest of the servants would do to anyone who ruined things for all of us."

It had taken her the first two weeks to sort out who was with whom in Mr. Smith's household, and then some of them were always changing partners. Some didn't have partners—Jamie, Norris, and Albert were together, a trio that had apparently been with each other for over five years.

Yes, it was unlike any place she'd ever been.

The door to the kitchen opened and Three popped his head in. "The master's carriage is coming."

Jo immediately stood and nodded to the others. "Well, that's me on, then."

There were a chorus of *g'night*s as she made her way swiftly up the stairs.

Mr. Smith's room was already prepared the way he liked and all she had to do was be there waiting for him.

The door opened and Mr. Smith smiled at her—that was another thing, he always seemed happy to see her. "Good evening, Leather."

"How was your evening, sir?" She helped him from his heavy wool overcoat, which was flecked with diamonds of water.

"Cold. Wet." His lips quirked as he reached into his coat pocket and pulled out a thick roll of bills. "Profitable." Jo took the roll from him. "See that gets down to Bevin, will you."

"Of course, sir." Jo put the money on the salver by the door and returned to unbutton Mr. Smith's coat. Unlike the prevailing fashion for loose sack coats, Mr. Smith carved out his own fashion with his solid black wardrobe, tailored to display what she now knew was a magnificent body.

"I was at Bernina's tonight and Madame Cecile said to give you her best," he said as Jo went behind him to help removed the closely fitted garment. At a hair over five foot ten, Jo was actually a bit taller than her new master, so it was not the stretch it had been with Mr. Chatham.

His comment about the brothel made her realize he'd been with somebody earlier tonight, taken his pleasure in another body. A sexual frisson shot through her at his admission. She'd imagined him with others more than once, while lying in her lonely bed.

"That was kind of her," Jo said. Mr. Smith knew she patronized the brothel, indeed, he seemed to find it natural.

She hadn't gone more often to Bernina's now that she had more free time, but she *had* met Cecile for tea once a week since she'd been at Mr. Smith's, which was almost as lovely as her Mondays.

"Cecile wanted you to know she would not be there on your next day. Her family is acting up, it seems."

Jo worked the jet buttons on his double-breasted waistcoat. Cecile's massive, demanding, disastrous family was a thing of legend.

"I think she enjoys the excitement they add to her life, sir."

And that was *another* thing—Mr. Smith had *ordered* her to speak her mind. In fact, it was the only time he'd looked annoyed since she'd been here—when she'd given a placating answer to one of his questions.

"I don't want a mindless cypher, Leather, I enjoy an active, curious mind," he'd said, his voice as soft as ever, but cold iron beneath his words. She was getting better at it every day—sharing her opinions, even when unsolicited.

"I think you are right, Leather."

Jo unbuttoned the remarkably fine black cotton shirt, keeping her eyes on her hands, but intensely aware of the man standing across from her. The effect he had on her seemed to intensify with each day that passed, no matter that she did all she could to suppress it. Her career as a valet would be curtailed rather quickly if she constantly fantasized about her masters while stripping them naked.

If she looked up, their eyes would be level. Controlling her breathing was taking every bit of effort she had. And if she could just make it to the last—

A hand landed over both of hers. "You're trembling. Do I frighten you?"

Did he? He kept his hand lightly over hers. Jo could have easily pulled away, but she didn't.

Jo knew that Mr. Smith did not, as a matter of course, invite his servants into his bed. He and Nash had been lovers for years, but neither man had been exclusive.

"It was not a condition of Nash's employment," Malcolm had told her. They'd both been down in the laundry room, Malcolm helping her with Mr. Smith's linens—mainly so the two of them could chat.

Malcolm swallowed and said, "I'd give a lot to have—" he'd stopped. But Jo knew what he'd been about to say, and Malcolm wasn't the only one in the house who would have warmed the master's bed in a heartbeat.

"I'm not frightened of you, sir." Jo finally admitted.

There was a long pause, and then, "Will you not look at me?"

Jo's head creaked on her neck, like something rusted and hard to move. When she met his eyes, she remembered why. She'd thought Mr. Chatham had a piercing stare—and he did—but he'd not been able to penetrate her mask to see who she was. Not even on that last, dreadful, day. Mr. Smith seemed to have access to every part of her.

This close she saw his irises were the dark brown of a whiskey barrel. His lashes were long but without a curl—spikey and somehow aggressive. Jo smiled at the description.

His lips curled up along with hers, the smile lines that were always there deepening. "That is a rare expression, Leather. Did I do something to earn it?"

Jo felt her face heat at her stupid thought. But this was the man who'd said to tell her everything—no matter how small. "Your eyelashes—they are long, but straight and seem rather, well, aggressive."

He chuckled, his eyes lighting with humor, his sensual lips parting to reveal teeth that were crooked—and two were chipped—but somehow very charming.

"And your lashes are a pale brown—a fawn color. They are long and I would say . . . defensive."

Jo grinned.

His eyebrows rose. "Ah," he said, the sound barely audible. His big brown eyes flickered over her face, their expression as unreadable as ever.

He dropped his hand and Jo finished the last button and then removed his cuffs.

By the time she turned from replacing the links in his jewelry drawer—in their precisely allotted position—he'd shrugged out of his shirt.

Jo took his linen and tried not to stare at the smooth, almost hairless, expanse of olive skin stretched attractively over a body that was breathtakingly toned and powerful. Like Mr. Chatham, he exercised every day—sometimes twice. Jo thought his need to keep himself fit was almost a mania—but she appreciated the results.

She deposited the linen in the basket just inside the door of the dressing room. When she returned, he was sitting in his chair. Jo felt his eyes on her again as she knelt, unbuttoning his ankle boots. Yes, she was moving slowly, and she knew why. This ritual had become more charged every evening.

Jo slipped off his shoes and set them aside before inserting her hands up his trouser legs and removing his stockings. How was it that anyone could do such an intimate service for another human and not feel *something*? Or was it just Jo—fatally flawed to become aroused by serving someone? No, not just someone, but some *men,* powerful men, especially.

But she'd never wanted the banker she'd worked for, or the Colonel. That was something, wasn't it?

Jo realized that she was kneeling holding his stockings, not moving, and stood.

When she returned to him, he'd already unbuttoned his trousers and untied his drawers, letting both fall to the floor.

Jo lowered her eyes from his naked, and, yes, hard body, holding out his heavy black silk robe and only raising her gaze when he'd wrapped it around himself.

His expression was as amiable as ever, but his enlarged pupils told her that she was the reason for his current condition.

Jo bent to retrieve his trousers and drawers and also to help him into his slippers. He had elegant feet that matched the rest of him, high arched and well-formed, and it was almost as much a pleasure to maintain them as it was his lovely hands.

She felt the slightest touch on the top of her head, perhaps the brush of a finger.

"Thank you, Leather. That will be all for tonight."

Jo stood and bowed her head, keeping her eyes lowered—for self-preservation as much as respect. "Thank you, sir. Sleep well."

She collected the shoes and clothing and walked the short distance to her room, closing the door and then closing her eyes and leaning back against it.

***

Smith watched his valet disappear behind the door to his room and then went to pour himself a glass of port before taking a seat in the chair closest to the fire.

He was not insensible to the charge of electricity between them and was also aware it was growing daily. But he knew the difference between physical attraction and deeper feelings.

It was Smith's belief that Leather had only begun to become comfortable with his sexuality recently. Indeed, it was bursting out of his every pore. He'd spent his life repressing who he was and this household—with its openness and freedoms—would be a revelation.

Smith knew his valet would willingly kneel and give him pleasure if he were to ask it. Indeed, Leather being who he was—a man who'd been bred to never deny his master—he would be pleased to do *whatever* Smith wanted.

As much as Smith loved blind obedience in his lovers, he didn't want it without any emotion.

Leather still belonged to Chatham, and might do so forever, for all that he shivered with barely suppressed desire when he dressed and undressed Smith each day.

Smith smiled and took a sip of port, enjoying the heavy feeling in his groin, but doing nothing to stimulate his already hard organ. He'd enjoyed release earlier this evening at Bernina's. There was nobody there who resembled Leather, and Smith didn't think he would have engaged him or her if there had been.

Instead, he'd taken the American, again—Lucien . He was a boy of twenty-two, sweet and not too smart, but he possessed a hulking, muscular body and a cock to match.

Smith had found it challenging to throat the entire monster, but he'd succeeded to the younger man's intense pleasure.

Afterward, he'd ridden Lucien, reveling in the sight of so much masculine power submitting to him. He'd made their joining last, fucking him with exquisite slowness, drawing out his pleasure over and over again, until the pressure in his balls gave way and he exploded, pumping the younger man full.

It had been a good night and it had eased his need—a need that hadn't diminished with more time spent with his reserved valet.

Smith had learned long ago not to try and dissect his attraction to people. Leather was neither beautiful nor ugly. He was not flamboyant or eye-catching. He was the sort of man you would pass on the street without noticing—his thick spectacles the only remarkable thing about him.

It wasn't until you watched him in action that anything stood out. At least it did to Smith and he knew that was only because of his *quirks*. He wanted this man to worship him the way Leather had so clearly worshipped Chatham.

That blend of regard, loyalty, and adoration was rare and worth more than gold.

Smith was almost positive that Chatham would be realizing now how his quiet, unobtrusive valet had somehow gotten into his blood, under his skin—into his very bones—and made him stronger, more contented, and, ultimately, happier.

And Chatham had thrown all that away.

It remained to be seen if Smith would be lucky enough to retrieve it.

Chapter Twenty-Eight

tephen looked up at the knock on the door.

"Excuse me, sir, but there is somebody here to see you," his secretary said.

He stared irritably at the tangled mess of accounting Gideon Banks had messengered to him last night and then took off his glasses. "Who is it, Knowles?"

"A man looking for Mr. Leather, he says he is Benjamin Leather, er, Mr. Leather's brother. He asked if anyone knew where Mr. Leather had gone, but I'm afraid I had no forwarding address to give him. I thought you might know, sir."

Knowles's words were like a brick to the stomach. "Send him in."

"Very good, Sir."

The door closed and Stephen sat back in his chair. He knew about Benjamin Leather's existence, but he knew nothing more than the story of his dismissal from Tarland's household. He had to confess to a burning curiosity to meet one of the few people who knew Leather's real identity.

The door opened to admit a man so remarkably like Leather that Stephen was temporarily confused.

Benjamin Leather held his hat in his hand and stood uncertain, but not fidgeting, just a few steps inside the door.

"Come in," Stephen said, gesturing to one of the seats across from his desk even though he knew it was unusual to behave thus to a servant.

Benjamin Leather looked nonplussed at the offer but he came forward and sat, spine ramrod straight like Leather's. He was bespectacled, but his lenses were not nearly so thick. His hair was a similar mid-brown but cut short, rather than shorn. And he had the same full lips on his narrow face. It was . . . eerie.

Stephen realized he'd been staring. "You look remarkably like Leather," he said foolishly.

Benjamin smiled, an open expression so unlike Leather's that the resemblance faded. "Yes, we've been told that often."

"I'm afraid your brother is no longer in my employ," Stephen said, the words unpleasant in his mouth. He took one of his cards from his desk and jotted Smith's address and name on the back. "He's gone to work for one of my business associates." He held out the card and the other man rose quickly to take it.

"Thank you, sir," he said, not sitting down again, clearly ready to be on his way.

But Stephen felt an almost physical need to detain him—even if only for a few minutes. "I'm surprised he's not contacted you with his information," he said, shamelessly fishing for something—anything.

Benjamin grimaced. "I'm afraid we've become, well, estranged." His cheeks flushed, and then he added, "I've only recently returned from Spain, but my master has been appointed to France, so I won't be here long before we head off again."

Stephen was flailing for something to say—whatever normal people said when they held conversations.

"Are you happy to be leaving again so soon?" he asked, feeling like a jackass.

He must have been doing an adequate job of acting like a normal human being because Benjamin did not look at him askance. "I'm actually eager to go as it will allow me to use my French on actual Frenchmen."

Stephen blinked. "You speak French?" What an idiot he was—the man had just *said* as much.

"Yes, as well as Spanish and a smattering of German. But Joseph was always much better at languages than I was, yet it appears I am the one getting the opportunity to use them."

Stephen simply could not wrap his mind around this. "How is it that you both learned foreign languages?" His face heated at his skeptical tone. "I'm sorry—that s-sounds insulting," he said, now doubly ashamed at offending *and* stuttering.

But Benjamin Leather just smiled. "Not at all—I know it's unusual among English servants to speak another language. It was my father's doing, sir. As you may know, he worked all his life for the Duke of Tarland. He never travelled with His Grace—indeed, he never left Scotland—as His Grace's other valet was a gentleman schooled in several languages and accompanied the duke on his journeys to the Continent. My father determined his sons would have such chances so we were trained in languages and also spent a good deal of study on European politics and history." His lips twisted slightly and Stephen could see not all of Benjamin Leather's memories of his driven father were pleasant—or at least not comfortable.

He also realized he'd employed a man who was more educated than he was. That wouldn't be difficult as Stephen had never paid attention to anything other than mathematics. Still, it was . . . humbling.

"Thank you for this, sir." Benjamin held up the card, his expression hesitant.

Stephen knew the other man wanted to know what had happened, but of course he would never ask a stranger—and his brother's ex-employer, at that—such a question.

"Of course. Your brother is an excellent valet and Mr. Smith is a fine employer." Stephen stood and walked him toward the door. As he came closer to the other man he realized Benjamin was not as tall as Leather. Nor did he have that odd sense of stillness that Leather carried with him.

Stephen opened the door, and saw a footman waiting just beside the door, likely Knowles had sent him here to escort Benjamin to the front door. "I wish you well in France."

"Thank you, sir."

He watched until the two men disappeared down the stairs before shutting the door.

Without meaning to, his feet took him to the window where he knew he could see Benjamin Leather leave the house. The valet paused at the top of the steps, his stick tucked under his elbow as he pulled on his gloves. He moved with the same precise movements as Leather and his clothes were almost identical.

Mr. Jonathan Leather had produced two identical sons.

Stephen gave a soft snort of amazement; except one of them was a woman.

***

Jo escorted Ben to the servant entrance and opened the door. "I'm so glad you came to see me," she said.

Ben nodded, his expression sheepish. "So am I. We're all the family we have left and——" he shrugged.

Jo laid a hand on Ben's shoulder and squeezed. "I know."

Ben's lip trembled. "Blast!" He grabbed Jo in a tight embrace and squeezed hard. "I love you, Jo," he whispered in her ear. "Take care of yourself." And then he released her just as suddenly as he'd hugged her and turned on his heel, striding off into the dusk.

Jo closed the door and slowly mounted the servant stairs. It had been a shock when Ben called—a pleasant shock, but a shock all the same. And going to France, now. She smiled and shook her head as she strode down the corridor to Mr. Smith's rooms.

They'd always taunted each other about who would get to travel first, and now Ben would go to his second foreign country.

Ben had come just as Jo was finishing cleaning Mr. Smith's bedchamber. As he wasn't expected back until after ten o'clock tonight Jo had felt that she could take a half hour to see her brother.

It was seven-thirty now and she resumed her work. Mr. Smith liked his bed linens changed daily. It was more often than she'd seen in the past, but he was meticulous about cleanliness. She didn't mind. In fact, she enjoyed handling the fine silks, cottons, and even leathers that comprised his bedding.

Today she was dressing the bed with a black silk set that was sinful. Especially with him lying in it, which she'd seen more than once.

He read every evening, no matter how late he returned. And he liked to read in bed, propped up against a mountain of pillows, his silver-framed glasses perched on his high-bridged blade of a nose, bare from the chest up. Jo swallowed at the memory as she smoothed the butter soft silk over the down quilt.

He slept naked and it was difficult for her to get to sleep these days thinking about it—about him—only feet away, his body lying between crisp sheets, not wearing even a stitch.

263

The bell in her bedroom rang and she frowned; it would only ring if he were home early.

"Drat!" she muttered. She'd finished his bed and dusted, but she'd wanted to clean the baseboards and use the special oil that went on the leather furniture to keep it supple and soft.

She cut a quick glance around his chambers and saw all was neat and tidy, she would have to—

The door opened and Jo strode toward it. "Good evening, sir. You are back early tonight."

Rather than be annoyed by her observations. Mr. Smith seemed to expect them.

"Hello Leather," he said shrugging out of his overcoat as Jo went to stand behind him. "Yes, I decided against going to Number 14 tonight."

"The fog, sir," Jo said as she came around the front of him and unbuttoned his coat.

"That and the fact I'm tired." He yawned as if to demonstrate. "Your master is an old man, Leather. I will be forty-five in two days," he confessed.

Jo glanced up in surprise.

He smiled at whatever he saw on her face. "Confess—you thought me older."

Jo went around back to remove his coat, lightly pulling as he rolled his shoulders, allowing the garment to slide more easily.

"Actually, sir," she said as she draped the coat over the horse, "I would've guessed you as younger." She hesitated and then threw caution to the wind. "No more than forty-three."

Smith threw back his head and laughed, his rock-hard body shaking beneath her fingers as she unbuttoned his waistcoat.

"I deserved that for my shameful fishing," he said as he slipped out of the vest.

"I should have actually said you were in your late thirties, sir," she said honestly as she began to unbutton his shirt.

"And how old are you, Leather?"

"Almost twenty-eight, sir." Jo felt his eyes on her as she removed his cuff links—tiny, cunningly made compasses that actually worked.

"Ah."

Jo wondered if he were thinking the same thing she was: that he was almost twenty years her senior.

"I'd like you to order a tray sent up," he said as she replaced the jewelry in its drawer.

"Anything in particular, sir?" Jo stood behind him to remove his shirt, her mouth watering at the sight of his muscular shoulders flexing.

"I'll leave it to your discretion."

She returned to find him waiting in his chair and dropped to her knees. Jo felt distracted and knew that Ben's visit—while enjoyable—had been an unexpected break in her day. She also knew she should tell Mr. Smith that her brother had visited, as he deserved to know who came into his house.

She held his calf in her palm while she slipped off his boot, turning it over and frowning. She would need to replace the leather sole; Mr. Smith tended to tread heavily on the outside of his right foot.

She set aside the boot and looked up before moving to the next. She tried not to look at the expanse of muscular chest before meeting his eyes, but she knew her face would have those red spots over her cheekbones she despised so much.

"My brother came to see me today, sir, I hope that was all right. I, er, well, I brought him up to my room."

He smiled down at her, his hands resting lightly on the arms of his chair, making him look like carvings of the Egyptian kings she'd seen on a visit to the British Museum. She'd never realized before just how exotic he looked.

"Of course, you may have visitors. Does your brother live in London, or is he visiting?"

"He lives here but will soon be moving with his employer. He is the valet of a diplomat who has just been posted to Paris." Jo was relieved to look away from his too-knowing eyes, slipping her hands inside his trouser leg and removing one stocking and then the other.

"That sounds impressive."

Jo smiled, Ben certainly thought so.

He waited until she'd returned from depositing his stockings in the basket before standing, his hands going to his trouser front. "Are you competitive?" he asked.

"When we were younger, yes." Oh, how Jo had envied her brother's job serving Lord Staunton. Which of them would valet the new duke? It had been a plum, the prize in their own, personal Greek epic. Who would be the fortunate one? Who would be the best?

Mr. Smith's trousers and drawers dropped to the floor and he stepped out of them, his smile wry. "I'm sorry, I suppose a diplomat beats a mere businessman."

"I'm content where I am," Jo said as she bent to pick up his discarded clothing, allowing herself one quick glance at his swollen, but not fully erect cock.

She drew in a shaky breath and stood, only to find him waiting for her. He wasn't smiling or frowning, his was just looking, *intently.* "Are you?"

"I beg your pardon, sir?"

"Content—do you like your position here?" he clarified, his muscles seeming to relax, but so subtly that Jo didn't see the transformation until it had already happened and he was once again her smiling, pleasant employer.

"Very much, sir." She met his eyes, wanting him to know she meant it. "And I'm grateful to you for taking me, even though—" she broke off, suddenly aware she still didn't know *just* what it was he knew.

"You are welcome, Leather. It was my pleasure."

Jo nodded rather abruptly and picked up his robe, which she'd brought back from the dressing room with her. Once he was garbed, he padded softly to his study.

Jo quickly put away his clothing and shoes—he did not care to see clutter, even temporarily—and made her way down to the kitchen.

The kitchen staff were already waiting. Jo knew it sometimes made them nervous that they so very rare seemed to "earn their keep" when it came to cooking for the master of the house. Mr. Smith hardly ever ate at home and when he did, he was not gluttonous, preferring a few dishes, rather than full courses.

"Does he want dinner?" Cook asked, looking poised and eager.

"Just a tray in his room. Do you have some of the squab pie? Perhaps that Taunton cheese he received from the earl. Oh, and two slices of fresh bread, a portion of that rare roast, and what do you have for his dessert?"

Cook smiled proudly. "I've got a lovely flummery with pear compote and I can whip up Madeleines in a jiffy."

"That sounds excellent. Send it with coffee. Also send a flagon of ale with his meal, just in case. I'll go to the cellar and fetch up a bottle of Burgundy Thorins, the 1865. It will be lovely with that roast."

"Very good, sir."

Mr. Smith kept an impressive wine cellar and seemed to know and appreciate its contents. Mr. Chatham had always relied on his secretary, Mr. Knowles, to stock his cellar. It had been a job Jo had itched to take over as Knowles was a dreadful judge of wines and bought solely on the basis of price—if it was expensive, it must good. As a result, the cellar was a bit of an embarrassment.

The cellar was not locked as it had been in Mr. Chatham's house and every other house she'd worked in. But nobody stole from Mr. Smith. Ever.

She fetched the bottle and headed back upstairs. She kept glasses and openers as well as other necessities in what she thought of as the valet's pantry that separated her quarters from Mr. Smith's.

When she returned to his room he was sitting beside the fire, one leg crossed over the other, reading something he must have taken from the satchel that sat open beside his chair.

"Would you care for a glass, sir?" She held out the bottle to show him and he smiled.

"You read my mind, Leather. That should be ready by the time I'm finished with this." He gestured to the class of whiskey beside him.

Jo enjoyed her own private smile as she went to the small pantry to open the wine and let it breathe. She knew it was a pitiful remnant of her father's training to enjoy anticipating his needs so perfectly, but it genuinely made her happy.

She was curious as to why he was home so early in the day. He'd never come home before ten o'clock before. In general, she stayed down in the kitchen after dinner and then came up a few hours before his expected return and worked on small projects or perhaps read while she waited.

It was unfortunate that today was the first day she'd not finished her cleaning early and it was bothering her, even though she knew he'd likely not notice.

She could hardly crawl around cleaning baseboards, so she'd fetch the shoes he'd worn today and work on those.

As she passed through the study, he looked up. "It occurs to me that by coming home at such an unprecedented hour I might have interrupted your schedule. If I did, please go about what you have planned. I don't mind if you work around me." He paused and gave her a mocking smile. "As long as you don't plan to beat rugs."

She smiled. "No sir, that has been taken care of. Today was furniture oiling and base boards, and I will have plenty of time tomorrow to finish them without bothering you with strong smelling concoctions."

"As you will, then. I've been meaning to tell you that your work has pleased me greatly. I'm aware I am rather methodical—I saw that slight flash of humor, Leather."

Jo couldn't help chuckling.

"As I was saying, I know my requirements in some regards are demanding and you have done a superlative job meeting them."

Her face heated with a blend of happiness and pride. "Thank you sir, it's my pleasure. And I don't find your needs demanding." She hesitated, her mind flickering back to the banker she'd served. He'd been a nice enough man but had changed his mind at least twice a week about something or other. "You're consistent, sir, which is the most important thing—to me, at least."

He smiled, nodded, and turned back to his reading.

Jo busied herself until his food arrived and then set it out for him at the table she'd had two footmen bring closer to the fire. She dismissed the men as she would wait on him at table.

"This looks perfect," he said as she pulled out his chair and seated him.

Jo stood behind and slightly to the side of his chair while he ate and read, assisting him with his needs as necessary.

When the dessert arrived, she could see he was genuinely pleased. "Ah, blancmange—my favorite."

Both Jo and his cook knew that.

He enjoyed his coffee and desert in a leisured fashion and when Jo went to clear his plates, he closed the thick folder of documents he'd been reading. "That is enough work for one night." He cocked his head and looked up at her as she filled the tray with crockery. "I fancy a game of something, Leather. Do you play piquet?"

"I'm afraid I'm not in your league, sir." It horrified her to think of playing cards against a man who seemed to win thousands of pounds without even trying.

He chuckled. "Coward. But as you will be my guest, you get to choose the game."

"I used to beat my brother at Spillikins," Jo said, putting the last of the dishes on the tray and ringing the bell, which was answered almost instantly. The whole household would be on their toes with the master's unexpected presence.

Mr. Smith laughed at that. "Unfortunately, you're out of luck as I've loaned my set out. But how about chess? Backgammon? Draughts, even?"

"I am middling at all three, I'm afraid."

"Good, so am I. Ring for the chess table," he said.

Jo did so and soon they were set up in front of the fireplace.

If the footmen who delivered the game table thought anything odd about their master playing chess with his valet, neither showed it.

"Who taught you to play chess?" Mr. Smith asked as they set up their pieces.

"My father."

"He enjoyed games, did he?"

Jo hesitated and he looked up.

"You must tell me if my questions are too prying. I'm afraid I have a bad habit of being curious."

Jo knew that, and it wasn't just about her—he was curious about everyone and everything around him. She'd never met a more curious person.

"I didn't find the question prying, I was just thinking about my father. I don't believe he enjoyed games, but he believed it was part of our training—mine and my brother's—to know such things."

"Oh, and why was that?" He put the last of his pawns in place and Jo realized she'd lagged behind while looking at him. Specifically, while looking at his chest. The robe had slipped open and she was being treated to a hard, beautiful expanse of skin and muscle.

"A gentleman's gentleman should be prepared for every eventuality," she said, dropping her eyes to her pieces.

"That sounds like a famous quote—Shakespeare?"

His words surprised a laugh out of her and she looked up to find him staring, arrested.

Her face slid immediately back into its usual expression and he shook his head. "Don't."

She didn't ask what he meant; she knew. But the laughter had already gone.

They played in silence, only the ticking of the clock and crackling of the fire keeping them company.

They were well-matched—at least he was pretending they were—and the game ended in a draw.

"Well," he said as they put away the pieces, "If you are middling, I guess I must be, too."

Jo stood once the lovely ivory pieces had all been returned to their spots. "Thank you, sir, that was enjoyable."

"You didn't just let me win because I'm your employer, did you?" he asked with a look that was only partly joking.

"If I told you, that would defeat the purpose, wouldn't it, sir?"

He laughed.

"Are you ready for bed, sir?" she asked, suddenly aware just how that sounded.

"Not yet," he said, "But off with you—I shan't need you again tonight."

Jo hesitated and he smiled and made a shooing gestured that opened his robe a little more.

She swallowed and bowed. "Good night, sir. And thank you for the game."

"You're welcome. Good night."

Jo felt his eyes on her as she walked toward one of the two doors that separated their beds.

Chapter Twenty-Nine

After that evening, Mr. Smith didn't come home before two in the morning for a week. The only times Jo saw him were the mornings.

"Don't wait up for me this week," he'd told her two days after their chess game. "I don't know when I'll return."

"It's my pleasure to wait, sir."

Smith's eyes had narrowed slightly. His expression didn't change, but she would have sworn there was a coolness emanating from him.

Jo hastily bowed her head. "As you wish, sir."

There had been five more nights without seeing him at night and in the mornings, he'd been distracted and had not chatted.

Just when Jo had begun to accept this new, unwanted, distance between them—by reminding herself that she was his bloody servant, not his lover—he announced one morning that he would be home early that night. And then again the next night, and the next.

He had come home before ten o'clock every night for two weeks.

Every night they played a game before going to bed.

Every night he asked a handful of questions about her. Not always personal, sometimes just her opinion.

And every night it became harder and harder to fall asleep in her bed—her body aroused, her mind stimulated by the enigma in the next room.

He encouraged her to ask him questions, but the few times she found an opportunity, he either deflected the questions with something amusing that made her forget, or his answers were so vague as to be non-answers.

Somewhere around the eighth night, Jo realized that he was courting her.

Not with flowers and jewels, but with companionship. And not just any companionship, but company so charged with sexual tension that her body was primed to come by the time she dropped into her lonely bed.

She knew how much of her mind Mr. Smith had come to occupy, and it scared the hell out of her. Was she falling in love again—*already*? When she'd not even fallen out of love from the first time?

Or was she in love with two men?

Because if her waking hours belonged to Mr. Smith, when Jo closed her eyes, it was always Mr. Chatham she saw in her dreams. Even now, when her days were spent eagerly awaiting her master's return, she could not rid herself of Mr. Chatham's specter.

***

Mr. Smith was telling her an amusing anecdote about an acquaintance of his who kept a pet magpie.

"You can't set anything down in his house—even for a minute—and be guaranteed to find it." Apparently, the bird had stolen a pair of his reading glasses he'd set down while stepping away for a moment.

Jo couldn't help smiling as she unbuttoned his shirt, and then removed his cufflinks—elegant jet set in silver—and put them in his tray.

"Well, I'm glad you're amused. I daresay you wouldn't be so jolly if it had been your spectacles," Mr. Smith said as he slipped out of his shirt.

Jo grinned. "I'd willingly hand them over to any magpie strong enough to fly off with my glasses—I'd be afraid not to."

She knelt to remove his shoes and stockings.

"*Are* they heavy?" he asked.

Jo looked up. "Very."

"Might I see them?"

Jo didn't hesitate to do as he asked, but that didn't mean her hands weren't trembling slightly as she took them off and handed them to him.

He whistled as he hefted them up and down in his hand, as if weighing them, and then looked from the spectacles to Jo. "Good Lord. Don't you get a headache?" he leaned forward in his chair, squinting at her. "You've got a line from where they rest." He lightly touched the high bridge of her nose and they both stilled, their eyes locked.

And for just a second, he let her see into his eyes—beyond the heavy veil: he wanted her—fiercely.

Her sex, which had been swollen and wet for him half an hour before he'd come home, clenched so hard she barely captured the soft grunt that almost slipped from her lips.

Jo dropped her head and slowly removed his second shoe and both stockings.

"Jo?"

Her head whipped up before she realized what he'd called her.

He cocked his head in the charming way he had, as if he were cutting through the vapid social pleasantries to get to know her better. "You know I want you."

"Yes." The word was hoarse and Jo wondered if he heard the amazement beneath it. She swallowed, her breathing so ragged she worried she'd not be able to get the words out. "I want you."

The nostrils of his prominent, hooked nose flared, as did his pupils and she wanted to push his thighs wide and suck him until he screamed her name. But she couldn't do that with yet another man who didn't know the truth.

"Sir?"

He leaned toward her. "Yes?"

She had to say it. For weeks it had eaten at her—she couldn't go through this again. "I'm a woman," she blurted.

He cocked his head. "Are you?"

Jo gaped. "You knew?"

"I know everything that goes on in my house."

Jo felt weak with relief that he'd known all along. Still, she had to tell him. "I'm not a female in a way that is normal."

He made a moue of distaste. "Normal. What a tedious, flat, uninteresting word." He held out his hand and Jo took it and he brought her to her feet as he stood.

When his mouth slanted over hers, her hands did what they'd been wanting to do for weeks and slid around his smooth, muscular torso. He groaned and pulled her against him, his arm like an iron strap around her waist.

His mouth was silken and tasted like liquor and smoke from his strangely fragrant cigars. His kisses were as firm and hot and powerful as he was.

Jo was starved from spending evening after evening with him but never touching him. She had no time for finesse, sucking his tongue into her mouth, and then suggestively massaging it with her lips.

He chuckled—or as much as a man can chuckle with his tongue being sucked. He was the one who broke contact and stepped back, leaving her opened mouthed and breathless.

"Your clothes," her master said. "I want to take them off."

Jo's fingers went to her buttons, but one side of his mouth pulled up into a slight, sensual smile as his hands covered hers and gently but firmly moved them away.

"*I* want to take them off. You can finish undressing me."

Jo looked at that part of him that drew her eyes like a magnet, moisture flooding her mouth at the sight of his arousal. Her fingers made short work of the seven buttons and she slid her hands between the soft wool and his fine muslin drawers to push them down.

His cheeks beneath her hands were tight muscular globes that she couldn't resist squeezing.

He gave a breathless laugh. "You're still dressed; I'm falling behind."

"I had the advantage," Jo said, her voice just as breathy as her fingers tugged the drawstring of his drawers. She filled her hand with hot, silky skin.

"Good Lord!" he hissed, "You've got powerful hands—that feels delicious."

Jo smirked to herself. He didn't know the half of it.

He stepped back and she realized his hands had been working the entire time.

"How's that for efficiency? I unbuttoned coat, vest, *and* shirt. You can shrug out of them all at once." He looked so pleased with himself that Jo gave a low laugh.

"Mmmm," he said leaning forward to give her a hard kiss. "I like the sound of that—I'm going to make it my new hobby to have you laugh more." His pushed all three of her garments off her shoulders together but got no further than her elbows.

He stood back to look at her, his pupils flaring as he lifted his hands, palm out and gently swirled them over her hard nipples.

Jo's body shuddered at the way his palms rubbed the fine muslin of her undershirt against the sensitive flesh. He leaned down and sucked her nipple through the material and Jo moaned, her back arching to push her breast closer. Her hands twitched to touch him but her arms were trapped within her clothing.

"Er, Mr. Smith—" she began

He laughed softly on her aching, erect nipple. "Just Smith when we're fucking, darling."

She jolted at the vulgar word, the first she'd heard him speak.

"You liked that, didn't you," he whispered into her breast, and then tried to suck all of her into his mouth.

Jo didn't deny it. "I'm trapped in my coats."

"I know. Clever of me, wasn't it?" He nipped the tender pebble and she gasped. He backed her toward his massive bed, his eyes devouring her.

"I've thought about you every damned night since you've been here. Just on the other side of my door." He pulled her undershirt out of her trousers and slid his hands up her belly to her chest, shoving up her shirt. And then he took her naked breast in his mouth and Jo bit her lip to keep from crying out.

She wanted to touch him so bad—his velvety almost hairless skin, the hard bulge of his biceps and the taut muscles of his hip

"Please, Smith," she begged as she shuddered against his mouth. "I need to touch you."

His lips curled against her nipple. "You'll need to convince me with something quite spectacular to talk me out of my current position of power." He grazed her breast with his teeth and she whimpered as he slid a hand down the front of her trousers, beneath the waistband, and then stopped on her mound, groaning. "Oh, God, I love a shaved cunt," he whispered into her breast before dropping into a crouch and grabbing both sides of her placket and then *ripping* her trousers right down the middle.

Jo gasped. "Oh, no, but—"

"Hush," he muttered, yanking the string that held up her drawers. "I'll buy you another dozen pairs. Good Lord your body is beautiful."

He dropped to his haunches and spread her lower lips with his thumbs and plunged his tongue into her, his moan vibrating through her body.

He ate her like a man dying of hunger, his tongue thrusting into her over and over while he fingered her to orgasm with shocking ease. When she was shaking and whimpering he slid his hands around her naked arse and then stood, tossing her up onto his bed, yanking off first one wadded-up sleeve and then the other, freeing her arms, before pulling off her shoes and ruined trousers and flinging them behind him.

"Stockings stay on while I fuck you, I think," he said, panting as he knelt between her spread thighs, staring down at her with black eyes that were heavy with need. "This is an emergency, darling, and I'm going to ejaculate with shocking haste. But the next time will be up to my usual standards."

Jo laughed breathlessly and spread wide for him as he placed his beautiful cock at her soaking entrance and slammed into her, pulling her tight to his body as he entered. He held her full for a moment, his eyes locked with hers, his chest rising and falling as if he were being chased.

"How do you want it? Hard, hard, *or hard?*" he asked.

Jo couldn't help laughing. "What was that third one agai—"

He began to fuck her with furious, violent thrusts, his teeth gritted and his jaw clenched as he pounded into her, angling his hips for the deepest penetration. He worked her so savagely she knew there would be bruises.

"Coming now," he grated, and then pulled out, grabbing his cock and pumping it, jetting onto her belly in hot splashes. He made sure to cover every part of her exposed torso. The action was filthy and wonderful and he was beautiful and wild—almost crazed, his eyes never leaving hers as he marked her with his seed.

He was right about making it up to her—not later, but sooner. Jo had never been with such an enthusiastic, demanding lover. He was hard all the time—and he was almost forty-five. What must he have been like at twenty? It was terrifying to contemplate.

He was insatiable that night, taking each of her holes—as if claiming them, claiming *her*. Jo adored each and every savage thrust and splash of hot seed.

But when her head fell back against her own pillow and she closed her eyes, after hours of intense pleasure, the man she saw in her mind's eye was still Stephen.

Chapter Thirty

The third month without Leather was even worse than the first two. Perhaps because it had finally sunk into his thick skull that she really wasn't coming back.

Leather was gone but the hole she'd left in Stephen's life just grew bigger every day.

He'd stayed away from Smith except to see him at their weekly meetings. Even those had become tense and he knew that was down to him. Smith was as pleasant and suave and witty as ever—at least on the surface. Stephen had never been good at being any of those three things, even on a good day, and he could barely force a civil word out now, when there *were* no good days to be had.

Edward and Gideon were aware of the tension, but neither said anything to him about it.

As for Smith? Well, who knew what the hell the man thought? But Stephen knew one thing: what he was doing with Leather was no game to thwart or tease Stephen. The man was in deadly earnest about his new valet: he wanted her, *badly*.

Stephen couldn't allow his mind to travel down that path—not without eventually hurting somebody.

As for Leather? Stephen hadn't seen her since the day she left. Now that he knew Leather went to Bernina's he avoided the place—no matter how very tempting it was to go on the first Monday just to catch a glimpse of her.

But although he'd not *seen* his ex-valet, he knew that whatever else Leather was doing these days, she was treating Smith exceptionally well.

It enraged him to the point of violence every time he saw Smith's sleek, well-tended body, knowing full well who was dressing him, keeping his hair and nails perfect, shaving and bathing and *massaging* him.

"Christ." Stephen dropped his forehead onto his desk. He simply couldn't bear to think about that—Leather's skilled throat and lips around Smith's—

He shuddered. No.

There was a knock on the door and he pushed himself up slowly, groaning. "Come."

He was sore, so bloody sore. He'd even gone to a bathhouse, but the one he'd ended up in was a whorehouse pretending to offer massages.

It was his butler. "Mr. Dawkins is here to see you, sir."

Stephen sat up straighter, his heart galloping; it was about bloody time. "Send him in immediately."

It was only two in the afternoon, but Stephen needed *something* to calm down, so he poured himself a Scotch whiskey, which he'd developed a liking for in Glasgow.

"Want one?" he asked Dawkins when he entered, lifting his glass.

"Er, no thank you, sir." Dawkins was a lumbering man but got the best results of any detective he'd ever had on his payroll.

"I'm sorry I was gone so long, sir."

"Have a seat," Stephen said, dropping heavily into his and then grimacing at the pain in his neck and shoulder.

Dawkins removed his notepad from his coat pocket, knowing how Stephen despised small talk.

"I wasn't in the village of Tarland the whole time, sir. I followed a lead I found to the cottage that belongs to Mr. Joseph Leather and spent five days in a place called Boddam. Back of beyond," he muttered, still turning pages. "Ah, yes, here it is."

He took a deep breath. "All right, first things first. His Grace of Tarland was unexpectedly at his castle when I got there." He looked up. "That meant tongues were battened down. That said, the duke was thrilled to meet with any representative of Stephen Chatham. I think the pennies must be tight because he was amenable to having men come and mine his dining room table if they thought it was likely to yield coal." He shook his head, a bitter twist of amusement on his face. "How a man can be so foolish as to believe there was coal up there, I'll never know."

Stephen knew how Tarland could believe it: desperation. The young duke was deeply below the hatches. Not only that, but the ducal seat wasn't entailed and the man had borrowed heavily against it. He was such a reckless gambler there should be a new word for him. He'd dissipated a sizeable fortune in the seven years he'd held the title.

"He's willing to meet with you when he comes to London next month."

Stephen's eyebrows shot up. "Don't tell me he's one of the representative peers?"

Dawkins chuckled. "No, he's not. But they're Scots, you know—clannish. They treat coming to London like riding to hounds and they all follow the sixteen representatives. He's quite hot to discuss the possibility of a lease and investment opportunities."

"All right, what else?"

Dawkins flipped a few pages. "Not much else on His Grace. He's not married although he certainly has a raft of children. He's been scattering bastards since he was fourteen. The old duke took care of them when he was around, but now there's grumbling. Tarland just takes what he wants and leaves bairns with nobody to pay for them—this is according to a few townsfolk. Couldn't get anything out of anyone who actually relies on the duke for a living. "

He cleared his throat. "As to my visit to the village of Boddam. Well, the old duke certainly found a spot that's dropped off the edge of the world. A number of people recall a woman coming to stay at Cairn Cottage—named for its proximity to a cairn. Nobody recalls the woman coming into town—they say she kept to herself. I thought I'd hit a dead end when one of the locals I was lubricating at the town's one pub, mentioned something about a doctor having visited the cottage. Apparently, the quack had gotten lost in town and this bloke remembered." He snorted. "A stranger is big doings in a village like Boddam. The man didn't recall a name or where the doctor came from, but he reckoned Peterhead—the largest village in that area—to be my best bet. To cut a long story short, the doctor that visited Cairn Cottage almost ten years ago when Joseph Leather stayed there is now dead."

Stephen sighed.

Dawkins reached into the battered old bag and extracted a slim brown paper wrapped packet. "*However*, the young doctor who took over his practice is struggling and was willing to trade an old file that nobody ever asked about for a few bob." He stood and handed it to Stephen.

Stephen turned it over and saw a faded blob of sealing wax over the string that tied the folder shut. He looked up.

"It was sealed when the young doctor found it—I know that because I was looking through a crate of folders right beside him. He wanted to open it, but I paid double to take it the way it is. I figured anything the old doctor had gone to the trouble of sealing like that must be important. Or private. Or both."

"That was the right thing to do, Dawkins." The name on the front of the faded paper was Jonathan Leather.

"So, that's what I got, sir."

Stephen looked up and remembered it was customary to smile when pleased. He did so and Dawkins almost fell off his chair.

"You did well," Stephen said, flabbergasting him even more. "Now, I'd like you to get a plan together for His Grace when he visits—something convincing enough to make him so eager he'll want to invest immediately. Hire whoever you need and buy whatever it takes, just make sure that when Tarland arrives in town I have a suitably irresistible business proposition to make him." He gave Dawkins a hard look, wondering if the man knew what he meant.

"You want something that will leave him in the poorhouse," Dawkins said, a little green around the gills at the thought of bringing down a duke. But the man nodded, smart enough to know where the power lay in this exchange.

"I might not exercise that option, but I want it ready and waiting."

"Yes, sir." Dawkins hefted his bulk to his feet. "I'll keep you abreast as it develops."

Stephen waited until the door had shut behind Dawkins before turning back to the sealed packet that bore a dead man's name.

He stood and poured himself a second drink. This would require a very great deal of thought before he broke that seal.

Chapter Thirty-One

Jo woke in utter darkness, a body crouched over top of hers, breath hot on her neck.

"I want to fuck your ass," Smith hissed in her ear, his hard, slick cock pressed between her cheeks.

Jo grinned into the darkness and spread her thighs, canting her hips in welcome.

He chuckled smugly and slid his hands beneath her hips, jerking her up onto her knees.

"Did you miss me?" he asked as he slid a hand between her thighs, two fingers penetrating her entrance while a third flicked her clitoris— or what he affectionately called her *clit*.

"Yes, Smith. I missed you." She moaned as he slowly, deeply, fucked her.

"Did you touch yourself?" he asked, his hand pausing.

"No."

He grunted, his slippery fingers sliding out of her and then pressing into her back entrance, his thumb testing the tight ring of muscle gently, but firmly. "I thought of you while I got my cock sucked at a brothel Banks dragged me to."

Jo felt a mild twinge of jealousy, but only enough to be pleasurable; it was nothing like the searing burning torments that had almost ripped her in two when Smith casually mentioned seeing Chatham at the Birch Palace a week ago. Her body clenched in mute fury at the thought of him with another.

"Mmm, that's nice," Smith murmured as she tightened around him, making her feel ashamed that she was thinking of another man when he was so primed for her.

"Was it good, sir?" she asked, turning her thoughts to the arousing image of Smith getting orally pleasured by some muscular, likely beautiful, young man.

"His mouth was nothing like yours, Jojo." He pushed his thumb into her slick hole, breaching her slowly. "I dreamed about your mouth," he murmured, "your hot cunt, your tight little rose." He pulled out and then pushed back in. "I couldn't decide which of your holes I should fuck first." He paused. "So I asked John Coachman which part of your body he thought about the most."

Smith chuckled when she bucked and thrust back against him, aroused as much by his filthy words as his invading thumb, which was rhythmically preparing her.

Smith had a gorgeous body, a perfectly shaped cock, and a mouth that brought her to orgasm faster than any lover she'd ever enjoyed, male *or* female. But it was his ribald, titillating, and crude language she loved the best. Although his body and skills tied for a close second.

He pulled his thumb out and she felt cool oil dribbling between her cheeks.

"God, I wish I could see you," he muttered. Rubbing the oil into her with the head of his cock. "I almost broke my bloody foot coming in here in the dark. I want you to sleep in my bedroom from now on when I'm gone," he said, pulling her hips up more, while sliding one oily hand down her back and pushing her head and shoulders low, the resulting position one of delicious supplication. "And leave a light on, so I can find you easily and slide right inside you."

Jo groaned with pleasure as he massaged her back hole with his cock.

He gave her buttock a stinging slap. "What did you say?"

She jolted and smiled. "Yes, Smith."

He made a noise of satisfaction and rubbed his crown against her entrance. "Push sweetheart, I'm coming in."

He entered her slowly, sucking in a noisy breath as he breached the tight muscle and then paused, letting her stretch to accommodate his girth. "I can't wait to pump you full of my hot spend," he said roughly, his hips beginning to rock back and forth. "Do you want it?

She wiggled her bottom, pushing against him. "More, Smith. All of it."

"Greedy bitch," he said, slapping her other cheek hard enough to bring tears to her eyes.

He fucked her slowly and deeply, taking care not to tear or hurt her.

They'd been sharing a bed—or a floor or the table or the wall—for three weeks, and she'd learned that Smith—and that really *was* the only name he went by—was a generous but extremely demanding lover.

He didn't seem to need much sleep and often kept her up talking after they'd already had sex two or three times.

He'd told her, that first night, that he needed to know *exactly* what she wanted, all the way down to what she liked being called and who she was. Not in her dreams had Jo ever imagined a lover being so receptive or that she would have any choice in such matters.

"You don't have to choose, Jo. You can be either, both, or something else entirely with me."

He often seemed to understand her better than *she* did. Jo had told him she needed to give his questions some thought.

But on the subject of how she wanted to go on with him, she knew exactly what she wanted. "If I warm your bed, do you want another valet, sir?" she'd asked, half-afraid of his answer.

"You're the valet I want, Jojo. But just because I'm fucking you doesn't mean you can skimp when it comes to polishing my boots."

She'd opened her mouth to protest when she'd noticed he was grinning.

"You're the perfect valet and serve needs I never even knew I had," he'd murmured against her throat, before biting her hard enough to leave a mark and making her squeal in the process. "I'd like to eat you," he'd murmured. "Then I could keep you inside me."

"Not for long," she'd pointed out, her vulgar comment making them both laugh like children.

Jo adored him, but she didn't love him. She had no idea what he felt for her. All these nights together and the only things she knew about him were what he liked in bed. Otherwise, he was a blank slate. He was a ferocious, uninhibited lover, but polite and unknowable and charming outside the bedroom.

"Jo! Your mind is wandering," he grated, not pausing his violent fucking.

Jo focused her attention where it belonged and pressed against him.

"I'm close now, Jojo," he said, his voice raw with barely restrained need.

Jo pushed her arse up maybe another inch higher and then tightened her inner muscles around him.

"Jojo!" he yelled and then slammed into her so hard they both fell forward on the bed, his slick torso tight against her back. He didn't pause for a second, his powerful hips drumming and pounding before he thrust one last time and his body stiffened, his cock rippling as he filled her with warmth.

"Jojo," he whispered as he jerked inside her, his movements weaker each time, until his muscles relaxed completely and sighed, "my Jojo."

Jo's heart clenched at the contentment in his words and tears slid down her cheeks as he slept, still inside her.

***

Smith was sitting in his study, working through a series of mechanical drawings Gideon had sent from his country house—the Earl of Taunton's ancestral estate—where Smith was supposed to be joining his partners soon for a small country house party.

He closed the folder after assessing the last of the schematics. He wasn't an engineer—he'd never even had a basic mathematics course in his life—but he could follow the logic of Gideon's clear, almost beautiful, renderings of his mind's eye. Gideon Banks, now the Earl of Taunton, was a train wreck of a man when it came to emotional and personal matters, but his mind, when it came to engineering, was one of the most meticulous and rigidly disciplined Smith had ever had the pleasure to work with.

He sat back in his chair and stared unseeingly at the opposite wall— a wall he usually enjoyed because it held one of Nora Fanshawe's paintings.

Smith didn't have friends—he had business partners he liked to keep happy and healthy so they made more money and—by extension—made *him* more money.

But the closest person he *had* to a friend was Nora. Smith wasn't sure how it happened, but in the process of trying to fix a problem for Edward Fanshawe—a personal problem that had been jeopardizing the business syndicate that brought them all so much money—he'd somehow gotten to know the woman who'd been driving Edward crazy.

Nora had been a whore at a brothel called Tosca's the first time Smith met her.

He'd gone to Nora one night mainly to drive poor Edward crazier. But he'd enjoyed the sex as well as the conversation. So much so that he began putting himself in positions where he might get opportunities to know her better. While he'd never fucked her again after that night, he'd developed an unusually close relationship with her. So, yes, perhaps she *was* a friend.

Now that she was Edward's wife, they didn't see each other as often as when she'd been on her own.

He was looking forward to seeing both Nora and Edward at Gideon's new country home, Foxrun.

Chatham would be there, too.

Smith knew he had to go to Gideon's home, but the question was, did he take Leather with him, or leave him here?

The burn he felt in his belly told him how the primitive part of his mind—still the greater part, despite all his years trying to civilize it— viewed taking his valet to a place where she would see the man she'd been in love with—and perhaps still loved.

Smith knew beyond a doubt that Chatham's feelings—maybe love, maybe obsession—had only become stronger in the months since Leather had left his service. Chatham hated Smith so much he could barely look at him at the weekly meetings. Smith knew the other man could scent his happiness and would easily guess the cause. After all, he'd once been fortunate enough to possess without effort what Smith fought tooth and claw to have: Leather's regard and attention.

Smith had no idea whether his extremely reserved and complex lover still loved Chatham. He'd probed Leather's mind as often and as deeply as he'd probed her body these past weeks, and he still knew so little about her.

But at least he now knew how she viewed herself. "I don't care what you call me—Joseph or Josephine. I'm both and neither at the same time, so use whichever words you please. But I want you to *treat* me like a man, Smith. Both in bed and out of it. I'm not a piece of spun glass. I like—well—"

"You like it rough," Smith said.

She'd blushed furiously and nodded.

Smith had become so bloody hard at her declaration that he'd treated her like a man right then and there, against the door to his bedchamber.

He called her Jojo, his own name for this person who was so much more than the sum of her parts. He adored her naked female body but he also lusted for the suited and booted man who dressed and tended his body so sedulously while viewing him dispassionately through lenses that obscured more than they clarified—at least for Smith.

The only other lover who'd captivated him even a fraction as much was Charles.

But Jojo was something more than Charles. Smith wasn't sure he wanted to experience what was happening; especially as he had no idea what Leather wanted or felt.

Charles had *always* made his feelings—his *love*—for Smith open and apparent. Of course, that had been part of the problem—ultimately *the* problem. Smith simply didn't do love—or at least if he did it never lasted for long. But he did obsession, and he did it quite well.

And he'd never been obsessed by anyone more than he was with Joseph Leather.

He chuckled softly. What a bloody fool he was—and also a coward to be afraid to take her to a place where Leather would see her former employer and lover.

Smith got up and poured himself a whiskey. He took a sip and went to stand in front of Nora's painting. It was a portrait of him—a gift she'd surprised him with. Unlike the nude in his bedroom—the one with Charles—he could display this in a public area.

Smith found the portrait remarkably powerful, but it always left him uneasy. The man Nora had captured was indisputably not English—or not entirely—although his ethnicity would be difficult to pinpoint. Was he an Arab? Greek? Or perhaps even Rom?

His smile was pleasant, the curve of his lips subtle. But there was something about the man's eyes that left the viewer unsettled—some intensity or even dangerous glint. It bothered Smith that she saw that in him because it meant others—people he did not like as he did Nora—

might also see the same thing. He took great pains to portray himself as an urbane, intelligent, and civilized man of business.

This portrait held a man in a business suit, but the veneer of civility was a thin patina that had worn off in places. And beneath was . . . Well, beneath was Smith. The real Smith.

He turned away from himself and threw back his drink.

There was a knock on the door just as he laid his hand on the handle so he opened it.

"Oh!" Donovan startled.

"You were looking for me?"

"Yes, sir, Mr. Chatham is here to see you."

Smith blinked. It was as if he'd summoned the man just thinking of him.

"Of course," he said to the waiting servant, his public smile already in place. "Show him in."

Chapter Thirty-Two

"Ah, Stephen, what a pleasant surprise," Smith said, standing behind his unnaturally bare desk.

The hair prickled on the back of Stephen's neck as he entered Smith's black study, which somehow made him feel like a fly entering a spider's web.

Stephen dismissed the uncharacteristically whimsical thought and nodded. "Thank you for seeing me on such short notice."

"We should never stand on such ceremony, Stephen. Would you like a drink?"

"No."

Smith smiled, as if amused by his abrupt answer. "Very well, I shall abstain, also." He sat. "What can I do for you?"

"I want to know what your intentions are with Leather."

Smith's smile grew and he stood. "Perhaps I'll have that drink after all. Are you sure you won't change your mind?"

"Can't you just answer me for once without playing any of your f-f-f-*fucking* word games," he retorted, *infuriated* at himself.

Smith was still smiling, but it had shifted; it was now the smile of a poisonous snake: a snake that was willing to kill to protect what was his.

"Jesus!" Stephen blurted. "You're in l-love w-with her!" He surged out of his chair toward the desk, propelled by fury as he slammed his hands down on the smooth, cool surface and leaned toward the man behind it. "Confess it."

Smith, for all that he was half a foot shorter and at least three stone lighter, pushed right up into his face. "You have chosen the wrong man to bully, Stephen." His words were cool, low, and even had a spark of humor in them.

Stephen swallowed as he stared down at the much smaller man, whose pupils were mere pinpricks.

But then Smith's lips suddenly curled at the corners and the dangerous predator that had briefly inhabited his eyes was gone. "Come. Let's handle this like the businessmen we are. I'm pouring us both a drink. You can drink it, or not." He turned and strode without haste toward his decanters.

Stephen had to blink to clear the haze of red from his eyes and swallow down the hatred and fear and self-loathing; he was behaving like a stammering lunatic. He needed to regain control of himself because God knew he had no control over anyone else in this situation.

Whatever was between Smith and Leather, Smith would die before disclosing it. And Leather? Well, Stephen had lost the right to ask her *anything* the day he'd hurled such hideous accusations at her and then tossed her onto the street.

Stephen dropped into his chair and wordlessly took the glass when Smith handed it to him. "You were right about Tarland," he said.

Smith nodded, not smugly, but grimly. "I know."

Stephen put down the glass, untouched. "You do?"

"Yes, the man's reputation is that of an inveterate gambler and rapist." He took a sip and gave Stephen a hard look. "Leather would never voluntarily service such a man. Nor would he stoop to blackmail."

Stephen's pulse pounded at the words, "Leather" and "service." But he swallowed several times before nodding.

"I was foolish to think otherwise," he said, his face darkening at the admission—an admission he wanted to give to Leather but was too much of a coward to face her.

"Do you know what really happened?" he asked Smith.

Smith hesitated for only a second, but then shook his head. "No. I sent someone, twice. But I came up with nothing."

Stephen reached into his satchel and took out the brown packet. "I have the truth in here."

Smith sat forward and put down his glass, his gaze on the packet.

"I'll show it to you, but I want two assurances first."

"Fine, you have my word." He spoke without hesitation.

"That's not enough."

Smith barked a laugh. "You must be the most awkward, offensive bastard I know, Chatham."

Stephen shrugged. "I know you lie without even realizing it, Smith. I want you to swear on something you value. Swear on your regard for Leather that you'll abide by what I ask."

Smith's eyes narrowed dangerously—hell, *more* dangerously—but he nodded. "Very well."

Stephen tossed the packet onto Smith's desk. "Read this and then I'll tell you what I want from you."

Stephen stood, unable to sit still while he thought about what the other man was reading. He went to stare at one of the paintings, a portrait of Smith he'd noticed the only other time he'd been here. He recognized Nora Fanshawe's work, although he owned none of it.

He found her paintings powerful but wouldn't want to be the subject of one. She had an eye like a physician's knife and tended to expose her subject on the canvas. This portrait was no exception. The man in the painting was taut—almost brittle. It was a remarkable picture—an attractive, urbane façade that was barely holding at the seams. The predatory eyes were those of a wolf or a shark or some other beautiful but lethal creature.

Smith was . . . well, he made Stephen feel as innocent and fresh as a toddler by comparison. Whoever the man really was, Stephen had no desire to find out. Nor did he want to get any closer to him than he already was.

"Chatham." The voice was so soft he almost didn't hear it. When he turned, it was the wolf that waited for him. "Tell me your conditions."

"First, you don't kill him."

Smith urbane façade disintegrated and Stephen recoiled at what was behind the mask. "You're making a grave mistake, Stephen."

"You gave your word."

Smith's chest rose and fell, the sound of his harsh breathing filling the room. "And you still have it," he said, his voice so quiet that Stephen could barely make out the words. "What's the other condition?"

Stephen smiled and it was Smith's turn to recoil. "I need your help to bring him down. And if we do it the right way, Tarland will see to his own destruction."

Chapter Thirty-Three

*S*mith had been behaving oddly all week long—even for Smith. He'd taken Jo several times every night and while that wasn't out of the ordinary, there'd been an odd sense of . . . *urgency* in his lovemaking.

Jo wanted to ask him if something was wrong, but she was in the middle of dressing him and never mixed what they did at night with her valeting. She would ask him tonight if there was something amiss.

"Are you leaving after breakfast?" Smith asked as she knelt to hook the buttons on his boots. She looked up frowning.

"It's your Monday," he reminded her with his slight smile.

"Oh." She frowned, her mind spinning. She'd not gone to Bernina's the last time because Smith had surprised her with a suite at the Clarendon and a rather lovely young man he'd discovered at Tosca's. It had been a very memorable evening.

"I need to pay a visit on one of our prospective investors," he said, standing when she'd finished, making a minute adjustment to his tie in the mirror. "So, you might as well go out and enjoy yourself." He gave her a warm look in the mirror. "Try to think of me a little while you're engaging in pleasure."

Jo's lips twitched. "Thank you, sir. I shall do so."

Smith spun abruptly and caught her shoulders before putting one strong hand beneath her chin and holding her face steady. "I shall miss you," he said quietly, and then he kissed her hard and quick, turning away before she could respond, striding toward the door.

Yes, Smith was a mysterious, unreadable man.

Jo set about cleaning his chambers and changing his bedding. Malcolm would valet him while Jo was gone. Jo knew the younger man adored those rare opportunities and envied Jo both her job and her place in the master's bed.

She dismissed the slight twinge of jealousy she experienced at the thought of Malcolm seeing her lover's naked body. Smith did not belong to her any more than she belonged to him—as his suggestion for this evening clearly demonstrated.

As she went to her chambers and put a few items into her satchel she thought about that. It was true that it had surprised her that he'd suggested Bernina's, but perhaps he felt she was in need of reminding. He was likely right. The truth was, the more time she spent with him, the more she suspected it would be easy to fall in love with him. Although her feelings for Mr. Chatham had never diminished, she'd begun to realize she would simply need to wall off a chamber of her heart for him and set about finding a new occupant for the rest. Not that Smith had indicated he wanted to occupy such a position.

Once Jo was hatted and coated and gloved she took a last look at Mr. Smith's chambers to make sure everything was perfect in case he returned unexpectedly.

Mr. Smith had left instructions that a carriage was to be put at her disposal and Jo smiled at his thoughtfulness.

"Thank you," she said to John Coachman, a darkly handsome man who cut her a stimulatingly subtle but lascivious look. "I'm going to Bernina's."

He grinned, his teeth a white flash between full lips. "Lucky Bernina's," he muttered as Jo climbed into the carriage.

Jo relaxed and watched the day flicker past through the carriage window. She wasn't unhappy—she loved working for Mr. Smith and greatly enjoyed his household—but she wasn't exactly happy, either. Part of that was because Mr. Chatham always weighed heavily at the back of her mind, but that would lessen over time, wouldn't it? After all, it had only been a few months since she'd last seen him.

The other part of her unease was that her relationship with Smith, no matter how sexually and professionally fulfilling, did not have the feel of permanence to it. It had seemed to be heading in that direction, but he'd begun to pull away this past week and she suspected he was tiring of her. She'd expected that, of course. He'd never promised her anything and his servants had indicated he was a man whose affection did not remain fixed. Even Charles, who they seemed to believe Mr. Smith might have loved, had been with him barely a year.

The carriage slowed and Jo was ready to get out when it stopped. She was tired of being with her thoughts this morning.

"Thank you," she told the coachman.

"Enjoy yourself," he said before clucking his tongue and sending the team on its way.

Daniel opened the door as she got to the top step.

"Ah, Mr. Leather, welcome, nice to see you again."

"How have you been?" she asked, shrugging out of her coat.

"Excellent, thank you, sir. Madam Cecile is waiting for you in her study." He leaned close and whispered. "I believe she has something spe—"

"Mr. Leather, what a pleasure."

Jo turned to find Cecile at the top of the stairs, attired in one of the spectacular dressing gowns she favored, this one a frothy sea green that brought out the blue in her tilted eyes.

"Hello, darling," she enfolded Jo into a delicious smelling embrace. "It's been too long," she said, holding her at arm's length. "It seems I either miss our teas or you miss your Mondays."

Jo smiled. "I hope your family issues have been resolved."

Cecile laughed. "Never! They are endless." She walked past her study and smiled. "I'm sorry, my friend, but I'm afraid I had an appointment I couldn't get out of today. But I wanted to walk you to your room. I hope you don't mind, but I have something special for you."

"Oh. Well, thank you." Jo was a bit non-plussed. She'd hoped to choose her own entertainment. This time she was considering trying one of the men Smith came to see on occasion but she didn't want to seem ungrateful and reject Cecile's kindness.

Cecile gave her an odd smile. "I'm sorry, I know it was high-handed of me, but I—well, don't be mad at me." She leaned forward and kissed Jo on the forehead, the gesture oddly solemn, her words worrying.

"It's all right, Cecile. I'm sure I shall be delighted."

Cecile opened the door for her without another word and Jo went inside and then stopped, her mouth dropping open.

"Hello, Leather," Mr. Chatham said.

***

Stephen had heard about people having their hearts in their throats, but he'd not actually believed you could feel that way; he'd been wrong.

"Mr. Chatham," Leather said, her voice oddly breathy, but her expression the same impassive mask.

Stephen swallowed several times, but the obstruction was there to stay. He went toward her but stopped well shy of her, not wishing to *loom*. "I apologize for surprising you this way," he said, speaking slowly when all he wanted to do was pour everything out in a messy pile. "I'm afraid this was the best way I could come up with to speak to you. I promise I shall leave when I've said my piece."

"I don't understand, sir. What do you want?"

He heard the slight warble in her voice, which gave him hope; she wasn't untouched by him, no matter that her face was an impervious wall.

"I just want a chance to explain myself—and to apologize."

Her eyebrows rose slightly. "Very well. Would you like to sit?"

He was so weak with gratitude he almost collapsed at her feet. Indeed, he'd given that approach a great deal of thought and would use it if his first attempt failed.

"Thank you," he said, sitting in the biggest chair in the small seating area, drinking in the sight of her. She was so still, so self-contained, so familiar and yet such an enigma.

Stephen saw she was waiting. "This is not an easy thing to tell you. I shan't beat around the bush. I know what your half-brother—then Lord Staunton—did to you. I know the truth about what happened when you were eighteen."

Her body jolted, but her face remained expressionless.

Stephen handed her Doctor Willard's brief report.

She glanced at it and then up at him. "Where did you get this?"

"It was in a storage box."

"It's addressed to my father."

He nodded, his face heating. "Yes."

She laid the report on the side table. "Was that what you had to tell me—that you continued prying into my past and that you've stolen something private and meant for my father?" Her words were cool and even, but Stephen knew she was very, very angry.

"You're correct, I did pry. If you want to leave here now, I'll understand. I know you owe me nothing—quite the reverse—but I beg you to give me a chance to explain."

His impassive valet had fled and left in his place an angry stranger. "Go on," she ordered.

"It was Smith who gave me the idea of investigating the duke." She startled at the other man's name but said nothing. "He had the wisdom to know you would never do the thing I accused you of—he asked me what I knew about the man I'd accused you of blackmailing." His face was so bloody hot he wished it would just catch on fire and spare him this humiliating confession. But it was the least of what he owed her. "I decided to see who the Duke of Tarland was. I regret to say things were even worse than I expected." He didn't bother to keep the distaste from his voice. "You were not his only victim. He's—"

"I can guess what he's been doing. Are you here to tell me I should have spoken out—said something? And that maybe some of his victims would have been spared?"

Stephen was aghast. "Of course not. How could you—"

"What? How could I believe you would think such a thing of me?" Her brows descended and he saw a look of fury on her face that made him shiver. "You mean other than what you said to me the day you threw me out of your house?"

"I beg your pardon for that, although I will understand if you cannot give it."

Her jaw clenched tight and she stared at him from behind her thick, distorting lenses, which were like castle doors, keeping the real Leather safely locked behind them.

"What you said was—unjust, but the evidence was damning and you knew nothing about me other than I'd deceived you." She stood. "If that was what you came for—my forgiveness—you have it."

Stephen stood with her and took a step toward her. She glared up at him. "What do you want from me?" Her lip trembled and she bit down ruthlessly on it.

"I deeply regret what I said, Leather. I'd do anything I could to unsay it. But I cannot."

"I said I forgave you. Just forget it all. Why do you care about this?"

Well, here it was, the chance Smith had given him. "I care because I love you. I think I've loved you for quite some time but having never felt anything like it before it took me longer than I sh-should have to realize it."

Her lips parted and she reached out to steady herself on the chair. "Why are you doing this?" she whispered, her face pale, her hand shaking. "I've spent *months* trying to forget you."

He put his hand over hers and squeezed so hard she winced. "And have you? I will l-l-leave you be if you tell me you no longer care for me."

She snatched her hand away. "What do you want from me, Mr. Chatham?"

It wasn't the answer he wanted, but it was better than the *Go to hell* he deserved.

"I want *you*, anyway I can have you."

Her gaze went vague, as if she were hearing something other than his words.

"So," she said, her eyes refocusing, and fixing on Stephen. "You would be satisfied to have me as a lover if I remained Mr. Smith's valet?"

Just hearing her speak *his* name made his head buzz. Once again, he found himself swallowing repeatedly before he could speak. "You're correct," he forced the words through gritted teeth. "I couldn't . . . *bear* that. I know you are his lover and, well, I could not share you with him."

"I see. So you want to set me up as your mistress? Give me a nice—"

"No, for God's sake. I want to marry you, if you'll have me."

"You want to make me your wife?" She'd not raised her voice, but the question had a razor-sharp edge and he knew what it meant. Stephen had given this matter hours and hours and hours of thought.

"I would only want marriage if that was what you wanted."

She made a noise of irritation and took a step toward him—his gentle, quiet Leather menacing him. "What do *you* want, Mr. Chatham?"

"I want *you*."

She was breathing rapidly now, her eyes blinking behind their thick shields.

Stephen dared to reach out and take her hands. She flinched but didn't pull away. "I was terribly wrong and cruelly vicious to you. All I can say in my defense—and it's not much—is that the last woman I thought I loved," he gritted his teeth. "Louise," he forced himself to say. "We were to marry, but a few weeks before the wedding I discovered she was already married and that Loiuse and her husband had pulled their ploy more than once."

Her mouth formed a horrified O.

"I daresay most men would have gotten over such a thing in fourteen years, but I'm," he grimaced. "Well, I think you know me well enough to understand I'm not gregarious and it takes a tremendous effort to socialize. I took the route of less resistance and," he gestured to the place where they stood. "This was easier, safer." He hesitated and then said, "Will you sit with me for a moment and let me tell you about my past? I've violated your privacy so profoundly that I feel I owe you something of myself."

In answer, she walked to the settee—but she didn't release his hand.

They sat, side-by-side, and he prepared to tell her a story he'd never told another. "Do you recall I told you I grew up in an orphanage?"

"You said the people had been kind." Her face creased with apprehension. "Was that not true?"

He squeezed her hand lightly. "It was true. I wasn't a typical resident in the small institution. I'd been born to a well-off family in Leeds. My father was the youngest son of a baronet and was a successful barrister. I was the middle child out of five. My parents were . . . well, proud. Very proud. I was not a normal child—I developed later in areas like walking and speech. Indeed, I did not speak a word until I was five. When I did, I had a crippling stammer."

She made a sympathetic noise and squeezed his hands and Stephen couldn't help smiling.

"You will think I'm softening you up with my tale of woe," he jested.

"Tell me."

"I would get furious at not being able to speak and fall into rages. My parents were terrified of allowing me in public. For a while they engaged a sort of . . . well, a tutor/jailor. I lived almost separately with him, seeing my family rarely. He must have represented himself as a person skilled in eradicating stammers. His methods were," Stephen swallowed uncomfortably. "He was a cruel man. My parents eventually intervened when they discovered my shoulder had been dislocated. They took me to a physician who found the burns." He released her hand and opened his coat and vest before pulling up his shirt, exposing his side.

She bent closer and then gasped and covered her mouth. "Why, there are *dozens* of them." She looked at up at him. "I've noticed them, but I suppose I thought—" she broke off, "Good God. I never imagined—"

"It was a long time ago," he soothed.

"What *are* they?"

"He would light cigars and put them out on me whenever I stammered."

Tears ran down her cheeks.

"Shh, don't. Please," he begged, horrified that he'd made her cry.

She roughly scrubbed away the tears. "Go on, please."

"When my parents saw what he'd been doing they were furious—and guilty, I'm sure. Looking at me was a constant reminder of their failure, so they sent me to a series of places that were called different names, but they all offered the same thing: that they would make me normal. Their last resort was a special orphanage—a school for idiots."

Yet another tear slid down her cheek.

"Shhh," he whispered, gently stroking it away. "This story has a happy ending—at least for me."

She nodded, her lips pursed tightly.

"As I said before, the couple was kind. Many of the children were quite badly off—either mentally or physically crippled and unable to do for themselves. My problem seemed miniscule in comparison. I went there when I was ten—after four years of various attempts in other places. My parents must have been exhausted. They came to visit at first, but we brought no joy to each other and their last visit was on my eleventh birthday—when I still couldn't get a sentence out without butchering it. And becoming angry." He shrugged. "When I was twelve a young man came to teach—he didn't stay long, but he'd been a fellow sufferer. He taught me how to lessen the problem, perhaps even one day eradicate it if I worked hard enough."

She tilted her head. "How did you do it? Your speech is—well, impeccable."

"Hardly that," he said, his face heating. "But if I spoke slowly, I found I could control it. This was no overnight cure—I stammered well into my twenties. I was better each year, but for obvious reasons that kept me from meeting people, especially women."

"What happened to your family? Have you seen them?"

"No. I never went back. But I think something must have happened because the money stopped coming when I was fourteen. I could have stayed—a helper of sorts, as I was accustomed to working with the less fortunate students by then. But I wanted to get away, so I took a position in—"

"Some stables."

Stephen cocked his head and then smiled. "Ah yes, I told you about that, didn't I?" He took a deep breath and let it out. "There isn't much more to tell. I was good with figures and when I was seventeen I took a job at a manufactory in their counting house. I was there for ten years." He hesitated and then said. "It was Smith who first discovered me. The syndicate had purchased the company by then and I presented them with books that had proof of embezzlement. He and Edward Fanshawe took me on, and the rest is, as they say, history."

She was absently rubbing her thumb over his hand and he didn't want to move—to draw her attention and cause her to stop. So he kept babbling.

"I *love* you. I will understand if you don't want me. But you already have my heart, I would be honored if you took the rest of me."

She sniffed and brought both hands to her face, removing her spectacles and wiping her cheeks with her free hand before replacing them and turning back to him. "I still don't understand what you want."

"I want *you*. I want you to be my valet. And my lover. I don't know exactly how the hell we would wor-work such a thing, but I want you to mend my stockings, blacken my boots, and suck my cock. I want you to rub my body with those magical hands of yours and I want you to teach me to rub yours. I want you in my bed. I want to pleasure you with my fingers and tongue and fuck you until you scream my name. And then make you do it again. *Those* are a c-couple of the things I want."

She gave a breathless laugh but shook her head. "You don't understand—I can never marry you, Stephen. My birth certificate says Joseph Leather. And even if I could marry you—" she shook her head. "I wouldn't. I can't be the woman on your arm at dinners with your business associates. I can't be a mother to your children—" her voice broke on the last word, but she went on, "I don't *want* to be that person. I cannot be that person—it would never make me happy."

"I know that and can accept it. We could go on much as before—but with significant changes. I would settle an amount on you and make arrangements so that you never had to worry that—"

She laid a finger across his lips. "No. No settling of money. I'll be your valet. I'll press your shirts, clean your chambers, and suck your cock. I'll warm your bed and let you pleasure me. Those are the things I have to offer. Only that."

"*Only* that?" Stephen smiled and her eyes widened. "That is the world to me—all I want and more than I deserve. I'd be honored if you'd agree to be my valet."

Her lips twisted into a shaky smile, her tears falling freely now. "I accept. And I respectfully request that you get up off your knees as you're quite ruining those trousers, sir."

***

"I have a foolish question," Stephen said, his breathing still fast, the sweat cooling on his bare skin.

She turned to him, naked, no spectacles, and unmasked beside him. It was Leather, but it was Josephine, too.

Her full lips—still reddened from the vigorous work he'd just given them—curled up at the corners. "Yes?"

"What do you wish me to call you? Josephine? Joseph?"

She turned on her side and Stephen couldn't resist a quick journey with his eyes down her sleek body. He'd always believed a woman should have full breasts and shapely hips to be sexually appealing; he'd been monumentally wrong on that matter, as he'd been wrong in so many other ways when it came to this still very mysterious woman beside him.

"Call me Jo when we're together like this." Her cheeks darkened and her mouth pulled up slightly on one side in a way that sent blood rushing to his softening cock. "And Leather the rest of the time." She reached out and ran a warm, firm hand over his chest and he purred beneath her touch. "Has Charles been taking care of you? I noticed your right shoe was a bit worn in the instep."

Stephen threw back his head and laughed, and when he looked down, he found her staring, her lips parted and eyes wide.

He smiled—a bit sheepishly. "I know," he said, "I rarely laugh. Well, I'm hoping that will change." He slid a hand around her slender waist, his eyes holding hers as they laid side-by-side. "You're correct, I've been suffering terribly under Charles's ministrations—the man gives an awful massage."

A quick, thrilling look of possessiveness flickered across her beloved features.

Stephen knew he had to quit putting the moment off. "I need to tell you something, Jo."

Her body stiffened. "Yes?"

"It's about Tarland." She didn't move. "I—well, I wanted to make sure he couldn't do what he did to you, to anyone else."

"Is he dead? Did you—"

"No," Stephen quickly assured her, and then added as an afterthought. "At least not yet. I can't promise he won't put a period to himself." But Stephen bloody well wished he would. "I'm afraid he's in a bit of trouble."

"Stephen, what did you do?"

He couldn't help reveling in the sound of his name in her mouth for just a second. "I set up a business opportunity he couldn't resist." He hesitated, not wanting to mention Smith's name, but also not wanting to act as if all of this was his doing. "Smith helped me." She jolted slightly but said nothing. "Suffice it to say that Tarland jumped at an opportunity from two men known to offer high returns on investments. He did something that only a skilled businessman should ever do: he borrowed against everything he had and much he didn't, expecting profits to be bigger than the interest he would have to pay on his loans." He stopped, seeing from her expression that she understood.

She took a deep breath and Stephen appreciated the effect her action had on her slim ribcage and small, delicious breasts. "What will happen to the people who depend on him?"

Stephen suspected this would be her first concern and he gave her a gentle squeeze. "They will have more responsible masters—men who will see they are paid their salaries on time and that their daughters don't have to live in fear."

Her brow furrowed. "You?"

He nodded. "And Smith."

Her lips trembled and then stretched into a smile. "You're in possession of a ducal estate?"

Stephen heard the suppressed mirth in her voice. "What?" he demanded, mockingly indignant. "Are you saying I lack the ducal presence?"

She chuckled and he was embarrassingly pleased at having elicited such a reaction.

"So, you're not too angry with me? With us, for interfering?" he asked when it seemed she would say nothing.

"How could I be? You did it for me—both of you."

Stephen nodded, swallowing the burning jealousy that rose in his throat at having to share this moment—no matter how remotely—with a man she obviously cared for. But it was fair, and it was nothing compared to what Smith had done for him.

"You must have met him?"

Stephen looked up from his jealous thoughts to find her staring at him, pensive. He knew which *him* she meant.

"Yes."

Her lips twisted into a bitter smile. "And did you see a resemblance?" Stephen hesitated. "Oh, don't worry about offending me," she said, "I know we are very much alike."

"Only in appearance," Stephen said quietly. But she was right: it had been an eerie resemblance, much closer than between her and Benjamin.

"I was Her Grace's page the first time I saw him up close," she said, her expression vague and distant. "Lord Staunton." She snorted. "I'd heard the whispering—servants are terribly cruel—but I hadn't understood until we were face to face. Staunton was a year older and I know he couldn't understand any better than I did at the time, but he hated me fiercely—I could see it in his face." Jo pulled her eyes from the past and looked at him. "The person I really wonder about is the duchess. How do you think she could look at me day after day?"

"I don't know," Stephen said, honestly. "Was she cruel to you?"

"No, she treated me the same as any other servant, distantly. Staunton, however, took great pleasure in inflicting pain—boxing my ears and claiming I was slow to respond, or stupid, or insolent. My father whipped me numerous times because of Staunton's accusations."

Stephen's head heated and he reminded himself he'd already made Staunton pay. "And your real father? The duke?"

She shrugged, staring off into the distance. "I honestly believe he never remembered who we—Ben and I—were. By the time I was old enough to understand such things I know he had another woman—a girl, really. The very pretty daughter of one of the grooms. She gave him two children that I knew of. There were more besides."

"Christ," Stephen said, the word more explosive than he'd intended.

"It was something that was accepted—not only by my father." Stephen heard the defensiveness in her voice and knew the deceased Jonathan Leather, for all his many faults, was not somebody he could ever pass judgement on in front of his daughter. She loved her father fiercely, that much was clear.

Jo looked at him as if he'd spoken aloud. "My brother Ben has never forgiven our father for how he looked the other way. Ben never made that girl pregnant—the one he was dismissed for—that was Staunton."

Stephen nodded. "I'd assumed as much."

"It was true that Father did nothing to clear him, but he *did* go to His Grace." She shook her head. "Oh, if you only knew how difficult that was for him. He worshipped the duke," she cut him a sharp look. "It wasn't his fault; it had been *bred* into him by *his* father. My grandfather was an intimidating man, I remember him. I know my father never felt he was as good." Her jaw worked from side to side. "He gave His Grace everything."

Stephen had to bite back his fury at the sympathy she felt for a father whose only way of protecting her had warped her life—and even then, he'd not been able to save her from predation, had he?

"Staunton took whatever he wanted and it wasn't long before he decided he wanted me. He found out about me when he told me to strip because he was going to fuck my ass, just as he'd done my brother."

"Good God," Stephen breathed.

"Ben never said anything—he still doesn't believe I know, although he must suspect."

Stephen had to clench his jaws at that—it wasn't his place to point out what her brother *should* have done before allowing her to wander into that spider's nest.

"When Staunton discovered what I was, he beat me—badly." She stopped and set her hand on Stephen's chest, which he realized only then was rumbling: he was growling like an animal. "Shhh, Stephen. Do you want me to stop?"

"No. I want to hear it, Jo. I want to know."

"He beat me but then he took me." She cleared her throat, her hand trembling as she rubbed his shoulder. "He told me he was going to put a child into me, just as his father had into my mother."

"Christ!" Stephen couldn't help himself, he sat up and wrapped his arms around her, holding her trembling body tightly.

She clung to him, but she wasn't finished. "I didn't want to, but I had to ask Father for help. I had cracked ribs and I was badly torn and bleeding. I'd never seen his face like that before. He bandaged me and then he took me to see His Grace." She choked out a sound that was half sob and half laugh. *'Your son has raped your daughter,'* he said." She gulped nosily. "It was agreed I would go away someplace where I wasn't known, to wait and see."

She sat back and met his gaze. "What the doctor's letter did not say is that they never told me about the baby until after he'd gotten rid of it. An abomination, he told me when I woke after the procedure. He never told me to my face about what he'd done to make certain I never had children. My father confessed what he'd done in a letter just before he died. I'd suspected as much, but it hardly mattered as I had no plans in that direction." She snorted softly. "How could I?"

Stephen didn't trust himself to speak.

"The duke wanted me to stay in that cottage—to live out my life there, a pariah. He never knew what really happened. It was my father who stole his seal and wrote the letter of reference you read. The duke suffered a stroke not long after and never regained his faculties. I think, for all his faults, His Grace was gravely shaken by what had happened. He knew what Staunton was, but there wasn't a thing he could do about it. My father died not long after the duke. So then the only two who knew were me and Staunton. Well," she admitted, "And that doctor." She smiled at him. "And now you."

***

Leaving Stephen today had been wrenching, but Jo had to return to Mr. Smith's at her regular time—she *owed* him that much for several reasons.

"He's not just my employer, he's been my lover, Stephen, I cannot leave him without an explanation. I owe him that much at least," she said as they lay in bed together, the time for her departure drawing nearer.

He'd flinched at the word lover but nodded, looking jealous, unhappy, but resigned. "I agree this is the right thing to do—but that doesn't mean I like it." He hesitated and then said, "You must be on your guard. He is Smith and he is devious and deceitful and you need to expect he'll attempt to keep you. I know this will hit him hard and—"

Jo turned and then crawled on top of him. "Shhh," she said, lowering her mouth over his nipple to distract him. Besides, Jo knew he was mistaken about how Smith would take her departure. He'd be annoyed about losing another valet, but he felt no more strongly about her than any other lover.

She didn't know how to explain to Stephen that Smith was almost more friend and savior than lover, nor did she feel comfortable discussing one man with the other.

"How long will you stay?" he asked

"I will offer to stay until he engages another valet."

He groaned. "He'll keep you forever."

Jo laughed. "I never knew you could be such a baby," she teased.

He eyed her breast and then latched onto a nipple, making her hiss and laugh. "You *are* a baby. A very big one."

"I want you once more before you go," he'd whispered, putting his hands around her waist and flipping her onto her back as if she weighed no more than a feather. His head disappeared beneath the bedding and she felt his hot mouth on her thighs before his slick tongue began to stroke her.

306

Jo shivered at the memory as she sat alone in her cab back to Smith's house. Part of her mind was still in shock. Stephen loved her, and she didn't have to pretend to be somebody else to be with him. And he knew every sordid and horrid thing about her. He didn't want to change her—he didn't need to dress her in finery and make her his wife; they could be together the way she'd always dreamed.

But the other part of her mind was in an odd sort of mourning: leaving Smith wouldn't hurt him as Stephen believed, but there was no denying that what they'd had these past weeks was precious. She wanted to keep his friendship, although the thought of a powerful man like Smith wanting to remain even on nodding acquaintance with a valet was wishful thinking.

She went in through the servant entrance but found the kitchen empty—a situation she couldn't recall happening before.

Not until she was half-way up the stairs did she see Malcolm coming down with two suitcases.

"Oh, there you are, Leather."

"What's going on," Jo asked, her heart beating faster. "Did something happen?"

Malcolm shrugged. "You know how himself is—always something new. We're removing to some place up North for a month or so. I don't know, he didn't say how long."

Jo shook her head, baffled. "But when did he mention this?"

"Just this morning."

"I need to go and pack his—"

Malcolm lifted up the two cases. "He took what he needed to travel but asked for more to be sent. He's given everyone a two-week holiday except a few of us who are to join him." Malcolm cocked his head. "I guess you missed all this, seeing as yesterday was your free day. There was a letter for you. I daresay it will have your instructions. Well," he said, "I've got to go. I'm to be on the next train."

Jo watched him clomp down the stairs before taking the remaining steps two at a time. Something was wrong; something had happened. Why hadn't he mentioned this yesterday?

His room was pristine—the way it always was, as if nobody lived there.

On the chess table was an envelope with her name.

Pulse pounding, she slit open the flap with her thumb.

My Dear Jojo,
I knew if you stayed the night with Stephen, you would no longer need your port in the storm.
I'm off on sudden business. Don't worry about leaving me in a valeting lurch, my needs are well met and you needn't stay. Please go to Stephen before he drives every one of his business partners mad.
I'll always be here for you should you ever need a friend. But I suspect Chatham—as awkward and rude and abrupt as he is—will not make the same mistake and let you slip through his fingers twice in a lifetime.
If I have guessed incorrectly, please accept a two-week holiday and then await my return.
I wish you the best, Jojo.
Your servant and friend always,
Smith

Jo saw the tear before she knew she'd shed it. She read the letter through again, and then again. But that really was *it*.

It didn't surprise her that he'd known where she was going last night and who she'd see—when did Smith *not* know everything about everyone around him?

Jo had grown to love him in the months she'd been here—how could she not after all they'd shared? But she was not *in* love with him. He was witty and smart and an excellent companion and she hoped, one day, she might see him again—as a friend—without hurting Stephen.

Jo stared down at the letter, the neat, perfectly formed letters blurring on the page; she would *miss* him.

She folded the letter and tucked it into her breast pocket and then took out her handkerchief and dried her tears, a smile already forming as she imagined Stephen's face when she walked into his chambers this evening.

***

Smith was sitting in an old hackney across the street from his house, waiting. It wasn't the lowest point in his life this last decade, but it was close.

308

The driver had complained about waiting until Smith gave him a bill big enough to buy his bloody carriage.

Smith couldn't help smiling at how pathetic he was.

Waiting like a lovelorn swain.

He'd done the same last night. He'd waited in his bed for somebody he knew was never coming. And it was all his fault.

Smith thought back to Stephen's response: "You're telling me that you'll tell Leather to go to Bernina's tomorrow and Cecile will make sure I see her?" His voice had dripped with so much suspicion the air had been thick with it.

"Yes, that is what I'm saying, Stephen," Smith confirmed, smiling tightly at the openly skeptical man.

Stephen shook his head. "Why? Why are you giving me this chance?" His eyes narrowed and his breathing quickened. "I *know* you want her, Smith—I can smell the want on you."

Chatham's words had fed the fury he'd barely kept restrained since the day the other man had come to him with his plan—a plan Smith had voluntarily engaged in with vicious glee.

But that was over and now it was just the two of them and Leather between them.

As Smith stared into Chatham's confused, suspicious gray eyes he'd been so bloody close to telling the other man that yes, he *had* been jesting and Leather was *his*.

Instead, he'd stubbed out his cigar and stood. "I need to be off. Do whatever you want tomorrow, Stephen, it makes no odds to me," he'd lied. And then he'd left him sitting alone in their private room at Number 14.

So, that was one task done. After Chatham, the only thing he'd had to do was go home and pretend it wasn't his last night with his valet: pretend that nothing was different.

But then Smith was an expert at pretending.

A flash of dark wool pulled Smith from his brooding thoughts and he turned toward the window just in time to see Leather walking past the front entrance to Smith's house and then going left, heading down the alley toward the servant entrance.

For some reason that made Smith smile; Leather was either entering his house as his lover, or as the new consort of another very wealthy man, yet he did so on his own terms: always a servant, and proud of it.

Once again Smith waited, as if he didn't already know what he was waiting for. Still, he had nothing more pressing. The next train didn't leave for hours, and it wasn't taking him anywhere he urgently needed to go, just away from here.

Smith saw his carriage emerge from the mews with Malcolm on the box beside John Coachman. That meant the only person left in the house was Leather.

It was simple, really. She would do one of two things when she read the letter: stay or go.

Smith, for once, had not spied on her or Stephen yesterday and today. He had no idea whether she'd kicked Chatham in the crotch or kissed him.

But there was one thing he knew for sure: if she came out of the house within the next hour, he would know exactly where she was going.

But if she didn't come out? His lips began to curve into a smile but stopped when a flicker of black caught his eye.

Smith watched, his chest heavy as she emerged once more from the alley beside his house.

In her hand she carried her cloth traveling bag, the one that was large enough to hold her few possessions. Her step was light and she was smiling.

Smith followed her progress away from him and his house, watching until she was just a small dark speck that finally turned a corner and disappeared.

He looked down at the hand-carved wooden box he'd been holding so tightly that his fingers ached. It was lovely, one of a kind, just like the person he'd bought it for.

He placed it carefully on the torn leather seat and opened the door.

"Sir, where you goin'?" the grizzled old driver called as Smith shut the carriage door with a hollow *thud* and began walking.

Smith didn't answer him, because he didn't know.

Jo was sitting on her bed in her room, staring at the article in the paper she'd found face up on Mr. Chatham's breakfast tray after he'd left this morning.

He'd left it for her, knowing she'd want to read it in privacy.

She'd sat and read it one time and then had put it aside to go about her duties.

The day was a busy one. Tomorrow they would be going to stay for a week at the country house of the Earl of Taunton and Jo had a good deal to do before they left.

Their lives had quickly fallen back into a familiar rhythm in the weeks since they'd been back together—with a few important exceptions.

Jo kept her room and still slept part of most nights in her own bed. Although they'd never discussed it, they were two private people and needed the time alone to regenerate after the passionate hours they spent together.

Jo doubted she would ever be able to sleep a night through beside him and knew he was equally solitary when it came to such matters. The time apart also allowed her to go to him each morning as Leather—his valet rather than his lover.

The truth was that Jo loved both positions in his life equally. She craved the time she served him almost as much as the time they spent together in his bed. Jo knew that her lover lived this way for her, and she'd done something a week ago that was especially for him.

His expression had been wondrous when she'd shown up in his bedroom, dressed in the red gown and black gloves he'd liked so much, as well as the bracelet he'd given her. Of course she'd also had to wear an expensively coiffured wig to complete the outfit.

"I thought you might take me to the theater," she'd said. "And debauch me in your box before taking me out for a shamefully expensive dinner."

"Ah, is *that* what you thought?" he'd teased, seizing her and kissing her breathless. But when he'd released her, he'd met her eyes, serious. "You don't need to do this for me, Jo—I love you the way you are."

"I know." She hesitated and then said, for the first time. "I love you, Stephen, and you know I can sometimes be adventurous."

He'd almost crushed her spine in his fierce embrace. "My Jo," he'd whispered. "My Leather."

The night had proven a success and Jo knew they would do the same again from time to time. Indeed, she suspected they would try many new things over the coming years.

Her heart and life were so full she sometimes thought she could scarcely contain all the happiness.

And then she'd seen this headline this morning:

"The Duke of Tarland Dies on His Yacht."

The story had gone into detail about the young duke's finances. Although the reporter had never said it, the general belief was that the unpopular and dissolute young aristocrat had taken the coward's way out. Jo's lips had twitched to read that, *"mystery millionaire businessman Mr. S_____ had recently taken up residence at Tarland Castle."*

Jo wondered if Benjamin had seen it yet and if he'd connected the name of Smith to her prior employer. She'd written to Ben in France to tell him that she'd come back to Mr. Chatham, who knew her story—all of it. She knew her brother would never understand the relationship they had, but at least he no longer needed to fear her discovery. And, perhaps, he might be able to now find somebody of his own to love.

***

Stephen was floating in a pleasurable haze of bliss when Leather spoke.

"Are you ready to turn, sir?"

He smirked to himself. Yes, he was quite ready.

Firm hands helped him turn on the padded table they now employed for his delicious massages. His staid valet's eyes barely flickered over the thrusting proof of his arousal.

"I have something different in mind for tonight." Stephen laced his hands behind his head and flexed his hips, enjoying the sudden tightening of his valet's jaw as Leather took in the rippling muscles of Stephen's torso. The flare of hunger in her distorted eyes told him she'd be wet and hot between her thighs. That knowledge alone made the almost two hours a day he spent sweating in his gymnasium more than worth it. He had a young lover; he needed to keep fit.

"Yes, sir?" Leather asked, mildly, the pulse in her temple telling a different story.

"Go fetch that box on my dresser and bring it to me."

She complied with her usual swift obedience and Stephen stared down his body at his throbbing cock, gloating over his newest idea.

She returned with a long black leather box, which she offered to him with both hands.

"It's for you. Open it."

"Thank you, sir." Her slender, oil sheened fingers trembled slightly as she opened the box and then her lips parted, her breath quickening. She looked up, her eyes wide. "Sir?"

Stephen smiled. "Do you like it?"

She swallowed hard, her gaze drawn back to the item in the box, and then nodded slowly before raising her blue eyes to his. "Yes, sir. Very much. But—"

Stephen let her question hang in the air for a moment before sitting up, reveling in the way her eyes consumed him as he slid from the table. "I thought you might enjoy using that—on me." He stared down at her as she looked, slack-jawed, from the enormous double-headed dildo in the box to Stephen.

"Truly?"

Stephen grinned at her squeaky tone; finally, he'd managed to flap his unflappable valet. "Truly."

Her pupils flared, but she lowered the box. "Stephen? Are you sure?"

Her step out of character—away from a role she protected zealously—told him just how concerned—and excited—she was by his offer.

"Yes," he said, stroking her jaw and letting his fingers drift up until he could palm the fuzzy cropped hair that he loved so much. "I'm very serious." And not a little nervous, but she didn't need to know that. "I know how much you adored fucking Julian. I wanted to give you that pleasure. I—" he hesitated, his face heating. "Well, we both know I will likely enjoy it. With you." He cleared his throat. "Only you, Leather."

Stephen saw the instant she understood what he meant: he wanted her to take him as a man, not as Jo, but as his servant. There was a brilliant flash of lust and happiness and anticipation, and then it was gone.

"Very good, sir," she said without expression, and then unbuttoned the middle buttons of her trouser placket, her eyes not leaving his.

Stephen's blood pounded in his ears and he slid a hand around his aching shaft as she took the heavy ivory cock from the box and deliberately spread her legs. He almost came when she put the thick crown at her entrance and pushed, her hips undulating and her body so primed it smoothly accommodated the length. Once she'd taken all of it, she shifted until the scrotum pressed against her spread, shaved lips.

She reached for the bottle of oil.

"I want to do it," Stephen said gruffly, holding out the hand he wasn't using on himself.

"Of course, sir." She poured a generous amount of oil into his palm.

Stephen smiled down at her and stepped forward, taking both their shafts in one hand and slowly, firmly stroking them together.

She shivered and whimpered as he worked them. "Feel good?" he whispered hoarsely.

"Yes, sir," she said in between gasps.

"Are you going to be kind when you fuck me, Leather?" he asked, a feral smile twisting his lips when she shuddered at his crude words.

"I always endeavor to please, sir."

Stephen smirked at her very Leather answer and then released her. "Tell me, how do you want me, Leather?"

A hint of a smile pulled at her stern lips. "Please turn and face the bed, sir. Spread your legs—wide—and then bend over."

Wisely, Stephen did exactly as his valet ordered.

About the Author

SM LaViolette has been a criminal prosecutor, college history teacher, B&B operator, dock worker, ice cream manufacturer, reader for the blind, motel maid, and bounty hunter.
Okay, so the part about being a bounty hunter is a lie.
SM does, however, know how to hypnotize a Dungeness crab, sew her own Regency Era clothing, knit a frog hat, juggle, rebuild a 1959 American Rambler, and gain control of Asia (and hold on to it) in the game of RISK.

S.M. also writes under the name Minerva Spencer

Read more about SM at: www.MinervaSpencer.com

www.ingramcontent.com/pod-product-compliance
Lightning Source LLC
Chambersburg PA
CBHW051639180726
48284CB00006B/1788